This special signed edition
is limited to
1500 numbered copies.

This is copy ___369___.

JOE R. LANSDALE

DEAD on the BONES
Pulp on Fire

DEAD on the BONES
Pulp on Fire

by Joe R. Lansdale

SUBTERRANEAN PRESS 2016

First Edition

ISBN

978-1-59606-747-9

Subterranean Press
PO Box 190106
Burton, MI 48519

subterraneanpress.com

To Timothy Truman

TABLE of CONTENTS

PULP FURY

BEFORE I TALK about pulps, I need to talk about TV. When I was very young and TV was relatively new, I was infatuated with it, like pretty much everyone else in the fifties. TV had been around since the 20s, but since there were no TV stations, there were no TV shows. It lingered as a novelty for years.

Originally, it was used as a sort of video phone. Images were transmitted across vast distances via phone wires. Herbert Hoover in 1927 had a long distance conversation with the President of American Telephone and Telegraph. The telephone company president could see Hoover on the other end. I don't know if it worked both ways, but here was the beginning of a technology that would lead to so many things it's almost impossible to list them.

By 1928 there was even a color television system, but that would lie dormant for some time. By 1929 there was an actual live broadcast from an airplane, so if you should ever watch old serials, say Buck Rogers or Flash Gordon, their nifty, video machines are not too unlike what actually existed at the time. Even so, it would be years before the general public had access to these devices, and in fact, most Americans probably had little idea, if any, that such a thing existed, since only an elite group were capable of having them, and they were at that point little more than a novelty.

When I was growing up in the 1950s, TV began to appear in homes. Even then, it was still rare, at least in the part of the country where I lived, and I think the first TV programs I saw were on my grandmother's TV, possibly one of my uncles'. We were invited to their house to watch it. I have no recollection what we watched at that time, as this was early in the fifties and I was young, but by the time I was four TV began to have its impact on me.

I think the first television shows I really remember were *I Love Lucy, Lassie*, and somewhere in there, *Jack Benny*.

Around this time *The Tonight Show* came into being as well, with its original host, Steve Allen, but the bottom line was there really wasn't much on TV. Not right then. That began to change rapidly. They had to fill the time and air waves with material. In a short time old movies, film shorts, and serials, made their way to the little box in the living room.

I remember when we got our first TV, which must have been around 1954. It amazed me. A TV screen back then was small and had a kind of glow band around it and the screen was more round than rectangle.

The shows that began to pop up on it amazed me even more, because as the fifties progressed, not only were these old films and serials seeping into our everyday life, so were original shows like *The Edge of Night*, an early soap opera my mother watched. I became fascinated by it during those times I was able to watch it, probably during summer months, or when I pretended to be sick so I could find out what happened next and not have to go to school and be bored.

The Edge of Night was a soap opera, but it was also a crime show, and had to do with New York detectives. One name associated with the program was the first writer's name I ever remembered from TV, Henry Slesar, who was also a fine short story writer and novelist, though I wouldn't discover that for quite a few years.

PULP FURY

These days *The Edge of Night* is terribly dated, and of course shot in what would now be thought of as a primitive manner, but as a child I was riveted, and it may well have helped develop my taste for crime and mystery. But even more important to me than *The Edge of Night*, was *Alfred Hitchcock Presents*. This bent me out of shape, and became required viewing for our entire family. Near the end of the decade *The Twilight Zone* showed up, and then for me it was game over. I was deep into the idea of telling stories. I wanted to give others the feelings and emotions I got from these shows.

Thing about a lot of these programs was they were either borrowed from old radio shows, which were frequently inspired by the pulps, or they were direct stories from the pulps or digest magazines. The digest magazines were merely extensions of the pulps; pulps dressed up and presented as more sophisticated.

What was happening was all of us who watched TV were unconsciously being fed a steady diet of the pulps by way of these shows. *Thriller* broadcasted numerous tales originally written for pulp magazines by authors like Robert Bloch, one of my earliest influences, Charles Beaumont, John Tomerlin, Robert E. Howard, and others.

The incredible "Pigeons from Hell," based on a Howard story, was one of those shows. It is impossible at this date for a younger generation to understand the impact that episode had on viewers. For many years it was the most powerful thing ever broadcast on television, and it's still well worth viewing if you can find it. That one locked in my head like a tick in an armpit, and echoes of it, and the original pulp story, which I later read, have filtered into my work throughout my career, which has now spanned over forty years. *The Outer Limits* came along a little later, and the stories were frequently based on classic science fiction pulp tales.

The pulps were the source for many programs, including westerns, detective shows, private eye adventures, mysteries, crime, science fiction, fantasy and horror.

The point is to let you know the pulps were with us long after they supposedly died out, and the same could be said of radio shows, because so many shows that made their way to the boob tube had originally been on radio. *Gunsmoke* pops immediately to mind, as well as *The Adventures of Superman*, which came from comics to radio to television, but Superman, like many comics, was inspired by the pulp heroes of an earlier generation. To carry it even farther, it could be said that many of the pulp characters were inspired by mythology, primarily Greek and Roman, and like those heroes they somehow transcend the general idea of a character with everyday problems who in the face of rather trite situations can't find the gumption to get past it all. They are heroes in the truest meaning of the word.

On Saturday mornings I watched old Tarzan movies, all of them were played and replayed constantly, watched and re-watched. My favorites were the Johnny Weissmuller ones, and to this date, though there have been attempts to update Tarzan, and in many ways pull him closer to the original creation, in my mind the Weissmuller films are the only ones that ever actually made me fully believe a man could run through the jungle, swing on vines, climb trees like a monkey, swim rivers, and whip the hell out of crocodiles, and if that wasn't enough, the son-of-a-bitch lived in a cool tree house and was living with a hot blond lady with very little clothes on. Oh, and there was a chimpanzee, Cheetah, and later a boy, who Tarzan cleverly named Boy.

These Saturday morning programs were followed, or preceded, by Flash Gordon or Buck Rogers sequels, both of which starred Buster Crabbe. The biggest difference in the series was Buster's hair color. As Flash he was blond, as Buck his hair was darker. Buster also played Tarzan and other assorted heroes, including Captain Gallant of the Foreign Legion, and so on. Like Weissmuller he was once a champion swimmer, and one of my early heroes. As actors, they were the pulps personified. Buster ended up selling swimming pools, and when Weissmuller got too heavy to play Tarzan, he became Jungle

Jim, another program that popped up on Saturday mornings, and if Tarzan didn't show, then he was replaced by the Bomba movies, Bomba played by Johnny Sheffield, who when he was younger played Tarzan's son, Boy. These kind of sucked, actually, and the books on which Bomba was based were even worse. Still, for a kid, they were all pretty amazing.

All of these shows, the power of television, the fact that I was an avid reader of comics, a medium also inspired by the pulps, were shaping me, twisting me, molding me. It affected my reading. I was no longer consuming only comic books by this time. When the bookmobile rolled around, I found myself prowling within its tight confines, shoving against other scrambling kids for something similar to the shows I was watching, the comics I was reading.

Not all of what I read had appeared in the pulps, but many had inspired pulp writers. Authors like Jack London, Rudyard Kipling, and Robert Louis Stevenson, but one of those I read that was directly from the pulps, was Edgar Rice Burroughs.

After discovering Burroughs, from that point on, I was ruined. I wanted to be a writer before, but he made me crazy to be one, and what I wanted to be was a pulp writer. I was living in a pulp writer fury, a storm of imagination. I was so excited about wanting to write these kinds of stories, I could hardly sleep.

I had no idea the pulps, by that point, were gone. I had no idea they had existed, or even what a deceased pulp magazine looked like, but their leftover juice was in my blood, like unnamed parasites.

I wrote my own stories and novels in composition notebooks. Some of those still survive. One of the novels I wrote, and never finished, was about a character named Braxton Hooker. You will find the roots of that novel here, in "Under the Warrior Star," though I changed the last name to Booker. I wrote the original between the ages of eleven and thirteen, updated it later, and it was published under the current title. The original name for my hero was taken from Joe Hooker, a Civil War general I was reading about in some book or another, and I liked his last name. Braxton may well have come from the same book; another general. Later I discovered Hooker's name was the origin for the word hooker, as Joe was said to supply his troops with prostitutes, thereafter known as hookers. So for the updated version of my adolescent story, he became Braxton Booker.

"Under the Warrior Star" was written as my love letter to Burroughs. It isn't particularly original, as the idea was to capture the Burroughs feel as closely as possible, while eliminating the racism and sexism of the era in which Burroughs originally created his works. I don't claim this story is going to break new ground, but I do believe it is as close to modern pulp pastiche as I am capable of writing, and is only one of two or three times when I consciously tried to write like someone else, or at least ring the bells of that writer so close to his own cathedral.

Equally in that vein is "Wizard of the Trees," a long story written for Gardner Dozois and George R. R. Martin's *Old Venus*, which was meant to be a throwback anthology with stories in it that resembled and were inspired by the stories of the pulp era, specifically about the planet Venus. There was a companion volume about Mars, and the Heinlein-inspired story I wrote for that one, "Kings of the Cheap Romance" is also included here, and has a female lead.

Like "Under the Warrior Star," "Wizard of the Trees," is mostly inspired by Edgar Rice Burroughs. I did something, however, you didn't see in the pulps when it came to heroic warriors on other planets. My main character is Black, and a former Buffalo Soldier.

To complete my Edgar Rice Burroughs-influenced stories, an actual Tarzan story is included here, "Tarzan and the Land That Time Forgot." Permission was given to write this story by the Burroughs estate, and it was part of a number of Burroughs-inspired stories that appeared in *The Worlds of Edgar Rice Burroughs*.

I got the chance to loosely combine Tarzan and Pellucidar, a Burroughs inner-world creation, inspired by *Tarzan at the Earth's Core*, and then place the bulk of the action on another Burroughs world, inspired by his Land That Time Forgot series.

If you should want more Burroughs pastiches, then you might check out the anthology *Under the Moons of Mars*, which has plenty, including a story by me titled "The Metal Men of Mars," another pulp pastiche of a Burroughs character, and my favorite of his creations, John Carter.

Better yet, check out Burroughs originals. They have dated in some ways, but they are still rollicking adventures, especially suited to younger readers, and probably best suited to young boys, as women aren't exactly given big roles, though one might claim that in some ways he provided better roles for women than many pulp writers of his era. Dejah Thoris can be quite the fighter when she needs to be, and there are other female characters in Burroughs books that deserve recognition for their spunk and warrior ability. It should also be noted, that racist as Burroughs could be—and boy he could be— he almost redeemed himself with the race of Black Martian warriors that appear in the John Carter series, and did much the same with the Waziri, a tribe of Black warriors who were friends to Tarzan, but true to the times, the warriors seem a bit too uncomfortably like servants to "The Big Bwana," as Tarzan is called. Burroughs even has Tarzan think of the Waziri as like children, so we're not talking about huge leaps in racial activism here. My Black Buffalo Soldier hero on Venus would not have made it in the original science fiction pulp magazines.

The other stories here are all pulp-inspired, though some, like "Dead on the Bones," are combined with more modern, character-driven sensibilities.

The bottom line is when I got older all I heard was how the pulps were crap, and frankly, if you read a lot of old pulp magazines, you will discover this is true. This might be said of a variety of other types of magazines, but the pulps, the word pulp, became a brand name for bad writing, which is why even to this day I cringe a little when someone calls me a modern pulp writer, though with the stories in this book, that would be accurate. These are very much inspired by the pulps.

It is often forgotten that some of our greatest writers, both literary and popular, started out in the pulps. Tennessee Williams first appeared in *Weird Tales*, as did Ray Bradbury. Dashiell Hammett and Raymond Chandler in *Black Mask*, MacKinlay Kantor, and so many others great writers began their careers in the pulps. Even Hemingway tried to write for them, unsuccessfully, I might add.

Still, the bulk of it was tripe, and for that reason, so many writers of my generation wore the brand of pulp writer begrudgingly.

After *Pulp Fiction*, the film by Tarantino appeared, the meaning of the word changed. It began to mean a certain off-the-wall approach, lots of color, action, all the better aspects of the pulps, which are the same as the best aspects of other kinds of fiction; storytelling, characters, dialogue and style.

Though I have been influenced heavily by the pulps, I have tried to weld the better aspects of literary writing with the raw and appealing aspects of pure storytelling and vivid imagination, as well as cinematic viewpoint, all of which are hallmarks of the pulps. The pulps were just the opposite of the kind of literary story that boils down to two people in Connecticut are having trouble with their marriage, or a character so overcome by personal disappointment, they can't find the energy to mow the grass.

Truth is, I like all manner of stories, but have never been able, or willing, to shake entirely those original inspirations. Still, I generally like stories, as both reader and writer, that demand a little more of me than watching a hero go through his or her paces. I have never been one to like it when someone says, "I only want to be entertained."

Not everyone is entertained by the same thing, and not everything that is entertaining is slight. One can be entertained by Robert E. Howard's Conan (something that is harder for me these days) or Franz Kafka's stories of alienation.

Now and again, however, I prefer to go back and dig directly into that pulp well in my head and come out with a story that might actually have appeared in those old, long defunct magazines. This book is an example of that. I hope now and again, like me, you like to read that sort of story as well. If you do, here is a book of them.

Read with pleasure.

Written in Salem, Mass., by way of Nacogdoches, Tex. 2015

THE GRUESOME AFFAIR OF THE ELECTRIC BLUE LIGHTNING

From the Files of Auguste Dupin

TRANSLATED LOOSELY FROM THE FRENCH

THIS STORY CAN only be described as fantastic in nature, and with no exaggeration, it deals with nothing less than the destruction of the world, but before I continue, I should make an immediate confession. Some of this is untrue. I do not mean the events themselves, for they are accurate, but I have disguised the names of several individuals, and certain locations have been re-imagined—for lack of a better word—to suit my own conscience. The end of the cosmos and our world as we know it is of considerable concern, of course, but no reason to abandon manners.

These decisions were made primarily due to the possibility of certain actors in this drama being unnecessarily scandalized or embarrassed, even though they are only mentioned in passing and have little to nothing to do with the events themselves. I do not think historians, warehouse owners and the like should have to bear the burden of my story, especially as it will undoubtedly be disbelieved.

There are, however, specific players in my article, story if you prefer, that have their own names to contend with, old as those names may be, and I have not made any effort whatsoever to alter these. This is owed to the fact that these particular personages are well enough recognized by name, and any attempt to disguise them would be a ridiculous and wasted effort.

This begins where many of my true stories begin. I was in the apartment I share with Auguste Dupin, perhaps the wisest and most rational man I have ever known, if a bit of a curmudgeon and a self-centered ass. A touch of background, should you be interested: we share an apartment, having met while looking for the same obscure book in a library, which brought about a discussion of the tome in question, which in turn we decided to share in the reading, along with the price of an apartment, as neither of us could afford the rental of one alone. Dupin is a Chevalier, and had some financial means in the past, but his wealth had somehow been lost—how this occurred, we have by unspoken agreement never discussed, and this suits me, for I would rather not go into great detail about my own circumstances.

In spite of his haughty nature, Dupin is quite obviously of gentlemanly countenance and bearing, if, like myself he is a threadbare gentleman; I should also add, one who in manners is frequently not a gentleman at all. He is also a sometime investigator. This began merely as a hobby, something he did for his own amusement, until I assured him that regular employment might aid in his problems with the rent, and that I could assist him, for a small fee, of course. He agreed.

What I call "The Gruesome Affair of the Electric Blue Lightning" began quite casually, and certainly by accident. I was telling Dupin how I had read that the intense lightning storm of the night before had been so radical, producing such powerful bolts, it had started fires all along the Rue ——————. In fact, the very newspaper that had recorded the article lay before him, and it wasn't until I had finished telling him about the irregular events, that I saw it lying there, and admonished him for not revealing to me he had read the article and knew my comments even before disclosing them for his consideration.

"Yes," Dupin said, leaning back in his chair and clasping his fingers together. "But I appreciate your telling of it. It was far more dramatic and interesting than the newspaper article itself. I was especially interested in, and impressed with, your descriptions of the lightning, for yours was a practical explanation, but not an actual recollection, and therefore perhaps faulty."

"Excuse me," I said.

His eyes brightened and his lean face seemed to stretch even longer as he said, "You described to me lightning that you did not see, and in so doing, you described it as it should appear, not as the newspaper depicted it. Or to be more precise, you only said that the fires had been started by a lightning strike. The newspaper said it was a blue-white fulmination that appeared to climb up to the sky from the rooftops of a portion of the warehouse district rather than come down from the heavens. To be more precise, the newspaper was supposedly quoting a man named F——————, who said he saw the peculiar lightning and the beginnings of the warehouse fire with his own eyes. He swore it rose upward, instead of the other way around. Out of the ordinary, don't you think?"

"A mistake on his part," I said. "I had forgotten all about his saying that. I didn't remember it that way."

"Perhaps," said Dupin, filling his meerschaum pipe and studying the rain outside the apartment window, "because it didn't make sense to you. It goes against common sense. So, you dismissed it."

"I suppose so," I said. "Isn't that what you do in your investigations? Dismiss items that are nonsensical? Use only what you know to be true? You are always admonishing me for filling in what is not there, what could not be, that which faults ratiocination."

Dupin nodded. "That's correct. But, isn't that what you're doing now? You are filling in what is not there. Or deciding quite by your own contemplations that which should not be there."

"You confuse me, Dupin."

"No doubt," he said. "Unlike you, I do not dismiss something as false until I have considered it fully and examined all the evidence. There is also the part of the article where F————'s statement was validated by a child named P————."

"But, the word of a child?" I said.

"Sometimes they have the clearest eyes," Dupin said. "They have not had time to think what they *should* see, as you have, but only what they *have* seen. They can be mistaken. Eye witnesses often are, of course. But it's odd that the child validated the sighting of the other witness, and if what the article says is true, the man and child did not know one another. They were on very distant sides of the event. Due to this—and of course I would question their not knowing one another until I have made a full examination—perhaps more can be made of the child's recollections. I certainly believe we can rule out coincidence of such an observation. The child and the man either colluded on their story, which I find unlikely, because to what purpose would they say such an unbelievable thing? Or, the other possibility is they did in fact see the same event, and their description is accurate, at least as far as they conceive it."

"That lightning rose up from the ground?" I said. "You say that makes more sense than it coming down from the heavens? I would think suggesting Jove threw a bolt of lightning would be just as irrational as to suggest the lightning rose up from the earth!"

"From a warehouse rooftop, not the earth," he said. "And it was blue-white in color?"

"Ridiculous," I said.

"It is peculiar, I admit, but my suggestion is we do not make a judgment on the matter until we know more facts."

"I didn't realize we cared to make a judgment."

"I am considering it."

"This interests you that much? Why would we bother? It's not a true investigation, just the soothing of a curiosity, which, I might add, pays absolutely nothing."

"What interest me are the deaths from the warehouse fire," Dupin said. "Though, since, as you noted, we haven't been hired to examine the facts, that pays the same absence of price."

"Horrid business," I said. "But I believe you are making much of nothing. I know that area, and those buildings are rats' nests just waiting for a spark to ignite them. They are also the squatting grounds for vagrants. Lightning struck the building. It caught ablaze rapidly, and sleeping vagrants were burned to death in the fire. It is as simple as that."

"Perhaps," Dupin said. He leaned back and puffed on his pipe, blowing blue clouds of smoke from between his teeth and from the bowl. "But how do you explain that our own acquaintance the Police Prefect, G————, was quoted as saying that they found a singed but still identifiable arm, and that it appeared to have been sawed off at the elbow, rather than burned?"

I had no answer for that.

"Of course, G———— is often wrong, so in his case I might suspect an error before suspecting one from the witnessing child. G———— solves most of his crimes by accident, confession, or by beating his suspect until he will admit to having started the French Revolution over the theft of a ham hock. However, when he has solved his cases, if indeed one can actually consider them solved, it is seldom by any true form of detection. I should also note that there has been a rash of grave robbings of late, all of them involving freshly buried bodies."

Now, as he often did, Dupin had piqued my curiosity. I arose, poured the both of us a bit of wine, sat back down and watched Dupin smoke his pipe, the stench of which was cheap and foul as if burning the twilled ticking of an old sweat-stained mattress.

"For me to have an opinion on this matter, I would suggest we make a trip of it tomorrow, to see where this all occurred. Interview those that were spoken to by the newspaper. I know you have contacts, so I would like you to use them to determine the exact location of these witnesses who observed the lightning and the resulting fire. Does this suit you?"

I nodded. "Very well, then."

That was the end of our discussion about these unique, but to my mind, insignificant events, for the time being. We instead turned our attention to the smoking of pipes and the drinking of wine. Dupin read while he smoked and drank, and I sat there contemplating that which we had discussed, finding the whole matter more and more mysterious with the thinking. Later, I decided I would like to take a stroll before retiring, so that I might clear my head of the drinking and heavy smoke.

I also had in mind the ideas that Dupin had suggested, and wanted to digest them. I have always found a walk to be satisfying not only to the legs and heart, but to the mind as well; many a problem such as this one I had considered while walking, and though, after talking to Dupin, I still turned out to be mistaken in my thinking, I had at least eliminated a large number of my fallacies of thought before speaking to him.

Outside the apartment, I found the rain had ceased; the wind had picked up, however, and was quite cool, almost chilly. I pulled my collar up against the breeze and swinging my cane before me, headed in the direction of the lightning fire in the warehouse district along the Rue ——————. I didn't realize I was going there until my legs began to take me. I knew the location well, and no research was required to locate the site of the events, so I thought that for once, having seen the ruins, I might actually have a leg up on Dupin, and what he called his investigative methods of ratiocination.

—

I WILL NOT name the exact place, due to this area having recently been renovated, and keep in mind these events took place some years back, so there is no need to besmirch the name of the new owners. But for then, it was an area not considered a wisely traveled pathway by night. It was well known for unsavory characters and poor lighting. That being the case, I was fully aware it was not the best of ideas to be about my business in this vicinity, but what Dupin had said to me was gnawing at my thoughts like a terrier at a rug. I felt reasonably confident that my cane would defend me, as I am—if I say so myself—like Dupin, quite skilled in the art of the cane, and if I should be set upon by more than one ruffian, it contained a fine sword that could help trim my attackers' numbers.

I came to where the warehouse section lay, and found the burned buildings instantly, not far from a large allotment of land where other warehouses were still maintained. I stood for a moment in front of the burned section, going over it with eyes and mind. What remained were blackened shells and teetering lumber; the rain had stirred the charred shambles and the stench of it filled and itched my nostrils.

I walked along the pathway in front of it, and tried to imagine where the fire had started, determining that the areas where the structure of the buildings were most ruined might be the source. I could imagine that the fire jumped from those ruined remains to the other buildings, which, though burned beyond use, were still more structurally sound, suggesting that the fire had raged hottest before it reached them.

I was contemplating all of this, when from the ruins I heard a noise, and saw a shape rise up from the earth clothed in hat and overcoat. It was some distance away from me, and even as it rose, it paused for a moment, looking down in the manner of a man who has dropped pocket change.

I can't explain exactly why I thought I should engage, but I immediately set off in that direction, and called out to it. As I neared, the shape looked up, seeing me. I took note of the fact that it carried something, clutched tightly to it, and that this undefined individual was in a kind of panic; it began to run. I wondered then if it might be a thief, looking for some surviving relic that could be swapped or sold, and part of its loot had been dropped when it came up from wherever it had been lurking, and before it could be found, I had startled the prowler.

I took it upon myself to call out again, and when I did, the shape ceased to run, turned and looked at me. I was overcome with fear and awe, for I was certain, even though the being stood back in the shadows, wore an overcoat and had the brim of a hat pulled down tight over its face, that staring back at me was some kind of hairy upright ape clutching a bagged burden to its breast.

Unconsciously, I lifted the shaft of my walking stick and revealed an inch of the hidden sword. The beast—for I can think of it no other way—turned, and once more proceeded to run, its hat blowing off as it went. In a flash, it disappeared behind one of the standing warehouses. I remained where I was for a moment, rooted to the spot, and then, overcome with curiosity, I pursued it, running through the burnt lumber, on out into the clearing that led to the street where I had seen the beast standing. As I turned the corner, I found it waiting for me. It had dropped the bag at its feet, and was lifting up a large garbage container that was dripping refuse. I was granted a glimpse of its teeth and fiery eyes just before it threw the receptacle at me. I was able to duck, just in time, and as the container clattered along the cobblestones behind me, the thing grabbed up its bag, broke and ran toward a warehouse wall. I knew then I had it trapped, but considering that what it had thrown at me was heavier than anything I could lift, perhaps it would be I who was trapped. These thoughts were there, but my forward motion and determination succeeded in trampling my common sense.

As I came near it again, my previous astonishment was nothing compared to what I witnessed now. The creature divested itself of the overcoat, slung the bag over its shoulder, and with one hand grasped a drainpipe, and using its feet to assist, began to climb effortlessly upwards until it reached the summit of the warehouse. I watched in bewilderment as it moved across the rain-misted night-line, then raced out of sight down the opposite side of the warehouse wall, or so I suspected when it was no longer visible.

I darted down an alley, splashing in puddles as I went, and came to the edge of the warehouse where I was certain the ape-man had descended. Before me was a narrow, wet, street, the R——————, but the ape-man was not in sight.

I leaned against the wall of the warehouse, for at this point in time I needed support, the reality of what I had just witnessed finally sinking into my bones. I momentarily tried to convince myself that I had been suffering the effects of the wine Dupin and I had drunk, but knew this was wishful thinking. I drew the sword from the cane, and strolled down the R—————— in search of the ape, but saw nothing, and frankly, was glad of it, having finally had time to consider how close I may have come to disaster.

Replacing the sword in its housing, I walked back to the ruins of the warehouse. Using my cane to move burnt lumber about, throwing up a light cloud of damp ash, I examined the spot where I had seen the thing pulling something from the rubble; that's when I found the arm, severed at the elbow, lying on top of the ash. It had no doubt been dropped there after the fire, for it appeared un-charred, not even smoke-damaged. I knelt down and struck a Lucifer against the tip of the cane, then held it close. It was a small arm with a delicate hand. I looked about and saw that nearby were a series of steps that dipped beneath ground level. It seemed obvious this was where the creature had originated when it appeared to rise out of the very earth. It also seemed obvious this opening had been covered by the collapse of the warehouse, and that the creature had uncovered it and retrieved something from below and tucked it away in the large bag it was carrying. The obvious thing appeared to be body parts, for if he had dropped one, then perhaps others existed and were tucked away in its bag. I lit another Lucifer, went down the narrow steps into the basement, waved my flickering light so that it threw small shadows about. The area below was larger than I would have expected. It was filled with tables and crates, and what I determined to be laboratory equipment—test tubes, beakers, burners and the like. I had to light several matches to complete my examination— though complete is a loose word, considering I could only see by the small fluttering of a meager flame.

I came upon an open metal container, about the size of a coffin, and was startled as I dipped the match into its shadowy interior. I found two human heads contained within, as well as an assortment of amputated legs, arms, feet and hands, all of them submerged in water.

I jerked back with such revulsion that the match went out. I scrambled about for another, only to discover I had used my entire store. Using what little moonlight was tumbling down the basement stairs as my guide, and almost in a panic, I ran up them and practically leapt into the open. There was more moonlight now than before. The rain had passed and the clouds had sailed; it was a mild relief.

Fearing the ape, or whatever it was, might return, and considering what I had found below, I hurried away from there.

I should have gone straight to the police, but having had dealings with the Police Prefect, G————————, I was less than enthusiastic about the matter. Neither Dupin nor myself were well liked in the halls of the law for the simple reason Dupin had solved a number of cases the police had been unable to, thereby making them look foolish. It was they who came to us in time of need, not us to them. I hastened my steps back to the apartment, only to be confronted by yet another oddity. The moon was turning to blood. Or so it appeared, for a strange crimson cloud, the likes of which I had never before seen, or even heard of, was enveloping the moon, as if it were a vanilla biscuit tucked away in a bloody-red sack. The sight of it caused me deep discomfort.

—

IT WAS LATE when I arrived at our lodgings. Dupin was sitting by candlelight, still reading. He had a stack of books next to him on the table, and when I came in he lifted his eyes as I lit the gas lamp by the doorway to further illuminate the apartment. I was nearly breathless, and when I turned to expound on my adventures, Dupin said, "I see you have been to the site of the warehouses, an obvious deduction by the fact that your pants and boots are dusted heavily in ash and soot and are damp from the rain. I see too that you have discovered body parts in the wreckage. I will also conjecture we can ignore having a discussion with the lightning witnesses, for you have made some progress on your own."

My mouth fell open. "How could you know that I discovered body parts?"

"Logic. The newspaper account spoke of such a thing, and you come rushing in the door, obviously excited, even a little frightened. So if a severed arm was found there the other day, it stands to reason that you too discovered something of that nature. That is a bit of speculation, I admit, but it seems a fair analysis."

I sat down in a chair. "It is accurate, but I have seen one thing that you can not begin to decipher, and it is more fantastic than even severed body parts."

"An ape that ran upright?"

"*Impossible!*" I exclaimed. "You could not possibly know."

"But I did." Dupin paused a moment, lit his pipe. He seemed only mildly curious. "Continue."

It took me a moment to collect myself, but finally I began to reveal my adventures.

"It was carrying a package of some kind. I believe it contained body parts because I found an arm lying in the burned wreckage, as you surmised. Something I believe the ape dropped."

"Male or female?" Dupin said.

"What?"

"The arm, male or female?"

I thought for a moment.

"I suppose it was female. I didn't give it considerable evaluation, dark as it was, surprised as I was. But I would venture to guess—and a guess is all I am attempting—that it was female."

Joe R. Lansdale

"That is interesting," Dupin said. "And the ape?"

"You mean was the ape male or female?"

"Exactly," Dupin said.

"What difference does it make?"

"Perhaps none. Was it clothed?"

"A hat and overcoat. Both of which it abandoned."

"In that case, could you determine its sex?" Dupin asked.

"I suppose since no external male equipment was visible, it was most probably female."

"And it saw you?"

"Yes. It ran from me. I pursued. It climbed to the top of a warehouse with its bag, did so effortlessly, and disappeared on the other side of the building. Prior to that, it tried to hit me with a trash receptacle. A large and heavy one it lifted as easily as you lift your pipe."

"Obviously it failed in this endeavor," Dupin commented. "How long did it take you to get to the other side of the warehouse, as I am presuming you made careful examination there as well?"

"Hasty would be a better word. By then I had become concerned for my own safety. I suppose it took the creature less than five minutes to go over the roof."

"Did you arrive there quickly? The opposite side of the building, I mean?"

"Yes. You could say that."

"And the ape was no longer visible?"

"Correct."

"That is quite rapid, even for an animal, don't you think?"

"Indeed," I said, having caught the intent of Dupin's question. "Which implies it did not necessarily run away, or even descend to the other side. I merely presumed."

"Now, you see the error of your thinking."

"But you've made presumptions tonight," I said.

"Perhaps, but more reasonable presumptions than yours, I am certain. It is my impression that your simian is still in the vicinity, and did not scale the warehouse merely to climb down the other side

30

and run down the street, when it could just as easily have taken the alley you used. And if the creature did climb down the other side, I believe it concealed itself. You might have walked right by it."

That gave me a shiver. "I admit that is logical, but I also admit that I didn't walk all that far for fear that it might be lurking about."

"That seems fair enough," Dupin said.

"There is something else," I said, and I told him about the basement and the body parts floating in water in the casement. I mentioned the red cloud that lay thick against the moon.

When I finished, he nodded, as if my presentation was the most normal event in the world. Thunder crashed then, lightning ripped across the sky, and rain began to hammer the street; a rain far more vigorous than earlier in the evening. For all his calm, when Dupin spoke, I thought I detected the faintest hint of concern.

"You say the moon was red?"

"A red cloud was over it. I have never seen such a thing before. At first I thought it a trick of the eye."

"It is not," Dupin said. "I should tell you about something I have researched while you were out chasing ape-women and observing the odd redness of the night's full moon, an event that suggests things are far more desperate than I first suspected."

I had seated myself by this time, had taken up my own pipe, and with nervous hand, found matches to light it.

Dupin broke open one of the books near the candle. "I thought I had read of that kind of electric blue lightning before, and the severed limbs also struck a chord of remembrance, as did the ape, which is why I was able to determine what you had seen, and that gives even further credence to my suspicions. Johann Conrad Dipple."

"Who?"

"Dipple. He was born in Germany in the late sixteen hundreds. He was a philosopher and something of a theologian. He was also considered a heretic, as his views on religion were certainly outside the lines of normal society."

"The same might be said of us," I remarked.

Dupin nodded. "True. But Dipple was thought to be an alchemist and a dabbler in the dark arts. He was in actuality a man of science. He was also an expert on all manner of ancient documents. He is known today for the creation of Dipple's oil, which is used in producing a dye we know as Prussian Blue, but he also claimed to have invented an elixir of life. He lived for a time in Germany at a place known as Castle Frankenstein. This is where many of his experiments were performed, including one that led to such a tremendous explosion it destroyed a tower of the castle, and led to a breaking of his lease. It was said by those who witnessed the explosion that a kind of lightning, a blue-white lightning, lifted up from the stones to the sky, followed by a burst of flame and an explosion that tore the turret apart and rained stones down on the countryside."

"So that is why you were so interested in the lightning, the story about it rising up from the warehouse instead of falling out of the sky?"

Dupin nodded, relit his pipe and continued. "It was rumored that he was attempting to transfer the souls of the living into freshly exhumed corpses. Exhumed clandestinely, by the way. He was said to use a funnel by which the souls of the living could be channeled into the bodies of the dead."

"Ridiculous," I said.

"Perhaps," Dupin replied. "It was also said his experiments caused the emergence of a blue-white lightning that he claimed to have pulled from a kind of borderland, and that he was able to open a path to this netherworld by means of certain mathematical formulas gleaned from what he called a renowned, rare, and accursed book. For this he was branded a devil worshiper, an interloper with demonic forces."

"Dupin," I said. "You have always ridiculed the supernatural."

"I did not say it was supernatural. I said he was a scientist that was branded as a demonologist. What intrigues me is his treatise titled *Maladies and Remedies of the Life of the Flesh*, as well as the mention of even rarer books and documents within it. One that was of special interest was called *The Necronomicon*, a book that was thought by many to be mythical."

"You have seen such a book?"

"I discovered it in the Paris library some years ago. It was pointed out to me by the historian M——————. No one at the library was aware of its significance, not even M——————. He knew only of its name and that it held some historical importance. He thought it may have something to do with witchcraft, which it does not. I was surprised to find it there. I considered it to be more than a little intriguing. It led me to further investigations into Dipple as not only the owner of such a book, but as a vivisectionist and a resurrectionist. He claimed to have discovered a formula that would allow him to live for 135 years, and later amended this to eternal life."

"Drivel," I said. "I am surprised you would concern yourself with such."

"It was his scientific method and deep understanding of mathematics that interested me. My dear friend, much of what has become acceptable science was first ridiculed as heresy. I need not point out to you the long list of scientists opposed by the Catholic church and labeled heretics. The points of interest concerning Dipple have to do with what I have already told you about the similarity of the blue-white lightning, and the interesting connection with the found body parts, the ape, and the curious event of the blood-stained moon, which I will come back to shortly. Firstly, however was Dipple's mention of the rare book. *The Necronomicon*, written by Abdul Alhazred in 950 AD, partially in math equations and partly in verse. He was sometimes referred to as 'the Mad Arab' by his detractors, though he was also given the moniker of 'Arab Poet of Yemen' by those less vicious. Of course, knowing my penchant for poetry, you might readily surmise that this is what first drew my attention to him. The other aspect of his personality, as mathematician and conjuror, was merely, at that time, of side interest, although I must say that later in life he certainly did go mad. He claimed to have discovered mathematical equations that could be used to open our world into another where powerful forces and beings existed. Not gods or demons, mind you, but different and true life forms that he called the Old Ones. It was in this book that Dipple believed he found the key to eternal life."

"What became of Dipple?"

"He died," Dupin said, and smiled.

"So much for eternal life."

"Perhaps."

"Perhaps? You clearly said he died."

"His body died, but his assistant, who was imprisoned for a time, said his soul was passed on to another form. According to what little documentation there is on the matter, Dipple's experiments were concerned with removing a person's soul from a living form and transferring it to a corpse. It was successful, if his assistant, Hans Grimm can be believed. Grimm was a relative of Jacob Grimm, the future creator of *Grimm's Fairy Tales*. But of more immediate interest to us is something he reported, that a young lady Dipple was charmed by, and who he thought would be his companion, took a fall from a horse and was paralyzed. Grimm claimed they successfully transferred her soul from her ruined body into the corpse of a recently dead young lady, who had been procured by what one might call midnight gardening. She was 'animated with life,' as Grimm described her, 'but was always of some strangeness.' That is a direct quote."

"Dupin, surely you don't take this nonsense seriously."

He didn't seem to hear me. "She was disgusted with her new form and was quoted by Grimm as saying 'she felt as if she was inside a house with empty rooms.' She leaped to her death from Castle Frankenstein. Lost to him, Dipple decided to concentrate on a greater love—himself. Being short of human volunteers who wanted to evacuate their soul and allow a visitor to inhabit their living form, he turned to animals for experimentation. The most important experiment was the night he died, or so says Grimm."

"The ancestor of the creator of *Grimm's Fairy Tales* seems an unlikely person to trust on matters of this sort."

"That could be. But during this time Dipple was having exotic animals shipped to him in Germany, and among these was a creature called a chimpanzee. Knowing himself sickly, and soon to die, he put his experiments to the ultimate test. He had his assistant, Grimm, by use of the formula and his funnel, transfer his soul from his disintegrating shell into the animal, which in turn eliminated the soul of the creature; the ape's body became the house of his soul. I should add that I have some doubts about the existence of a soul, so perhaps essence would be a more appropriate word. That said, soul has a nice sound to it, I think. The experiment, according to Grimm, resulted in an abundance of blue-white lightning that caused the explosion and left Grimm injured. In fact, later Grimm disappeared from the hospital where he was being held under observation, and arrest for alchemy. He was in a room with padded walls and a barred window. The bars were ripped out. It was determined the bars were pulled loose from the outside. Another curious matter was that the room in which he was contained was three floors up, a considerable drop. How did he get down without being injured? No rope or ladder was found. It was as if he had been carried away by something unknown."

"Come, Dupin, you cannot be serious? Are you suggesting this ape pulled out the bars and carried him down the side of the wall?"

"There are certainly more than a few points of similarity between the story of Dipple and the events of tonight, don't you think? Consider your description of how effortlessly the ape climbed the warehouse wall."

"But, if this is Dipple, and he is in Paris, my question is how? And his ape body would be old. Very old."

"If he managed eternal life by soul transference, then perhaps the ape body does not age as quickly as would be normal."

"If this were true, and I'm not saying I believe it, how would he go about his life? An ape certainly could not ride the train or stroll the street without being noticed."

"I am of the opinion that Grimm is still with him."

"But he would be very old as well."

"Considerably," Dupin agreed. "I believe that the body parts you saw are for Grimm. It is my theory that Grimm received a wound that put him near death when Castle Frankenstein blew up. Dipple saved him by transferring his soul to a corpse. Unlike Dipple's lady love, he managed to accept the transfer and survived."

"So why did Dipple go after the body parts himself? Wouldn't he have Grimm procure such things? It would be easier for the one with a human body to move about without drawing so much attention."

"It would. My take is that the human soul when transferred to the soul of a corpse has one considerable drawback. The body rots. The ape body was a living body. It does not; it may age, but not in the way it would otherwise due to this transformation. Grimm's body, on the other hand, has to be repaired from time to time with fresh parts. It may be that he was further damaged by the more recent explosion. Which indicates to me that they have not acquired the healthy ability to learn from their mistakes."

"After all this time, wouldn't Dipple have transferred Grimm's essence, or his own, into a living human being? Why would he maintain the body of an ape? And a female ape at that?"

"My thought on the matter is that Dipple may find the powerful body of an ape to his advantage. And to keep Grimm bent to his will, to maintain him as a servant, he only repairs him when he wears out a part, so to speak. Be it male or female parts, it is a matter of availability. If Grimm's soul were transferred into a living creature, and he could live for eternity, as male or female, then he might be willing to abandon Dipple. This way, with the ape's strength, and Dipple's knowledge of how to repair a corpse, and perhaps the constant promise of eventually giving Grimm a living human body, he keeps him at his side. Grimm knows full well if he leaves Dipple he will eventually rot. I think this is the Sword of Damocles that he holds over Grimm's head."

"That is outrageous," I said. "And wicked."

"Absolutely, but that does not make it untrue."

—

I FELT COLD. My pipe had died, as I had forgotten to smoke it. I relit it. "It's just too extraordinary," I said.

"Yet *The Necronomicon* suggests it is possible." With that, Dupin dug into the pile of books and produced a large volume, thrusting it into my hands. Looking at it, I saw that it was covered in leather, and that in the dead center was an eye-slit. I knew immediately that what I was looking at was the tanned skin of a human face. Worse, holding the book I felt nauseated. It was as if its very substance was made of bile. I managed to open the book. There was writing in Arabic, as well as a number of mathematical formulas; the words and numbers appeared to crawl. I slammed the book shut again. "Take it back," I said, and practically tossed it at him.

"I see you are bewildered, old friend," Dupin said, "but do keep in mind, as amazing as this sounds, it's science we are talking about, not the supernatural."

"It's a revolting book," I said.

"When I first found it in the library, I could only look at it for short periods of time. I had to become accustomed to it, like becoming acclimated to sailing at sea, and no longer suffering sea sickness. I am ashamed to admit that after a short time I stole the book. I felt somehow justified in doing this, it being rarely touched by anyone— for good reason, as you have experienced—and in one way I thought I might be doing the world a justice, hiding it away from the wrong eyes and hands. That was several years ago. I have studied Arabic, read the volume repeatedly, and already being reasonably versed in mathematics, rapidly began to understand the intent of it. Though, until reading the newspaper account, I had been skeptical. And then there is Dipple's history, the words of his companion, Grimm. I believe there is logic behind these calculations and ruminations, even if at first they seem to defy human comprehension. The reason for this is simple; it is not the logic of humans, but that of powerful beings who exist in the borderland. I have come to uncomfortably understand some of that logic, as much as is humanly possible to grasp. To carry this even farther, I say that Dipple is no longer himself, in not only body, but in thought. His constant tampering with the powers of the borderland have given the beings on the other side an entry into his mind, and they are learning to control him, to assist him in his desires, until their own plans come to fruition. It has taken time, but soon, he will not only be able to replace body parts, he will be capable of opening the gate to this borderland. We are fortunate he has not managed it already. These monsters are powerful, as powerful as any god man can create, and malicious without measure. When the situation is right, when Dipple's mind completely succumbs to theirs, and he is willing to use the formulas and spells to clear the path for their entry, they will cross over and claim this world. That will be the end of humankind, my friend. And let me tell you the thing I have been holding back. The redness of the moon is an indication that there is a rip in the fabric of that which protects us from these horrid things lying in wait. Having wasted their world to nothing, they lust after ours, and Dipple is opening the gate so they might enter."

"But how would Dipple profit from that? Allowing such things into our world?"

"Perhaps he has been made promises of power, whispers in his head that make him outrageous offers. Perhaps he is little more than a tool by now. All that matters, good friend, is that we can not allow him to continue his work."

"If the red cloud over the moon is a sign, how much time do we have?"

"Let me put it this way: We will not wait until morning, and we will not need to question either the boy or the man who saw the lightning. By that time, I believe it will be too late."

There was a part of me that wondered if Dupin's studies had affected his mind. It wasn't an idea that held, however. I had seen what I had seen, and what Dupin had told me seemed to validate it. We immediately set out on our escapade, Dupin carrying a small bag slung over one shoulder by a strap.

The rain had blown itself out and the streets were washed clean. The air smelled as fresh as the first breath of life. We went along the streets briskly, swinging our canes, pausing only to look up at the moon. The red cloud was no longer visible, but there was still a scarlet tint to the moon that seemed unnatural. Sight of that gave even more spring to my step. When we arrived at our destination, there was no one about, and the ashes had been settled by the rain.

"Keep yourself alert," Dupin said, "in case our simian friend has returned and is in the basement collecting body parts."

We crossed the wet soot, stood at the mouth of the basement, and after a glance around to verify no one was in sight, we descended.

Red-tinged moonlight slipped down the stairs and brightened the basement. Everything was as it was the night before. Dupin looked about, used his cane to tap gently at a few of the empty beakers and tubes. He then made his way to the container where I had seen the amputated limbs and decapitated heads. They were still inside, more than a bit of rain water having flooded into the casement, and there was a ripe stench of decaying flesh.

"These would no longer be of use to Dipple," Dupin said. "So we need not worry about him coming back for them."

I showed him where I had last seen the ape, then we walked to the other side. Dupin looked up and down the wall of the warehouse. We walked along its length. Nothing was found.

"Perhaps we should find a way to climb to the top," I said.

Dupin was staring at a puff of steam rising from the street. "No, I don't think so," he said.

He hastened to where the steam was thickest. It was rising up from a grate. He used his cane to pry at it, and I used mine to

Joe R. Lansdale

assist him. We lifted it and looked down at the dark, mist-coated water of the sewer rushing below. The stench was, to put it mildly, outstanding.

"This would make sense," Dupin said. "You were correct, he did indeed climb down on this side, but he disappeared quickly because he had an underground path."

"We're going down there?" I asked.

"You do wish to save the world and our cosmos, do you not?"

"When you put it that way, I suppose we must," I said. I was trying to add a joking atmosphere to the events, but it came out as serious as a diagnosis of leprosy.

We descended into the dark, resting our feet upon the brick ledge of the sewer. There was light from above to assist us, but if we were to move forward, we would be walking along the slick, brick runway into utter darkness. Or so I thought.

It was then that Dupin produced twists of paper, heavily oiled and waxed, from the pack he was carrying. As he removed them, I saw *The Necronomicon* was in the bag as well. It lay next to two dueling pistols. I had been frightened before, but somehow, seeing that dreadful book and those weapons, I was almost overwhelmed with terror, a sensation I would experience more than once that night. It was all I could do to take one of the twists and wait for Dupin to light it, for my mind was telling me to climb out of that dank hole and run. But if Dipple succeeded in letting the beings from the borderland through, run to where?

"Here," Dupin said, holding the flaming twist close to the damp brick wall. "It went this way."

I looked. A few coarse hairs were caught in the bricks.

With that as our guide, we proceeded. Even with the lit twists of wax and oil, the light was dim and there was a steam, or mist, rising from the sewer. We had to proceed slowly and carefully. The sewer rumbled along near us, heightened to near flood level by the tremendous rain. It was ever to our right, threatening to wash up over the walk. There were drips from the brick walls and the overhead streets.

40

Each time a cold drop fell down my collar I started, as if icy finger-tips had touched my neck.

We had gone a good distance when Dupin said, "Look. Ahead."

There was a pumpkin-colored glow from around a bend in the sewer, and we immediately tossed our twists into the water. Dupin produced the pistols from his bag, and gave me one.

"I presume they are powder-charged and loaded," I said.

"Of course," Dupin replied, "did you think I might want to beat an ape to death with the grips?"

Thus armed, we continued onward toward the light.

There was a widening of the sewer, and there was in fact a great space made of brick that I presumed might be for workmen, or might even have been a forgotten portion of the sewer that had once been part of the upper streets of Paris. There were several lamps placed here and there, some hung on nails driven into the brick, others placed on the flooring, some on rickety tables and chairs. It was a makeshift laboratory, and had most likely been thrown together from the ruins of the warehouse explosion.

On a tilted board a nude woman…or a man, or a little of both, was strapped. Its head was male, but the rest of its body was female, except for the feet, which were absurdly masculine. This body breathed in a labored manner, its head was thrown back, and a funnel was stuck down its throat. A hose rose out of the funnel and stretched to another makeshift platform nearby. There was a thin insect-like antenna attached to the middle of the hose, and it wiggled erratically at the air.

The other platform held a cadaverously thin and nude human with a head that looked shriveled, the hair appearing as if it were a handful of strings fastened there with paste. The arms and legs showed heavy scarring, and it was obvious that much sewing had been done to secure the limbs, much like the hurried repair of an old rag doll. The lifeless head was tilted back, and the opposite end of the hose was shoved into another wooden funnel that was jammed into the corpse's mouth. One arm of the cadaver was short, the other long, while the legs varied in thickness. The lower half of the face was totally incongruous with the upper half. The features were sharp-boned and stood up beneath the flesh like rough furniture under a sheet. They were masculine, while the forehead and hairline, ragged as it was, had obviously been that of a woman, one recently dead and elderly was my conjecture.

The center of the corpse was blocked by the body of the ape, which was sewing hastily with a large needle and dark thread, fastening on an ankle and foot in the way you might lace up a shoe. It was so absurd, so grotesque, it was almost comic, like a grisly play at the Theater of the Grand Guignol. One thing was clear, the corpse being sewn together was soon to house the life force of the other living, but obviously ill body. It had been cobbled together in the past in much the same way that the other was now being prepared.

Dupin pushed me gently into a darkened corner protected by a partial brick wall. We spoke in whispers.

"What are we waiting for?" I said.

"The borderland to be opened."

Of course I knew to what he referred, but it seemed to me that waiting for it to be opened, if indeed that was to happen, seemed like the height of folly. But it was Dupin, and now, arriving here, seeing what I was seeing, it all fit securely with the theory he had expounded; I decided to continue believing he knew of what he spoke. Dupin withdrew *The Necronomicon* from the bag, propped it against the wall.

"When I tell you," he said, "light up a twist and hold it so that I might read."

"From that loathsome book?" I gasped.

"It has the power to do evil, but it also to restrain it."

I nodded, took one of the twists from the bag and a few matches and tucked them into my coat pocket. It was then I heard the chanting, and peeked carefully around the barrier.

The ape, or Dipple I suppose, held a copy of a book that looked to be a twin of the one Dupin held. It was open and propped on a makeshift pedestal of two stacked chairs. Dipple was reading from it by dim lamp light. It was disconcerting to hear those chants coming from the mouth of an ape, sounding human-like, yet touched with the vocalizations of an animal. Though he spoke the words quickly and carefully, it was clear to me that he was more than casually familiar with them.

That was when the air above the quivering antenna opened in a swirl of light and dark floundering shapes. I can think of no other way to describe it. The opening widened. Tentacles whipped in and out of the gap. Blue-white lightning flashed from it and nearly struck the ape, but still he read. The corpse on the platform began to writhe and wiggle and the blue-white lightning leaped from the swirling mass and struck the corpse repeatedly and vibrated the antenna. The dead body glowed and heaved and tugged at its bonds, and then I saw its eyes flash wide. Across the way, the formerly living body had grown limp and gray as ash.

I looked at Dupin, who had come to my shoulder to observe what was happening.

"He is not bringing him back, as in the past," Dupin said. "He is offering Grimm's soul for sacrifice. After all this time, their partnership has ended. It is the beginning; the door has been opened a crack."

My body felt chilled. The hair on my head, as on Dupin's, stood up due to the electrical charge in the air. There was an obnoxious smell, reminiscent of the stink of decaying fish, rotting garbage, and foul disease.

"Yes, we have chosen the right moment," Dupin said, looking at the growing gap that had appeared in mid-air. "Take both pistols, and light the twist."

He handed me his weapon. I stuck both pistols in the waistband of my trousers, and lit the twist. Dupin took it from me, and stuck it in a gap in the bricks. He opened *The Necronomicon* to where he had marked it with a torn piece of paper, and began to read from it. The words poured from his mouth like living beings, taking on the form of dark shadows and lightning-bright color. His voice was loud and sonorous, as we were no longer attempting to conceal ourselves. I stepped out of the shadows and into the open. Dipple, alerted by Dupin's reading, turned and glared at me with his dark, simian eyes.

It was hard for me to concentrate on anything. Hearing the words from *The Necronomicon* made my skin feel as if it were crawling up from my heels, across my legs and back, and slithering underneath my scalp. The swirling gap of blue-white lightning revealed lashing tentacles, a massive squid-like eye, then a beak. It was all I could do not to fall to my knees in dread, or bolt and run like an asylum escapee.

That said, I was given courage when I realized that whatever Dupin was doing was having some effect, for the gash in the air began to shimmer and wrinkle and blink like an eye. The ape howled at this development, for it had glanced back at the rip in the air, then turned again to look at me, twisted its face into what could almost pass as a dark knot. It dropped the book on the chair, and rushed for me. First it charged upright, like a human, then it was on all fours, its knuckles pounding against the bricks. I drew my sword from the cane, held the cane itself in my left hand, the blade in my right, and awaited Dipple's dynamic charge.

—

IT BOUNDED TOWARDS me. I thrust at it with my sword. The strike was good, hitting no bone, and went directly through the ape's chest, but the beast's momentum drove me backwards. I lost the cane itself, and used both hands to hold the sword in place. I glanced at Dupin for help. None was forthcoming. He was reading from the book and utterly ignoring my plight.

Blue, white, red and green fire danced around Dipple's head and poured from his mouth. I was able to hold the monster back with the sword, for it was a good thrust, and had brought about a horrible wound, yet its long arms thrashed out and hit my jaw, nearly knocking me senseless. I struggled to maintain consciousness, pushed back

the sword with both hands, coiled my legs, and kicked out at the ape. I managed to knock him off me, but only for a moment.

I sat up and drew both pistols. It was loping towards me, pounding its fists against the bricks as it barreled along on all fours, letting forth an indescribable and ear-shattering sound that was neither human nor animal. I let loose an involuntary yell, and fired both pistols. The shots rang out as one. The ape threw up its hands, wheeled about and staggered back toward the stacked chairs, the book. It grabbed at the book for support, pulled that and the chairs down on top of it. Its chest heaved as though pumped with a bellows.

And then the freshly animated thing on the platform spat out the funnel as if it were light as air. Spat it out and yelled. It was a sound that came all the way from the primeval; a savage cry of creation. The body on the platform squirmed and writhed and snapped its bonds. It slid from the board, staggered forward, looked in my direction. Both pistols had been fired; the sword was still in Dipple. I grabbed up the hollow cane that had housed the sword, to use as a weapon.

This thing, this patchwork creation I assumed was Grimm, its private parts wrapped in a kind of swaddling, took one step in my direction, the blue-white fire crackling in its eyes, and then the patchwork creature turned to see the blinking eye staring out of the open door to the borderlands.

Grimm yanked the chairs off Dipple, lifted the ape-body up as easily as if it had been a feather pillow. It spread its legs wide for position, cocked its arms, and flung the ape upwards. The whirlpool from beyond sucked at Dipple, turning the old man in the old ape's body into a streak of dark fur, dragging it upwards. In that moment, Dipple was taken by those from beyond the borderland, pulled into their world like a hungry mouth taking in a tasty treat. Grimm, stumbling about on unfamiliar legs, grabbed *The Necronomicon* and tossed it at the wound in the air.

All this activity had not distracted Dupin from his reading. Still he chanted. There was a weak glow from behind the brick wall. I stumbled over there, putting a hand against the wall to hold myself up. When Dupin read the last passage with an oratory flourish, the air was sucked out of the room and out of my lungs. I gasped for breath, fell to the floor, momentarily unconscious. Within a heartbeat the air came back, and with it, that horrid rotting smell, then as instantly as it arrived, it was gone. The air smelled only of foul sewer, which, considering the stench of what had gone before, was in that moment as pleasant and welcome as a young Parisian lady's perfume.

—

THERE WAS A flare of a match as Dupin rose from the floor where he, like me, had fallen. He lit a twist from the bag and held it up. There was little that we could see. Pulling the sword from his cane, he trudged forward with the light, and I followed. In its illumination we saw Grimm. Or what was left of him. The creatures of the borderlands had not only taken Dipple and his *Necronomicon*, they had ripped Grimm into a dozen pieces and plastered him across the ceiling and along the wall like an exploded dumpling.

"Dipple failed," Dupin said. "And Grimm finished him off. And the Old Ones took him before they were forced to retreat."

"At least one of those terrible books has been destroyed," I said.

"I think we should make it two," Dupin said.

We broke up the chairs and used the greasy twists of paper we still had, along with the bag itself, and started a fire. The chair wood was old and rotten and caught fast, crackling and snapping as it burned. On top of this Dupin, placed the remaining copy of *The Necronomicon*. The book was slow to catch, but when it did the cover blew open and the pages flared. The eye hole in the cover filled with a gold pupil, a long black slit for an iris. It blinked once, then the fire claimed it. The pages flapped like a bird, lifted upward with a howling noise, before collapsing into a burst of black ash.

Standing there, we watched as the ash dissolved into the bricks like black snow on a warm windowpane.

I took a deep breath. "No regrets about the book?"

"Not after glimpsing what lay beyond," Dupin said. "I understand Dipple's curiosity, and though mine is considerable, it is not that strong."

"I don't even know what I saw," I said, "but whatever it was, whatever world the Old Ones live in, I could sense in that void every kind of evil I have ever known or suspected, and then some. I know you don't believe in fate, Dupin, but it's as if we were placed here to stop Dipple, to be present when Grimm had had enough of Dipple's plans."

"Nonsense," Dupin said. "Coincidence. As I said before. More common than you think. And had I not been acquainted with that horrid book, and Dipple's writings, we would have gone to bed to awake to a world we could not understand, and one in which we would not long survive. I should add that this is one adventure of ours that you might want to call fiction, and confine it to a magazine of melodrama; if you should write of it at all."

We went along the brick pathway then, with one last lit paper twist we had saved for light. It burned out before we made it back, but we were able to find our way by keeping in touch with the wall, finally arriving where moonlight spilled through the grating we had replaced upon entering the sewer. When we were on the street, the world looked strange, as if bathed in a bloody light, and that gave me pause. Looking up, we saw that a scarlet cloud was flowing in front of the sinking moon. The cloud was thick, and for a moment it covered the face of the moon completely. Then the cloud passed and faded and the sky was clear and tinted silver with the common light of stars and moon.

I looked at Dupin.

"It's quite all right," he said. "A last remnant of the borderland. Its calling card has been taken away."

"You're sure?"

"As sure as I can be," he said.

With that, we strolled homeward, the moon and the stars falling down behind the city of Paris. As we went, the sun rose, bloomed red, but a different kind of red to the cloud that had covered the moon; warm and inspiring, a bright badge of normalcy, that from here on out I knew was a lie.

The REDHEADED DEAD

In memory and tribute to Robert E. Howard

REVEREND MERCER KNEW it was coming because the clouds were being plucked down into a black funnel, making the midday sky go dark. It was the last of many omens, and he knew from experience it smacked of more than a prediction of bad weather. There had been the shooting star of last night, bleeding across the sky in a looping red wound. He had never seen one like it. And there had been the angry face he had seen in the morning clouds, ever so briefly, but long enough to know that God was sending him another task in his endless list.

He paused on his horse on a high hill and pushed his hat up slightly, determining the direction of the storm. When the funnels were yanked earthward and touched, he saw, as he expected, that the twister was tearing up earth and heading swiftly in his direction. He cursed the God he served unwillingly and plunged his mount down the hill as the sky spat rain and the wind began to howl and blow at his back like the damp breath of a pursuing giant. Down the hill and into the depths of the forest his horse plunged, thundering along the pine needle trail, dashing for any cover he might find.

As he rode, to his left, mixed in with the pines and a great oak that dipped its boughs almost to the ground, was a graveyard. He saw at a glance the gravestones had slipped and cracked, been torn up by tree roots, erosion, and time. One grave had a long metal rod poking up from it, nearly six feet out of the ground; the rod was leaning from the ground at a precarious due west. It appeared as if it were about to fall loose of the earth.

The pine needle trail wound around the trees and dipped down into a clay path that was becoming wet and slick and bloodred. When he turned yet another curve, he saw tucked into the side of a hill a crude cabin made of logs and the dirt that surrounded it. The roof was covered in dried mud, probably packed down and over some kind of pine slab roofing.

The Reverend rode his horse right up to the door and called out. No one answered. Reverend Mercer dismounted. The door was held in place by a flip-up switch of wood. The Reverend pressed it and opened it, led his horse inside. There was a bar of crudely split wood against the wall. He lifted it and clunked it into position between two rusted metal hooks on either side of the doorway. There was a window with fragments of parchment paper in place of glass; there was more open space than parchment, and the pieces that remained fluttered in the wind like peeling, dead skin. Rain splattered through.

Down through the trees swirled the black meanness from heaven, gnawing trees out of the ground and turning them upside down and throwing their roots to the sky like desperate fingers, the fingers shedding wads of red clay as if it were clotted blood.

The Reverend's horse did a strange thing; it went to its knees and ducked its head, as if in prayer. The storm tumbled down the mountain in a rumbling wave of blackness, gave off a locomotive sound. This was followed by trees and the hill sliding down toward the cabin at tremendous speed, like mashed potatoes slipping along a leaning plate.

The Redheaded Dead

The Reverend threw himself to the floor, but just before he did, he saw gravestones flying through the air, as well as that great iron bar, sailing his way like a javelin.

All the world screamed. The Reverend lay flat, his back wet from rain flashing through the window. He did not pray, having decided long ago his boss had already made up his mind about things.

The cabin groaned and the roof peeled at the center and a gap was torn open in the roof. The rain came through it in a deluge, splattering heavily on the Reverend's back as he lay face down, expecting at any moment to be lifted up by the wind and drawn and quartered by the Four Horsemen of the Apocalypse.

Then, it was over. There was no light at the window because mud and trees had plugged it. The roof was open at the top, and there was a bit of daylight coming from there. It filled the room with a kind of hazy shade of gold.

When the Reverend rose up, he discovered the steel bar had come through the window and gone straight through his horse's head; the animal still rested forward on its front legs, its butt up, the bar having gone into one ear and out the other. The horse had gone dead before it knew it was struck.

The only advantage to his dead mount, the Reverend thought, was that now he would have fresh meat. He had been surviving on corn dodgers for a week, going where God sent him by directions nestled inside his head. In that moment, the Reverend realized that God had brought him here for a reason. It was never a pleasant reason. There would be some horror, as always, and he would be pitted against it, less he thought for need of destroying evil, but more out of heavenly entertainment, like burning ants to a crisp with the magnified heat of the sun shining through the lens off a pair of spectacles.

The Reverend studied the iron bar that had killed his horse. There was writing on it. He knelt down and looked at it. It was Latin, and the words trailed off into the horse's ear. The Reverend grabbed the bar and twisted the horse's head toward the floor, put his boot against the horse's skull, and pulled. The bar came out with

a pop and a slurp, covered in blood and brain matter. The Reverend took a rag from the saddle bag on the horse and wiped the rod clean.

Knowing Latin, he read the words. They simply said: And this shall hold him down.

"Ah, hell," the Reverend said, and tossed the bar to the floor.

This would be where God had sent him, and what was coming he could only guess, but a bar like that one, made of pure iron, was often used to pin something in its grave. Iron was a nemesis of evil, and Latin, besides being a nemesis to a student of language, often contained more powerful spells than any other tongue, alive or dead. And if what was out there was in need of pinning, then the fact the twister had pulled the bar free by means of the literal wet and windy hand of God, meant something that should not be free was loose.

For the first time in a long time, Reverend Mercer thought he might defy God, and find his way out of here if he could. But he knew it was useless. Whatever had been freed was coming, and it was his job to stop it. If he didn't stop it, then it would stop him, and not only would his life end, but his soul would be flung from him to who knows where. Heaven as a possibility would not be on the list. If there was in fact a heaven.

There was a clatter on the roof and the Reverend looked up, caught sight of something leering through the gap. When he did, it pulled back and out of sight. The Reverend lifted his guns out of their holsters, a .44 converted Colt at his hip, and a .36 Navy Colt in the shoulder holster under his arm. He had the .44 in his right fist, the Navy in his left. His bullets were touched with drops of silver, blessed by himself with readings from the Bible. Against hell's minions it was better than nothing, which was a little like saying it was better than a poke in the eye with a sharp stick.

The face had sent a chill up his back like a wet-leg scorpion scuttling along his spine. It was hardly a face at all. Mostly bone with rags of flesh where cheeks once were, dark pads of rotting meat above its eyes. The top of its head had been curiously full of fire-red hair, all of it wild and wadded and touched with clay. The mouth had been drawn back in the grin of a ghoul, long fangs showing. The eyes had been the worst; red as blood spots, hot as fire.

Reverend Mercer knew immediately what it was; the progeny of Judas. A vampire, those that had descended from he who had given death to Christ for a handful of silver. Christ, that ineffectual demigod that had fooled many into thinking the heart of God had changed; it had not, that delusion was all part of the great bastard's game.

There was movement on the roof, heavy as an elephant one moment, and then light and skittering like an excited squirrel.

The Reverend backed across the room and found a corner just as the thing stuck its head through the gap in the roof again. It stretched its neck, which was long and barely covered in skin, showing a little greasy disk of bone that creaked when its long neck swayed.

Like a serpent, it stretched through the roof, dropping its hands forward, the fingers long and multiple-jointed, clicking together like bug legs. It was hanging from the gap by its feet. It was naked, but whatever its sex, that had long dissolved to dust, and there was only a parchment of skin over its ribs and its pelvis was nothing more than bone, its legs being little more than withered gray muscle tight against the bone. It twisted its head and looked at the Reverend. The Reverend cocked his revolvers.

It snapped its feet together, disengaging from the roof, allowing it to fall. It dropped lightly, landed on the damp horse, lifted its head and sniffed the air. It gazed at the Reverend, but the dead animal was too inviting. It swung its head and snapped its teeth into the side of the dead horse's neck, made a sucking noise that brought blood out of the beast in a spray that decorated the vampire's face and mouth. Spots of blood fell on the sun-lit floor like rose petals.

It roved one red eye toward the Reverend as it ate, had the kind of look that said: "You're next."

The Reverend shot it several times.

The bullets tore into it and blue hell-fire blew out of the holes the bullets made. The thing sprang like a cricket, came across the floor toward the Reverend, who fired both revolvers rapidly, emptying them, knocking wounds in the thing that spurted sanctified flames, but still it came.

The Reverend let loose with a grunt and a groan, racked the monster up side the head with the heavy .44. It was like striking a tree. Then he was flung backwards by two strong arms, against the window packed with limbs and leaves and mud. The impact knocked the revolvers from his hands.

It came at him like a shot, hissing as if it were a snake. The Reverend's boot caught the skin and bone brute in the chest and drove it back until it hit the floor. It bounced up immediately, charged again. The Reverend snapped out a left jab and hooked with a right, caught the thing with both punches, rocked its rotten head. But still it came. The Reverend jabbed again, crossed with a right, upper cut with a left, and slammed a right hook to the ribs. When he hit the ribs, one of them popped loose and poked thought the skin like a barrel stave that had come undone.

It sprang forward and clutched the Reverend's throat with both hands, and would have dove its teeth into his face, had the Reverend not grabbed it under the chin and shoved it back and kicked it hard in the chest, sending it tumbling over the horse's body.

The Reverend sprang toward the iron bar, grabbed it, swung it and hit the fiend a brisk blow across the neck, driving it to the ground. His next move was to plunge the bar into it, pinning it once again to the ground in the manner it had been pinned in its grave. But he was too slow.

The creature scrambled across the floor on all fours, avoiding the stab, which clunked into the hard dirt floor. It sprang up and through the hole in the roof before the Reverend could react. As the last of it disappeared, the Reverend fell back, exhausted, watching the gap for its reemergence.

Nothing.

The Reverend found his pistols and reloaded. They hadn't done much to kill the thing, but he liked to believe his blessed loads had at least hampered it some. He worked the saddle bag off his horse, flung it over his shoulder. He tried the door and couldn't open it. Too much debris had rammed up against it. He stood on his dead mount and poked the bar through the hole, pushed it through the gap far enough that he could use both ends of it to rest on the roof and chin himself up. On the roof he looked about for it, saw it scuttling over a mass of mud and broken trees like a spider, toward a darkening horizon; night was coming, dripping in on wet, dark feet.

The Reverend thought that if his reading on the subject was right, this descendant of Judas would gain strength as the night came. Not a good thing for a man that had almost been whipped and eaten by it during the time when it was supposed to be at its weakest.

Once again, the Reverend considered defying that which God had given him to do, but he knew it was pointless. Terror would come to him if he did not go to it. And any reward he might have had in heaven would instead be a punishment in hell. As it was, even doing God's bidding he was uncertain of reward, or of heaven's existence. All he knew was there was a God and it didn't like much of anything besides its sport.

The Reverend climbed down from the roof with the rod, stepping on the mass of debris covering the door and window, wiggled his way through broken trees, went in the direction the vampire had gone. He went fast, like a deranged mouse eager to throw itself into the jaws of a lion.

As he wound his way up the hill it started to rain again. This was followed by hail the size of .44 slugs. He noticed off to his left a bit of the graveyard that remained; a few stones and a great, shadowy hole where the rod had been. With the night coming he was sure the vampire would be close by, and though he didn't think it would return to the grave where it had been pinned for who knew how long, he went there to check. The grave was dark and empty except for rising rain water. It was a deep hole, that grave, maybe ten feet deep. Someone had known what that thing was and how to stop it, at least until time released it.

The light of the day was completely gone now, and there was no moon. With the way the weather had turned, he would be better off to flee back to the house, wait until morning to pursue. He knew where it would be going if it didn't come back for him. The first available town and a free lunch. He was about to fulfill that plan of hole up and wait and see, when the dark became darker, and in that instant he knew it was coming up behind him. It was said these things did not cast a reflection, but they certainly cast a shadow, even when it was thought too dark for there to be one.

The Reverend wheeled with the iron bar in hand. The thing hit him with a flying leap and knocked him backwards into the grave, splashing them down into the water. The bar ended up lying across the grave above them. The Reverend pulled his .44. It was on him as he fired, clamping its teeth over the barrel of the revolver. The Reverend's shot took out a huge chunk at the back of the thing's head, but still it survived, growling and gnawing and shaking the barrel of the gun like a dog worrying a bone.

The barrel snapped like a rotten twig. The vampire spat it out. The Reverend hit him with what remained of the gun. It had about as much effect as swatting a bull with a feather. The Reverend dropped the weapon and grasped the thing at its biceps, attempting to hold it back, the vampire trying to bring its teeth close to the Reverend's face. The Reverend slugged the thing repeatedly.

Using a wrestling move, the Reverend rolled the thing off of him, came to his feet, leaped and grabbed the bar, swung up on it, and out of the grave. Still clutching the bar he stumbled backwards. The vampire hopped out of the hole effortlessly, as if it the grave had been no deeper than the depth of a cup.

As it sprang, the Reverend, weary, fell back and brought the rod up. The sky grew darker as the thing came down in a blind lunge of shape and shadow. Its body caught the tip of the rod and the point of it tore through the monster with a sound like someone bending too-quick in tight pants and tearing the ass out of them. The vampire screamed so loud and oddly the Reverend thought the sound might knock him out with the sureness of a blow. But he held fast, the world wavering, the thing struggling on the end of the rod, slowly sliding down, its body swirling around the metal spear like a snake on a spit, then bunching up like a doodle bug to make a knot at the center of the rod. Then it was still.

The Reverend dropped the rod and came up on one knee and looked at the thing pinned on it. It was nothing more now than a ball of bone and tattered flesh. The Reverend lifted the rod and vampire into the wet grave, shoved the iron shaft into the ground, hard. Rain and hail pounded the Reverend's back, but still he pushed at the bar until it was deep and the thing was beneath the rising water in the grave.

Weakly, the Reverend staggered down the hill, climbed over the debris in the cabin, and dropped through the roof. He found a place in the corner where he could sit upright, rest his back against the wall. He pulled out his .36 Navy and sat there with it on his thigh, not quite sleeping, but dozing off and on like a cat.

As he slept, he dreamed the thing came loose of the grave several times during the night. Each time he awoke, snapping his eyes open in fright, the fiend he expected was nothing more than a dream. He breathed a sigh of relief. He was fine. He was in the cabin. There was no vampire, only the pounding of rain and hail through the hole in the roof, splashing and smacking against the corpse of his horse.

The next morning, the Reverend climbed out of the cabin by means of his horse foot-stool, and went out through the hole in the roof. He walked back to the grave. He found his saddle bags on the edge of it where they had fallen during the attack. He had forgotten all about them.

Pistol drawn, he looked into the grave. It was near filled with muddy water. He put the revolver away, grabbed hold of the rod, and worked it loose, lifted it out to see if the thing was still pinned.

It was knotted up on the rod like a horrid ball of messy twine.

The Reverend worked it back into the grave, pushing the bar as deep as he could, then dropped to his knees and set about pushing mud and debris into the hole.

It took him all of the morning, and past high noon to finish up.

When he was done, he took a Bible from his saddle bags and read some verses. Then he poked the book into the mud on top of the grave. It and the rod would help to hold the thing down. With luck, the redheaded dead would stay truly dead for a long time.

When he was done, the Reverend opened his saddle bags and found that his matches wrapped in wax paper had stayed dry. He sighed with relief. With the saddle bags flung over his shoulder, he went back to the cabin to cut off a slab of horse meat. He had hopes he could find enough dry wood to cook it before starting his long walk out, going to where he was led by the godly fire that burned in his head.

KING OF THE CHEAP ROMANCE

IN MEMORY OF ARDATH MAYHAR

I GLANCED AT the body and trembled. I looked at the blue ice directly in front of me, and beyond that at the vast polar regions of Mars, stretched out flat, and way beyond that was a mountain rise. Past that rise was where I needed to go. I felt cold and miserable and sad, and for one long moment I wanted to quit. Then I told myself, that's not what Dad would have wanted. That's not what he would have wanted his daughter to do.

We Kings, we weren't quitters. It had been drummed into my head since birth. I looked down at Dad's corpse, all that was left of my family, wrapped in silver bedding, lying on the sled, and it was as if I could hear him now. "Angela, put your ears back and your nose forward, and keep going. That's how we do. Just like an old mule. That's how we Kings are. We keep on going when everyone else has already quit."

That made me feel strong for a moment or two, and then I was thinking back on how I had ended up where I was, and that took the zip out of me again. I couldn't get hold of being here on the ice, after only moments before being high in the air. It felt as if it were all some kind of dream, some astral visitation of someone else's life who looked like me and had a dead dad. But the real me was somewhere else, and at any moment I'd snap awake and find myself back in the silver airship, cruising high above the Martian ice.

I didn't though.

It was really me. Angela King. Out on the ice, breathing out air puffy and white as clouds, the body of my father lying on a sled at my feet.

I took a deep breath of chilly air and determined then that I had to get over my feelings of defeat. I was a King. I couldn't quit. Something might quit me, but I wouldn't quit. Not until I was as dead as Dad.

—

WHAT HAPPENED WAS this.

The fever hit the Far Side, as we called the city long beyond the mountains. The Martian fever is a nasty beast. It comes on sudden and hot and burns the mind right out of a person, turns them red, mounds up pus-filled lesions quick-time, makes a person quiver, scream and rave, go completely off their nut. No one really knew how it got started, but it happened now and then, came out of nowhere like rain from a clear, sunny sky. It was thought to have something to do with certain kinds of Martian water, melted snow that flowed down out of the mountains and joined up in streams and creeks that got into the water supply. Mars was mostly hot, dry desert, but up around the ice caps it was rich in water, cold and savage.

Though the fever was brutal, there was a cure, and it was mighty effective, if not readily available. That's what my father and I were trying to do, make it available. It was considered a routine trip, though any trip on Mars can blow out and go bad in quick-time. Just when you thought things were good and the land was tamed, Mars would throw a trick at you.

KING of the CHEAP ROMANCE

The ship we had was quick and light. It held us and a couple of sleds, which we didn't think we'd need, an emergency stash of supplies, and a small, padded, leather bag of vaccine. That's all it took, a small bag containing a few vials. A bit of it went a long ways. In fact, Dad said a drop would fix the fever and keep you from having it again, which mean it didn't take much at all to cure an entire Martian city, and on Mars a city was about two to three thousand. Dad said on Earth you'd call that kind of gathering a town, maybe even a community. But on Mars it was a city. I didn't remember Earth too well, and had yet to go back, the return trip being so expensive and me not really wanting to go. I liked it on the Red Planet, out in the area where it wasn't red at all, but blue and white with freezing ice.

Anyway, Dad said a drop of vaccine would do, and he ought to know. He was a doctor before he died out there on the ice.

Dad had not wanted me to come. He always said, "On Mars things can, and do go wrong, regular as clockwork, and irregularly too."

But since my mom was dead and I would have had to stay with people I didn't know well, I whined my way into the glider, and up we went, powered by sunlight, carried by whining turbines, darting fast through the thin-aired Martian sky. When we started out both moons were up and shiny as silver. Dad said he could never quite get used to two moons. I didn't remember much about Earth, but I did remember it had one moon in the sky. That seemed pretty deficient after living on Mars with one moon fast and one moon slow, both bright in the sky and looking not so far, as if you could stand on a ladder and touch them.

We sailed along under the moonlight. The night air sucked into the turbines and fed them and charged them along with solar and whatever those pellets were that Dad put in the sliding tray that slid in and out of the instrument panel.

I sat in the co-pilot chair, having learned a thing or two about navigation, and we cruised through the last of the dying night; and then the light rose up and the world below went from shiny black to blue and white ice. What I think about is how if we'd have left a few seconds earlier, or a few seconds later, none of it might have happened. But there we were with first light on the windshield, and then the shield turned dark, and there was a whomp, a sound like some kind of machine tearing metal. It wasn't metal though. It wasn't the ship. It was the scream of the Martian bat. The damn things are huge, and unlike Earth bats, which Dad says travel by night, Martian bats travel day and night, but are blind, their eyes huge and white as snow. They are guided by some kind of in-built radar. That radar helps them find prey, and I guess the bat thought we were one of the great blue birds that fly over the ice, for it came at us and let out with its horrid scream that sounded like metal ripping. The craft twisted and swirled, but held to the sky all right, at least until the bat bit us and clawed us and we started to come apart.

The craft killed the bat due to collision of its wings or part of the beast being sucked into a turbine. Whatever did it, we both went down. I remember seeing out the windshield a glimpse of the bat's wings, a near subliminal glimpse of those white eyes and that toothy mouth. The front end of the ship bent up, and down we went. Had the bat not had hold of us, had what was left of its massive wings not held and glided, we would have dropped faster than a stone and with the sudden impact of ripe fruit being slammed on rocks.

Still, when we hit I was knocked unconscious.

Coming to, I discovered I was lying on the ice. I had on my insulated suit. Dad had insisted I wear it, even in the craft, and I was glad then I had. I didn't have the hood pulled up though, and when I sat up on the ice, stiff and sore, I pulled it over my head and lifted up the goggles and the chin cover that had been lying on my chest, suspended there by a dangling strap.

I tried to get up, but it was like I was wrestling someone invisible. I just couldn't do it, least not at first. It was as if whatever kept me balanced had been knocked off its gyro. I finally got my feet under me, which took me so long I though maybe a Martian year had passed. When I did get to my feet, I looked around for Dad, but couldn't find him. Over the hill I saw the Martian buzzards gathering, their red-tipped wings catching the rays of the sun. I stumbled over a little mound of snow, and there was the ship. Or what was left of it. It was so wadded up with the bat, which was about the same size, that it looked as if a great leathery black animal had mated with a silver bird and then fallen to earth in blind passion.

Moving that way, I soon saw Dad, lying out on the ice. When I trudged to where he lay, I saw the snow around him had blossomed red and had frozen, like a strawberry ice drink. I got down on my knees, and tried to help him. He put out a hand.

"Don't touch me," he said. "It hurts too much."

"Oh, Dad," I said.

"There's nothing for it," he said. "Not a thing. I'm bleeding out."

"I know how to sew you up," I said. "You taught me."

He shook his head. "Won't do any good. I'm all torn up inside. I can feel how stuff has moved around, and I'm not getting any stronger here. Prop me up."

There was a loose seat cushion, and I grabbed it, gently lifted his head and rested it on that.

He said, "When the sun gets to the middle there, I won't be with you."

"Don't say that," I said.

"I'm not trying to scare you," he said. "I'm telling you how things are, and I'm about to tell you how things have to be, before I'm too weak to do it. I'm going to die, and you should leave me here and take the medicine, if it survived, if you can find it, and you got to take one of the sleds and go across the ice, into the mountains and make your way over to Far Side."

"That's miles and miles," I said.

"It is, but you can do it. I have faith. Those people have to have the cure."

"What about you?" I said.

"I told you how that's going to turn out. I love you. I did my best. You have to do the same."

"Jesus," I said.

"He didn't have anything to do with it. Alive or dead, he never shows up. You got to do it on your own, and the thing that's got to carry you is knowing you're a King. Think of it like an adventure, like those cheap romance novels I used to read to you."

He meant adventure novels. They were old stories, like *Ivanhoe*, and he said they were called romances, but they were primarily stories of high adventure. Right then, I didn't feel too terribly adventurous. I wanted to lie down beside him and die right along with him. When I was dead I didn't care what happened to us. Frozen in ice, or eaten by snow runners, or those buzzards with red-tipped wings. It was all the same to me.

"You got to see yourself as a hero," Dad said. "You got to see yourself as a savior. I know that sounds prideful, but you got to see yourself that way. You got to find that bag, and you got to put it and you on a sled and start out. The supplies may have survived too. You'll need them. There's plenty of things out there on the Martian ice, so you got to stay alert. You'll be able to make it. Go quick as you can. But watch for the ice, and what's under the ice, and what flies above it, and what lives on it."

I nodded.

Dad grinned then. "I'm not making it sound easy."

"No," I said. "You're not."

"Well, it isn't easy. But you're a King. You can do it."

And I swear right then, no sooner had he said those words, he closed his eyes and was as long gone as the day before.

—

THE SMART THING to do was to leave him, but I couldn't. Not to be eaten by Martian birds, and whatever else might come along. I strapped him onto one of the sleds that I found in the wreckage. There were two. The other had been crunched up and was nearly in a ball. The one I used had some bends and gaps in the metal, but it was serviceable. I searched around for the medicine and supplies. They were easy to find. I put them on the sled.

The supplies had food and water and lighting, first aid, flares, blankets, tubes of this and that, and even a pair of snowshoes, all tightened up in a little bundle; but with a touch of a finger they would spread out and form to any foot.

I went then and got Dad and dragged him over to the sled. Being so confused, I didn't have enough sense to take the sled to him. I pulled one of the five weather blankets from the supply packet and wrapped him in it. It fastened up easy on the sides, and over his feet and head. I managed him into the sled, up near the front. I put the supplies and the medicine in there with him.

I took my place in the seat and pulled the clear lid over me and sat there and thought a moment. Looking out in front of me, seeing Dad's body shaped in the blanket, I started to cry. That went on for a while. I won't lie to you. It was a tough moment, and right then, once again, I thought maybe the Kings did quit; at least this one might.

Finally, I got myself together and turned the switch and hit the throttle. The sled jumped forward and I steered. As I went, I popped one of the compass pills. I didn't feel anything at first, but then there was a subtle twist in my brain, like a hot worm trying to find a place to rest, and then I knew. I knew how to go. The pills were like that. One could get you set in the direction you needed. They were made from a Martian worm, which is why I said I felt like a worm was in my head. It was that kind of sensation. Something in the worm's DNA allowed it to travel from one end of Mars to another, consuming one, you got the same ability. You knew what the worm knew, and all it knew was direction. You didn't have to wait as long for it to kick in. It was nearly an instant sensation.

The sled hummed and the rig beneath it split the snow and slid across the ice. It had some lift about it too. I needed it, the machine could float up to ten or twelve feet, and I could float on water, and it was air tight enough to act for a short time like a mini-submarine. It sure beat snowshoes.

—

ALL THIS WORLD, and all the worlds there are, and all the stars, and all that is our universe, are connected. That's what Dad used to tell me. I, however, felt anything but connected. I felt like a particle to which no thing could be fastened.

I sled-bumped a few spots where the snow had drifted across the ice, and then there were no drifts, just this long expanse of blue and white like a sheet stretched tight, and far away a thin line of mountains on the horizon that seemed to recede, not come closer. Probably because they were actually moving, because the Martian Mountain range slides and shifts and moves back and forth, a little from side to side. It's something to do with the bedrock. It's a shift of as much as fifty miles in either direction, ten side to side, and right now, subtle as it was, slow as it happened, I knew it was moving away from me.

After some time, I stopped and popped the lid on the sled and got out. Inside the sled it was comfortable because there was a heater and I had wrapped my legs in one of the thermal blankets, same sort Dad's body was wrapped in. Outside the air cut like a frozen knife. I found a spot to relieve myself that looked like all the other spots available. I dropped my pants and squatted to pee. It was cold on my butt. Anyway, I did my business, and while I was doing it, I saw it coming.

At first I thought it was an illusion, mirage. But no, it was real. A black fin had broken the ice, and it had broken it violently enough I heard it crack, though I figure I was a quarter mile from that fin. I didn't know what it was from experience, but I had read about it, and recognized it that way.

It was an ice shark, big as killer whales on earth, but sleeker with a black fin and tentacles that exploded from its head like confetti strands, but were considerably more dangerous. It could travel on the surface or underneath, and could even crawl on land for a long time. Its fin was harder than any known metal and could crack the ice without effort. The ice shark had a tremendous sense of smell, a bit of radar, not as highly developed as the bat, but effective enough. It could squeeze into tight places, like oatmeal sliding through a colander. It had most likely smelled my urine and had come for lunch.

I yanked up my pants and made a quick-step trip back to the sled, slid into place and closed the lid and gave it the juice. Too much juice. It jumped, came back down with a smack. For a horrid moment I thought maybe I had done myself in, destroyed my transportation and shelter, but then, away it went.

I pulled the view screen over and took a look through the back view cameras. It was still coming, and it looked closer, and I knew those cameras were not entirely accurate; the shark was considerably closer than it appeared.

The sled had more juice to be given, but I saved it, because the more you used, the more sunlight you needed to keep it charged, and now, to make matters worse, the light was dropping down over the moving mountains. When nightfall came I would have power, but it sometimes faltered then, if the sled was given full throttle. Still, if I slowed too much, the shark would catch me. Crunch the craft in its great teeth, snapping it apart, getting to the gooey, tasty center inside, meaning, of course, me and my dad.

—

THAT SHARK COULDN'T have known I would be more vulnerable come night, but it sure seemed to. It came fast behind me, but was never able to catch me, even though I had only pushed the throttle a little more than before. Yet, it was like it knew I had limitations. That if all it did was wait, I would have to slow down and it would have me.

It was growing dark, but I could still see the line of mountains and the vast expanse of nothing around me, and then all of a sudden the light washed out and the moons rose up. I turned on the lights.

And then it happened.

Even inside the sled I could hear the ice crack, and then I could see them. I had never actually seen them for real, just vids, but there they were, cracking up through the ice and rising up and sliding along—the Climbing Bergs. They were rises of solid ice that came down from the depths where it was cold and wet and where the old, old Mars was. They would break open the surface and slide along and suck in the air. They were mounds of ice full of living organisms that owned them. Living organisms that came up for air and pulled it in and renewed themselves like Southern Earth ladies with hand-shaking fans on a hot day in church. Sometimes they were empty ice—clear ice you could see all the way through. And sometimes the ice held the ancient Mars inside of it. I had heard of that, extinct animals, and even Martians themselves, though there had only been fragments of that discovered, and most stories about them were legends, as the ice soon sank back down into the depths, taking their ancient treasures and information with them.

The ice cracked loud as doom and rose up and the moons flashed on the clean, clear ice, and the moonlight shone through it. It covered my entire path, and inside of the ice I could see things; a dark shadow. The shadow was in the center of the ice, and it was a shadow that covered acres and rose up high. Then I was close enough I could see better what the shadow was. It almost took my breath away, almost made me forget about what was behind me. It was a slanting slide of ice that went directly up against the icy wall of the berg, and inside the berg was a huge set of stone stairs that rose up to a stone pyramid, and the stairs went inside and dipped into the dark. The ice between the outside and the pyramid looked thin, as if it might be hollow inside the berg.

I knew this much. I couldn't keep outrunning the shark. In time the sunlight would wear, and the sled would slow. I had a sudden wild thought, but it was the only one I had. Besides, going around the berg might take hours; it was that big.

I glanced in the mirror and saw the shark's fin, poking high, and I could see its shape shimmering beneath the ice. A huge shape, and

I could see that it was as said, a monster that in spite of its name was really nothing like a shark. It was a dark form that was formless; it moved like gelatin, except for the fin, which stayed steady, sawing through the ice effortlessly.

Aiming the sled for the natural slide of ice, I gave the machine full throttle. I knew I was sacrificing some of my juice, but it was as good a plan as any I could think of.

I slid up the ice and came hard against the cold, clear wall of the berg, killed the engine. I flipped the top and got out, leaned over and tore the supply bag open. Jerking out three of the thermal sticks, better known as flares, I gave them a twist, and tossed them against the ice. They blossomed with flame. The flames rose up high and the heat singed my hair, made a kind of hissing sound as it melted a big hole in the ice. It was as I had hoped, a thin wall of ice, and inside, it was open; it was as if the ice were a glass cake cover of unusual shape and design, dipped over a pyramidal cake.

I looked back. The shark tore its whole body through the ice. It shifted and twisted and wadded, and finally it roared. It was a roar so loud I felt the ice beneath me shake. The roar and the wind carried its horrid breath to me. It was so foul I thought I might throw up. Its shape changed, became less flat and more solid, tentacles flashed out from its head, and I could see flippers on its belly, between those dipped little legs with bony hooks for feet. It was slithering and clawing its way across the cold space between me and it.

Back in the sled with the lid pulled down, I gunned forward and drove in and bounced up the steps, and then I was inside the pyramid. The lights on the sled showed me the way. I went along a large hallway, if something that large could be called a hall. On either side were strange statues of tall, thin creatures that resembled men. I zoomed by them and came to two wide open doors made of something I couldn't identify. They were wide enough for me to sled through, leaving several feet on either side.

Once I was inside, I grabbed a light from the supply bag, got out and tried to push one of the doors, but it was too heavy. Then I had an idea. I got back in the sled and circled it back against one of the doors and pushed, and it moved, slammed shut. I did the same with the other. I got out to make sure, flashed the light around. I could see there was a lock on the doors. It was too large for me to handle. I saw on one side of the door a rectangular gap. Running over there, I poked the light inside. There was a switch in there. I grabbed hold of it and tugged. It creaked and made a noise like a begging child, then I heard the lock slam into place. I had taken a guess, and I had been lucky. I had pulled the right switch, and the amazing thing still worked. It had most likely not moved since before the beginnings of civilization on Earth, and yet, no rust, no decay. It worked. A little squeaky, but otherwise, fully serviceable. If I hadn't been in such a tight spot, I might have marveled even more at this turn of events.

It wasn't really damp inside the pyramid. Inside its icy den it was clean and clear and there was air. If I remembered what I had read about the microscopic things in the ice, they would rise every now and then—maybe centuries passed before they rose—and they would suck at the air, and they would give off air as well, they would fill the void around them with it. Before this had merely been specu- lation, but I was breathing that air and I could verify it. In fact, the atmosphere inside the pyramid was so rich it made me feel a little light-headed.

Then I heard the shark hit the door. It had come out of the ice and onto the steps. It struck the door hard. The door shook, but held. I crawled back inside the sled, and with the lights guiding my path, I drove it deeper into the structure's interior.

—

I FINALLY CAME to a large room, and even more amazing, it was lighted. The lights were like huge blisters on the walls, and there were plenty of them. They gave off an orange glow. They were not strong lights, but they were more than adequate to see by. I killed the sled's beams and engine, got out and looked around. It was amazing. First off, I couldn't understand at first how the lights could exist, but then I thought about the old Martian technology that had been uncovered over the years. Things that had existed and survived and not decayed for millennia; like that door lock. They had been so far ahead of us in many ways it was impossible to comprehend. Add to that this strange iceberg, this thing made of ice and creatures that sealed off this world from water and decay, provided oxygen, and then sunk back to the bottom of the sea, and it was enough to make my head spin.

There were sheets of ice where one wall of the pyramid had actually been destroyed by what looked like an explosion. That part of the wall had a large bubble of ice that swelled out from it, and there was a sheet of ice on the outside of the pyramid, and inside the enclosed bubble there were beings. I blinked. They were in great stone chairs and they were frozen solid. They were easily eight feet high and golden skinned, with smooth heads and closed eyes. Their noses were flat against their face and their mouths were slightly open, and I could see yellow teeth that looked hard and like little carved stones. They had long fingers, and leaning against the seats, or thrones on which they rested, were weapons. Things that may have been guns, long and lean of barrel, without any real stock, but with apparatus on both sides that looked like sights and triggers. There were harpoons, twelve feet long at least, with long blue-black blades. They looked heavy.

Whatever had broken the outside wall, it had caused these beings to be frozen, instantly. I could only imagine a war in ages past; an explosion that opened them to the outside air, which must have been freezing. But the truth is, I can't really explain it. All I can say is there they were and I have seen them.

I walked about the huge palace room, for that was what I had concluded it was. That was only a guess, of course, but it was the one I decided on. Now that my eyes had adjusted, I could see that there were thumb-sized red worms on the floor, and my feet were crunching them as I walked. There were worms in the walls, at least where the stones had separated, and when I looked up I could see movement on the high ceiling. I flashed my light up there, to help brighten the orange glow of the room. I saw that it was the worms. They skittered over the ceiling on caterpillar legs, fell to the floor now and again like bloody rain.

In the distance I could hear a booming sound. I realized it was the ice shark, slamming itself against the great doors of the pyramid. My idea was to find a back way out. Use a couple of the thermal flares to cut the ice cover loose and flee, maybe without the monster knowing I was gone. But all I found was a gap in the wall and a split of six tall and wide corridors that fled into darkness.

Hurrying back to the sled, I closed the lid and fired it up, moving across the floor with the sled's lights sweeping before me. I came to the divided corridors and hesitated. I had no idea which one I should take, or if any of them led to an exit. I sat there and thought about it, finally decided to take the middle one. I reached out and gently touched Dad's wrapped body, for luck, and then I throttled off into the middle corridor.

IN THE LIGHTS the red worms seemed to leak from the stones. As I went, behind me I heard a loud shattering sound. The doors. The ice shark had broken them down. That had to be it. I couldn't believe it. The damn thing was not a quitter. Like a King, it stayed on track.

All I could do was concentrate on what was in front of me. Along I went and it was deep dark in there. My sled lights had begun to flicker and waver. I had probably used more of its energy than I thought while fleeing the ice shark. I didn't know what to do, other than to keep going forward, so I did. When I felt I would go on forever, there was a glow, and then I was out of the tunnel which emptied out onto an icy ridge. It was the moons that gave the glow, and in front of the ridge was a great long, sleek ship of shiny metal, a seagoing ship with massive paper-thin, metal sails. It took a moment before I realized it too was inside the icy bubble. The bubble had broken in spots, and new barriers of ice had developed, and there were sheets that dipped down from above and onto the ship, like ice-fairy slides. The stern of the ship was open, and there was a drop door that lay on what had once been the dock. I directed the sled that way and drove inside.

I drove along the open path, and it was wide and tall, for it had been made for the golden Martians. That made it so I could use it like a road. I drove into the depths of the ship and along a corridor. Finally I stopped and got out and pulled open a partially opened door and looked inside. It was a large room. The sled, though powerful when completely charged, is light as a feather. I pushed it inside the room effortlessly, came out, and closed the door. I thought I would leave it there for safe-keeping while I looked about for a way out on foot. I wanted to preserve what power it had left. If I could get out on the ice, and if I could manage to keep it moving until daylight, it would start soaking up the rays of the sun again, and the more sun it got the faster it would go.

Moving along quickly, I came to a vast opening with great portholes on either side. In front of me, I saw an immense chair in front of a wide stretch of viewing shield.

I eased in that direction and saw a long, massive leg poking out. When I went around and looked, there was one of the Martians. Golden and huge. Bigger than the others. His hands lay on a large wheel, and at his right, and on his left, were gears and buttons and all manner of devices, and beneath them were squiggle shapes that I figured were some kind of long-lost language.

I examined his face. His eyes were open, and he still had eyeballs. They had not rotted. They were frosted over, like icing on doughnuts. Part of his skin had fallen away in a few spots, and I determined this wasn't from decay. It was from wounds that had been inflicted. He had been attacked while he sat in this chair. Perhaps trying to direct the ship to sea. On the wall to the far right was a row of harpoons like those I had seen earlier. They were on racks and I figured they were for show, maybe old, ceremonial weapons more than ones they might have used when their world went from top to bottom, from air to ice, but those blades looked mighty sharp and dangerous nonetheless.

It took some work, but I climbed on the control panel and looked out through the great view glass in front of the Martian and his chair. The moons were bright and there was a thin see-through icy barrier in front of the ship and beyond it more flat ice, and way, way off, the dark pattern of the mountains. It looked so far away, right then I felt sick to my stomach.

Then came a wheezing sound, a cracking of things, and I knew instinctively the ice shark had followed me here.

—

I'LL BE HONEST. I thought the ice shark would quit. They can survive off the ice and out of the sea, but I didn't know they could stay out so long, but sure enough it was the shark; I could smell it. I couldn't see it, but that odor it had was of things long dead in water, of all its recent meals come up in gassy bubbles from its stomach (stomachs, I'm told) and it had all oozed out in an aroma so bitter I felt as if my eyebrows were curling.

I went and stood on a counter in front of the rack that held the weapons, and picked the smallest harpoon there. This one would have been really small in the hands of that seated Martian, a light throwing spear for him, but for me it was heavy, yet manageable. I pulled the harpoon down, jumped to the floor and moved swiftly to the opening that led out, then I heard it coming down the hall. It was wheezing and slipping and sliding over that ship's ancient floor, and it sounded near.

Back in the control room, I climbed up on the counter again. It ran along the wall and past the portholes. I hustled to one of the portholes and used the tip of the harpoon to pry at it. I worked hard but it didn't move. I could hear the ice shark coming, and its smell was overwhelming. Just when I thought the thing was in the room with me, the porthole snapped beneath my prodding; popped completely out and went shattering onto the deck below. I tossed the harpoon out then, lowered myself out of the hole, and dropped about eight feet to the deck. I picked up the harpoon and hustled along the deck and tried to find my way to the room where I had left the sled and my poor dad's body.

When I glanced back that monstrous thing was easing out of the porthole like it was made of grease. When its dark head poked through it ballooned wide again and the rows of teeth reassembled and tentacles popped from its head. Its bright white china plate eyes turned toward me on a thin neck swelling large as it eased out of the porthole. I knew then that it would never give up. I remembered my dad said: "The ice shark is a big booger, but it's got a brain about the size of an apple. A small apple. It rests right between the bad thing's eyes. That's what makes it dangerous. That small brain. It doesn't consider alternatives. It's a lot like a lot of people in that respect. It makes a decision and sticks to it, if it makes any sense or not. It finds its prey and it doesn't give up until it eats it or it gets away."

The shark's head hit the deck with a plop, and it began to slither. As the rest of it came out of the porthole, it swelled, and tentacles popped from the rest of its gooey form and those little legs sprang out. What was coming out of the porthole was at least twenty times bigger than me.

For too long a moment I was welded to that spot by fear, and then the spell broke. I think it was the stink that did it; struck me like a fist. I turned and ran along the deck. Behind me the ice shark wailed so loud my ears ached. I grabbed at a door that led inside. Locked. I tried another. More of the same.

I finally found one that was not locked, but it wasn't coming open easy. I put my whole 140 pounds and six feet against it (I'm a big girl) but it still didn't move. Along came the shark, slithering and making that unpleasant screeching noise. I gathered up all the strength I had, and some I borrowed from somewhere I didn't know existed, and shoved and shoved at that door with all my might. The door moved. It made a crack wide enough for me to slip inside. On the floor by the door was the corpse of one of the Martians. It had fallen there some ages ago in combat, perhaps against invaders that had killed it and the others and went away with heaps of spoils. Its head was almost lopped off its body, and a dark goo had run from it and dried to the floor and turned solid as stone.

I jumped over the body and scrambled down the hall just as the shark broke through. I turned my head to see both of its eyes looking at me in the near dark. They glowed like white fire. Then it dipped its head and took to that long dead Martian's body, began gobbling it up with a sound like a turkey choking to death on too much corn. I wondered if it had done the same to the Martian in the chair, gobbled it up, but I must admit, neither of those long dead creatures were a big concern. What I was worrying about was if I was going to get away.

Doors were closed in the hall, and the only light was the dual moonlight slanting through portholes on my right side. And then the hall came to an end. It emptied at a wide open door that was not an exit, but was in fact, a row of shelves, and the shelves had dividers, like a bee's honeycomb. There was nowhere for me to go now.

I was trapped.

—

THERE'S NO TRUE description of how I felt. You can't put that kind of desperate emptiness into real words. I can say it was like a pit opened up and I dropped through, but that can't be right, because that's at least some place to go. I could say everything fell in on me, but that would have either killed me outright or given me something to hide behind. No. I was out there. Naked in state of mind. The ice shark was coming. I could hear it slurping along the floor, wailing so loud the ship's walls shook. My heart beat so hard against my chest I thought it was going to spring out of me. It was as the old Earth saying went: It was die dog or eat the hatchet time.

The shelves were large and easy to climb, so I took that route. It was a route to nowhere, but I took it anyway. I pushed the harpoon into one, and then climbed up on it, pushed the harpoon into the higher shelf, and climbed into that one. When I got to the top, the shark entered the room. I turned just in time, clutched my harpoon and put my back against the wall of my cubby hole, pushed the haft of the harpoon under my arm so that it was braced against the wall too, and waited for it, knowing full well it wouldn't have any problem entering that little space where I waited; not with what its body could do.

Let me tell you how it came.

Like the proverbial bullet, that's how. There was the space before me, empty, and then there was the stink and then—

—it was there.

It thrust forward hard against the opening of the shelf with a flash of teeth, a glow of white eyes, like head beams, and it hit the harpoon point and let out with a scream like an old woman on fire. It writhed and slammed against the walls of the shelf hard enough I heard them crack, and then its head flexed rapidly, and it became smaller and it tried to dart into the shelf with me. I shifted the harpoon, remembering what Dad had said about that small brain, that little apple between its eyes, and I poked at that. It popped back and away, throwing out wide those tentacles that were some-times concealed in its head. They flexed and flashed in the air like Medusa's snakes. It came again, and I screamed with fear and anger, lunged, stuck it deep with that harpoon. I kept lunging and ichors like a stomped caterpillar sputtered out of it and splashed my face. It felt like pus from exploded pimples. I kept jabbing, and it kept shrieking, and then—

—it went away.

Or rather, moved out of my sight.

I sat there trembling with fear, my body covered in its innards, or brains, or whatever that mess was.

Had I killed it? Walking on my knees I made my way to the edge of the shelf, poked my head out—

—it rose up like a serpent and struck with a screech.

It was reflex. I screamed almost as loud as it was screeching, poked out with the harpoon, not at any target mind you, just poking at it, poking in fear. The harpoon went in deep, and the shark jerked back and that yanked the harpoon from my grasp. I thought: Okay, Angela, this is it, you might as well hang your head between your legs and kiss your ass goodbye, because in the next few moments it will have you, and the last thing you'll hear is a crunch as it bites through you, and then for you it's ice shark digestion and a bowel release of your remains beneath the icy sea.

It slammed against me then, cracked the shelf. The haft of the harpoon, which had been jerked from me, hit me between the eyes. Stars gathered up and filled my head. The shelf cracked more, and then I fell and the stars dropped backwards into the blackness.

———

WHEN I AWOKE I was on the shark, and it had gone flat, like a dish rag. I got up slowly and looked about. Only its head was a mound, and I could see the harpoon sticking out of it like a unicorn horn.

The thing had spread out so much it filled and trailed all the way down the long hall. I got up slowly and fell back against the wall by a porthole. I had, by accident, not by design, hit that apple between its eyes. I had tried repeatedly to do that without success, and then, due to fear, desperation, and happy accident, I had managed it.

I laughed. I don't know why. But I laughed way loud.

Gathering myself, and let me tell you, at that point there was a lot to gather, I started looking for my sled. I went down the corridor, walking on the ice shark for a long ways, and finally I came to another corridor, and that led to another. I realized I was getting more confused, so I backtracked the way I had come, and finally I came to where the Martian body had lain by the door, but was now gone, consumed by the dead ice shark. I went out that door and along the deck of the ship, looked up at the porthole I had dropped out of. It was too high up to climb. And if that wasn't bad enough, I felt the ship shift. Then shift again.

I assumed for a moment that the berg was merely moving, but when I looked past the bubble of ice that contained the ship, I saw that the frozen surface over the sea was cracking. The berg was about to settle again, way down in the deeps like an enormous stone. And I was trapped.

I couldn't leave Dad, not here in this icy grave, so I rushed along the deck and followed it around. Eventually, I came to the stern of the ship. There was a staircase there. I took it. I went down and found where the ship was open at the rear, where I had driven in with the sled, and I ran back inside, the way I had come earlier. Finally, I arrived at the room where I had left the sled and Dad's body. Pulling the sled out, I opened its top and slipped in behind the controls and started it up and let the lights sweep before me. I drove back the way I had come, through the long corridor, to where those incredible red worms climbed the walls. I drove on, and as I did I could hear ice cracking and there was starting to be water on the floor of the pyramid.

By the time I came to the mouth of the pyramid the water was rushing in, and then it covered the sled as the iceberg sank, taking me down with it, pushing me back with the might of the sea.

As I said, the sled had submergible abilities. The lid was fastened tight. The lights cut at the dark water, but the problem was I was still inside the mammoth berg, and it was going down hurriedly, and the sea was darker down there. Ice was crashing all about and bits of it were sliding in through the gap I had made with the flares, banging against the sled like mermaids tapping to get in.

I levered it forward and bounced against the sides of the pyramid, fighting the power of the water with all the juice there was in my little machine. I saw a bit of light, the moons piercing the water, making a glow like spoiled milk poured on top of cracked glass. And then that light began to disappear.

I pushed on, and though I had some idea where the gap in the ice was, I had a hard time finding it. I couldn't figure it. Then I realized that it had begun to ice over already; the creatures in the ice, they were sealing it up. I went for where I thought the gap had been, hit it hard with the nose of the sled. The sled bounced back. I went at it again, and this time I heard a cracking sound. I thought at first it was the sled coming to pieces. But the lights showed me it was the ice shattering. It was just a glimpse, a spiderweb of lines against the cold barrier. I hit it again. The sled broke through and the ice went all around me in slivers. Up and out I went. And then the lights began to blink.

The sled slowed. It drifted momentarily, started going back down into the jet-black, following the descending pyramid and ship. I tugged back on the throttle and the engine caught again, and up I went, like an earthly porpoise. The sled shot up through a hole in the ice, clattered on the surface of the frozen water. The lights blinked, but they kept shining.

Tooling the sled out wide and turning, I headed in the direction of the dark bumps that were the Martian mountains.

For a moment I felt invigorated, and then I began to feel weak. I thought it was food, and I was about to dig in the bag of goods, when I realized that wasn't the problem at all. My shoulder was wet, not with cold water, but with warm blood. The ice shark had hit me with one of its teeth, more than one. It had torn a gap in my shoulder that my adrenaline had not allowed me to notice until then.

I thought I might pass out, something I had been doing a lot of lately. I aimed the sled the way my head said go; the way the worm pill in my body said go. I dug in the bag and got out a first aid kit, tore it open, found some bandages. I pushed them against the wound. They grew wet, through and through. I pulled them off and put on some more. Same thing. I let them stay, sticking damp to my flesh. I dug in the bag and found a container of water, something to eat in hard, chewy bar form. It tasted like sawdust. The water hit my throat and tasted better than any water I had ever drank, cool and refreshing.

The sled was heading straight toward the mountains. Depending on how long the charge lasted, I should be there in about eighteen hours. I knew that as easy as I knew my name was Angela King. I knew that because Dad had taught me to judge distance. Beyond the mountains, on the Far Side, I had no idea how much more I would have to go. I was living what my dad had called a cheap romance. I had found a lost word of dead Martians encased by ice and busy microbes; I had fought a Martian ice shark with a harpoon and won. I had gone down in an iceberg, down into a deep, dark, cold sea; and now I was gliding along the ice, bleeding out. I knew I'd never make it as far as the mountains; I damn sure wouldn't make it to the other side. If I didn't die first, the engine on the sled would go, out of sun-juice. By the time morning came and the sun rose up hot and slowly charged the engine, I'd be a corpse, same as my dad. That was all right. I had done my best and I hadn't quit. Not on purpose. I looked out once more at the moonlit ice and the rolling mountains. I laughed. I can't tell you why, but I did. I lifted my head and laughed. My eyes closed then. I didn't close them. They were hot and heavy and I couldn't keep them open.

I reached out with the toe of my foot and touched Dad's covered head, and then I passed out. That was starting to be a habit, but I figured this would be the last time.

—

If you die on Mars, do you go to Martian heaven? Did the old, gold Martians have a heaven? I know I didn't believe in one, but I was thinking about it because I seemed to be going there. Only I was starting to feel warm, and I thought, uh-oh, that's the other end of the bargain, the hot part, hell. I was going right on quick to Martian hell, for whatever reason. I was going there to dance with big tall Martians carrying harpoons, dancing down below with the ice sharks and the other beasts that lived at the bottom of it all, dancing in lava pits of scalding fire. That wouldn't be so bad. Being warm. I was so tired of being cold. Martian hell, I welcome you.

Then I awoke. The sled was no longer moving. I was warm now and comfortable, and not long before I had been cold. It took me a moment, but finally I knew what had happened. The sled had quit going, and the heater inside had quit, and it had grown cold, and I had dreamed, but here I was alive, and the sun was up, and the sled had been pulling in the rays for a few hours now, heating up the solar cells, and it was roaring to warm, vigorous life. The throttle was still in forward thrust position, and the sled began to move again without me touching a thing.

I couldn't believe it. I wasn't dead. Glancing out at the ice, I saw the mountains, but I knew by the worm in my head I had drifted off course a bit, though I had gone farther than I expected. Placing my hand on the throttle made my whole body hurt. My shoulder had stopped bleeding and the bandage I had made was nothing now but a wet mess. But it had done the job. I was careful not to move too much, not to tear too much.

Over the ice the sled fled, and I adjusted its navigation, kept it pointed in the right direction.

When I came to the mountains it was late afternoon, and they were moving toward me. They had shifted again. Something was in my favor for a change. I began to look for a trail through them. My body was hot and I felt so strange, but I kept at it, and finally I came to a little path that split through the mountains, and I took it. I went along smoothly and thought it would break up eventually, or suddenly a high wall of rock would appear in front of me, but it didn't. The path wasn't straight, but it was true and it split through the mountains like a knife through butter.

It was nightfall again when I came to a larger split of land, and below me where it dipped was a valley lit bright with lights. Far Side.

Plunging down the slope, away I went, driving fast. It all seemed to be coming together, working out. I was going to make it just fine. And then in the headbeams a rock jumped up. I hit the throttle in such a way the sled rose high as it could go. For a moment I thought I was going to clear the rock, but it caught the bottom of the sled and tore it and then it went crashing, spinning, the see-through cover breaking around me, throwing me out where the valley sloped off on a hill of wet winter grass. I went sliding, and then something bumped up against me.

It was my father's body. I grabbed at it, and then the two of us were going down that hill, me clinging to him, climbing on him, riding his torso down at rocket speed.

Down

Down

Down we went, Dad and me, making really good time.

Until we hit the outside wall of a house. Hit it hard.

———

THERE'S NOT MUCH to tell after that. Making it to my feet, I staggered along the side of the house and beat on a door. I was taken inside by an old couple, and then the whole town was awake. People were sent up the hill to find the sled, to look for the vaccine, and my dad's body next to the wall. The sled was ruined, the vaccine was found, and my dad was still dead. People came in and looked at me like I was a rare animal freshly brought into captivity. I don't remember who was who or what anyone looked like, just that they came and stared and went away and new people took their place.

After the curious had gone, I sat in a chair in the old couple's house, and they fed me soup. The doctor came in and fixed my wound as best he could, said it was infected, that I had a concussion, maybe several, and I shouldn't sleep, that it was best not to lie down.

So, I didn't.

I took some kind of medicine from him, sat in that chair till morning climbed up over the mountain like it was fatigued and would rather have stayed down in the dark, and then I couldn't sit anymore. I slid out of the chair and sat on my butt a long while, and then lay on the floor and didn't care if I died because I had no idea if I was dying or getting well; I just plain had no idea about anything at all.

Someone got me in a bed, because when I awoke that's where I was. I was bandaged up tight and was wearing a nightgown, the old woman's I figured. The bed felt good. I didn't want to get out of it. I was surprised when the old woman told me I had been there three days.

I guess what happens in those cheap romances Dad talked about, is they end in a hot moment of glory, with all guns blazing and fists flying, but my romance, if you can truly call it that, ended with a funeral.

They kept Dad's body in an open barn, so the cold air would keep him chilled, protect him from growing too ripe. But in time, even that couldn't hold him, and down he had to go, so they came and got me ready in some clothes that almost fit, and helped me along. The entire town showed up for the burying. Me and Dad were considered heroes for bringing the vaccine. Good words were said about us, and I appreciated them. Pretty much overnight the whole place was cured because of that vaccine.

Hours after Dad was buried I got the goddamn Martian fever and had to have the vaccine myself and stay in bed for another two or three days, having been already weak and made even more poorly by it. It was ironic when you think about it. I had brought the vaccine, but had never thought to immunize myself, and neither had Dad, and he was a doctor.

I won't lie. I cried a lot. Then I tucked Dad's memory in the back of mind in a place where I could get to it when I wanted, crawled out of bed, and got over it.

That's what we Kings do.

NAKED ANGEL

DEEP IN THE alley, lit by the beam of the patrolman's flashlight, she looked like a naked angel in midflight, sky-swimming toward a dark heaven.

One arm reached up as if to pull air. Her head was lifted and her shoulder-length blond hair was as solid as a helmet. Her face was smooth and snow white. Her eyes were blue ice. Her body was well shaped. One sweet knee was lifted like she had just pushed off from the earth. There was a birthmark on it that looked like a dog paw. She was frozen in a large block of ice, a thin pool of water spreading out below it. At the bottom of the block, the ice was cut in a serrated manner.

Patrolman Adam Coats pushed his cop hat back on his head and looked at her and moved the light around. He could hear the boy beside him breathing heavily.

"She's so pretty," the boy said. "And she ain't got no clothes on."

Coats looked down at the boy. Ten, twelve at the most, wearing a cap and ragged clothes, shoes that looked as if they were one scuff short of coming apart.

"What's your name, son?" Coats asked.

"Tim," said the boy.

"Whole name."

"Tim Trevor."

"You found her like this? No one else was around?"

"I come through here on my way home."

Coats flicked off the light and turned to talk to the boy in the dark. "It's a dead-end alley."

"There's a ladder."

Coats popped the light on again, poked it in the direction the boy was pointing. There was a wall of red brick there, and, indeed, there was a metal ladder fastened up the side of it, all the way to the top.

"You go across the roof?"

"Yes, sir, there's a ladder on the other side, too, goes down to the street. I come through here and saw her."

"Your parents know you're out this late?"

"Don't have any. My sister takes care of me. She's got to work, though, so, you know—"

"You run around some?"

"Yes, sir."

"You stay with me. I've got to get to a call box, then you got to get home."

———

DETECTIVE GALLOWAY CAME down the alley with Coats, who led the way, his flashlight bouncing its beam ahead of them. Coats thought it was pretty odd they were about to look at a lady in ice and they were sweating. It was hot in Los Angeles. The Santa Ana winds were blowing down from the mountains like dog breath. It made everything sticky, made you want to strip out of your clothes, find the ocean, and take a dip.

When they came to the frozen woman, Galloway said, "She's in ice, all right."

"You didn't believe me?"

"I believed you, but I thought you were wrong," Galloway said. "Something crazy as this, I thought maybe you had gone to drinking."

Coats laughed a little.

"Odd birthmark," Galloway said.

Coats nodded. "I couldn't figure if this was murder, vice, or God dropped an ice cube."

"Lot of guys would have liked to have put this baby in their tea," Galloway said.

The ice had begun to melt a little, and the angel had shifted slightly.

Galloway studied the body and said, "She probably didn't climb into that ice all by herself, so I think murder will cover it."

When he finished up his paperwork at the precinct, Coats walked home and up a creaky flight of stairs to his apartment. Apartment. The word did more justice to the place than it deserved. Inside, Coats stripped down to his underwear, and, out of habit, carried his holstered gun with him to the bathroom.

A few years back a doped-up goon had broken into the apartment while Coats lay sleeping on the couch. There was a struggle. The intruder got the gun, and though Coats disarmed him and beat him down with it, he carried it with him from room to room ever since. He did this based on experience and what his ex-wife called trust issues.

Sitting on the toilet, which rocked precariously, Coats thought about the woman. It wasn't his problem. He wasn't a detective. He didn't solve murders. But still, he thought about her through his toilet and through his shower, and he thought about her after he climbed into bed. How in the world had she come to that? And who had thought of such a thing, freezing her body in a block of ice and leaving it in a dark alley? Then there was the paw print. It worried him, like an itchy scar.

It was too hot to sleep. He got up and poured water in a glass and came back and splashed it around on the bedsheet. He opened a couple of windows over the street. It was louder but cooler that way. He lay back down.

And then it hit him.

The dog paw.

He sat up in bed and reached for his pants.

—

DOWNTOWN AT THE morgue the night attendant, Bowen, greeted him with a little wave from behind his desk. Bowen was wearing a white smock covered in red splotches that looked like blood but weren't. There was a messy meatball sandwich on a brown paper wrapper in front of him, half eaten. He had a pulp-Western magazine in his hands. He laid it on the desk and showed Coats some teeth.

"Hey, Coats, you got some late hours, don't you? No uniform? You make detective?"

"Not hardly," Coats said, pushing his hat up on his forehead. "I'm off the clock. How's the reading?"

"The cowboys are winning. You got nothing better to do this time of morning than come down to look at the meat?"

"The lady in ice."

Bowen nodded. "Yeah. Damnedest thing ever."

"Kid found her. Came and got me," Coats said, and he gave Bowen the general story.

"How the hell did she get there?" Bowen said. "And why?"

"I knew that," Coats said, "I might be a detective. May I see the body?"

Bowen slipped out from behind the desk and Coats followed. They went through another set of double doors and into a room lined with big drawers in the wall. The air had a tang of disinfectant about it. Bowen stopped at a drawer with the number 28 on it and rolled it out.

"Me and another guy, we had to chop her out with ice picks. They could have set her out front on the sidewalk and it would have melted quick enough. Even a back room with a drain. But no, they had us get her out right away. I got a sore arm from all that chopping."

"That's the excuse you use," Coats said. "But I bet the sore arm is from something else."

"Oh, that's funny," Bowen said, and patted the sheet-covered body on the head. The sheet was damp. Where her head and breasts and pubic area and feet pushed against it there were dark spots.

Bowen pulled down the sheet, said, "Only time I get to see something like that and she's dead. That don't seem right."

Coats looked at her face, so serene. "Roll it on back," he said.

Bowen pulled the sheet down below her knees. Coats looked at the birthmark. The dog paw. It had struck a chord when he saw it, but he didn't know what it was right then. Now he was certain.

"Looks like a puppy with a muddy foot stepped on her," Bowen said.

"Got an identity on her yet?" Coats asked.

"Not yet."

"Then I can help you out. Her name is Megdaline Jackson, unless she got married, changed her last name. She's somewhere around twenty-four."

"You know her?"

"When she was a kid, kind of," Coats said. "It was her older sister I knew. That birthmark, where I had seen it, came to me after I got home. Her sister had a much smaller one like it, higher up on the leg. It threw me because I knew she wasn't the older sister, Ali. Too young. But then I remembered the kid, and that she'd be about twenty-four now. She was just a snot-nosed little brat then, but it makes sense she would have inherited that mark same as Ali."

"Considering you seem to have done some leg work in the past, that saves some leg work of another kind."

"That ice block," Coats said. "Seen anything like it?"

"Nope. Closest thing to it was we had a couple of naked dead babes in alleys lately. But not in blocks of ice."

"All right," Coats said. "That'll do."

Bowen pulled the sheet back, said, "Okay I turn in who this is, now that you've identified her?"

Coats studied the girl's pale, smooth face. "Sure. Any idea how she died?"

"No wounds on her that I can see, but we got to cut her up a bit to know more."

"Let me know what you find?"

"Sure," Bowen said. "But that five dollars I owe you for poker—"

"Forget about it."

COATS DROVE TO an all-night diner and had coffee and breakfast about the time the sun was crawling up. He bought a paper off the rack in the diner, sat in a booth, and read it and drank more coffee until it was firm daylight; by that time he had drank enough so he thought he could feel his hair crawling across his scalp. He drove over where Ali lived.

Last time he had seen Ali she had lived in a nice part of town on a quiet street in a tall house with a lot of fine trees out front. The house was still there and so were the trees, but the trees were tired this morning, crinkled, and darkened by the hot Santa Ana winds.

Coats parked at the curb and strolled up the long walk. The air was stiff, so much so you could have buttered it like toast. Coats looked at his pocket watch. It was still pretty early, but he leaned on the doorbell anyway. After a long time a big man in a too-tight jacket came and answered the door. He looked like he could tie a knot in a fire poker, eat it, and crap it out straight.

Coats reached in his pants pocket, pulled out his patrol badge, and showed it to him. The big man looked at it like he had just seen something foul, went away, and after what seemed like enough time for a crippled mouse to have built a nest the size of the Taj Mahal, he came back.

Coats made it about three feet inside the door with his hat in his hand before the big man said, "You got to wait right there."

"All right," Coats said.

"Right there and don't go nowhere else."

"Wouldn't think of it."

The big man nodded, walked off, and the wait was started all over again. The crippled mouse was probably halfway into a more ambitious project by the time Ali showed up. She was wearing white silk pajamas and her blond hair looked like stirred honey. She had on white house slippers. She was so gorgeous for a moment Coats thought he might weep.

"I'll be damned," she said, and smiled. "You."

"Yeah," Coats said. "Me."

She came over smiling and took his hand and led him along the corridor until they came to a room with a table and chairs. He put his hat on the table. They sat in chairs next to one another and she reached out and clung to his hand.

"That's some butler you got," Coats said.

"Warren. He's butler, bodyguard, and makes a hell of a martini. He said it was the police."

"It is the police," Coats said. He took out his badge and showed it to her.

"So you did become a cop," she said. "Always said you wanted to."

She reached up and touched his face. "I should have stuck with you. Look at you, you look great."

"So do you," he said.

She touched her hair. "I'm a mess."

"I've seen you messy before."

"So you have, and fresh out of bed, too."

"I saw you while you were in bed," he said.

She didn't look directly at him when she said, "You know my husband, Harris, died, don't you?"

"Old as he was when you married him," Coats said, "I didn't expect him to outlive you. Of course, he had a lot of young friends and they liked you, too."

"Don't talk that way, baby," she said.

As he thought back on it all, bitterness churned inside Coats for a moment, then settled. They had had something together, but there had been one major holdup. His bank account was lower than a snake's belly, and the best he wanted out of life was to be a cop. The old man she married was well-heeled and well-connected to some rich people and a lot of bad people; he knew a lot of young men with money, too, and Ali, she saw it as an all-around win, no matter how those people made their money.

In the end, looks like they both got what they wanted.

"This isn't a personal call, Ali," Coats said. "It's about Meg."

And then he told her.

When he finished telling her, Ali looked stunned for a long moment, got up, walked around the table as if she were searching for something, then sat back down. She crossed her legs. A slipper fell off. She got up again, but Coats reached up and took her hand and gently pulled her back to the chair.

"I'm sorry," Coats said.

"You're sure?" she asked.

"The dog paw, like you have."

"Oh," she said. "Oh."

They sat for a long time, Coats holding her hand, telling her about the block of ice, the boy finding it.

"Any idea who might have wanted her dead?" Coats asked.

"She had slipped a little," Ali said. "That's all I know."

"Slipped?"

"Guess it was my fault. I tried to help her, but I didn't know how. I married Harris and I had money, and I gave her a lot of it, but it didn't help. It wasn't money she needed, but what she needed I didn't know how to give. The only thing I ever taught her was how to make the best of an opportunity."

Coats looked around the room and had to agree about Ali knowing about opportunity. The joint wasn't quite as fancy as the queen of England's place, but it would damn sure do.

"I couldn't replace Mother and Father," she said. "Them dying while she was so young. I didn't know what to do."

"You can't blame yourself," Coats said. "You weren't much more than a kid."

"I think I can blame myself," she said. "And I will."

Coats patted her hand. "Anyone have something against her?"

"She had gotten into dope, and she had gotten into the life," Ali said. "I tried to pull her out, but she wasn't coming. I might as well have been tugging on an elephant's trunk, trying to drag the beast uphill. She just wouldn't come out."

"By the life, you mean prostitute?" Adam asked.

Tears leaked out of Ali's eyes. She nodded.

"Where'd she do her work?"

"I couldn't say," she said. "She was high-dollar, that's all I know."

Coats comforted her some more. When he was ready to leave, he picked up his hat and she walked him to the door, clutching his arm like a life preserver, her head on his shoulder.

"I can't believe it, and I can," she said. "Does that make any sense?"

"Sure," he said.

"You got married, I heard."

"Yeah," he said. "It was great. For about six days."

When Coats opened the front door the hot wind wrapped around them like a blanket. Coats put on his hat.

"It's just awful out there," Ali said.

When he stepped down the first step, Ali said, "You could come back and stay here, you know. There's plenty of room. You could stay as long as you like. You could stay forever."

He turned and looked at her. He looked at the house. It was one hell of a place and she was one hell of a woman. But it was too much of either one.

"I don't think so, Ali."

—

THE UPSCALE PART didn't tell Coats much about Meg's work habits. She could have worked anywhere. The only thing it told him is she gave sexual favors to people with money. Coats didn't like to think it, but she and Ali weren't really all that different. It's just that Ali made her deal the legal way.

On the way back to his apartment, Coats drove by the now-defunct Polar Bear Ice Company. It was just another reminder of what he had found in the alley, and it made his head hurt. He drove a little farther and an idea hit him. He turned around and went back.

He parked out front of the ice company in a no-parking zone and walked around back. There was a chain through the sliding back door and there were boards over the windows. The boards over one of the windows were easy to pull loose, and Coats did just that. He crawled inside and looked around.

Before today, last time he had seen Ali was through the prism of a polar bear made of ice. She had decided he was a bad prospect, and started seeing Old Man Harris from way uptown. He heard she was at a party and he went over to see her, thinking maybe he'd make a scene; went inside like he belonged there. And then it hit him. Everyone there had an air about them that spoke of privilege and entitlement. They were everything he was not. Suddenly, what he was wearing, what he had thought was a nice-enough jacket, nice-enough shoes, felt like rags and animal hides. He saw Ali across the way, her head thrown back, and above the music from the orchestra in the background he heard her laugh. A deep chortle of pleasure that went with the music and the light. She was laughing with a man who wasn't the man she married. She was laughing with Johnny Ditto; a gangster, drug seller, and prostitute wrangler. He was known for handling the best girls, high-end stuff. Johnny was tall, dark, and handsome, splendid in a powder-blue suit with hair that was afraid to do anything but lay down tight and hold its part.

Coats stepped aside so that a table mounted with a big ice sculpture of a polar bear on an ice floe was between him and them. Below the ice was a ring of shrimp, tight up against the sawlike cut at the bottom. Through the sculpture he could see Ali, made jagged by the cuts and imperfections in the carving. He lowered his head, feeling as out of place as a goat at the ballet. He slipped out quick. Until today, it was the last time he had seen Ali.

What he realized now was that the sawlike cut at the bottom of the ice that night was locked in his head, and it was the same jagged cut he had seen on the ice block in the alley. And that polar bear on the table—was that the ice company's emblem? It made sense, connected up like bees and honey.

Coats walked around and found a room in the back with a bed and camera and some pull-down backdrops. He toured all over, came to the ice freezers with faucets and hoses and frames for shaping the ice. One of the frames was about the size of the big block of ice in the alley. The kind of block an ice sculptor might chop into a polar bear, or use to house a cold, dead angel.

Coats drove along Sunset, and for a moment he thought he was being followed, but the car, a big blue sedan, turned right, and he decided against it.

Downtown he stopped at the morgue to see Bowen.

"What we got is her belly was full of water, and so were her lungs," Bowen said.

"So she drowned?" Coats asked.

"Yeah, but the way her throat looks, I think someone ran a hose into her mouth, pumped her up. Figure they squirted it in her nose, too. Unpleasant business."

"When did she die?" Coats asked.

"The ice throws that off. It's hard to know body temperature to figure how long she was laying there, messes up rigor—" He stopped in midsentence.

Coats was nodding all the time Bowen was talking.

"Oh, I get it," Bowen said. "That was the point. Harder to know when she died, harder to break an alibi someone might use. They could kill her and walk away, and the ice melts, body's found, it doesn't show signs of being dead as long. They could kill her, one, two, three days before and keep her frozen, drop her off when they wanted."

"If the boy hadn't gone through the alley, she'd just be a dead prostitute," Coats said.

"It kind of figures now," Bowen said. "We found, let me see, three other girls in the past week in alleys. All of them stripped and lying on the bricks. One of them, she was in a pool of water. It wasn't urine. We couldn't figure it. Now it makes sense. She melted out of her block."

"I think they may have killed them all at the same time," Coats said. "Kept them frozen, put them out when they wanted to, made it look like a string of nut murders. But this time the ice didn't melt soon enough before she was found."

"And all this means...what?"

"I'll get back to you on it," Coats said.

—

At the Hall of Records a snooty woman with her hair in a knot so tight it pulled her cheeks up under her ears showed Coats where he could look up what he wanted. What he wanted was to know who owned the Polar Bear Ice Company. When he saw who it was, his stomach ached.

He went home and called in sick for his shift, took off all his clothes, sprinkled the bed with water, and lay there with the window open listening to traffic. The sunlight went deep pink and hit the buildings across the way, made them look as if they were being set on fire by celestial arsonists. He thought about what he had found out at the Hall of Records and decided it didn't necessarily mean anything, but he could never quite come to the conclusion that it meant nothing. He was thinking about what he should do, how he should go about it all. He eventually decided whatever it was, tomorrow was soon enough, after he got some rest.

In the middle of the night he came awake to a click like someone snapping a knife blade open. He slogged out of his dreams and got up and picked his gun off the nightstand. Naked as a jaybird, he walked into the kitchen and looked at the front door, which is where the snicking sound was coming from. Someone was working the lock.

The door slipped open a crack and when it did, Coats lifted his pistol. Then the door went wider. Framed by the outside streetlights was a woman.

"Come on in," Coats said.

"It's me, Ali," the woman said.

"All right," he said.

She came in and closed the door and they stood in the dark. Coats said, "You always work men's locks at night?"

"I was going to surprise you."

"I thought you might be someone else," he said, and turned on a small light over the kitchen sink. She looked at him and smiled.

"Who would you be expecting?"

"Oh, someone about Warren's size. Maybe drove you over in a big blue sedan. Maybe he's standing out there right now with a lock pick in his hand."

"I didn't know you liked Warren that much," she said.

"I don't like Warren at all."

"It's just me," she said. "Don't be silly." She smiled and looked Coats over good. "I certainly like your lack of dress, though a hat and tie might spruce it some."

"Your husband, he never owned the Polar Bear Ice Company."

"What?" she said.

"That means you didn't inherit it."

"Make some sense, baby," she said. "I didn't come here to talk ice. I came to see you and make some heat."

"That's all right," Coats said. "It's plenty hot enough."

"I don't know," Ali said. "I'm starting to feel a little chilly."

"You own the Polar Bear Ice Company. You bought it. And it's not out of business. It's just closed off and secret and the only time they make ice now they put someone in it. And you got a partner. Johnny Ditto. He's on the books with you, honey. That doesn't bode well. He's not what you'd call your stand-up businessman."

"In business, you have all kinds of partners. You can't know them all. Is that a gun?"

"It is," Coats said. "You know what I think, Ali? I think you're just what you've always been, only more so. Your sister, you were running her with your high-end stable. You were her madam, her and the other girls. Somewhere along the line, you and her, you got sideways, and you had to have her wings clipped."

"Me? That's ridiculous."

"You got a good act," Coats said. "I believed it. That walking around the table bit, that was good. And I didn't tell you my address. So how'd you come here?"

"I know people who know people," she said.

"At the ice house, I found a camera, and I figure that's where some special pictures were made; reels for smokers. But I also got to figure a girl like Meg, she might have made a film for one of the owners. Someone like Johnny Ditto, a little keepsake for him to take home and watch on lonely nights. But she decided maybe to keep the film, take it out of the private realm. I think she may have made other films, her and some of the other girls. Maybe not just for Johnny. But films for big-name guys who wanted to watch themselves do the deed with some fine-looking babe. Only the babes kept the films. Threatened blackmail. Asked for money. Johnny might not have cared who saw him do what. But some of the clients you and him were servicing, they might have been more worried. You couldn't have that. So you had to have the films and you had to get rid of any girls in on the scheme. They had to pay. Even your sister had to pay."

"Don't be silly," Ali said. "She was my sister. I wouldn't hurt her."

"But you might let someone else do it for you."

Ali's face changed. She looked older. She looked tougher. It was like the devil had surfaced under her skin.

"You're too damn smart for your own good," she said. "It wasn't exactly like that, but you're near enough you get the Kewpie doll."

"I got to take you in," Coats said.

She said, "Warren."

Even though Coats expected it, he was still surprised. He thought Warren would have to open the door. But he came through it. The door blew off the hinges like it had been hit by cannon shot and Warren came speeding through the gap. He rushed straight at Coats. Coats brought his gun up and fired, but it didn't stop Warren. Warren hit him and knocked him back over the table and into the wall. It made cabinet doors fly open and it made dishes fly out; they popped and shattered on the floor.

Coats lay on the floor with Warren on top of him, choking him with both hands. Coats's vision crawled with black dots and there was a drumbeat in his head. He tried to get his feet stuck up in Warren's belly to push him back, but Warren was too close. Coats felt around for the gun, but couldn't find it.

Then he saw Ali, leaning over them, looking down at him. She had his gun in her hand.

"I got nothing against you," she said. "It isn't personal. But business is business, and it's what runs the world. You finish up here, Warren. Make it look like a robbery. Mess things up some more."

Warren didn't seem to be listening. He was concentrating on choking the life out of Coats. Ali wandered off, sat in a chair at the table, and coiled one leg over the other.

"You are quite the waste, baby," she said.

Coats pushed his shoulders up. It helped a little, lessened the choke. There were fewer black dots. He glanced sideways, saw a broken cup from the cabinet. He snatched it up and dragged it hard across the side of Warren's neck. Warren yelled and sat up. One hand flew to his neck, the other still clutched Coats's throat. Blood crept through Warren's fingers, leaked onto the floor.

Coats smashed what was left of the cup into Warren's nose and rolled him off. There was a shot. Coats felt a bit of a pinch in his side. He scuttled his feet underneath him and rushed at Ali. She was coming out of the chair, pointing the gun. Coats dropped down and the gun barked and his ears rang. He kept coming. She tried to fire again, but he had her wrist now and was shoving her into the wall. When he did he lost his grip on her, but she lost the gun. It went sailing across the room. He struck her with a hard right to the side of the head. She dropped like a brick and didn't move.

A big hand grabbed Coats's shoulder and jerked him backward. He went tumbling across the floor. When he looked up, Warren was looking at him. He had one hand to his cut neck. His nose was flat and bloody. His teeth were bared and there was a look in his eye that made Coats feel weak, as if from a blow. Warren trudged forward a couple of steps. Coats lifted his fists, ready to fight. He figured he might as well be bear hunting with a switch.

Warren's face changed. He had a look that reminded Coats of a man who's forgotten his money. Warren swallowed, then coughed. Blood flew out of his mouth. He pulled his hand away from his neck and blood squirted high and wide. Warren looked at his bloody hand as if it had been replaced with a catcher's mitt. Coats saw now that the first shot he had fired had hit Warren in the side. The big galoot hadn't even noticed.

Warren sat down on the floor and tried to put his hand against his neck again, but he was too weak. It kept sliding off.

"Damn it," Warren said. Blood gurgled out of his mouth. He carefully stretched himself out on the floor and made a sound like someone trying to swallow a pineapple. Then he didn't move again. He was as dead as last year's Christmas.

Coats went over and looked at Ali. She was breathing heavily, and she had a blue knot on the side of her head, but that was the worst of it. When he stood up, he went weak. The hole in his side was dripping big time. He leaned against a chair for a moment, got it together.

Outside, through the doorway, he saw lights. The shots had been heard and someone had called. Pretty soon, cops would be coming up the stairs. He grinned, thought maybe it would look better all around if he could at least put on his pants.

DEAD ON THE BONES

IT WAS SOLID night out there in the woods down by the river, but we had plenty of light cause there was a big fire built up in the middle of the clearing for just that reason, and there was a dozen kerosene lanterns hung in the trees. The trees was mostly willows, though there was some giant oaks, and I was under one of the oaks getting ready to clean three catfish that was going to be grilled up for supper.

Uncle Johnny said, "Now you skin them catfish out good," and he gave me a knife and a pair of pliers, wandered toward the fire to pile on some big-sized logs.

I ain't one to love cleaning fish, but at least catfish you don't have all them scales, like a bass or such. You can hang them up and make a cut around the head and take the pliers and pull the skin off, like helping a lady out of a jacket.

Uncle Johnny got him a bottle of beer out of a tub of ice, sauntered back over. He had on a chambray shirt half buttoned up and some loose pants and boxing shoes he only wore on nights like this. Them boxing shoes had cost him a pretty penny. That was why he kept them stored in the closet most of the time. They wasn't for wearing around, but for boxing only.

He had cut his hair close to his head. He always cut it skin-close on fight nights. The firelight crackling and jumping lit it up like it had been shined with floor wax and a polish rag. I could see cuts here and there where he hadn't been smooth with the razor. It looked like the top of his head had been in a briar patch.

He said something about making sure to look inside the catfish guts when I broke them open, cause he had found some stuff in them that was mighty curious from time to time. He even had a pocket knife he said he'd cut out of one of them once, a long one with a yellow-bone handle. That was the one he'd given me to clean the fish with. It was a good knife, and I knew when I got the skins off the fish and touched the point of it to their bellies, they'd split open like a hot watermelon in the sun. I was thinking I'd love to stick it in him, see how he split open, on account of he may have found some stuff inside catfish, but that knife wasn't one of them. He ought to know I knew who it belonged to. I had sharpened it enough.

I don't think he cared. I think he just told that story because he liked to tell it, and maybe he half-believed it himself, and maybe it was just his way of messing with me. That knife had belonged to my pap. Pap told me someday he was going to give it to me, and I thought about saying something about it, but figured it might not be the thing to do. Not the smart thing anyway.

If Johnny would kill my pap, I figured he might kill me too. Mama wasn't all that fond of me either, when you got right down to it. She put Uncle Johnny over me and Pap. I guess it could be she was scared of him, and I could understand that. I was scared of him, and everyone else was too.

There was good reason. He was big and strong and in plenty good shape and had a temper like hot water about to boil. I had actually seen him run a wild boar down once, jump on it and kill it with a knife, and it trying to get its tusks in him. It had already killed two of Uncle Johnny's dogs, which is what made him so mad.

He didn't care for much, but he loved them dogs. As for Mama, he had wanted her because he didn't have her. Once he got her, he didn't want her, least not all the time. Everyone knew he had other women. Everyone knew he had killed several men and one woman, and there was rumor of a child. A baby that was drowned. One of the men he killed was a lawman that came after him, and the woman that was killed was his first wife. It was pretty well understood, if not proved, that he and Mama had killed my pap.

Like I said, there was good reason to be scared.

Uncle Johnny stood over me for a moment, a bottle of Jax in his hand, sipping at it like a kitten at its mother's tit, then said, spraying me with beer breath, that I ought to hurry on up, cause the grease was hot and the cornmeal was ready to roll the fish in.

I had the three catfish hung up on a limb by a rope run through their gills, and they was huge. I had a kerosene lantern dangling from a nubbin of a limb, broken off by drought and wind, and I was working mostly by that light. I took the lantern down from time to time to hold up next to the fish to make sure I was doing the job right. One alone would have made a meal for five or six, but we had three of them, all of them caught by Uncle Johnny. He had snagged them out of the river that day. They had been kept fresh on lines that let them hang in the water and swim about. I ain't stretching it too much to say them fish was as big as me, and I'm twelve years old and pretty tall and solid of weight. Smaller catfish are supposed to taste better, but when Mama Mooney rolled the cuts of them fat old fish in cornmeal with salt and pepper, put them in a big cooking pot full of boiling, hot grease, it would all come out sweet and tender as the first breath of spring.

While I was working, I could see the grown-ups starting to drive down there in the bottoms. In bad wet weather they couldn't have done that. The river would have been all the way up to the woods and the dirt road, and sometimes over it.

I watched them get out of their cars and trucks and gather around the fire that was too hot for the night but gave plenty of light. They gathered and greeted each other. There was a lot of them, which was how it was expected, this being about the only thing around to do outside of squirrel hunting or drinking potato skin liquor.

Mama was there too, of course. Her long blonde hair hung way down her back and she had on a long dress, the way Pentecostals are supposed to wear, but it fit her a little tight, and when she moved she moved like a fish in its skin. I figured there was plenty of Pentecostal men that night would look at her and think of sin, which I figured fit since they was also drinking. Of course, what they had all come to see didn't have much to do with religion either.

There was side dishes brought by all the ladies. Shelled corn, beans and breads, casseroles, pies and cakes and all manner of fixings. I watched as they stacked them on a row of long, plank tables. The men and their wives had also brought gifts for Conjure Man, and those they laid out on a table that had been put away from the food and the fire. The gifts was in brown sacks or wrapped up in newspaper.

I was right seriously scared of Conjure Man, on account of not only how he looked, but because of what he could do. I was scared of Uncle Johnny, but I was more scared of Conjure Man, and nervous about what I was going to be seeing, 'cause I had seen it all before.

When I had the fish cleaned, their guts spilled out on the ground, I checked through their innards by using a stick to push them around, but there wasn't nothing inside them that interested me. Only thing was one of them had swallowed an old white china cup with blue flowers painted on it. It wasn't broke up even a little bit, until Uncle Johnny came over, saw it lying by the bluish intestines of the fish, stepped on it and smashed it. He didn't like nothing that was whole. Anything like that, a cup, a person, he wanted to break it.

"Ain't them cleaned yet?" he said.

"They got to be filleted," I said, "that's all that's left to it."

"I can see that. Get 'em on over to the cutting table," he said. "Quit messing around."

He took a gulp of his Jax and went back to the fire. Pretty soon I could hear all of them men and women talking amongst one another about this and that, but mostly about the Depression that was going on, and how the President said all we had to fear was fear itself. One man said, "Yeah, that and starving to death."

That might be, but wasn't nobody going to starve this night. I pulled the fish one at a time off their hanging lines and carried them the cutting table where Mama Mooney was. She was smooth-skinned and black as the night. She was meaty and always smelled sweet like honeysuckle. I asked her about it once. She said it was her soap. That it was made with ash and hog lard or bacon squeezings, and sometimes store-bought lye. Said she broke honeysuckles into it when she made it, or mint when she had that, and sometimes both. She said if she didn't do that, the bacon squeezings she used to make the soap would make her smell like breakfast. She said that wasn't entirely a bad thing. Her husband liked it.

Mama Mooney had already started cutting up the catfish when Uncle Johnny came over. He was impatient and nervous, getting ready for what was to come. "You getting it done, auntie?"

"Yes, sir, Mr. Johnny," she said. "I'm working on it right smart."

"Get on it smarter," he said. "We got a crowd here already and more coming."

"Yes, sir," she said, as if she was getting paid a king's ransom instead of five dollars.

I seen then Uncle Johnny had a look on his face that made me feel uncomfortable. He had that Jax half-lifted to his mouth, and was watching the younger girls that had come with their folks and was helping lay out the food. They was maybe thirteen or fourteen.

"Looks like them girls is getting pretty near ripe," Uncle Johnny said.

I felt cold all over. Mama Mooney reached out and got me by the elbow, said, "You come on over here and help me sort out these cuts of fish."

Me and Mama Mooney took the fish she had rolled in her mix of cornmeal and spices, and dropped them carefully into the boiling pot of grease so it didn't splash up on us and burn our skin to the bone. It wasn't hardly no sooner than them cuts was in the grease, than they was fried and Mama Mooney was scooping them out with a wooden ladle long as me.

She dipped the fish out and put them in large bowls on the cook table. She filled bowl after bowl after bowl. Fact was, we run out of bowls and had to put some of the fish out on a white, table cloth folded up thick on the far end of the table. The chunks stained the table cloth and filled the air with a sweet, hungry smell. My mouth watered.

It was time to eat, and a little later on would be the Conjure Man.

—

MY PAP WAS a bad-luck fella, and he wore that bad luck like a suit coat on a bum.

He treated me all right, though. He worked hard at the cotton gin, but the job wasn't good like it had been 'cause the cotton crop was smaller, and what things was made from cotton wasn't selling like it once was. Folks didn't have money and were making do with what they had, so the need for cotton wasn't as high as it might have been, least not at the gin where Pap worked. They gave him fewer hours, and this meant he worked a lot of pick up jobs while Mama stayed home, such as it was, and painted her nails and read magazines and was messing around with Pap's brother, my Uncle Johnny.

Now, I didn't know this right away, though I reckon Pap did, but didn't say nothing. I never could understand that. Guess he was so in love with Mama he wouldn't dare to say anything 'cause that would make it real. As for me, I have to say I didn't much care for her, even if she was my mama. She didn't like me neither. I think it's because I look just like Pap.

I found out about her and Uncle Johnny one afternoon when I come in from the river, fishing for our supper. I brought the fish I'd cleaned into the house, heard moaning, the kind you might make when you sat yourself down in a wash tub full of clean, hot water.

I saw what was making the moaning pretty quick, 'cause our house wasn't so big you had to hunt for anybody. The door to the bedroom was wide open, and there was Mama and Uncle Johnny on the bed, neither of them with a stitch of clothing on, and what Uncle Johnny was doing to Mama wasn't the sort of thing you'd mistake for a fella trying to help someone get a cinder out of their eye.

I knew enough about farm animals to have that figured, but there I stood, statue-stiff, watching, and then Uncle Johnny looked up and seen me, and smiled. Just smiled like wasn't nothing going on that anyone ought to be concerned about. I took myself and my fish out of there and started walking, and somewhere along the way I just tossed them clean fish and the pail they was in to the side of the road. I don't remember how long I walked. Finally I came back and there was Pap's old car in the yard, him home from work, and when I went in the house he was sitting in a chair, looking as if a rain cloud was right over his head and it was about to blow water and drown him.

Uncle Johnny and Mama was sitting at the table eating some cornbread with honey, and wasn't neither of them mindful of Pap or me. It was right then I knew Pap knew what I knew. I don't know that he found them in the same way I did, but I think they just told him and said for him to get over it. Pap was like that. He could take a lot and would. He wasn't really a strong person like his brother, Johnny. He just didn't have it in him to be forceful. He was strong all right. I had seen him lift the back end of a car up and hold it while a fella changed a tire, and he could bend a tire iron until it darn near looked like a horse shoe, but in his head and heart he wasn't strong. That part of him the wind could blow away.

Mama finally looked at me, and when she did, the look on her face was so odd it made me uncomfortable. Pap got up slowly, walked over to me, put a hand on my shoulder, and before I knew it he was guiding me out the door and to the car.

He drove us out in the country. The trees were high and green and the hills rose up and were split by the red clay roads. We drove on and on, and sometimes we drove back the way we had come, and on out again.

The night came down and the moon went up and we kept driving, out on the bad clay roads, on through the shadowy woods, and down to the edge of the Sabine River. Pap got out of the car and walked over and stood on the bank. I walked down there with him. The river smelled like wet dirt and fish and rotten things. There was on either side of us some tall reeds growing and there was a little bit of wind. The wind rattled the reeds and whistled in-between them in a way that could make your hide stand up off the bone.

Pap stood there and looked at that brown, moonlit water like it was calling to him, like he wanted it to swallow him up and wash him away, as if it were the River Jordon wanting to carry him wet and quick, way on out to the Promised Land.

I reached out and took his hand. His fingers wrapped around mine, and he turned and looked at me. The moonlight glistened off the wet stains on his cheeks and made his eyes glow like a deer's. He smiled. It was a slow smile, and he had to fish for it, but he hooked it and pulled it up.

Without saying a word he went back to the car, climbed into the front seat, stretched out, closed his eyes, and crossed his hands over his chest like a dead man. I got in the back seat and lay there and waited on him to say something, anything, but he didn't say a word. I could hear him breathing though, so I knew he was awake.

After a time the moon got sacked by some clouds and there was a rumbling of thunder and a sky-wide slash of white lightning made the sky brighten up. That lightning cracked so loud it was like someone had taken a whip to the roof of the car. When it cracked I hopped up a little and made a noise, and Pap said, "That's all right, son. It ain't gonna hurt you none. You try and sleep."

"Okay," I said.

I lay back down.

Pap said, "You know what's going on, don't you?"

I said I did, and he said, "That's too bad, son. It really is. But you're old enough to know sometimes things are just what they are and not what you want them to be, or what they ought to be, and then you got to decide if you're going to put up with it. I been putting up with it a long time, but today they're telling me to put up with it. It's one thing to put up with it, another to be told to put up with it."

I was a little confused on that at first, but finally it come to me what he meant. I lay there waiting for more, but there wasn't anymore. I watched the lightning for a long time, listened to it pop and crackle, listened to the thunder pound and roar, and then there was the rain. It fell down on the car roof, and at first it was loud, but then it got a kind of evenness to it, and that caused me to close my eyes. With my eyes closed I could still hear the thunder and the sizzle of lightning. Now and then there was such a hot blast the light came right through my eyelids. But I didn't open them. I just lay there, and pretty soon, lightning or no lightning, thunder or no thunder, I was asleep.

In the morning, when I woke and sat up, the rain was gone. Pap was sitting up in the front seat with the window down. The air was turning warm and steamy from the rain, and flies had come into the car and were buzzing around. I waved my hand at them to keep them off my face. Pap shooed them out of the car window, and when they was all out, he rolled up the window and we sat there for a bit. With the window rolled up it was terrible hot, so Pap started up the car and drove us away.

I climbed up front with him as he drove. We rolled down our windows and let the wind come in then, cause the flies couldn't, not at the speed we was driving, which was pretty damn fast on wet clay roads. Finally Pap slowed down and drove right. We came off the clay roads and onto a gravel road and rode into town.

Pap drove us to the café, which was something we hardly ever done. We went inside and he ordered up some coffee and breakfast, and while we ate, Pap said, "I once fought your Uncle Johnny. We was both wanting to box. We fought each other all over the place. I had some skill, more than him. I was stronger and the same quick as him, but I didn't have no backbone. Still don't. When it came to the getting place I didn't get any. I gave in because I couldn't stand it and didn't want to stand it. My will wilted like a flower in winter. I ain't one to care much for my brother right now, and haven't cared much for him in a long time, but what I want to say to you is you got to have backbone, not be like me. It ain't got me nowhere in life, not having any. You don't got to be mean or cruel or just wrong acting like your Uncle Johnny, but you might want to get that other part, the backbone, and wear it up tight under your skin."

"Pap," I said, "it's you I want to be like."

Papa didn't seem to hear what I said. He sat there with the coffee still full in his cup, his food untouched. He said, "I tell you what. I'd like one more crack at Uncle Johnny, gloves on, or gloves off. Just a hard, square fight, and not even square, now that I think about it, but a fight to the death, cause I think maybe now I could find some backbone."

That was the last real conversation we had, cause a few days later they found him dead and dumped out by the river with a bullet in the back of his head. Wasn't no way to prove it, but I knew, and everyone else knew, it was Mama and Uncle Johnny that had done it, Johnny being the one to pull the trigger. With Pap shot in the back of the head I got to figuring maybe Uncle Johnny didn't have all that much backbone after all. But then there were fights, and who he fought went against that thinking, because so far he had fought Bob Fitzsimmons, Gentleman Jim Corbett, and John L. Sullivan, who gave him the best fight, cause he was more like a street brawler and strong too. He had fought them all and won, and them wasn't men you fought if you didn't have no backbone; you fought them that backbone had to be made of steel.

No one was at the funeral or the grave burying besides me and a preacher and the colored folks that worked with him at the cotton gin. One of the men when he come by me at the grave, said, "Your daddy was all right. He was a good man."

I thought maybe he was too good. So good he didn't have that backbone he said he needed.

Right after that I went home and got to thinking on how I could kill Uncle Johnny. I wasn't feeling all that favorable toward Mama neither. This went on for a year, me thinking, and watching my back, cause I didn't know for sure I wasn't next. I didn't stay at home anymore than I had to, to sleep mostly, cause that's where my bed was, on the screened-in back porch. But I slept nervous. It was like the sheep in the Bible that was supposed to lie down with the lion. He might do that, but I figured he'd keep an eye open, and that was me, one eye open. And maybe like the sheep, I lay there thinking on how to kill the lions in my life. I was thinking on this one night, lying in my bed on the back porch, when Pap came to see me.

He came and sat on the edge of the bed. The front of his head was all torn open where the bullet had come out of it. He said, "I had one more straight out crack at Johnny, I could take him."

I said, "I know, Pap," though I didn't know no such thing at all. And then he was gone. I wondered was I dreaming. But I felt wide awake. I got out of bed, went to breathe the air through the porch screen. It seemed like real air. The moths that were clinging to the screen wire seemed real. I pinched myself. I was awake all right.

I figured it was Pap come back from the grave, and not a dream. It was easy for me to believe that, because I had seen Conjure Man and what he could do, so it wasn't much of a jump to think Pap had come on out from behind the veil to speak to me.

I sat up in bed and waited for him to come back, but he didn't never show.

—

WHEN WE FINISHED up eating the catfish and all the sides we wanted, the men took to whisky flasks, or pulled Jax beer from a tub of ice, and everyone set about digesting. I hadn't felt hungry at first, but the smell of that cooking fish had made my belly gnaw, and I had eaten my fill.

I noticed the men was starting to check their pocket watches. It had to be getting along time for Conjure Man and the bout. And sure enough, it wasn't five minutes later that I heard Conjure Man's old truck, its loose parts clanking along the road, its motor grumbling like a hungry lion. As the sound came nearer you could see the women was looking nervous and the men was trying not to. Only Uncle Johnny seemed solid, like that backbone of his, the one Pap had talked about, had latched in tight and was packed with fire.

Conjure Man's old black truck come into view and along with it a cloud of red dust, and the dust crawled around that truck like a dusty snake. The truck drove on past the crowd and parked out by the table with all the gifts on it. The door creaked open and Conjure Man stepped out. Something inside the truck stirred but didn't come out, even though the door was left open.

Conjure Man was tall and thin and his skin was night-sky-black. He wore a black hat, black shirt, pants and coat, and black cowboy boots. It was as if him and that old black truck had peeled themselves out of the dark.

He had a clay jar under his arm, and he come along to the tables smiling. Not like no other colored, the ones that knew they best act a certain way around whites, but in a way my Uncle Johnny said was uppity, but he didn't never say that to Conjure Man.

Conjure Man seemed to float up close to the fire. He had a smell about him, sweet and sharp to the nose, like old flowers dying. Big blue-bottle flies came with him and made a halo around his head. He set that clay jar on the table with the food, and without a word to nobody, got himself one of the metal plates, a fork and spoon, went along picking up a little of this and that, heaping it on his plate. Now and again he'd pick something up and bite into it, frown, and toss it over his shoulder. After he had done that a couple of times, a big black dog with a head the size of a well bucket and a slink to its walk, come out of the shadows of the truck, out of the open door, and loped over and took to eating what Conjure Man had tossed.

No one said nothing, just watched. Conjure Man finally had his plate the way he wanted it, and he found him one of the wooden chairs and set down and enjoyed it, got up when the plate was nothing but greasy, heaped some great spoonfuls of banana pudding onto it, sat back down and ate with a lot of smacking and smiling. When he was done, he tossed the plate on the ground and burped louder than a bull frog. He went over and got him a couple of the Jax out of the ice tub, used the bottle opener on them. He drank one down like it was water, sipped on the other. It was then that he looked up and seemed for the first time to see everyone there.

He went over to the table that was laid out for him, looked through the sacks and boxes at the gifts that had been brought, said, "Load 'em up."

That meant us kids was to take all the gifts and put them in the back of the truck. None of us wanted to do that, because we knew what lay in the bed of the truck, but we had to do it. It was the way things got started, and what was in the pickup bed wasn't going to do us no harm, nor anyone else, least not yet.

We started doing that, and the dog went with us, making me nervous, on account of I figured he could rear up and grab my head in his teeth and pull it off. But all he did was get back in the truck and lay down.

It was cold around the truck and our breath puffed, and that didn't make no sense, it being dead summer, but that's how it was. When we had all the gifts in the truck bed, laid out away from the thing in the middle that was covered in oil cloth, we went back to the others, where the air was warm, and we didn't waste no time doing it.

Conjure Man finished his beer and got the clay jar, walked over to the clearing, said, "So, you all ready there, Johnny Man?" Had any colored man other than Conjure Man called him anything but Mr. Johnny, or sir, he'd have killed him. But Conjure Man had what Uncle Johnny wanted, and he was afraid of him too. Conjure Man had the darkness on his side, and he had a voice like someone who had just chewed and swallowed a mason jar, and that was something that gave you pause; you couldn't help but think that voice was coming from some place way down deep, so deep it went all the way into the ground.

"I'm ready," Uncle Johnny said. "I ate light and drank one, so I'm ready."

That's pretty much what he always said when Conjure Man asked him if he was ready.

I stood by Mama Mooney. She put her arm around my shoulders, and it made me feel good and warm in a way didn't have nothing to do with the summer heat. It was the way I figured a child ought to feel when his mama was nearby, and that mama was worth something.

The clearing was wide and surrounded by the tables of food. In the center of the clearing the dirt was worn from the shuffling of feet, for people had been coming here for bouts for a long time, bouts between men, and then the kind of bouts that Uncle Johnny fought. Pap always said he ought not to be messing with such things cause it couldn't have any good kind of ending. That was of course when Pap still tried to like his brother, even though he knew he wasn't worth the powder it would take to blow his ass up.

Now, let me tell you something here, so you'll know, as an old man down at the feed store says. Souls don't go to heaven or hell. Whatever is inside of us just goes, and when it gets where it is, it's just some place neither happy or unhappy. It's just a place. Pap explained all of this to me once, 'cause the Conjure Man explained it to him, way back, and how that talk between them come about I got no idea.

Pap said Conjure Man said all the souls that have ever lived and died are in this place between times and spaces, and someday our souls will be there too, just drifting and floating and mingling. It's a good enough place, Pap was told. It ain't got no strife or worry, and what you done in life is without reward or punishment.

As for them souls, well, Conjure Man could call them up with the right spells. They was kind of like ghosts, but if you had a place for them to go, a body they could slip into, they could come back. Conjure Man could control them to some extent, but they sure didn't like being here on this earth, not after being nothing for awhile. 'Cause when they come back they knew then the world was just a place where people was striving for this or that, or trying to get with this man or woman, or trying to take hold of some money, or get a new hat or drive a new car, always wanting this or that, and from their new point of view wasn't none of that worth spit.

So what Conjure Man done is he made it so people that liked to box could get their chance to fight the greatest that ever lived. He'd find a dead body about the size of the boxer in question, say his stuff, and that soul would come whistling into that body with all its old skills. What had to be done then was to get the fighter in front of that dead man with the soul stuffed in him, and let them go at it. See who was the better man.

Uncle Johnny had fought them fighters in them dead bodies, and he had always won, though like I was saying about John L. Sullivan, he had his time with that one, and after the fight he was laid up for nearly six weeks. Back then I kind of thought a little more of Uncle Johnny, 'cause he wasn't bothering Mama. But it was after that fight, after her seeing him fight, that she got the fixation. The need to breed, as I heard one man say when he saw Mama crossing the street and didn't know I was listening.

The fights was private, but there was plenty knew about them, and bets were made on who would win. Lots voted for Uncle Johnny, but lots would vote tonight for the shade of Jack Johnson, who was said by many to be the best there ever was.

Out in the crowd was the General Store owner, the banker, the owner of Little Beaumont's Four Star Café, housewives and farmers, a preacher or two, a teacher and a mayor. Except for Mama Mooney and Conjure Man, everyone was white.

So Conjure Man takes that clay pot, sets it on the ground, takes off the lid, picks up a stick, pokes it inside and stirs something around. Whatever it was, it had a smell like a ripe outhouse. The stink filled the air, made it heavy as lead.

Conjure Man bent his face toward the mouth of the jar and spat a long, sticky stream of tobacco into it, set the jar on the ground and put the lid on it, plugging the stink inside. He yelled out toward his truck, "Come on over, Dead on the Bones. Come on over and into the light. Walk from the grave and out of the night. Come on over Dead on the Bones."

Then it happened like it always did. The air turned chill, even though it was the dead of summer. I could feel Mama Mooney's arm around my shoulders shake with the cool and she made a noise in her throat that reminded me of a scared dog under a porch.

Conjure Man's truck shook a little and then the oil cloth raised up as what was under it sat up. The cloth fell off it then, and there was the dead man. A big black man with shoulders wide as a milk truck, no shirt on.

Conjure Man called out again. "Come out of that shadow. Come out of that dead. Come out of that truck and into the light, you ole Dead on the Bones."

The dead man stood up in the bed of the truck, swung over the side of it in a way that was pretty brisk for a fella that had recently been dug up. That was how it worked when there was a fight. A dead body had to be found, one about the size of the boxer that the boxing man wanted to fight. There was always a body, one that was fresh with no meat falling off, and no questions were asked. That made one wonder if a grave was robbed or a man was made dead with a blow to the head or a sip of a poisoned drink.

But right then I was just thinking about what I was seeing. A dead man stumbling toward our camp, walking like he had one foot in a bucket and one made of lead. The hair on the back of my neck pricked up and chill bumps crawled up and down my arms like a nest of ants.

Dead on the Bones walked between the tables and into the firelight. He wasn't wearing nothing but pants held to his waist by a rope for a belt. His bare feet kicked up dust as he came. When Dead on the Bones was in the clearing where the fights took place, Conjure Man said, "Stop them bones."

Dead on the Bones stopped, weaving a little, like a drunk trying to make the world quit spinning and find which way was up and which way was down. The firelight licked over his black skin, made it glow like a wet chocolate bar, made his flat dead eyes seem almost alive. He was a young man, but he had lived and died rough. His face was pocked and there was a dent in his forehead.

Conjure Man cackled, took the stick he had stirred in the jar, used it to make a scratch line in the dirt in front of Dead on the Bones, then he made one where Uncle Johnny would stand.

The crowd moved. We was standing still one moment and the next we was making a circle around Dead on the Bones. Uncle Johnny stripped off his shirt and stepped up to his scratch line and took a deep breath.

"You know who I want," he said to Conjure Man.

"You want Jack Johnson. You want him in his prime. You want the man that might be the greatest boxer who ever lived. Him who beat a big white man like a circus monkey. Him that knocked out teeth and danced on his toes. Him that was quick as lies and strong as truth."

"Get on with it," Uncle Johnny said.

Conjure Man took Uncle Johnny's words like piss in the face. He turned his head slowly, glared at Uncle Johnny. I saw a flicker in Uncle Johnny's eyes. He had forgotten who he was speaking to. Conjure Man wasn't no field hand. Conjure Man didn't have any rules he had to live by, except his own. Conjure Man didn't have to say Yes, sir, and thank you kindly, and Uncle Johnny knew that.

"I'm ready," Uncle Johnny said, and he was so polite for a moment I forgot who he was.

"All right, then," Conjure Man said. "We gonna do it on my own time, when I get to it and say when. You understand them rules that are mine?"

"That's fine," Uncle Johnny said, then tagged it with: "Appreciated."

CONJURE MAN RELAXED. He was about his business, and I had seen his business before. Conjure Man would pick up the clay pot, take off the lid, and let that damn smell out. Then he'd lean forward and bathe his face in it. The wind would come from all its corners, come in cold and wet and through the trees, and howl like a wolf with its leg in a trap. Then Conjure Man would lean forward and call into that jar, call out the name of the one he wanted, and there would be a noise like all the world had done cracked open, and out of that jar would blow a mess of blue-bottle flies, same as them that circled Conjure Man's head like he was an old cow pie. With them flies would be a thick blue cloud. Flies and cloud would jump on the dead man's head and sink right in. When Dead on the Bones lifted his chin he'd be Dead on the Bones no more, but a rotting body full of someone yanked on out from the big beyond.

I don't really remember doing it, but somehow I eased around in that crowd and got closer to Conjure Man. Closer than anybody, 'cause wasn't no one wanted to be that near him. He cocked his right eye toward me, and studied me. His eyes didn't have no whites because they was red with blood, and his black eyes had what looked to be a gold streak from top to bottom, like someone had cut them down the center and found light behind them.

That eye that was watching me flicked away. Conjure Man picked up the clay pot, took off the lid, and, like he always did, stuck his face right over the jar. Oh, Lordy, that stink come out of there was strong enough to lift a Buick, came out and wrapped all around Conjure Man's big old head. I felt the wind stirring. I could hear the branches creak and the leaves rustle. Then he spit the tobacco he was chewing into the jar. I seen then that he was about to shout Jack Johnson's name.

I don't know I had a real idea I was going to do it before I did it, but I leaped forward, snatched the jar away from Conjure Man, stuck my face down into that stink and yelled out my pap's name.

Well, now, that stink punched me in the face and knocked me backwards. I dropped the jar and it broke. The wind stirred up where the jar fell, and then there was more wind that came whistling cold and full from all four corners of the earth. That wind from everywhere was full of the stink in that jar and it had with it that blue cloud and those big, fat flies. The force of them winds and all that came with them dove right down onto Dead on the Bones, hit him in the top of the head with a sound like a slaughterhouse hammer smacking a big hog's head. Then there wasn't no wind and there wasn't no stink, no blue cloud and no fat flies.

All that business had gone inside him.

Dead on the Bones lifted his head and smiled.

—

DEAD ON THE Bones looked at me and chuckled. I knew that chuckle. It was the kind Pap had when he caught a fish, or gave me a smile. He had done come on out of that place for souls, and he was right there in that dead man's body, one toe on the scratch line. He looked then in the other direction, saw Mama standing there, holding a beer in her hand, and when he looked at her, she knew, 'cause she dropped that bottle of beer and it busted on the ground.

Pap chuckled again, looked straight ahead at Uncle Johnny.

"That can't be you," said Uncle Johnny.

Pap opened his Dead on the Bones mouth and tried to speak, but all he had was a gurgle.

"Do something," Uncle Johnny said to Conjure Man. "Send him back. This ain't the right man."

"No, it isn't," said Conjure Man. "But he won't go back until he's good and done. So you better fight, or you better run."

"I don't run," said Uncle Johnny. "I beat him before, and I'll beat him again. Go on, let it rip."

Dead on the Bones had his foot on the scratch line, ready to go. Uncle Johnny got set, and Conjure Man yelled, "Fight."

They shuffled toward each other, gathering up dust beneath their feet.

It started out like a bout. Uncle Johnny came in like a bull, and Pap shot out a left and hit him on the nose, then hooked a right into his body. Uncle Johnny slammed his shots home, and the thing was, Pap could feel it. Dead on the Bones didn't feel nothing, but Pap, his spirit, it felt it, and it made the dead body bend a little. Then Pap was back at it. He hit again and again, with lefts and rights, uppercuts and hooks, all kinds of combinations. At first Uncle Johnny did just fine, held his own. But then on came Pap, using that dead body like it was his, smashing and hitting, and finally there wasn't no rules anymore, and it wasn't a boxing match, it was a fight to the death.

They was slamming and jamming against one another, and though Pap's borrowed body couldn't bleed, you could see it was getting tired, same as a living man. Uncle Johnny was tired too. They clenched, and Uncle Johnny had his mouth close to Pap's ear, and I could hear him say, "For me, when we did it, she sang like a bird."

I heard that just as clear as a gunshot, and I reckon everyone else out there did too. I know when he said it Mama stepped back, crunching that broken beer bottle with her flat-heeled shoes.

"Your problem," Uncle Johnny said, "is you ain't got no backbone when it comes right down to it."

Pap made a noise like a growl, butted his head into Uncle Johnny's face, pushed him back with his left palm and swung his right in a short, sweet arch. Uncle Johnny took it right on the nose. Blood sprayed and Uncle Johnny staggered. Then came a left upper cut to Uncle Johnny's chin; it hit so hard Uncle Johnny's head flew up and there was a snapping sound, like someone had broken a green limb over their knee.

Pap grabbed Johnny's shoulders and kneed him in the potatoes. Uncle Johnny tried to clench, but Pap wouldn't let him. He'd dance back and jab, his raw knuckles cutting Uncle Johnny's face up like he was using a razor.

On this went until Uncle Johnny got savage-brave and come running at Pap. Pap stepped to the side and kicked out and hit Uncle

Johnny in his left thigh with his shin. Uncle Johnny tripped and cussed and fell flat on his face.

He was trying to get up when Pap got him around the neck with that borrowed dead man's arm, and squeezed his neck so hard that within a moment it looked like a deflated inner-tube. Then there was a cracking sound like a wishbone being pulled, and then Pap got Uncle Johnny around the waist, lifted him up so his head was down, marched to the fire and stuck Uncle Johnny's limp head right into the still hot cooking grease. The air sizzled and there was a smell like bacon in a pan.

Pap held him like that for awhile, then lifted him out of the grease and tossed him aside.

He turned then toward Mama.

She trembled. She said, "Now Phil, you don't want to do nothing. It's you I love."

But Pap did want to do something. He come charging toward her on those dead legs. She tried to mix in with the crowd, but they weren't having that. They didn't want no part of Pap. He came and they spread, and there she was, standing lonely as the last pine in a lumberjack run. She stood there like she was nailed to the spot. And then he had her. He picked her up by the waist, raised her high.

She looked down at him, he looked up at her.

I thought for a moment he was going to put her down, but he turned his head toward the fire and smiled, and ran right at that big ole blaze of crackling logs and sputtering fire, leapt right in with his heart's desire, dropped her on her back and lay down on top of her. The scream she let out was almost enough to make me feel sorry for her, but not quite. They squirmed there, overturning that grease pot. The hot grease splashed onto them and over them and the fire lapped it up.

The flames spread, ash and sparks flew. That fire wasn't like any fire I've ever seen. It ate them right down to the bones in seconds, burned the bones black, turned them to a powdery ash. A blue cloud swarming with flies and blown by wind, lifted out of the blaze and climbed on high, rode on up in front of the moon, weaved there like a drunk storm cloud, and then it was all gone and the air was still and the world was so quiet you could have heard a gnat clear its throat.

After awhile Conjure Man said, "Well, I guess that's all for the festivities, and now it's time for me to go. Thanks for the presents. Thanks for the food. I got the bets in my pocket, and I plan to keep them. You want entertainment, you know where to find me. If you want a spell to cure up that constipation, or make some man or woman love you like they was insane, you come see me. And bring your money."

He walked on out to his truck without nobody asking for their bets back. That big black dog come out of the truck and met him, licked his hand. They climbed inside, the engine got started, the lights came on, and away they went, clattering over the pasture and onto the road, driving around a wall of trees and out of sight.

People headed out of there quick like, leaving the food, the beers, the whole kit-and-caboodle. In a moment's time the place was clear of everyone but me and Mama Mooney and her old car nestled up under a heavy old willow.

She said, "You ought to come home with me, Sugar."

"I appreciate that," I said. "I sure ain't going back to our place. But I'm moving on, Mama Mooney. I'm moving on away from this place, going just as far as I can. I'll catch a train, I'll hitch a ride, I'll walk at night and sleep in the day, under a tree if I have to. But I'm away from the place, and away for good."

She gave me a smile and a soft pat on the shoulders, and that's how it was. Over and done.

I got hold of Uncle Johnny's shirt, 'cause I knew he had some money stuffed up in his pocket, a handful of bills. That was my seed money. I put it in my pocket with Pap's knife that I had hung onto, and then Mama Mooney drove me to the wide gravel road, gave me a hug and a kiss, and I got out.

She drove one way, I walked the other.

It was still night, the moon was bright, and I felt good about what I had done. I walked on and pretty soon Pap was walking beside me. I could hear his feet crunching on the gravel, same as mine.

He looked like he always had, except for his head being broken open in front. He said, "I showed them, didn't I?"

"You did," I said. "You showed them good."

"You're gonna be all right, son," he said. "You gonna be fine."

"I know," I said, and then he was gone.

I walked on.

TARZAN AND THE LAND THAT TIME FORGOT

THE GREAT CIGAR shaped zeppelin, the O-220, rose up from the great depths of Pellucidar, the underground world with its constant daylight and stationary sun, rose up and through a gap at the roof of the world. It floated high in the sky above the arctic waste, and set a course straight for England, where Tarzan, one of its passengers, was to meet up with his wife Jane; a trip promised him by Captain Zeppner, the commandant of the ship. Tarzan had made several trips to Pellucidar in the last year or so to aid his friend David Innes in numerous endeavors in the world inside the world, but now he was too long without Jane and wanted to be with her.

Two days out the wind changed and the heavens went dark with tumbling clouds and jags of lightning. The zeppelin, its crew and famous passenger, were blown way out and lost over the sea. The wind didn't stop, and the sky was so dark they were unsure of the change from night to day.

The ape man, standing in the wheelhouse of the zeppelin, clutching the railing, remembered once in Africa riding out a great storm like this in the top of a tree; the sky dumping rain, the wind as wild and ferocious as the rush of a lion. Tarzan was philosophical then as he was now. Had he fallen from the tree and hit the ground he would have died. This was a higher fall, and there was nothing but blackness before and above, around and below, but if they were to strike land or water from this height, he would be no less dead than if he had fallen from that tree. He had been in many scrapes and learned long ago that some things were beyond his or anyone's power. You only had to remain alert and look for opportunities. If none presented themselves, then so be it. That was fate.

"We've lost our bearings," said Captain Zeppner, trying to look out the view glass of the control room, but seeing only dark.

"This is not news to me," said Tarzan.

"I can't tell if we're high up, or near the sea," said the captain. "The controls aren't working. Nothing is working. Turning the wheel is a chore; it fights back. The compass is spinning."

The others in the wheelhouse were clinging to the railing that traveled the wheelhouse completely around, watching the dark skies, hoping for some miracle, like a split of light or a glimpse of land below. Then came the lightning again, ragged as a can opener. It struck the balloon and leaked out the helium with a sound like a mad child blowing water out of its mouth. The expelling of the gas shot the 0-220 across the darkness, throwing everyone against the walls, banging into rails, slamming the floor, knocking them up to meet the ceiling. Everything was coming apart. Fragments of the craft were awhirl on the wind, along with men, and the one woman who had been on board; a beautiful former savage of Pellucidar in modern aerial crew dress. Zamona was her name, a woman trained by Zeppner to crew the ship. She had been flung out of the craft by the blast of the storm, a white face and dark hair in blue clothing, looking like nothing more in the flash of lightning than a flying scarecrow. Then the lightning ended and she was gone from view.

What was left of the zeppelin hit the sea with a loud smack, a groan of metal, a split of wood, and screams from the remaining crew. The black waters raged over them. The residue of the O-220, containing Tarzan, went down into the wet, dark deeps. Tarzan eased out of a jagged gap in the broken wheelhouse, swam fiercely upward. When he broke free, a wave, like a father lifting a child on its shoulders, brought him up high, and during a flash of lightning he saw the nearly unconscious captain, clinging to a fragment of fraying wood. Tarzan swam hard, snatched Zeppner by the back of his coat collar as the lumber broke apart. He swam away from the clashing, sea-rolling debris, and after a few minutes, stopped and floated, rode the pitching waves up and down.

The storm raged through the night. Tarzan floated on his back, and clung to the captain. After what seemed like a century came daylight, the first true light in days. The storm had finally passed. Tarzan watched it rush away. It was a vast dark curtain of clouds with murky strands of rain falling out of it and touching the ocean. The sea gradually became calmer. The sky turned the color of bloody honey. An hour later it was hot and bright and blue.

Zeppner was now fully awake. He looked at Tarzan supporting him in the water, said, "You saved my life. I should hold you up awhile."

"I'm fine," said Tarzan. "You took quite a blow to the head. You've lost some blood."

The captain swung his arms at the water, kicked gently with his legs. "How can you not be tired? Let me loose. Help yourself."

"I am still alive," Tarzan said. "And there's land, my friend. I can see and smell it."

As a gentle wave lifted them, the Captain looked in the direction Tarzan had indicated, but he saw nothing, nor did he smell anything but the sea. Next time the wave tossed him, he saw what he thought was a fine brown line. Down again, and another ride up, and he saw big white birds sailing above the land. It appeared to be a great tan wall rising out of the blue-green water. It went for miles. Island or continent, he couldn't tell.

—

THEY HALF-SWAM, HALF-WASHED against the walls of the land mass. It appeared there was no way up. The walls were slick as glass. There was no beach. With the storm having passed, a mist gathered around the high walls and around them. It was as if they were insect specimens wrapped in balls of cotton.

"We will drown," said Zeppner, the waves push him against the rock wall.

"While I still live," Tarzan said, "I will assume that I will not drown, and you are not allowed to think otherwise."

Tarzan had been clothed in normal pants, shirt, shoes and a coat, as well as a belt that held a knife in a wood and leather sheath. The hilt of the knife was tied down tight. The belt and the knife were all that were left on his body. The raging ocean had taken everything else away. Zeppner was completely without clothes, or weapons. The ocean, unlike when they first fell into it, was warm near the great rock wall. Soon it was almost hot.

"The warm water is coming from inside the rock walls," said Tarzan. "The water has salt in it, but it is not purely sea water. Fresh water from inside is mixing with it. You have to try and stay close to the wall until I get back. Stay in this spot as much as possible."

"Get back," Zeppner said. "You are expecting a taxi?"

"Look," Tarzan said, and pointed. "There were limbs with leaves floating in the water, even a few flowers. Somehow those limbs managed to find their way out, probably by route of a fresh water river. If I can find it, swim against the flow, and inside these cliffs, we have a chance. And to my way of thinking, Captain, we always have a chance."

"I will say this for you, Tarzan, you are not a quitter."

"That could be my motto, Captain. Stay here, and do not give up."

Tarzan dove beneath the waves. Time fled by. The sun rose higher. Zeppner became weaker. Just as he thought he might be pulled beneath the water, a wooden beam from the flooring of the O-220 wheel house washed up, and he grabbed it. It bounced him against the great wall of rock, but clinging to it gave him some rest.

He decided Tarzan had drowned and now he had to face the ocean alone, with nothing but a plank of wood for a companion. He tried to encourage himself by remembering what Tarzan said about there always being a chance. He wondered how long he should remain here, waiting. Perhaps he should use the board like a boat, kick his legs and start to move along, hoping for some gap in the wall, a beach. But the main reason he felt weak had nothing to do with the storm and the waves and the wound to his head. It was Zamona. He had known for some time that he was in love with her. He had met her when she was a savage in Pellucidar. He had been the one to teach her English, to teach her about the O-220, which she took to like the proverbial duck to water. Her small and delicate features and her bright blue eyes were constantly before him. He became infatuated with her. He only hated that he had not acted upon his infatuation and told her how much he loved her when there was time. There always seemed to be another day. Now she was gone. He had seen her blown out from the O-220 by the blasts of the storm, lost forever, pulled down into wet nothingness, gone with his heart.

At that moment Tarzan shot up out of the water like a leaping porpoise. He swam over to Zeppner and his plank, grabbed one end of it, let it support him. What amazed Zeppner was that Tarzan didn't even look winded.

"As I suspected, the warm water is coming from a path beneath the wall," Tarzan said.

"A path?" Zeppner said.

"It's a long and hard swim, but it's a way inside."

"You made it all the way inside?"

"There's land. A lush land. It reminds me of Pellucidar, parts of Africa."

"I don't know that I can make it," Zeppner said.

"You can make a choice," Tarzan said. "You can ride this plank, or you can swim with me. It is your choice."

"How will I know where to go in the dark?"

"You won't be in the dark for long. You swim a short distance, toward where it seems lighter, and then it will be much brighter. Finally there will be plenty of light above you. Swim up and break the surface. It is that simple. Oh, and watch for some very large reptiles."

"What?"

"I am going to swim down again," Tarzan said. "Toward the light. You may follow, or you may stay here and cling to your plank until you are too exhausted to make the swim."

"I am already exhausted," said Zeppner.

"Stay close to me," Tarzan said, and without further comment, he took a deep breath and dove beneath the waves.

—

TAKING HIS OWN deep breath of air, Zeppner followed. Down he swam. There was no light, only darkness. He could not see Tarzan, but he could feel the water churning in front of him, stirred about by the kicking of Tarzan's feet. The water grew warmer, almost hot. He followed that unseen path, and then as Tarzan had said, the water became lighter. He could see the ape man's shape ahead of him. Finally the water was much brighter above him. When he thought his lungs would burst, it seemed as if a hole of golden, heavenly light was opening above them.

He and Tarzan burst to the surface. They came up in a great pool of warm water. Behind them, tumbling down high rocks, was a waterfall.

They swam to land. Red and yellow mud made up the bank. There were great masses of underbrush and high rises of trees all around them. No sooner had they crawled onto the muddy bank than Zeppner saw a large creature, a crocodile perhaps, but if so, the largest he had ever seen. It scooted swiftly out of the brush across the way, and into the water. It made waves as it crossed the pool toward them.

"Come," Tarzan said. "I think it is best we move away. Quickly."

Tarzan helped Zeppner to his feet, and within a moment they were deep into the jungle, greeted by bird calls and animal cries. A warm wind rustled leaves and shook the boughs of tall trees. Above them, monkeys swung from limb to limb.

Zeppner, feeling as if he was on his last legs, saw the ape man was moving easily ahead of him. Unlike himself, nudity did not bother him. It seemed to be his natural state. In time they came to the edge of a clearing. They stopped and stood amongst the trees, not venturing out onto the vast clearing. Tarzan said, "We should let you rest, see what we can do for that wound on your head."

Zeppner studied Tarzan. The ape man did not appear to need rest. He was stopping for him, to let him regain his strength. Zeppner started to protest, but put pride aside. He slid down to sit on the ground with his back against a tree. He could not go another step. Immediately, he was asleep. He dreamed of Zamona, alive.

—

WHEN ZEPPNER AWOKE, without having to ask, he knew Tarzan had not slept, but had watched over him as he did. He saw too that Tarzan had broken off a large limb and stripped it, making himself a crude club. As Tarzan stood there in the leaf-dappled sunlight, leaning on the club, Zeppner thought that he was the very embodiment of Hercules with his long black hair, dark, scarred body, and brutal countenance.

"I have found foot prints," said Tarzan. "Here, at the beginning of the clearing."

"Human?"

Tarzan nodded. "One foot is bare, the other wears a shoe."

Zeppner felt confused. "A shoe? One shoe?"

"A shoe like those worn by the crew of the O-220. A small shoe. A woman's foot."

"Zamona?"

"She too has somehow survived the storm and found her way here, most likely the same way we did. Minus a shoe."

"But how? She is so small and delicate."

Tarzan's mouth twisted into something that resembled a smile. "She may be small, but she is fierce. She is of Pellucidar, Captain. Zamona may have learned how to crew on the O-220, but she is a survivor of the first degree. She was raised a savage, like me, and at heart, no matter how much we learn about the outside world, how much we embrace it on the surface, we are always savages."

"My god," Zeppner said, jumping to his feet. "We have to save her."

"We have to find her," Tarzan said. "This world is not too much unlike her world. She will know better how to survive than you. Look up there."

Where Tarzan was pointing through a gap in the trees a great winged reptile was flying lazily overhead. At first glance it looked like a massive kite.

"This world has as many creatures out to kill us as Pellucidar," Tarzan said. "This is her world, and it is mine."

"We must find her," Zeppner said. "I...I love her, Tarzan."

"Does she know it?"

"No," Zeppner said, shaking his head. "I should have told her."

"We will find her," Tarzan said.

"Where could she be going?"

"In search of food, shelter. In Pellucidar the inhabitants are born with a sure ability to find their way home. My guess is she will go in whatever direction that she feels will bring her closer to that goal. She may not fully understand how far away her world is, that this land mass is not connected to her lost world, but is a lost world unto itself."

"Where are we?"

"I believe this is the lost continent mentioned by Caproni. He was an Italian explorer in the 1700s. He wrote that during his adventuring he passed a continent in the middle of the southern ocean, covered in mist. Most thought he was a fraud and a liar."

"It has remained hidden all these years?"

"It's not exactly on flight paths, and it would take a powerful plane to reach this spot. (1) Come, let me make you a weapon, and we will follow her tracks."

—

ZEPPNER COULD BARELY make out the tracks on the jungle trail, but Tarzan saw them easily. Before long, they found Zamona's shoe. She had abandoned it.

Tarzan picked up the little shoe, examined it. The loss of it didn't matter. Like Tarzan, her feet were as hard as cured leather.

"We at least know she came this way," Tarzan said.

Tarzan dropped the shoe and went on. Zeppner followed as quickly as he could, carrying the long, knife-sharpened stick Tarzan had given him. It was not too unlike having nothing more than a large pencil.

They spent a night in a tree, and the next morning, at daybreak, they were back on the trail. By the end of that day they had come to a break in the jungle and there was a large savannah spotted with trees and a sun-glistened water hole. They were a good distance away, and they squatted down to observe. There were a number of large cats surrounding the water hole, purring and growling, but mostly lying in the sun near the water.

"My God," Zeppner said. "Those are saber-tooth tigers. This place is like Pellucidar's cousin."

"More like a brother or sister, I would think," Tarzan said. (2) "But without the central and constant sun. At least here, we have sunset and sunrise."

Out of the sky came a shriek and a great shadow moved over the savannah. They looked up. A large leather-winged monster was swooping down on the water hole.

"It certainly is like Pellucidar," said Zeppner. "That's a pterodactyl."

The creature dove down, extended its claws, grabbed one of the great tigers by the scruff of the neck, whipped it up into the sky as easily as if it had been a rag doll. Zeppner's heart sank. Zamona had come this way, and savage or not, what chance did a small, unarmed woman have against these things? What chance did they have?

"I know what you're thinking," Tarzan said. "It doesn't necessarily mean a thing. Remember. Zamona is resourceful. She grew up in the wild. Come."

They dodged the cats, skirted the savannah, and after a while found another small watering hole visited by a herd of antelope. While Zeppner remained at the edge of the savannah, Tarzan crept through the grass toward the herd. When he was close, he leaped up and raced into them. Startled, they broke and ran. Zeppner couldn't believe the ape man's speed. Tarzan reached out, nabbed one of the antelope by its nub of a tail and jerked it down, struck it with his club. It was a brutal event, and ended with Tarzan dispatching the beast with his knife. After that Zeppner joined him. Tarzan skinned the beast rapidly and cut slabs of meat from it. They ate it raw. It was hard at first for Zeppner to get it down, but after a few bites he craved it and ate his fill. For the first time in a long time, he felt strong.

They drank from the spring that fed the watering hole, picked up Zamona's tracks again, crossed the savannah, and eventually arrived back at the jungle. The day was almost done. Long shadows were falling through the trees and across their path in coal-colored patterns of leaves and trees and leaping monkeys.

That's when they found the dead men.

—

THERE WERE TWO of them, strange men with thick brows and near-absent chins, barrel-chests and short, stumpy legs. They wore only loincloths. Beside them lay crude clubs, like the one Tarzan carried. One had an arrow through the eye, the other an arrow all the way through his throat.

While Zeppner leaned on his spear, Tarzan put his foot on the dead man's chest, and yanked the shaft from his neck. The arrow was a simple creation, the point made by snapping a thin stick in such a way it left a crude point.

"Zamona made these arrows," Tarzan said. "She found feathers in the jungle, used resin to connect them to the shaft. She was probably hunting, and they surprised her. There was a fight. She killed these two."

"Good for her."

"Yes," said Tarzan, "but they took her."

"Are you sure?" Zeppner asked.

"That's what the sign shows. Look there."

Zeppner saw a crude bow lying in the brush. Tarzan picked it up. It was a limber limb bent and bound by string made of twisted plant fibers. Tarzan slipped it over his shoulder, pulled the remaining arrow from the dead man's eye. He slung the bow over his shoulder, held the crude arrows in his left hand, the club in his right.

"They didn't bother to bury their dead," Zeppner said.

"Simple tribe. Simple ways. No sentimentality. Look there. Blood drops."

"I don't see anything," Zeppner said. Already it had grown too dark for him to define anything other than the general pathway.

"It is there nonetheless," Tarzan said. "I can see it, and I can smell it."

"Hers?" asked Zeppner.

Tarzan nodded. "The drops are small, so my guess is the wound is small. You can see where she put up a scuffle."

Zeppner didn't see anything other than shadows, but he remained silent.

"There are six sets of feet here," Tarzan said, "where before there were eight. They picked her up and are carrying her. Even if it is a minor wound, I have her scent full in my nostrils, and we can follow."

"You can follow her blood by smell?"

Tarzan grinned. "Like a bloodhound."

"Then follow we must," Zeppner said.

Tarzan in the lead, they rushed along the trail as night fell over them like a hood.

—

THE MOONLIGHT WEAVED in and out of the trees, allowing Zeppner to see Tarzan's back as the ape man moved swift and sure before him. It was all Zeppner could do to keep up. The jungle was full of sounds, chatters and roars, night birds and wind-rustled leaves.

Once a dark shape rushed in front of Tarzan, some kind of cat, Zeppner thought. Tarzan did not slow his stride, and as Zeppner passed the spot where the beast had rushed into the foliage, he saw two glowing eyes peeking out at him. They went along for a good ways like this. Zeppner was beginning to feel winded, but each time he thought he could not take another step, he thought of Zamona.

Eventually they saw the campfire. Where the jungle split there was a clearing, possibly made by a blaze sparked by lightning. In the clearing were a number of undefined human shapes huddled around the fire. They had killed something, and it had been tossed straight away into the flames with the hair still on it and the guts still intact, boiling in its own juices. Zeppner could smell the hair burning off of it.

Tarzan whispered to him. "The wind is on our side, and the fire is making a stink of the wood and carcass. They can't smell us."

Once again, Zeppner marveled at Tarzan's abilities. They squatted down, waited and observed. After a moment, Zeppner's eyes adjusted to the flickering of the fire. He could make out Zamona among the huddle. She sat on the ground on the far side of the fire. When the flames licked wide he could see her clearly. She was nude; the ocean having stolen her clothes same as theirs. She looked natural that way, not in the least bit prudish. She held her head high, haughty, proud. Her hands were tied behind her back, and she was bound at the ankles. There were five men in the group, and one of them, a big fellow, was squatting down next to her, holding a strand of her long black hair between his fingers. He made sounds that sounded to Zeppner at first like grunts and snaps, but he soon realized were language. The man showed his ragged teeth. Spittle on his lips sparkled in the firelight. As if by signal, the other men in the group slowly stood up, turned toward her.

The big man said something sharply to Zamona and bared his teeth. She spoke back to him; her words were almost a bark.

From their concealment Tarzan and Zeppner spoke in whispers.

"It is the language of the apes," Tarzan said. "My first language. They want her."

"Want her?" And then the reality of what Tarzan meant washed over Zeppner. He was grateful that he didn't speak the language of the apes; he wouldn't have wanted to understand what the man was suggesting coming directly from his lips. He felt as if someone had unscrewed a plug at the bottom of his foot and all that he was and ever would be was running out of it.

"We must fight," Zeppner said.

"We have no choice," Tarzan said, shoving the points of the two arrows into the dirt, pulling the bow off his shoulder. "I will take care of two of them from here, and then we charge."

Before Zeppner could respond, Tarzan strung an arrow and let it fly. Zeppner saw it as it reached the firelight, wobbling. But it struck true. It hit the big man in the ear as he squatted beside Zamona. It was such a swift and silent shot, that when the man fell over the other four didn't move for a long moment. By the time they were moving, another arrow was in flight, striking one of the men in his open mouth. The man stumbled, went to one knee, tugged at the arrow, dislodging it. Zeppner could see by the glow of the fire he was spitting gouts of blood.

Tarzan was moving. Zeppner followed.

The ape man swung his club over his head in a heavy arc as he entered into the firelight. The club struck one of the men, smashing his skull like a china cup. Zeppner rushed the man who was bleeding from his mouth and drove his spear against him. The point went in with some difficulty, but it went in. He forced the man to the ground and pushed the weapon deep into his gut. The man clutched at the spear and groaned for a moment, then gasped blood and stopped moving. When Zeppner turned, the remaining men were dead. Tarzan had dispatched them with the club. One had fallen into the fire to cook along with the crude dinner.

That's when the jungle broke open with a rattle of leaves and a cacophony of yells. More of the primitive men had arrived, and in that moment, Zeppner realized the party they had dispatched had been waiting on them.

They came out of the jungle in droves, came like ants swarming over a discarded picnic, rushed and yelled, swung clubs and fists. Tarzan met their charge with his whirling club. Heads knocked and heads exploded. Zeppner fought with his crude spear, stabbing, but the point was soon blunt, and he began to use it like a yeoman's staff.

As one of the wild warriors went down, another took his place. The shadowy jungle seemed to leak them. On they came, and finally Zeppner went down. He glanced at Zamona. She was still bound, struggling to get loose. She had rolled on her belly, and using her knees and wriggling her body, she was trying to crawl toward him. Then Zeppner was snatched up. He made a wild swing, missed, was hit again and again. He kept trying to cling to consciousness the way he had clung to that fragment of lumber in the midst of the ocean. It was a losing battle. But before he passed out he saw Tarzan swinging his club. He heard jaws shatter, heads crack, and then a horde of the men were on him, covering him thick as grapes on a vine. Then those men seemed to explode, flying up and catching the light of the fire, dropping down into shadow to leave Tarzan standing alone, a broken club in his fist.

They rushed again, covering him, even as Tarzan tossed aside the remains of the club and went at them with first his knife, which was knocked from his hand, and then his fists, and even his teeth. Zeppner smiled. He will not go easy, he thought, and then he passed out.

WHEN ZEPPNER AWOKE his head hurt and he feared he might have a concussion because the world was upside down and he was bouncing and everything was red.

It took awhile to realize his hands and feet were attached to a pole and he was being carried. The redness was the rising of the sun. He glanced to his right, saw Tarzan, bloodied, bound in the same way, being carried on a pole supported by the jungle dwellers. Glancing to his left he saw Zamona. She was looking right at him. A smile crossed her face. It was an odd thing to do considering their situation, but it warmed Zeppner and gave him a flash of courage.

Eventually they came to a clearing on the edge of a great cliff. Zeppner could hear water tumbling violently over rocks. A moment later he was hanging at a precarious position as they carried him down a narrow, rocky trail. They had all fallen into a single line now. Tarzan ahead of him, Zamona next, and him at the end of it. Down they went. The trail twisted and turned, and the men who carried him moved carefully so as not to slip and fall. Off to his left was a great gorge and he could see a tremendous waterfall; it came tumbling over glimpses of black stone with a roar like a den of lions. They continued down, and finally they came to a river where a large number of the tribe had gathered. Here there were women, as primitive looking as the men. They were tossed down roughly and left tied to the carrying limbs. Nude and bedraggled, bruised and insect-bit, they waited by the shore. A moment later Zeppner saw and heard something horrible, and realized their fate.

—

TARZAN HAD SMELLED the water long before they came to it. On the shore there were a dozen men stretched out on the ground, held down by the jungle men. They were not the same as the jungle men. They were more like Tarzan and his friends, longer and leaner with more common human features. They wore loincloths made from animal hides. As they were held by the arms and legs, large and strong members of the jungle tribe were standing over them with clubs, swinging their weapons, breaking leg and arm bones with single blows, turning those bones to jelly, causing the men on the ground to scream in agony.

Out in the water, floating, Tarzan could see the heads of the same sort of men, their necks supported by large wooden collars that helped them float. The collars were attached to ropes. After the club work the men could neither swim nor struggle, could only dangle like worms on hooks. On the shore were piles of skulls and bones. They were heaped together and Tarzan guessed they had been glued that way by some primitive form of cement. The skulls and bones were painted and marked with designs made from black soot from fires, as well as red and yellow clay. The designs were squiggles and circles and inside the circles a lot of teeth were drawn. In fact, this was the most common design on the bones—long, sharp teeth.

Tarzan watched as Zeppner turned to Zamona to say, "Zamona. It is bad timing to say the least. But I want you to know I love you. I have for sometime. And if it is not returned, I understand. But I won't let this moment, what may be one of our last, pass without me saying it."

Zamona's eyes crinkled. She spoke in English, but with that peculiar accent that is prevalent to the inhabitants of Pellucidar. "You foolish man. I know that. I have only been waiting for you to say as much."

Zeppner grinned. "It may be our last moments, but those words from you have made me the happiest man in the world."

Tarzan said, "Before you exchange wedding vows, you might wish to get out of this predicament."

"What magic will allow that?" Zeppner said.

"If there is to be any magic, we are it," Tarzan said.

"Why would they do this to those men?" Zeppner asked. "And who are they?"

"Another tribe, obviously farther along on the evolutionary scale," Tarzan said. "I have listened to the jungle folk and have caught a bit of their talk. What I believe the jungle men are doing is sacrificing these men as part of an important ritual. That's why the last ones we fought were meeting up with the men at the campfire. This isn't a village. This is where all the people of their ilk, people of other tribes, gather to appease some god, or some ritual. Unfortunately for us, we crossed paths with them just in time to be part of it. They break the bones, and then float their victims in the river, waiting for something to come, something with plenty of teeth."

"We are doomed then," Zeppner said.

"We still live," said Zamona.

"Good for you, Zamona," Tarzan said, speaking to her in English. "We are not done until we are done."

Tarzan looked toward the river. The men who had recently been broken up were crying and screaming and being dragged toward a stack of wooden collars. The collars were snapped open and fastened around their necks, then bound together with rope that passed through holes in the collars. The jungle men pushed the broken men out into the deep part of the river using long poles. The current kept them there and the ropes fastened to the collars kept them pegged to the shore. One of the jungle men carried a big club with pieces of what looked like stone or volcanic glass imbedded into it. He didn't use the weapon, but stood by with, perhaps as a sign of his office, his position in the tribe. He watched the others break the bones and push the jellied men into the water.

Then the jungle men and the man with the strange weapon came for Tarzan and the others.

Tarzan, Zeppner, and Zamona were lifted and carried toward the shoreline to have their turn.

—

THE MOMENT TARZAN awoke on the trail and found himself fastened to the pole, he had begun to flex his wrists and work at the ropes. By the time they were lifted and carried toward the shore, his efforts paid off. With a bend of his wrists, the ropes snapped.

Like a monkey, Tarzan dropped down and let his hands touch the earth, practically standing on his head. He flexed his legs and kicked up. The kick drove the pole upwards and caused it to crack, and when it did, Tarzan's bound feet slipped off of the pole and his ankles came loose of the rope. Tarzan bounded to his feet. The man with the strange weapon rushed him. Tarzan dodged his swing and hit him with his fist. It was a hard blow and the man's jaw broke and teeth flew and the man went down. Tarzan grabbed the club off the ground. By now other jungle men were closing in on him. Tarzan wielded the weapon as if it were as light as a fine willow limb. Jungle men flew left and right in sprays of flesh and blood and brains.

The other jungle men dropped Zamona and Zeppner to go after Tarzan, but the ape man plowed a path through them with the festooned club, and in a moment had created a space around his companions, as well as time enough to bend down and use the edge of one of the stone fragments in the club to cut their bonds. No sooner than it was done, then the jungle men had regrouped. Tarzan yelled, "Run for the water. Swim for your life."

Zeppner grabbed Zamona by the elbow and the two of them darted for the river. Tarzan held his ground, swinging the club, sending jungle men flying like chaff. And now the jungle men were coming on him from all sides. Tarzan turned and swung the club and cleared a path. The club finally snapped, came apart in the jungle lord's hands. The men grabbed at him, hung onto him like leeches, struck him and tried to choke him and pull him down. Tarzan trudged forward, dragging them with him until he reached the river's edge. Peeling off the jungle men with either arm, tossing them aside like confetti, he leapt into the river.

The water hit him like a cold fist. The current was swift and it carried him out and past the poor men floating in their collars, carried him to the center of the river and sent him swirling along. Well ahead of him he saw Zeppner and Zamona trying to swim with the rush of the river, going down and coming up, bobbing like corks.

One of the jungle men had followed Tarzan into the water, swimming rapidly in pursuit. The man grabbed at him. Tarzan intercepted the man's reach, snatching him by the wrist. He twisted it, heard the bones shatter over the rushing sound of the water. The man screamed. Tarzan let him go, and still screaming, the man went sailing right alongside Tarzan.

That's when the ape man saw what had been painted on the bones.

—

THEY DID NOT come out of the river as he expected. They came from the sky. He realized then the crude squiggles painted on the bones had been meant to represent the beating of wings. They were at first dots seen flying low and far down the length of the river. But then they came closer and their wings could be seen, and they could be seen; great of size and green of skin, mouths full of teeth. The flying lizard beasts were not like the pterodactyls they had observed before, they were impossible things the size of small airplanes, with their legs curled up under them as they flew, their skulls flared wide, their snouts long and tipped with massive nostrils. Tarzan would not have been surprised to see them breath fire, so much did they look like mythical dragons. On their backs were long, thin men with sloping, peaked heads painted blue and yellow, green and orange. The rest of their bodies were devoid of clothing or design. They seemed little more than skeletons wrapped in doughy flesh. They directed the flight of their mounts with reins. They sat in saddles held in place by harnesses. They had their feet in stirrups of a sort. They carried spears in one hand, held the reins to their mounts in the other. Slung on the right side of their monsters were long sheaths holding more spears. They flew in a V pattern, as if they were fighter pilots.

Tarzan saw Zamona and Zeppner swimming ahead of him. She touched Zeppner who was next to her, spoke something caught up and tossed away by the roar of the river. But Tarzan saw them dive.

Good girl, he thought. Good girl. She had given Zeppner proper advice. Then he too dove beneath the water, and not a moment too soon, for down swept one of the beasts and its claws snatched up the wounded primitive with the broken wrist, lifted him up and hauled him away, as lightly as one might lift a pillow.

—

THE WATER WAS savage and white with waves and ripples and suds-like foam. Soon there were slick mounds of rocks to clash against. When Tarzan came up for air, he looked back, saw the winged beasts, about ten of them, flying down to grab at the men in collars, lifting them, causing the ropes to trail into the air, then snap free and jerk up the pegs that had been driven into the shore. The creatures and their riders carried them aloft and away; the broken men dangled from their claws like wet socks.

Tarzan's attention was then turned back to the mounds of rocks. There was little he could do. The river slammed him against them. He clung to one and eased onto it. There were enough rocks he could walk across them before diving back into the water and swimming for the far shore.

Upon his arrival on the shoreline, Zeppner and Zamona came wet and dripping, banged and bruised, out of the thickness of the jungle and called to him. Tarzan was pleased to see that they too had survived. Tarzan glanced up, saw the flying creatures. They were lifting high and circling wide, most likely heading home with their prizes.

Then they realized, too late, there were more monster riders, gliding down from the heavens from behind, and before they could defend themselves, three of the beasts snatched at them and lifted them high into the sky.

—

WHEN TARZAN REALIZED what had happened—for it had happened so fast, that even his senses, dulled by exhaustion and cold water and a loss of blood, had failed him—he was already nabbed. The flying monstrosity had him gripped firmly, but its touch was also surprisingly soft, with the claws doing very little damage to his shoulder. By the time Tarzan thought he might rip himself free, even if he were to lose flesh in the process, he was already too high up.

Near him, Tarzan saw that his friends had been taken as well. The three of them were joining an aerial armada of the creatures and their riders, as well as their human prizes.

Tarzan could closely observe the riders on the winged reptiles next to him, and for the first time he got a solid look at them. They were much as they first appeared, pale, slender, with bulbous, bony heads. But what Tarzan previously thought was paint, was in fact their natural skull coloring. They had wide mouths with narrow lips that when open exposed rows of teeth, sharp and barbed like long, yellow thorns. This revelation made Tarzan reevaluate the images he had seen painted on the bones. The lines on the bones had been crude representations of the wings of the beasts, but the circles containing teeth were most likely meant to represent these bizarre pilots, not their mounts. In that moment Tarzan realized that the sacrifice had not been for the flying reptiles, but for these men; they were cannibals. He had some experience with man-eaters, and he knew without consideration that he was in the presence of the same sort of humans now, that the broken bones and the men in the water had been part of a kind of crude tenderization for these men who the jungle warriors must have thought of as gods. And why not? They flew on the backs of powerful winged creatures. They demanded sacrifice to keep from taking what they wanted from the tribe itself—meat. This way the tribe appeased their gods and protected their members by feeding them the broken bones and softened flesh of different tribes, men on a different part of the evolutionary chain.

As they flew, Tarzan looked down. He had learned that no matter what the situation, no matter how dire, he had to be observant. Something might be seen that could be of use for survival. So now that he had no choice but to go where the winged behemoths were taking him, he looked down. Below there was a steaming jungle and finally a great inland ocean. They passed along the edge of the ocean and flew over a large pool of water about which a number of men were congregated, entering into it slowly and with procession; there was something ritualistic about it. (3)

And then Tarzan saw something surprising. A large fort, made not too unlike one would expect Daniel Boone of old to build. A wall of pointed logs and inside the wall buildings and ramps and what Tarzan thought looked like a mounted gun. (4)

On they flew, and gradually the sky darkened and the ground below was nothing but a mass of shadows. Still they flew, against the face of the large full moon that appeared to rise like a god's head out of the sea. And then below the night became alight with flames.

—

IT WAS A big village and there were campfires everywhere. There was a lake next to the village, and the campfires tossed light on the water and the water rippled with flashes of orange and yellow. The moon's reflection made it appear to float on the water with the flames. Ahead of them the dragons, for now Tarzan thought of them as such, glided low over the lake and the riders yelled out in near unison, "Arboka." It was a word Tarzan recognized. It was a word from the ape language he had learned. The language the jungle men spoke. It was bastardized, but similar in the way Spanish is to Italian. Yet, even with its different accent he knew it meant "Drop." The dragons dropped the broken men. There were splashes as they were landed in the great lake below. They went under at first, then bobbed to the surface on their neck corks, able only to float.

Tarzan and his friends were not dropped. They were not already broken. The cannibals had other plans for them. Perhaps they too would be broken and collars would be fastened about their necks and they too would be lowered into the water. For now, they were

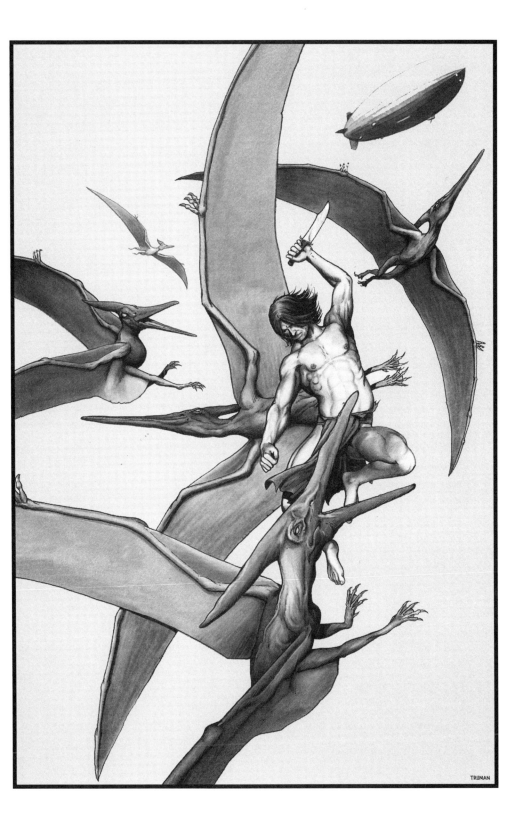

TRUMAN

carried over the lake toward the shore, and then just over the tops of tall jungle trees. Tarzan reached up with both hands and took hold of the creature's foot above the claws. He did this swiftly. He jerked his shoulder free as he did, causing the claws to tear his flesh. When he was loose the dragon began to whip its foot, trying to shake him loose, but he held. He was able to swing out and grab the belly strap that held the rider's saddle in place. He had hold of it before the rider knew what was happening. Tarzan climbed the strap and the rider tried to stab him with his spear. Tarzan snatched the spear and tugged, sent the man and his spear tumbling down and onto the ground near the lake. Even from where Tarzan was, some fifty feet above the ground, he heard the thump of the man as he struck earth.

Tarzan swung into the saddle and took the reins and yanked the dragon to the right, came in close over the rider carrying Zamona. The rider had seen what had occurred, and he threw one of his long spears at Tarzan. Tarzan caught it and flipped it, threw it at the rider, piercing his chest, knocking him from the winged monster. Tarzan swept in low and flew under the creature as it dropped down toward the trees. He reached out for Zamona, grasped her hand, yelled, "Arboka." The dragon holding her let her go and Tarzan swung her onto the saddle behind him. She clutched her arms around his waist and they flew toward the rider that carried Zeppner. The rider had seen all that occurred, so as vengeance, as they flew over the trees he yelled, "Arboka," and Zeppner was dropped.

There was a crash and a flutter, and Tarzan saw that Zeppner, having not dropped from too high, had fallen into a tree and was clinging to a limb. The rider who had dropped Zeppner pursued Tarzan. Tarzan gently tugged the reins, and the creature, easy as a trained quarter horse, responded, flew fast over the trees. Tarzan guided him up, saying to Zamona, "Hang tight."

They shot up like a bullet, the beast tilting to such an extent that Tarzan could feel Zamona's weight tugging back at him, a victim to gravity. Tarzan guided the monster into a surprising dive, and was hurtling straight toward the rider whose beast had moments before held Zeppner in its grasp. They sped directly toward each other like cannon shots.

—

TARZAN PULLED ONE of the spears from the tight sheath at the reptile's side. He cocked it into throwing position with one hand, managed the reins with the other. He continued to fly directly toward the rider. He stood up in the stirrups, leaned back and came forward as he loosed the spear. By that time they were about to have a head-on collision.

The spear flew straight. It hit the rider in the head and parted his skull the way a comb will part hair. The rider toppled from his mount, and at the last moment Tarzan was able to veer his beast and avoid them clashing together.

Tarzan directed his dragon toward the trees where Zeppner had fallen. When he came to the tree, he was able to see Zeppner, struggling to manage a sound position near the top of the tree. Tarzan slowed his flying monstrosity, hooked a heel on one side of the mount and swung out and extended his arm. It took a couple of tries, but Zeppner caught it, and Tarzan pulled him up. It was a tight fit, but he was able to slide on behind Zamona. He was bleeding from a number of places.

"Are you all right?" Tarzan said.

"All minor wounds," Zeppner said. "But now we have company."

Tarzan glanced back. The camp fires looked far away, like lightning bugs. Then there was a dark mass touched with moonlight. It was like a rising of mosquitoes from the face of a pond. They were many and they were coming fast. They appeared to change swiftly in the moonlight from mosquitoes to birds, and then Tarzan could see them clearly for what they were—men on their dragons. The ones who had dropped the broken men in the water were now in pursuit of Tarzan and his friends.

—

THERE WAS A wide path in the jungle. Tarzan guided the beast down close to the ground and they sped along the trail, which proved man-made. He saw a break in the trees, and he went off the main trail, down that. This was a path made by animals, most likely in pursuit of water. The reptile's wings beat at the edges of the trees. Leaves came loose and went fluttering about in the dark. Tarzan didn't believe he could stay hidden, but if he could merely confuse their pursuers for a time, they might have a chance.

Peeking back, he saw a flock of dragons flying low along the wide man-made trail adjacent to the path he had taken with his beast. He saw the last of them pass. In a few moments they would realize they had been duped and would double back, but for now Tarzan flew on, low as possible to the ground.

Then things changed. Ahead the trail was too narrow for their flying mount, so Tarzan had no choice but to rein the creature up and into the moonlight.

"They have spotted us," said Zamona.

Tarzan flew on, realizing their combined weight was slowing them. He flew over the great lake where the broken men bobbed like lily pads. He flew over great patches of jungle.

"They are falling back," Zeppner said.

Tarzan took a look. They were indeed falling back. He had gained quite a gap between them and himself. The little venture down that narrow trail had given them just enough of a break, and even after being discovered, they were too far ahead to make it worth the warriors' efforts. They already had their meals, broken and secure, tenderizing slowly in the river of the great lake. What were three more?

Zeppner laughed out loud. "We have beaten them, Tarzan."

"Seems that way," Tarzan said.

The great winged beast flapped on.

—

THEY REACHED THE great inland sea by morning and skirted the edge of it, stopping once to rest their mount. Tarzan tied the reins of the beast to a stout tree near the shore of the sea, left Zeppner and Zamona, took a spear from the sheath strapped to the monster, and trekked toward the deeper woods to hunt. Two hours later he returned with a deer over his shoulders.

Zeppner and Zamona had built a fire from deadwood because the sea air had turned surprisingly cool. Tarzan had lost his knife somewhere during their capture by the jungle men, so he broke one of the spears off near the blade to make a new knife. He was grateful that the knife he lost had not been the one he normally carried; his father's knife from long ago. It was safe at his plantation in Africa. He skinned the deer with the makeshift knife, gutted it, made a wooden rack for the body, and cooked it over the fire.

Tarzan gave a raw leg of the deer to their flying stallion of sorts, and then he and his friends sat down to eat.

"That flying thing is quite amazing," said Zeppner.

"For his size he is astonishingly light," Tarzan said. "His bones must be hollow. And yet, he is strong."

"I think we should name him," Zeppner said.

"I never name anything I might have to eat," said Tarzan.

Once they were filled with food, fresh water, and rested, they took to the air again, flew over the great inland sea. It took some time, but they finally reached the opposite shore. They rested again for awhile, and come morning they flew on with no set destination, just making sure they were putting space between themselves and the cannibals.

After a few days of travel, stopping to hunt and eat, they came to the great rock wall that surrounded the land that time forgot. Tarzan landed the beast. There was jungle and plenty of game along the edge of the wall. They made a good camp there. When the mist that surrounded the strange word thinned, they could see the ocean raging against the rock barrier below.

"How do we go home?" Zeppner said.

"Swimming won't do," Tarzan said.

Zeppner laughed. "I suppose not."

Zamona turned and looked back at the jungle and said nothing.

—

THEY BUILT A fine hut that housed them comfortably and had plenty of room left over. They left a gap at the top of it to let out the smoke. They built a well-made corral with a roof for the flying creature, and kept it fed with game, of which they found plenty. From time to time they flew in trio on the back of the beast, looking to see what they could find, but never traveling too far from camp.

After many days, the three of them walked to their spot on the wall, the place where they liked to look out at the ocean. As they stood there, watching the pounding waves break against the blockade of stone, Tarzan said, "When we were first carried off by the winged things, I saw below us a place with wooden walls, like a fort, with buildings inside of it. It looked to me that it might be a kind of civilized settlement. I thought I might try and go there. It will take many days, and I would have to stop to find water and food, but perhaps there might be someone there who could help us, or assist us. If so, I will come back for you. They might be enemies. On this world that seems more likely. But I thought I might try. I must find a way to go home. I must see my wife, Jane."

Zeppner looked at Zamona, then back at Tarzan.

"This may sound odd, Tarzan," Zeppner said, "but Zamona and I, we want to stay. Right here. Where the game is thick and there seems to be fewer dangerous predators. Most importantly, we have each other. This is a world not too unlike the one from which she came, and I have nothing to go back to. And to be honest, I have learned to love this life. All that I need is right here, with her. We talked it over and decided a few days back. We have wanted to tell you for quite some time, and now we must."

Tarzan almost smiled. "I have suspected. And I understand. If Jane were with me, I might stay. If she is by my side, I can be anywhere in the world and find happiness."

Tarzan clamped Zeppner on the shoulder and smiled at Zamona. "Have your life and your love, but I must go. I must find a way to leave and go home to Jane."

—

WHEN THE MORNING light came the mist was heavy. Tarzan and Zeppner and Zamona were all at the corral. Tarzan saddled up and reined the beast, guided it out through the open gate. It walked with a hobbling motion on its slightly bent legs. By the time he led the creature clear of the corral, the sun had started to penetrate the mist, but still they could not see the sky.

Tarzan had made himself a bow and arrows and a quiver of wood, and he had fashioned fresh spears with flint points to replace the broken ones from the quiver that was strapped to the reptile's saddle. He still had the knife he had made from one of the spears, the broken part of the shaft now wrapped in hide and strapped to his side in a sheath he had made from wild boar skin. He wore a loincloth of spotted antelope hide. He arranged his weapons, the bow over his shoulder, the quiver strapped to his back, the knife at his side, the spears tucked tight into the sheath next to the saddle. He climbed on top of the beast and looked down at Zeppner and Zamona.

"Make a life," he said.

"We will," said Zamona, looking beautiful in the gossamer-veiled light. "We still live."

Tarzan tugged at the reins. The dragon flapped its wings, lifted into the air, and finally high into the mist where it was swallowed up, wrapped tight in white. Zeppner and Zamona could hear the

Joe R. Lansdale

monster's wings beating for a while, and then there was only silence, leaving them to their life, and Tarzan to further adventure.

STORY NOTES

(1) Tarzan's adventure on the lost world would have taken place about 1929, when planes were nowhere as advanced or as able of flying long ranges. Besides, it's very likely that Tarzan's universe is an alternate universe that only crisscrosses ours from time to time.

(2) The sun of Pellucidar, the world inside our world, is always central and always bright. Pellucidar is a world of constant daylight.

(3) Although Tarzan could not discern the purpose of the pools, they are part of the evolutionary process of The Land That Time Forgot. When humans of a certain evolutionary scale are ready and prepared to move to a higher form, they enter the pools, and come out transformed. For more information on these pools, check out *The Land That Time Forgot*, *The People Time Forgot*, and *Out of Time's Abyss* by Edgar Rice Burroughs.

(4) He's looking down on Ft. Dinosaur, built by previous adventurers. Again, see the books in the *Land That Time Forgot* series by Burroughs.

UNDER THE WARRIOR STAR

DEDICATED TO THE GREAT CREATORS OF PLANET ADVENTURE
AND SWORD AND SORCERY: EDGAR RICE BURROUGHS, OTIS
KLINE, AND ROBERT E. HOWARD. GOODBYE TO NOSTALGIA.

Chapter One

My History

I WRITE HERE on yellow pad among the bones of the dead. The wind whistling through broken glass.

My name is Braxton Booker. This vast and empty underground structure, where I now sit, recording my experiences, is really where my story began, and now it is where it ends. But, to better understand what has happened to me, I'll move to an earlier beginning, and tell you about the events of my life that made me the perfect person for this strange adventure.

Not that I expect you to believe me. Providing anyone ever reads this. The bottom line is it is all so fantastic. If someone were to tell me what I am writing on my pad, or give it to me to read, I would think them either a liar or mad. But my experiences weigh on me like the tumbling stones of an avalanched mountain, and recording my adventures somewhat lifts that weight from my soul. So, here it is.

In a nutshell, when I was eleven, living in a small town in East Texas, my father, fearing that I was becoming a loner and that I lacked confidence, introduced me to an elderly man who taught jujitsu and fencing. His name was Jack Rimbauld.

Rimbauld was elderly, five-eight, weighing about one hundred and thirty pounds, soaking wet with change in his pocket. His age and size and appearance were misleading. He was the toughest, quickest, most physically capable man I ever knew. He had studied all over the world in his youth, both the physical arts and the arts of education. He was a warrior and an intellectual. He had settled in our small town to retire, for whatever reason. In time, we became not only student and teacher, but friends.

I never asked why he had come to live in East Texas. Never considered it. I was a young man and caught up in the skills he was teaching me. Each day after school I went to his home with great enthusiasm. The sight of the big fencing room and the matted room next to it were like the Holy of Holies for me.

I knew very little about my teacher beyond those training rooms and his library, where we often sat after class and he spoke to me of better understanding my skills. He wrote poetry, haiku mostly. He requested that I read them and try my hand at them. I tried. I also attempted the Japanese art of flower arranging, and the tea ceremony. I wasn't very good at any of that. My tea was sour, my flowers drooped. My poetry thudded.

He taught me meditation, and I swear I once saw him, sitting cross-legged on a mat, hands on his knees, eyes closed, slowly lift off the mat and hover there quietly for a full minute or so. Another time, I was looking right at him, and then he was gone. I heard him behind me. He had moved across the room by some weird means of teleportation. He told me it was just a trick of the mind. That he had never moved, but that he had in fact put the idea in my mind that he was behind me. Another time, in his office, he was at his desk and I was sitting in a chair across from him. The door opened, and in Jack walked, closing the door behind him.

This time, when I looked back at the man behind the desk, Jack was still there. There were two of him in the room. Slowly, the Jack behind the desk faded, and the Jack in the doorway smiled, turned, and walked right through the closed door. I stood there blinking for a long moment, not believing what I had seen.

When I rushed into the mat room, he was sitting there on one of the mats, cross-legged. The look on my face made him laugh out loud.

What I remember most about that, though, was right before the second Jack had entered the room, the Jack behind the desk had shaken my hand.

I had felt his touch, as sure and solid as if he were there.

He tried to teach me this power of mind over matter. It was difficult work. I didn't entirely understand it, though when I'm not caught up in the whirlwind of life, I make an effort to improve my ability. So far, my ability is me sitting cross-legged on the floor trying not to think about a cheeseburger.

But the combat arts, there I thrived.

If Jack Rimbauld had a family, I never heard of them. If there was someone dear to him, other than myself, I was never given an indication.

Looking back on it now, remembering certain things he said to me, I have the belated impression that he may have had some dark secret in his past. That, however, is nothing more than a guess, and comes in hindsight, and is ultimately unimportant to my story. Back then, I only knew that he was Mr. Rimbauld, maestro, sensei, friend and mentor.

I remember him saying to me, "Brax. You have an impulsive nature, and a temper. Neither serve a man well in the long run. The mind and the spirit and the body must be welded together by the tightest of glue."

This meant very little to me at the time.

I took lessons five days a week in fencing and jujitsu for three hours a day until I was twenty, and then three days a week in both arts until I was twenty-two and Jack became ill, and shortly thereafter died, surprising me by willing me not only his collection of swords, but his home and library and a fairly substantial savings. How he came about this money, I don't know. I never saw him teach another soul, other than myself, and I never knew of him to have a job or to go off to work. Perhaps these answers lie somewhere in the volumes of handwritten composition books he left me.

Before his death, he had taught me all there was to know about the sword, and not any one kind of sword, but all manner of swords and knives, and even some training in archery and spear casting. Anything with a point I could use with considerable skill. I was no slouch at jujitsu, either, and earned a third-degree black belt under his tutelage. He also spent time introducing me to books, and loaned me numerous volumes of rare editions of novels by the world's greatest authors. He was my education, and he was like a second father to me. I respected the information and skills he gave me.

Because of those skills I made a great mistake, and then those same skills saved my life. So, I owe Jack Rimbauld much praise, and I owe myself criticism for bad judgment. In the end, however, I would not undo what happened.

Though there are events leading up to my situation that are interesting, and under other circumstances might even be considered thrilling, they pale in comparison to the amazing events that came after. The events that I expect will be difficult for you to believe.

Because of that, I'll condense the early adventures, and simply say that I made the Olympic fencing team, and might have won a gold medal, if one of my comrades and I had not gotten into a quarrel over a young lady with long blonde hair and very nice figure.

He ended up with the girl. But it was not enough for him, and he, like in the old days, challenged me to a duel using sabers. I was foolish. I no longer cared about the girl, or at least not that much, but I did care—too much—about my pride. I accepted his challenge, and soon found it was not just a duel of skill, but that he fully intended to strike me down.

With a parry and a stroke, I cut him deeply in the face and shoulder, and dropped him. It was a frightful wound, but he wasn't dead. Being young, and foolish—and I am not far off that youth now, but in experience I am much older—I fled for fear of arrest. I most likely could have made a good legal defense, claiming accurately that he had tried to kill me and I was only defending myself. But at the time, it didn't occur to me. I was frightened.

What a funny word. Frightened.

Now, after all I have been through the idea of being frightened by merely wounding a man in self-defense strikes me as little more than amusing.

I ended up in Alaska. There I was able to hide and use a false name and not need anything much in the way of identification. I worked on a fishing boat briefly, and then ended up helping a fellow named Carruthers fly supplies, and I suspect stolen goods, to different locations in Alaska.

In over a period of a year I learned to operate the small prop planes, though I never acquired a pilot's license. I didn't need one. Carruthers had his own landing strip and flew his own flight plans and there was no one to stop him.

Alaska is truly the last frontier.

On Earth.

But somehow I was tracked by the law, and when I found out they were coming to get me, I panicked and stole one of the planes. I did all right until I was over a great patch of wilderness, flying low, and ended up with an eagle smashing into my propeller. It did damage. The plane went down. I tried to glide it to a landing, but when the plane hurtled earthward, it was as if I and the entire world were in a centrifuge.

I lost control. As I went down I thought of my parents, both dead some years back from a car wreck, and I thought of the girl I had lost to a man who had once been my friend. I thought of the Olympic opportunity I had missed, and I thought of my old mentor Jack Rimbauld.

I thought of a dog I had when young.

No more cheeseburgers.

And then the plane hit.

Chapter Two

The Invisible Project

WHEN I AWOKE I was warm. It was night and the main body of the plane was on fire, and pieces of it were scattered along the ground. I had been thrown free, and had somehow survived, perhaps because the plane had skidded on its belly in soft mud near a large body of water. I could see the marks of that slide imbedded in the shoreline near the water. I wasn't sure how I had managed that landing, or if I had. Perhaps it was nothing more than blind luck.

The impact had not only thrown me out of the plane, it had knocked me unconscious. And now, as I came slowly awake, saw the debris, felt the heat from the aircraft burning near the edge of the water, I was certain that I had broken more than a few bones.

In that estimation I was at least partially correct. I could see a bone in my leg jutting through a rip in my pants; it suck out like a jagged stick. The sight of it made me sick. I tried to pull myself up, so that I could rest my back against a large tree. I managed this, but passed out shortly thereafter. I blinked awake once, and saw a shadow moving along the shore in the firelight. And then the author of the shadow presented itself.

A grizzly bear.

I reached in my pocket for my clip knife, which was a little like pulling a toothpick, considering the size and strength of a bear, but it was not my nature to give in to anything without a fight. My old instructor, Jack Rimbauld, had established that in me, and it held to my being as tight as the skin on my bones.

In the process of drawing the knife, I realized my little finger on my right hand was twisted at an odd angle. It hurt to drag the knife from my pocket, but I managed, and was able to flick the blade open.

The bear turned its head toward me. It was outlined very well in the firelight. It sniffed the air. It was perhaps twenty feet away from me. It began to lumber slowly in my direction. I tried to pull myself even more upright against the tree trunk, but I was all out of energy.

Then I saw movement off to my left. Someone was coming along the edge of the bank, several people, in fact. Awareness of this was followed by a queasy feeling, perhaps the result of shock. The next thing I knew the world was blinking in and out and there was a popping sound that I recognized on some level, but for some reason could not put a proper thought to it. Later I would determine it came from rifles being fired in the air.

I passed out.

—

ONCE, I AWOKE and found myself being bounced along on some sort of support, covered in a warm blanket. I only had this awareness for an instant, and then I plunged back into blackness.

I don't know exactly how long I was out, but when I awoke completely, it was bright and the air smelled of disinfectant. I lay in a hard bed with crisp white sheets. My leg was in a cast. So was my hand and little finger. I pulled back the sheet and saw that I was bandaged all over. I had more wounds than I realized.

Joe R. Lansdale

I had been awake for only a few moments when a man came into the room. He was tall and thin and balding, except for a white tuft of hair that stood up on his head like a comb on a rooster. I thought he looked like a mad scientist. I wasn't entirely off in this judgment.

Leaning over me, he smiled, and gave me a container of water with a straw. My mouth was dry as the desert, so I sipped. He sat in a chair by my bed, waited patiently while I drank. He said, "So, are you feeling a mite better?"

I said that I was, and then, "Where am I?"

"Now, that is something I have to admit I'm not going to answer completely." It was a surprising statement, and I said so.

"No doubt it's confusing," he said, "but let me put it this way. This is a private facility, financed by a large number of rich, private investors. You are underground, son."

"Underground?"

He nodded. "That's right. Deep down. A few of those who work here, having lost interest, at least temporarily, in surviving like a mole, went above for a break, heard the plane crash. They went in search of the explosion, and found you. Good thing too. A bear was about to put you to the taste test. We ran it off by firing shots in the air, and we brought you here, doctored you up."

"Who is we?"

"Me and a hundred employees, fifty of them on site at the moment. I suppose you could say I'm the head honcho here. The question now is what to do with you."

I wasn't sure what he meant by that, so I lay silent.

"You rest and I'll think it over. By the way, you may call me Dr. Wright. What shall I call you?"

"Brax," I said. "That'll do."

I DIDN'T LEAVE that room for several days. Finally, I was allowed to visit Dr. Wright. He had an office down the hall from my room. The

170

room I was in was one of three rooms that provided hospital beds. There were a lot of other hallways that led to I knew not where.

I was given a motorized wheelchair and a large man dressed in black with a large black pistol on his hip. He was my escort. He made sure I went where I was supposed to go, and when he let me in Dr. Wright's office, he remained outside, the door closed.

Dr. Wright sat behind a big desk in a rolling leather chair. I could see mounted on the wall behind him a pair of crossed sabers. This, of course, caught my eye right away. He noticed, said, "You like swords?"

"I love swords," I said.

"You know how to use them?"

"Quite well," I said, and gave him my history. I planned to leave out the part about my problems in the lower states, but for some reason I let it all spill out. Maybe I was tired of the whole hide-and-seek business I had been conducting for the last year or so. Whatever my inner motives, I held nothing back.

"So, that one incident led to the plane crash?" he said.

"Yes," I said.

Dr. Wright nodded. He turned and looked at the sabers. "I was once quite good myself. That was a thousand years ago."

"What exactly is it you do here?"

"If I told you, I'd have to kill you," he said, and the smile that came across his face was narrow and hard, as if it had been pinned there.

"That wouldn't be good," I said.

"No. No," he said. "It wouldn't."

—

I LOST TRACK of time, but gradually my leg healed and so did my hand. I never really knew if it was day or night, being underground. My world was a world of electric lights. I was allowed the opportunity to move around on crutches, and sometimes I was allowed to venture down to Dr. Wright's office. I think he enjoyed the visits as much as I did, and he supplied me with books to read, and once we even played chess. I beat him the first time because he seemed distracted, but no time thereafter. It was a little like my relationship with Jack Rimbauld, but without the physical activity, and though Dr. Wright was pleasant enough, there always seemed to be a point at which he became reserved and unwilling to give more of himself emotionally.

One day, as we hovered over the chessboard, he said, "I suppose I can tell you something of our work here."

I didn't say anything, not wanting to show too much interest, but I didn't want to show lack of interest either. I lifted my head and tried to look no more curious than a puppy that has heard a noise.

"Have you heard of quantum physics?" he asked.

"Yes."

"What do you know about it?"

"That it's called quantum physics, and I believe it's mostly theoretical."

"No, it's not theoretical at all. There are many things about our universe that can be discovered by the study of it."

"I think I heard something about it having to do with, among other things, parallel dimensions."

"That's one thing, yes. One of many amazing things. What we're doing here, with our studies, and they are purely independent, and paid for by individuals so wealthy that their wealth cannot be measured, is we're creating a universe in a laboratory."

"A universe?"

He smiled at me. "That's right."

"You telling me this. Does it mean I'm going to be killed?"

"No. I don't think so."

"That doesn't seem certain enough."

"I'm certain," he said. "But it is top secret, and I'm not supposed to tell anyone, but it gets lonely here."

"With a hundred people?"

"With a hundred people who are scientists first and foremost. You, you have a good mind, but you have other interests. And, to tell you the truth, I have a proposal for you. I'm somewhat reluctant to mention it, but you seem like a young man that just might like the possible challenge."

"Possible?"

"Yes," he said. "Because if it doesn't work, you may die, or perhaps worse, be consigned to some place beyond our understanding, a kind of limbo."

"Sounds almost religious."

"If the creating of a universe is not an attempt to play God, what is?"

He leaned forward, supporting himself with his elbows on either side of the chessboard. "Our operation is top secret, and...well, I'm going to make the jump. I'm going to go ahead and tell you. As I said, it is financed by a large number of rich individuals, but those rich individuals do not spend a dime."

"Pardon," I said.

"They are shills. Fronts to what is in fact a government operation that is not on the books, and is therefore..." He grinned at me. "Not a government operation. It is an invisible project, an attempt to not only create a universe but to control it. Theoretically, many believe that if you can create a universe, then you can travel to that universe, and within are worlds that can be used for exploitation. The profit, creating one universe after another, could be beyond understanding, beyond reasoning."

"That seems like a considerable jump in thinking," I said.

He laughed a little. "I'm making it sound considerably more simple than it actually is. But to be frank, if I were to explain it completely, and in a scientific manner, you would be lost."

"I believe that," I said.

Dr. Wright nodded. "We have a problem. No volunteers to make the jump."

"The jump?"

"Into our new universe."

"You've actually created the universe?"

"We think so. The scientists we have here have been working on the project with me for twenty-five years. And, the truth is, to the layman's eye, there's not much to show. Because of that, we are on the verge of being shut down. Perhaps violently."

"Why violently?"

"Because, young man, as I said, we do not exist. And the main government has discovered the secret government's project. Citizens find out about us, the religions zealots find out about what we're doing here... Well, we would not only lose financing, we might, in fact, lose our lives. The whole project, knowledge of it, those involved, would have to be erased. Overnight, the most amazing discovery in the history of science would end. And we, who do not exist, would continue not to exist. Only for real."

Dr. Wright leaned back in his chair and studied me for a long moment. I thought the story sounded fantastic, but considering I was in their underground world, I was more than a little inclined to believe him. At least partly.

"All of the men and women who work here have families," he said. "They rotate in and out, spending part of the year at home, part of the year here."

"You're saying they all have something to go back to."

"I am."

"And you're saying I do not."

Dr. Wright slowly nodded. "From what you've told me, that seems to be the case. Your parents are dead. No close family. Wife or girlfriend. Not even a pet. You could go back, of course, possibly work out your problem, and go on with your life. It's also possible you could spend a few years in jail, if not for the injury you gave the young man, then for stealing an aircraft."

Dr. Wright gave me the adoring uncle look. "What I'm offering here, however, is something that is unique."

I understood then. Understood why he had been so friendly. He and his nonexistent organization saw me as nothing more than a lab rat.

Chapter Three

The Jump

I WAS ANGRY and insulted, and when I went back to my room my first thoughts were of escape, but then it occurred to me, I would be escaping to… Where?

Dr. Wright had befriended me, hastily winning my allegiance to benefit his plans, to show progress so his facility would not be closed down, even destroyed. It was underhanded, but the truth was, I saw it all as a new and amazing opportunity. A chance to try something that had never been tried. After my sojourn in Alaska, flying planes, living by my wits, to return to the lower states, to possibly spend time in prison, or to go about everyday life, a nine-to-five job, was not appealing. Like my old mentor, Rimbauld, I was an adventurer at heart.

To be part of something never before done… I found that vastly appealing. A day-to-day government project would never openly allow an outsider to put him- or herself in jeopardy. Here, however, in a place that was not supposed to exist, it could happen. I decided right then and there, as I sat in the darkness of my room in a soft chair, that I would make it easy for Dr. Wright. I would volunteer.

My guess was, there was a good chance that if I did not volunteer, I would be made a volunteer. There was no way in the world that he planned to let me go, to be a potential blabbermouth that might reveal not only what was being done here, but its general location.

I did not have, and had never had, a real choice.

And I didn't want one.

—

A DAY LATER Dr. Wright took me to the laboratory and showed me what was there. When I say laboratory it was a room the size of warehouse. There were busy men and women in white coats. There were computers with blinking lights on long wooden tables, and there were vials of this and that, and all manner of colors pulsing through tubes, and there were wires, red, blue, green, yellow, and the tubes and wires led to a glassed-in room at the far end of the lab. It was not a small room, but neither was it huge. There were rooms with windows, and looking through one of the windows, I saw spinning colors and stars and little bright planets, and dead center of it all, a prominent solar system revolving around a large star the color of a fresh egg yolk, which Dr. Wright identified as a sun. The room, that little universe behind glass, was breathtaking.

I was dazed, to say the least. I felt like a god looking in on that universe, those stars and worlds, that solar system, that bright yellow sun.

"It's a little like fine-tuning artillery, this traveling about," he said. "We have used mice up until now, trying to close in on that planet next to that sun in that solar system."

He pointed with his finger. "We now believe we can send a human visitor to that planet. We created that universe quite recently, but in the time of the universe itself, billions of years have passed. Life may have formed on those planets. Certainly, we believe the world close to that particular sun is hospitable. Different from what we know here, but maybe not too different. There are other solar systems, and other suns, and other planets, but from what we have researched, and perhaps guessed at a little bit, we feel that one dead center of it all is the most likely to house life, maintain a visitor."

"When you say a visitor, I assume you are no longer talking about mice," I said.

"No. Not mice. You."

"Once I'm there, provided I make it, can I return?"

"If we send you successfully, we can bring you back successfully. A timer. We brought three of the five mice back."

"What happened to the other two?"

"Can't say."

"Can't, or won't?"

"Can't."

From the moment I learned that Dr. Wright planned to use me as his guinea pig, and I assumed against my will if I chose not to agree, I looked at him differently. But I decided not to let it show. I wanted to go.

"How does it work?" I asked.

"Come."

I followed as he led me along a hall, into a room, over to a long metal table. There were computers on it, blinking lights and moving dots across their screens. It made no sense to me. On the table there was a little ball of metal, open in spots; it was shaped in the manner of fingers clutched loosely into a ball, with gaps between the fingers. The gaps were filled with hard glass or plastic, strips of windows.

"The mice traveled in this?"

"Yes."

"No space craft? I don't get it."

"You're not traveling through space, you're traveling… Ah, how to explain, son. You are traveling through dimensions, through time, and space is of no consequence. If the mice went, and came back, then the air on the particular planet where we plan for you to arrive can be breathed. We learned that."

"What planet?"

"The planet we call Fourth from the Sun. Meaning the particular sun in the particular solar system inside the universe we've made. The mice went there, and most of them survived."

"The ones that didn't survive. They went elsewhere?"

"No. They went to the same place. But they didn't come back."

"Did the vehicle come back?"

"Once, yes. It was empty. The other time. No, it didn't return."

I thought about that a moment. "All right, I presume that you do not intend for me to fit in that little ball."

He smiled at me and guided me toward a room that connected to the laboratory. Inside he closed the door. On a pedestal was a ball like the mice had traveled in, but it was, of course, huge, and there was a set of stairs that led up to it. Across from it was a glass, and it showed into the room containing the created universe I had seen before. Looking at it, it was amazing to think that that microcosmic universe housed stars and planets and suns, and maybe, life.

Dr. Wright walked up the steps and touched the ball. The silver fingers opened slowly. There was a seat inside with straps. There were a few simple controls.

"Is it like flying a plane?"

"You fly nothing. These switches," and he touched a red one and a yellow one, "are for opening and closing the ball. Once you arrive, you have one switch to set." He pointed at a larger yellow switch. "And then, it doesn't matter if you're inside again or not. You can be anywhere, and it will gather you up."

"Gather me up?" I asked. "How's that?"

"Once you're there, when the mechanism decides to return you, it will gather you into atoms and pull you inside the ball. It will find you, like a mother hen collecting her chicks. You need do nothing. Your atomic structure will be broken into fragments, so that it can make the journey back unharmed, and when you arrive, they will be pieced together again. Then, you touch a certain switch if all goes well, and you can open the ball, and come out. It's that simple."

"How long will I have there?"

"Here, your time gone could be seconds, minutes, days, a few weeks. Possibly a year. No way to tell for certain. But your time there, on that world, in that solar system, inside that universe... It could be a lifetime."

And then it struck me. The mice had traveled there and come back, and the life span of a mouse, compared to a human, is quite brief.

I said, "Did the mice age?"

"No," he said, smiling slightly. "We think that may be a peculiar side effect of the transfer. A freezing of the physical; an end to aging. From what we can tell from the mice, they have ceased to age. And they seem even more spry. None of this has worn off. Perhaps in time it will. But not so far. Not a bad side effect."

"Why?"

Dr. Wright shook his head. "I don't know. We don't even have a theory. It's a mystery."

"And you don't know that humans will be affected the same, do you?"

"No," he said. "We don't. But it seems highly likely."

"Of course," I said. "There were the two that didn't come back."

"True, Brax. Quite true."

As he escorted me out of there and back to my room, I thought: He has not even asked my last name, not once. And then I thought: Unless I made the round trip, there wasn't really any reason for him to know.

—

It was three days later when I awoke to find that through the slot in the door they had slipped me fresh clothes. Jeans and tee-shirt, fleece-lined jacket, socks and tennis shoes. I put them on, and an hour later I was brought breakfast. When I finished I was conducted by my guardian back to the room with the large ball in it. The last three days had been used to show me what I needed to do, which was minimal, and what I might expect, which was merely speculative. The only ones who might be able to explain that to me with any authority were the mice who had gone and come back, and they weren't talking.

Inside the ball I strapped myself in the chair. Dr. Wright said, "It will seem to spin. It isn't spinning, and it isn't moving, but it will feel that way. When you arrive, you should make sure the ball is in a safe place. It should, if all goes well, bring you back, as long as it isn't damaged. Do you understand?"

Of course I had heard this for the last few days, but I nodded as if it were the first time the information had been imparted to me. Before I pushed the button to close the door, which was almost all of the left side of the device, I noticed that Dr. Wright was teary-eyed.

I was uncertain if he felt some concern for my safety, or if he was merely excited to find that his human guinea pig had been so willing and so cooperative without him having to push the hard sell.

"Brax," Dr. Wright said. "I wish you all the luck there is."

He produced a broad belt with a little case fastened to its side, and gave me a fat pocket knife. It was one of those knives with all manner of gadgets attached. Awl, scissors, spoon, two different blades, as well as some devices I didn't recognize.

"You may need these things," he said. "They will all travel with you, will materialize with you when you come to a stop, wherever that may be."

"Provided it's not the middle of a star or underwater," I said.

"Yes, there's that," he said. "But remember, the mice came back."

"Most of them," I said.

He nodded. "The case on the belt contains first aid materials, some other odds and ends. It might come in handy."

I put the knife in the pack and fastened the belt.

"Before I go," I said, "I want you to know this. I know full well that I wouldn't have left here alive had I not chosen to go. Or at least someone would have tried to prevent me. I wouldn't go down easy. I just wanted you to understand I knew what my options were."

"Accident laid you in our hands," Dr. Wright said, and his voice was choked up, as if a knot had been tied in his throat. "I didn't want it this way, but the organization who sponsors us, they leave us little choice. And if we fail, or if the laboratory, our experiments are closed down, then I would suffer the same fate you might expect for yourself. I knew that going into this project. I had a chance to get out. I didn't take it."

"The difference is you chose to be here," I said. "But I will offer you this consolation, Doctor. I want this. I want it bad. I don't like not having a choice, but in this case, it's the choice I want to make."

"You're an odd one, Brax."

"This world is too tame for me, Dr. Wright."

"Then let's hope the next world excites you more."

I smiled at him. "Enough small talk. Let's do it."

I touched the button on the device. Dr. Wright left the room. A moment later all the colors of the universe leaped through the ball and the planets and stars charged toward me like bullets.

Then all was a swirl of darkness, and then the darkness was splattered with white stars. Then they were gone. There was a feeling as if my ears might break. I saw my hands, resting on the small console in front of me, come apart in a billion flakes of colorful energy. I tried to lift my arms, but they appeared to be dissolving. And then they were gone, and my memory of The Jump, as Dr. Wright called it, ended.

Chapter Four

Giants and Monsters

I WAS WHOLE again. I lifted up my hands and inspected them. Everything seemed okay, all the fingers were in the right place. I patted myself down. A superficial examination proved me to be sound and able-bodied. The belt with the pack Dr. Wright had given me was still strapped on me. I was a little dizzy, but other than that, I felt fine.

The ball was wrapped in a green color and the green color was full of light. It took me a moment to adjust, but I soon realized it was foliage around me; a big mass of leaves and boughs, and the leaves were easily the length of an average man's body, two feet or more across. The arrival, the impact after materialization in this mass of greenery, had cracked a band of the machine's see-through covering. It hadn't broken the clear plastic loose, but it had put quite a mark on it; it ran all the length of the glass, like a giant dueling scar. Maybe something similar had happened to one or both of the missing mice. One mouse got out, and something got it. The other mouse may have had its device damaged, and that's why it and the device failed to go back.

All I knew was I was a human mouse, and so far, so good in the physical department. As for my ride? At this point it was debatable. I had no idea how badly it had been damaged, or how little damage it took for it to be nonfunctional.

The leaves were pressed tight as a coat of paint against the clear parts of the ball, dotted with large dollops of dew, or recent rain. The light shining through the leaves made them appear artificial, almost like some kind of ornament.

I set the return button, and then pressed the hatch release. When I did, the powerful, but unseen, hinge that was one side of the ball sprang open and knocked the leaves back and the light from the sun shone in bright as a spotlight.

I unfastened my seat belt and got out of the ball, and when I was clear of it, it automatically closed and sealed with the quickness of a snapping turtle. There was no way to open it now. Not until it was ready. I wouldn't be going back inside until it dissolved me again, or whatever it was it did, and returned me to Earth. Provided it was still working.

Before me was a long stretch of brown ground that sloped off at one end. The ground was smooth for the most part, but there were bumps and rolls here and there. I moved away from the ball, and glanced back. The leaves that my machine had pushed aside, now that it had closed, were slowly wrapping themselves around it again. They did this until the only way you might see my traveling machine was to know it was there. And even then, it was doubtful. The sunlight was resting on the leaves, but unlike the view from inside the ball, the leaves appeared dark from the outside.

I looked up.

Above me were limbs and leaves. They climbed high, high, high. It was as if I were trying to see the top of a mountain. Light came through in gaps between the boughs. The gaps were enormous. Some of the limbs were the size of entire redwoods in California.

I walked where there was plenty of light shining through a break in the boughs and vegetation in the manner of great leaves and long needles and flowers, all of which were easily the size of rowboats and all kinds of colors. Through the gap I could see the sun, and assumed it was the star that had been pointed out to me in the laboratory. Now, here I was on the Fourth Planet from that sun.

The sky was as blue as a Robert Johnson song.

I ambled along, and soon I was walking along the dark brown surface with no limbs above me. I felt as if it should be hot, but it wasn't. I also realized that I felt really good. The air was terrific, so sweet and full of oxygen, I felt a little euphoric.

I walked for a long time. When I looked back, I realized that where I had landed was well in the distance. I turned and walked some more, and then the ground thinned on both sides, became narrow before me.

The land kept tapering. Soon, I could see a clutch of bushes. A moment later I realized they were not bushes at all. They were little growths off of what I was walking on, and what I was walking on wasn't ground.

I was walking on a mostly barren limb, except for that little eruption of greenery. My ground was in fact a limb larger than any tree I had ever seen. I finally came to where it forked and broke off in a jagged manner, most likely due to natural causes.

I carefully looked down.

The earth was miles below. I could make out rivers, like blue lines, and above the rivers, mountain peaks, even a few spotty clouds surrounding the mountains, as if someone who was about to pack it up and move it all were in the process of packing everything in cotton.

I turned around and looked back at the tree. The trunk of the tree was very thick around. It went for a far distance in either direction before it curved on either side. It was filled with massive limbs and all those big leaves, needles and flowers.

Next to that monstrous, strange tree, far away on either side were other trees, and next to them were more, on and on, beyond vision, into the depths of an unknown world. Between the trees were patches of light and shadow, spreading left and right, climbing high and expanding broadly, and like all the trees, it too was festooned with all manner of different leaves and needles and flowers, and some had round and oblong, multicolored fruit, like Christmas decorations, large as beach balls.

I was standing on one giant limb projecting from one monstrous tree that was merely one of many in a massive forest that rose higher than the mountains and clouds, and yet the air was thick and easy to breathe. I wasn't a scientist, but I knew enough to feel that this world violated certain base assumptions of scientific fact. It wasn't that I felt it lacked science, merely that when created, certain laws of physics had been altered in the creation.

So large were the trees, and so close to one another, the limbs so even and so wide, it would not be difficult to walk from one tree to another. I even determined that the bark of the trees was jagged, and could be grabbed and climbed like a mountain face. Vines hung from a large number of the limbs like ropes, and at a glance, I saw something monkey-like scramble up one and disappear into a wad of foliage.

It was overwhelming, and for a moment, so amazing, I felt as if my legs might fold out from under me and I would collapse.

Gladly as I had come, I now wondered what I was to do here. Then the words Dr. Wright had spoken to me about time here being different than time at home struck me.

I could be here on this fourth planet from this massive sun, for a long, long time.

If the ball no longer worked, if it no longer had the power to break me apart and gather me up in all my pieces, and throw me out of this miniature universe, through dimensional barriers, through time and space, back to my world, then this world of trees was my world forever.

As was often the case with my life, I had made a hasty, impulsive decision and thought it good at the time. I wasn't so sure now.

Of course, there was another factor.

If I had not made the decision, it would have been made for me.

A moment later, standing there on the tip of the branch, all of this running through my mind, my concerns were abruptly lost to me when I saw the most extraordinary sight. A sight that made me believe what I had seen so far was minor in comparison.

—

BETWEEN THE LARGE trees, some distance away on another smaller limb, I saw a man moving swiftly. He was on foot and was covering considerable ground (or to be more precise, tree) in great hopping strides, like an excited grasshopper. He was a small man, perhaps five feet in height, and he was lean and dark as the bark of the trees around him, his hair was long and red as a vicious wound. Short as he was, he was large-chested, long-legged, and long-armed. His only clothing was a loincloth. His feet were bare.

He rushed out on the limb, stood on the edge of it, and leaped from it, caught a dangling vine, swung across a vast gap, and landed on the base—again, quite some distance away—of the massive limb on which I stood.

I could see that he had a bow slung over his shoulder, and a quiver of arrows, and he also had what appeared to be a long spear slung by a cord of some kind over his back. He carried a long blue metal sword in his hand. When he spied me, he sort of crouched, as if I were a problem.

I didn't move.

In the distance I heard a sound akin to bamboo being knocked together by a violent wind, saw behind the man there was a stir between the trunks of the trees, where a thick growth of what in fact did look like bamboo grew along a patch of intertwined limbs. The tall green and brown stalks knocked together like angry children banging oversized chopsticks, then from between the long reeds something burst into view that seemed to be out of the imaginings of a lunatic. For a moment I considered the possibility that I might in fact still be lying on that Alaskan shore, my back against a tree, the plane I had stolen in ruins. Or perhaps I was in the spinning ball, somehow lost in limbo, as Dr. Wright said I might be, and my head was stuffed with confusion and imagination as I moved eternally through…nowhere.

For what parted the reeds and came into view was what I can only describe as something akin to a praying mantis. It was astride a great blue and yellow, multi-legged critter that looked like a humongous aphid or beetle. There really is no word to describe it. The mantis's mandibles snapped at the air like old-fashioned ice tongs.

Behind it, came another, and another, until three of the mounted creatures were in view, and their mounts were scrambling over limbs and vines with an almost magical grace.

It didn't take a genius to understand that the man was on the run.

There was no way for me to know if the manlike creature was in fact the worst of villains, and the Insectoids, as I named them at first sight, were just and correct in the matter of their pursuit. But, I suppose certain cultural instincts involving man and bug took over, and of course, the fact that he was one and they were three was a deciding factor as well, although I was soon to discover that there were more than three.

At that moment, I didn't consider anything deeply. I just responded, as was my nature, and was soon running toward them. This seems to be a Booker trait. When we should be silent and observe, or run away, we become loud and charge forward, directly into the mouth of trouble.

I was soon aware of the fact that I had incredible energy. Not just adrenaline, but as I ran I found that I was almost leaping. At first I thought it might be due to a lighter gravity, but soon realized it was another reason altogether. My muscles felt extraordinary. I'm not sure what the journey, the transmitter, or the planet, or this universe, had done to me, but it was as if I had been given an enormous transfusion of muscle, and power.

As I ran, the man gave me a look, but soon turned his attention to the mantises and the beetles. If that wasn't problem enough, the reeds parted again, and stepping from them, first one, then another, there were two beings perhaps twenty-five feet tall. They were humanoid in structure, but broad in the hips and narrow in the shoulders, slumped somewhat with wide mouths that went almost ear to ear, and they had a third eye in the center of their broad foreheads. They were nude except for large net bags that hung around their waists. In the netting were three or four humans on each hip. Men and women and children. They were screaming in a high-pitched language that meant about as much to me as the song of crickets. It amazed me, big as the giants were, that they were able to support these human beings in mesh bags without showing any sign of strain.

The giants had massive feet with long toes. Their hands were enormous, oversized for their bodies; with fingers so long they had an extra row of joints. They carried in one hand what I can only describe as a giant scoop, and in the other a long, loose, open net. At the back of their necks, partially on the rear of their skulls, was a strange-looking, squid-like creature. Tentacles thrashed all about like Medusa's hair. I couldn't determine if these things were in fact some kind of secondary creature, or just some structural accouterment that came with the giants at birth.

If that wasn't bad enough, the reeds rattled again, and two more of the creatures appeared, their waists dripping in netting filled with yelling humans.

The little man was brave. He stopped, stuck the sword in the limb at his feet, quickly swung the bow off his shoulder and flicked three arrows out between his fingers, laid them all against the bow, fired one right after the other, like bullets from a chamber.

One of the arrows went into the foremost giant, took an eye, the other lodged in the throat, and a third went into the chest. The last shot was about as effective as a porcupine quill in an elephant's knee. The eye and throat shot, however, yielded results.

The monster grabbed at the arrow, jerked it free, taking what was left of his eye with it, and then he grasped at the one in his throat. The blood was pouring from that wound like a crimson river. It had hit a vital spot, an artery, and the giant wavered and stumbled, and fell, dropping onto the netting and its contents, crushing them like overripe fruit beneath his massive body, squirting blood and innards from under him and in all directions, like lumpy jam.

The man who had loosed the arrows let out with a bellow. It was not a sound of triumph, but of heartache. He had killed one of his tormentors only to destroy a large number of his own kind. The death of his enemy brought the death of his kin. And by his own hand.

I was at his side now, and I snatched the spear off of his back with one clean move. He turned, as if to stop me, then saw me lunging forward with the spear, tossing it smoothly into the knee of one of the giants. It might as well have been a porcupine quill in an elephant's leg, but it was well placed. The giant stumbled and went to one knee.

The mantis creatures on their beetles had held back, to let the giants have their way, but now, seeing one dead, and one with his knee down, they rushed forward with a squealing and clicking kind of war cry.

One of my new comrade's arrows knocked a mantis from its mount. I jerked his sword from its stuck position in the tree, and sprang forward, landing on the head of one of the beetles, and driving the sword through the chitinous chest of its rider. It was a deathblow, and the mantis tumbled off in a crash that sounded like dry bones rolling over rocks.

I fell off the beetle and saw it scuttle away, but decided I could catch it with my newfound muscles. Springing forward, I landed on its back and caught the long, vine reins and pulled at them, discovered the beetle worked very much like a horse. I wheeled it and saw that the man had finally broken and run, which was, of course, the only sensible thing to do.

I charged after him, whipping the sword above my head. One of the mantises and its beetle were closing in on him, and as I came up behind the monstrosity, it turned its head and pulled from its belt a sword, tried to wheel its insect steed about to face me.

He was too slow. I was on him. I whipped an arc with my blade and clove his head from his shoulders with a single strike. I plunged the beetle forward, into the thickening foliage, came upon my new companion, darting for cover. I called out to him. Certainly he couldn't understand my words, but he understood my intent. He wheeled about and took my extended hand as I, with effortless ease, swung him up behind me on the beetle.

Behind us the giants and the remaining mantis and its beetle plunged toward us.

The man I had rescued swung around on the backside of the beetle, so that he was facing the rear, and let loose with a volley of arrows. I glanced back once, just in time to see the mantis catch a shaft and fall from its mount into a thick wad of greenery. Then we gained ground, leaving the remaining giants and their poor captives behind.

—

WHEN WE FINALLY stopped, I tied the beetle to a limb with the reins, not knowing what else to do. My companion pulled some leaves and grass here and there, gave it to the beetle. It squatted down with its many legs beneath it, and ate.

The man looked at me and smiled. His face was V-shaped, almost elfin. His hair was very red. I had never seen hair that red. He was all muscles, but the muscles, though similar in construct to mine, seemed somehow overlong and less pronounced, as if they had been drawn taught like a bow string.

He reached out cautiously for his sword, which I still held. I gave it up with minor reluctance. Then he gently touched my shoulder with the palm of his hand, and dipped his chin quickly. I assumed this was this world's equivalent of a handshake.

Joe R. Lansdale

I did the same in return. He moved away from me immediately, toward a clutch of strange plants that were blue in color, rose up high and were sharp tipped. As I followed, I realized these plants looked just like the blue sword I had been wielding, only longer. The sword, sharp as it was, was in fact a natural creation, and was some form of vegetation. It grew straight up in a large natural crop, and some of the growth was blue, some of it was red. The red blades drooped slightly, and I immediately had the impression that the red ones were a younger growth of the same plant.

My new partner bent down close to the tree into which the sharp plants grew, and got hold of it there. There was no blade there, just a kind of root. He pulled at it, and it came free from the great limb on which we stood; when it popped free, it did so loudly. He had picked one of the shorter growths, about six feet in length, and I saw that at least two feet of it was of the root. The root made a natural handle, except for a mass of fibrous vines that grew out of that portion. Bending down, he placed the fresh-pulled shaft on the tree trunk, and began shaving off the vines, or perhaps a more accurate description is smaller roots, until the larger root from which they grew was smooth. He chopped off part of that, left about seven inches of the haft remaining, the rest sword.

He handed it to me. I took it carefully. There was no guard, as such, but the root flared naturally close to where the blade part of the plant began, proving a kind of protection from your hand sliding up on the sharp edge. It was amazing that such a plant made a fine weapon. It was lighter than most swords of that size I had handled, by quite a bit, and its blade was of extraordinary sharpness and rivaled cold steel. I tapped it a few times on the base of the limb on which we stood, looked up and grinned at him.

He smiled. He took his sword and smashed up the root he had cut off of the sword, the part that was more like wood, and broke it open. He pushed it under my nose. It smelled sweet, kind of like a cross between the honey of a bee and a honeysuckle plant. He tasted it, made a universal yum noise to let me know it tasted good.

190

Handing it to me, I took it, and ripped into it with gusto. I was suddenly starving. And though it was sweet, there was a texture to it that was akin to meat, and after only a few bites, I was feeling strong again.

—

WE MOVED ON by beetleback until the great sun's light thinned through the trees and the sounds of wild animals, and what I assumed were birds, filled the air in recognition of the coming of the night. We stopped just before dark and my companion found a long green plant that sprouted out from the side of a tall tree, the base of which was of phenomenal diameter, and could not have been reached around by the entire east Texas town from which I came if they all linked hands. It went on for what appeared to be miles.

The green shaft of the plant was hollow, and my sword, with a bit of cutting, fit right into it. He handed me my natural sword and sheath, and then went about cutting vines. He took the sword and sheath back, fastened these to it so that I soon had a harness where I could sling the sword over my shoulder.

I thanked him, and though he didn't understand the words, again, the meaning was clear.

He took over control of the beetle, and I rode on the back, as the insect climbed up the side of the tree. There was a saddle for the rider, and an extension on which I could sit, and the back of the saddle had a kind of lift that supported me above my buttocks and kept me from falling. I also quickly learned to lean forward as the amazing bug climbed up into thicker foliage. There were also straps that I could use to harness myself in, and they were easily unstrapped; they were made of some kind of vegetation that worked much like Velcro.

I noticed there were great gaps in the larger limbs, like caverns. My companion soon picked one of these, which was perhaps ten feet high and twenty feet long, and guided our mount into it. Once there, he used some of the vines he had kept to hobble our bug, and went out and got more greenery for it to eat while I stood at the mouth of our cavern and looked out at the dying light.

It was as if the night was a curtain, and it dropped down slow and certain, and soon it was dead dark. Or at least for a moment, but then my eyes adjusted, and up through the limbs of the trees I could see a patch of night sky, and a huge star, pulsating red and blue.

When my partner returned he had some fruits for us to eat, and more food for the bug. He built a fire by using some kind of growth that lit up when touched with a blue root of some sort. I didn't understand it exactly, but it was a little like sticking a nine-volt battery against steel wool. It blazed.

When the fire was going, he pulled some large limbs around it and laid huge leaves over those to block out the direct light of the fire. It struck me that for anyone to see us up within this wood cavern, amidst this great clutch of foliage, deep in this wild and strange jungle, would have been a great feat, and more likely an accident, but I trusted my companion's judgment on this matter far more than mine.

After awhile, I went back to the edge of our immediate home and looked up again at the star. He joined me, stood and looked too.

"Badway," he said.

I looked at him.

He pointed up.

"Badway de Moola," he said.

This meant nothing to me. I pointed at the star. "Badway?"

He nodded. "Badway. Badway de Moola."

Whatever this meant, we were in agreement.

Back inside he gave me some heavy and very moldable large leaves. We lay on one and wrapped the other one around us. The leaves, like some kind of cocoon, enveloped us and held us loosely in its warmth.

We slept.

Chapter Five

The Horrors

IN THE NIGHT the rain came. It woke me with terrific lightning blasts and rolls of thunder like bowling balls being tumbled about inside a great steel drum. I sat up and saw that my partner sat up too. He lifted a hand, in a kind of wave, and lay back down. For him, I assumed, this was not uncommon. Soon I could hear his breathing, as he went back to sleep.

I got up and stood at the mouth of the tree cavern and watched great waves of rain splash through the jungle, caught up on a cool wind. It became so ferocious I had to back into my wooden cave, pressing my body near the rear. The rain smacked all the way inside of our cubby, and soon the air smelled wet and strange, the aromas fostered by stimulated plants. The smells were mostly unknown to me, but a few had some faint familiarity to boiled coffee and rich vanilla, a twist of lemon, a stinging sensation in the nostrils like sea salt. The rest were beyond my olfactory experience. The smells came in waves. And so did the rain.

I watched it for awhile. I found myself practicing the meditation that Jack had taught me. I didn't levitate, but I did manage to sleep well after I finished and turned back in between my sleeping leaves.

By morning, the water had seeped in, and I was damp. But I noticed a curious thing. The tree wood was sucking up the water. On earth, in this kind of environment, everything would have remained wet for a long time, and rot would have been a problem, but here, the water was absorbed deep into the tree in a short time, so the damp didn't stick around long enough to rot anything.

Physically, I had never felt better. As I said before, my muscles seemed imbued with strength and stamina. It was as if the very air I breathed had filled my veins with energy. I was contemplating all this, when I realized my new companion was up. He looked at me in my wet clothes and grinned. He, wearing only a loincloth, had fewer garments to contend with, and no shoes, and therefore was not as encumbered by water.

Our beetle was waiting patiently for a wad of breakfast greenery that we gave it. It ate contentedly, its sad eyes more like a deer's than an insect's, watching us while we ate stringy vegetation from a broken gourd. Something about our sad-eyed mount made me feel affection for it. I decided to call it Butch, at least to myself.

Although I had no idea where we were going or why, or even if we were on a mission other than continued flight from what might be chasing us, I fell in line like a soldier. Pretty soon we were mounted on Butch, heading into the twisting depths of the jungle that grew up from the massive boughs of the trees. It was a jungle contained on one massive tree that covered miles. Other trees with their own jungles could be accessed by our beetle. It was unique, to say the least. Jungles growing on massive trees that intersected with other trees and jungles. It was a world of jungle, populated by little jungles. I had never imagined the possibility of such a thing.

By midday the jungle had turned warm, but not hot. The rainwater had been sucked into the plants, and as we went, many of the leaves and branches reached out to touch us like curious children, and then jerked away as if frightened.

From my companion's manner, I was certain he was watching out behind us, to see if we still had pursuers. My thought was it would hardly be worth the trouble for that great band of giants, beetles and insect riders, to pursue a mere two men when they had so many already captured. Why they had been captured I was uncertain, but my guess was slavery.

It took me awhile, but on our second day out, I was able to ascertain that my new friend's name was Booloo. He taught me this by touching his chest and repeating the word until I understood. I taught him my name, or a derivative of it. Brax.

It took me yet another day to ascertain from the position of the sun that we were in fact not fleeing our pursuers, but circling back toward them; this seemed like a less than intelligent procedure, but I was uncertain how to pass this thought along to Booloo, nor was I positive that if I could, it would matter. I might be better off abandoning Booloo if he was going to go back into the jaws of his former captors, but I felt being alone in this world of strange plants and animals without a mount or knowledge of how to survive might be worse. I made the decision to stick with him. For what it was worth, he was now my only friend.

—

ONE AFTERNOON AS the sun began to dip, and a greenish glow slipped through the jungle, Booloo directed Butch high up into the trees (and I refer to the trees of the little jungle, not the tree that supported it). Our insect scuttled acrobatically over limbs and tangled vines and the tops of trees, with an up-and-down motion that I had finally gotten used to; it was like gaining your sea legs on a ship. It was a great way to observe the dipping sun, and I began to realize that the greenish glow that often persisted was most likely due to floating pollen. With my sinus problems, I was surprised I was not bothered, but I began to think it was the pollen from the trees that was in fact giving me my feelings of strength and stamina.

We came to a plunge in the forest, and Booloo guided Butch down into a grove of great trees, just as the wind picked up and came twisting through the forest like a wraith. The trees we were among were tall and white and had clumps of vegetation at their tops, but were otherwise limbless, smooth, and not that big around. When the wind blew the trees rattled together at their summits and the sound of their striking one another was like the clacking of thousands of hoofbeats.

We rode Butch between the trees, and just before the sun died down behind the world, we saw what looked like a great sheet of gray gauze stretched and wound about a dozen trunks. It twisted up to a height of thirty feet. As soon as we observed it, it was no longer there.

Booloo halted Butch and swung off, dropping the reins. Butch remained in his spot as I climbed down and moved with Booloo toward what had been there only moments ago, but was now nothing more than night. But as we grew closer, Booloo drew his sword, extended it, and slashed. There was a ripping sound, and then what had seemed like growing darkness split apart and dangled down, looking now like the gray gauze it had at first resembled. Whatever it was, it was a natural camouflage. Booloo seemed excited to have discovered it, and he knelt down with his sword and cut off two large swathes. He touched it with his sword, and the sword stuck. He tugged the sword free, and waited. The stickiness, which was white as puss, began to fade. Booloo reached down and picked it up. It was obvious it was no longer sticky. Once cut from its source, that aspect of it appeared to dissolve.

When Booloo saw my confusion, he smiled. It was a glorious smile. He stuck his sword into the ground, or the tree that served as our ground, and flicked the patch around his shoulders and let it fall over the front of his body. He clutched it tight, and a moment later, he seemed to be nothing more than a floating head. He had naturally been camouflaged.

The look on my face made him laugh. He whipped off the cloak, for that's how I now thought of it, and handed it to me. He picked up the other for himself. He bent down and proceeded to roll it up. I held my cloak in front of me. On one side was the part that served as camouflage, but the other side was transparent. I lifted it over my head, saw that I could see through it almost as clearly as if it were not there.

Booloo began to talk, and his words were like a stream. They wouldn't cease. He was telling me about the material he had just cut into patches, of that I was certain, and it seemed to excite him to no end. My guess is that he was trying to explain the rarity of it, and the good fortune of finding it.

It was during his explanation that behind him, on the greater expansion of the gauze, I saw something that made me realize the source of the material Booloo had just cut was not of its own making. A creature that looked very much like an earthly spider was crawling down from on high. It had twelve legs and large black eyes and dripping chelicerae; it scuttled rapidly on its hairy legs, and my immediate thought was that it was not hurrying down to give us an enthusiastic greeting. Booloo had just cut a portion of its web, and the beast resented the invasion.

I pulled my sword just as Booloo noticed its approach and pulled his, and then the thing leaped. I jumped out of its way, and was amazed to find that the leap was effortless and carried me a great distance. When I wheeled to look back, Booloo was under the spider, and its snapping "jaws" were trying to drive its fangs into him. He was managing to keep it at bay by pushing his sword crossways between the set of fangs, but the power of the creature was weakening his grip and his resolve.

With one step and a leap, I was on the creature's back. I drove my sword down hard into its head. It then bucked, like a horse, and threw me back into the hanging patch of gauze, which I knew now to be a web. I stuck there immediately, but my sword arm was free, and as the monster rushed at me, I stabbed out at it and planted my sword directly into one of its eyes, which exploded a kind of black goo that splattered on me and the web.

As the spider snapped its fangs in the air, I saw Booloo scrambling up over the top of the spider, clutching at it with one hand, while driving his sword deep into its broad back.

I pushed out as far as I could, and tried to cut backwards with my sword. Pinned as I was to the web, I found this difficult, but by slashing over my shoulder, I was able to cut loose enough of my restraint to fall forward and out of the web. Still, it clung to me. I stood and found myself twisted up in it. I cut at it viciously with the sword arm until it came free. A moment later, the web relaxed and fell away from me and onto the tree beneath my feet. The spider may have made it, but it seemed to be a living thing, and any section of it cut down and separated from the rest, lost its life and its stickiness, if not its camouflage.

I turned my attention to Booloo and the spider, saw that it was scuttling up one of the many branches that served as a tree on our giant base tree. Booloo was hanging to it like a parasite with one hand, and with the other, slashing at it with his sword.

I glanced around for Butch, planning to use him as a method of pursuit, and though he was normally content to stand by until we were ready to mount, he, or perhaps she, had scampered out of sight for fear of the spider, or perhaps he had sniffed out something to eat.

I stuck the light sword in my teeth and started to climb, and found that my newly acquired muscles had come with tremendous agility. I was able to scurry up the tree as effortlessly as a squirrel, my only impediment being my shoes, the soles of which slipped as I climbed.

Within instants, I had reached the spider, but had dropped my sword from my mouth. It had struck a limb as I climbed, cutting into the side of my mouth. It seemed the better part of valor was to let it fall than to have it inadvertently slice my head in half. Climbing onto the spider from the rear, dragging myself across its back by holding onto its thick hairs, which sprouted all over its body, I arrived at the spot where Booloo clung. He too had lost his sword, and was hanging for dear life as the spider navigated rapidly through the branches, trying to drag us off.

Finally, as if on cue, we both abandoned our mount, and nested ourselves onto a tree limb. We looked at each other. Booloo laughed. We looked up at the spider, still climbing, and then it stopped. It turned and we ceased to laugh.

It was coming back.

The spider-thing rushed down the tree, darting between limbs and leaves, set for the attack. Booloo and I moved off to the left and along a narrow limb. The limb parted, like a fork. I set out toward the thinner section of it, while Booloo veered right, climbing upwards and across to another tree. He called to me, repeating my name over and over, realizing we had gone in opposite directions. I ignored him. I had bigger problems. One of those big problems was a spider about the size of a delivery truck. I snatched a large yellow, oblong-shaped nut from one of tree's leafy boughs, wheeled and hurled it just as the monster was turning to pursue Booloo.

The nut hit the spider hard. There came from it a noise that was neither cry nor bark, but somewhere in between. It made the hairs on the back of my neck stand up.

Angry, it switched its path, darted after me. I went out as far on the limb as I could, then leaped to another, grabbing at a thick rope-like vine, feeling it give slightly, allowing me to swing out and down onto the bough of a tree below. When I looked up, the spider leapt from the limb where I had left it, light as a feather in the wind; it sailed across space and barely clutched its multiple legs into a netting of vines, and scrambled down after me. As it did, I jumped onto a narrow limb that rocked beneath my weight, saw there was another, quite some distance away. If I were on Earth I would have had no chance at all reaching it, but now, with my muscles hot-wired by the atmosphere and its strange pollen, I pivoted to watch the spider coming toward me at a leg-clicking run that was made all the more frightening by its leaking, savaged eye, its snapping jaws dripping green poison.

When it was twenty feet away, panic nearly caused me to retreat and leap. But I held my spot. Ten feet away. My knees coiled, and I half turned. Looking over my shoulder I saw that it was no more than six feet from me. I ran along the length of the limb, and jumped, successfully landed across the way on another limb. It gave beneath me, but sprang back to position, nearly tossing me from it.

I turned to see the spider hurtling toward me in midair, its legs flailing. I think both the beast and I knew simultaneously it wasn't going to make it. When it was three feet from my limb, it began to wag its legs and twist its head, and then it dipped and fell, splattering against limbs and tree trunks. It tangled briefly in vines, the vines snapped, and down it dropped, crashing almost directly in front of its web in a confusion of legs and body explosions.

I turned as I heard Booloo let out with a yip of triumph from a tree across the way. He leaped up and down on a limb like an excited monkey, chattering in his strange language.

Chapter Six

The Woman

WE GATHERED UP our cloaks from the web of the spider, and went looking for Butch. After some searching, we found the creature amongst a clutch of strange red and blue plants. Butch was munching them contentedly, having forgotten whatever had frightened it in the first place.

Riding Butch again, we continued on our way until we came to the plants from which Booloo had made my now-lost sword. Here we paused and made one apiece, using my pocket knife to cut the plants near their base where they were less strong, and more like common wood. The sword I now possessed was, frankly, not up to the one I had carried before. It was shorter and not as straight, but this was the condition of the entire plant, and no other plant of the same sort was currently within sight. It wasn't ideal, but under the circumstances it would have to do. The swords were still very serviceable.

Again, I was just going along for the ride because to do otherwise would leave me stranded in this strange land without assistance. I could easily starve surrounded by food, and not even know it. But, as we traveled, I carefully noted the fruits and vegetables Booloo chose, so that if we were ever separated I might at least have a fighting chance.

Two days later, after enduring windstorms and rainstorms, sleeping in tree caves, practicing my meditation, dancing about with my sword to accustom myself to its weight, riding until my butt ached, we came upon the giants and the mantis-things. We saw them from a distance. We were high up in a tree, strapped onto Butch, and when we dipped down slightly, letting the limbs of the tree predict our course, we could see through gaps in the leaves and limbs, a patch of devastated forest. Keep in mind that when I refer to forest, I refer to the trees that grew out of one of the great trees that on Earth would make up a small town. In fact, some of these forests, or jungles, were based on what would be a limb of a tree; though the term limb seems inadequate, considering the size of such a growth. To give you some idea of the size, in the distance, if we were high enough, we could see other great trees, looking like continents across an expanse of mist and blowing leaves.

But this smaller part of the forest to which I refer was hacked down and burnt, except for a few spotty, thin trees stripped of limbs. They were left standing, but their purpose was not an aesthetic one. Dangling from them by ropes were field-dressed bodies of men and women, headless, fastened to long hemp-style ropes; the corpses were split open and dripped blood; the corpses were those of men, women, and children.

It was a revolting sight, made all the more revolting, because as we watched, the giants approached one of the trees, tore down a few of the field-dressed bodies, and carried them toward a crackling fire. The fire was fueled by the trees they had chopped down. The meat was tossed directly onto the blazing pile amidst loud sounds of satisfaction from the giants; the meat hissed and popped in the flames. The mantis-things, dismounted, came forward then. They moved erratically, as if balanced on stilts. They squatted down, well outside the circle where the giants gathered.

Besides the corpses, there were living men and women—no children, they had all been disposed of by the giants—fixed firmly by long, yellow ropes that were attached to the tops of the trees. The ropes dangled down with the humans tied at their ends. They also had their arms and legs bound as well.

Seeing this, Booloo started to urge Butch forward, but I clasped his shoulder. He turned and looked at me. I shook my head, hoping the movement meant the same here as it did on Earth. He looked at me for a long moment, then dropped his head and turned back into his position on Butch's back. He trembled with anger.

It felt odd for me, for the first time in a long time, to be the rational one.

I gained his attention again, and by method of making signs with my hands, tried to make him realize that our chances were better if we waited until dark. I touched one of the folded up cloaks he had made from the spider's web. He nodded. We dismounted, and led Butch along the limb on which we were traveling, back into thicker foliage. There we tied Butch in a place where he could graze, and we went up a tall, thin tree, thick with foliage. At the top of it we found positions on limbs and looked out and down.

The giants were pulling smoking, blackened bodies from the fire and feeding themselves. They pushed and shoved one another and tore at the partially cooked flesh with their teeth like wild dogs. The things on the backs of their heads lay still, the tentacles not moving.

The mantises waited in a circle around them. From time to time the giants would toss a chunk of the meat outside the circle, and the mantises would scramble and fight for the scraps. After awhile, great gourds were brought forth. Soon the giants were gulping loudly from them.

It didn't take long to determine that the contents of the gourds consisted of some kind of alcoholic beverage, for soon the giants were pushing and shoving one another, fighting, and then falling down to sleep. As they did, the insectoids rushed in and grabbed at the disgusting remains of the meal, the last dregs in the gourds. It was a horrid spectacle.

As we observed, I noted that tied to one of the trees was a woman that stood out like fire on an ice floe. She was the most beautiful amongst a number of beautiful women. In fact, from what I had seen, a trademark of these people seemed to be their astonishing beauty. If the people of Earth could see them, each and every one of them, though constructed slightly different from Earthly humans, would have been thought models or movie stars. But even among a group of beautiful people, she was outstanding.

She was long and lean and curvaceous, with an almost elfin face framed by great waves of scarlet hair. Even from a distance, unable to see the detail of her features, she was striking. She was nude from the waist up, and her breasts were perfectly shaped and firm. Her only clothing was a kind of sarong of dark material fastened about her waist. She was shoeless. I was so stunned by her appearance, for a moment, I nearly lost my grip on a limb that held me in place.

As I was watching her, Booloo tapped my shoulder and pointed directly at her. He touched his chest. "Choona. Choona," he said.

I was uncertain of what he was actually saying, but the meaning seemed obvious. The beautiful redhead was his woman. It became evident now why we had made a wide circle to catch back up with the giants. He wanted to rescue her, though had he been left to his own devices, charging down amongst them on Butch's back, he would have most certainly been enslaved, killed or eaten.

I nodded to him, looked back at the woman, feeling weak, and even envious of Booloo. But when I turned back to him, I clasped his shoulder and nodded, hopefully letting him know I was a willing assistant in any enterprise to rescue her.

—

THE NIGHT CAME down like a drift of crepe paper and fell onto and twisted between the trees and coated them black. With it came the sounds of night birds and creatures, cries and squeaks and grunts and growls. The fires still raged below, and the light from them flickered across the standing trees that held the prisoners. The beautiful woman was nothing more than a shadow now, but I couldn't take my eyes off of her. When I had first seen her she had been standing, regal as a queen, but now she was sitting on the ground, her head hung. Seeing her that way made me angry and sick to my stomach.

If the giants were to move in her direction, perhaps to prepare her as food, I was certain I would hurry down there and do the best I could to save her. Of course, I felt for the others, but I must be honest and say the sight of her, the one Booloo referred to as Choona, gave me a strength and direction I had not felt in days. Without even knowing her, I knew I would give my life for her. I suppose this is what they call love at first sight.

Booloo fastened his bow to the side of Butch, because he had no arrows left, and we donned our cloaks and took our swords, and moved silently down among them on foot.

The cloaks made us dark as the night, but they were not perfect. When I looked at Booloo, I could see from time to time that he was like a patch of darkness coming loose from the gloom. I could see him moving, and could discern his shape, and occasionally, when the cloak slipped from where he gathered it at his head with his hand, I could glimpse his face.

But, if I were not expecting to see him, and if I were some distance away, then the probability of seeing him, or me, was small. Or so I hoped.

We stayed as far away as possible from the fires and the giants who were stretched out on the ground sleeping. The mantis creatures were standing near the trees, watching over the captives, stirring about restlessly with their stilt-like moves.

I slid in between two of them without being detected. I had my sword held close to my side, and when I was near the captives, I moved the cloak to reveal my face. One man, startled by my presence, let out a gasp. I threw a finger to my lips for silence, but it was too late. I could hear movement behind me. I gathered the cloak around me and moved as quietly as I could to the left, and turned ever so slightly, hoping no more than my eye was revealed by the cloak that went from my head to my feet.

One of the mantis-things came over to the man who had gasped, and kicked him. It was for no other reason than sport. I remained still. The mantis kicked the man again, made a noise in his throat like someone rattling dice in a tin cup, then moved away to join his chortling comrades.

I saw across the way that Booloo had already managed to cut a number of captives free, and they were slipping off into the darkness. I went about doing the same thing, cutting all those at the tree nearest me free. They drifted away into the gloom, toward where the forest grew thick. Moving quickly, I come to the tree where Choona was held, and arrived there at the same time he did. We actually collided slightly, not noticing one another, veiled as we were.

I'm proud to say it was my sword that sliced away Choona's bonds. As I did it, I let go of my cloak, allowing my face to be shown. Her eyebrows lifted when she saw me. Perhaps, because of the dark, there was little she could make of my features, and perhaps she was trying to associate me with one of her own tribe. When Booloo touched her arm, she smiled and hugged him beneath the cloak.

It was then that I heard a noise behind me. We had revealed too much of ourselves with our movements, and camouflaged or not, we had been seen. The insect warriors let out a series of snapping noises, drew swords and rushed toward us.

In the next moment, I flicked off my cloak, letting it hang over one shoulder. I rammed my sword through a sticklike body with a technique so smooth it was like pushing a hot knife through warm butter. The thing fell, and then the other mantis-things were on me.

By this time all the captives had been freed and were scrambling toward the forest outside the chopped and burned circle. I jetted like a bullet between foes, bobbing, weaving, stabbing, and slashing. Everything I had ever learned from Jack Rimbauld I used, and it was such a part of me, I never had to think about a particular move, or method. I was natural, precise, and deadly. Within moments, the mantises lay around me like stacked sticks.

The noise, however, had alerted the giants, who were up, and drunkenly weaving about, grabbing at their swords, swinging wildly, even managing to chop down a couple of their own. The weird growths, or whatever they were at the backs of their necks, flashed out their feet, or tentacle-like appendages, waved them in the air as if directing traffic from all directions.

I finished up with a mantis by dodging under its thrust and coming up with a backhand swing that took off its head, then I broke and ran, barely maintaining my weapon as I threw the cloak over me and dashed across the devastated ground toward where the forest grew thick again.

Chapter Seven

The Warrior Star

IN THE FOREST I was able to climb up a tree and find a broad limb on which to rest. I pulled the cloak tight about me, left it open slightly around my face so that I could see.

Below me, the mantises were scrambling about through the forest, and the torch-wielding giants were hacking at the underbrush and small trees with their great broadswords, felling them like they were nothing more than cardboard tubes. Behind them, I could still see the great fires raging. I could also see that some of the humans we had cut loose had been apprehended, and the monsters, both mantis and giant, were making short work of them, not trying to capture them, but going straight for the kill.

A short time later, the giants were setting fire to the forest. The blaze caught slowly, but finally it caught, and I was forced to abandon my tree, move across to another.

Like a monkey, I fled from one tree to the next, grabbing limbs and vines. I couldn't believe how this planet had changed my muscles and abilities. I came to a great dip in the vegetation and finally a deep ravine. I scuttled down the tree that was on the edge of that divide, losing my cloak in the process, but I maintained my sword. I had just touched ground, when I heard a whisper, and a soft voice speaking in the language of Booloo.

It was Booloo himself, and Choona. There were two others with them, two men. I had accidentally come upon my new companions.

Booloo, like me, had lost his cloak, but had held onto his sword. We had little time celebrate our reunion. Looking up, I saw bobbing licks of light, realized it was the torches of the giants. I could see a great blaze behind them. They had been trapped by their own fire, and the fire was driving them toward the deep ravine.

Soon, we could see their heads rising up amongst the trees like trees themselves, their three eyes reflecting the flickering light of their torches, their teeth glistening wetly. It was as if I had been caught inside an old Grimm's fairy tale of giants and monsters, for below them, some on the backs of their beetles, some on foot, were the mantises.

A great flash of torchlight fell over us, and one of the giants let out a bellow, and charged forward. I sprang forward with my sword, leaping so that my foot landed on the bent knee of the closest giant. From there I sprang effortlessly until I landed on his belt, and with another leap, I was even with his neck. While in the air, I slashed at his throat with all my might.

Even as I took the long fall down, his hot blood gushed from his throat like a fountain and splashed down on me. I hit the ground with amazing lightness that even I didn't understand. Then I was bounding up a tree, using my free arm to grab and my feet to climb. I leapt from limb to limb and hurtled myself out of the tree and into the face of another giant, grabbing at a long strand of his hair, clutching my fists into it, and plunging my sword into his middle eye with such savage force I felt it touch the back of his skull. My blade had gone through and pierced the thing that clutched to the back of his head; it fell loose from him with a screech, and splattered below.

The giant still stood. He bellowed and grabbed at me, but I swung the sword and severed one of his fingers, swung around on the strand of hair until I was behind him, dangling down his back.

With a quick move, I was up and on his shoulder. I reached around and cut his throat from ear to ear with a whipsaw motion.

As he toppled, I rode him to the ground, like a falling tree.

On my feet again, I wheeled and saw that Booloo was attacking the legs of one of the giants, and his two male companions were grabbing a mantis, jerking him off of his beetle mount. I turned again, looking for the girl. She had snatched up the fallen mantis's sword and was jolting across a clear patch of ground. As I watched, she sprang and hit one of the insects, knocking him off the back of his beetle, coming down on him and driving the purloined sword with all her force through his chest. Then she was up, whipping the sword about, doing battle with two other mantises trying to close in on her from left and right.

Choona moved with incredible dexterity, causing one of the mantis's slashes to swing above her and instead find its mark in the side of his companion. And then Choona was up on the beetle behind the remaining mantis, ramming the sword into his back, the point of it leaping out of his chest like an arrow shot from his innards. She dumped him off the beetle, kicked her heels into the bug, and caught up with the other beetle, grabbed its reins and called out to the others of her kind.

The two others were soon on the mount, riding double. Choona loped over to where Booloo and I had joined together, stuck out a hand and pulled Booloo up behind her. He in turn pulled me up behind him. I barely fit back there. Riding double was all right, but triple?

More giants came through the forest, and more mounted mantises, all of them driven forward by the fire and the chugs of foul-smelling smoke. Choona clicked to our bug and rode him down the side of the deep ravine, with me clutching to Booloo so as not to fall.

I thought of poor Butch, back there tied to a branch, waiting. It was my guess that he would eventually work himself free, perhaps even eat his reins, and find his way in the wild. But at that moment,

Butch was the least of my worries. Our adversaries were gaining on us. The giants stopped at the edge of the ravine and yelled insults, jerked up small trees and tossed them at us. We saw our companions on their mounts take a hit and tumble off and fall screaming down into the deep ravine; we could hear their bodies strike the water below.

Debris whistled by us, but none of it hit home. We went into the deeper dark of the ravine, and when I turned and looked up, I saw that the fire had made its way nearly to the edge. The giants were blaring out in pain. Flames had enveloped several, and they collapsed inside the inferno. Several of them leaped over the edge of the ravine, into the dark, and moments later I heard the crash of their bodies below.

The mantises, on the backs of the surefooted beetles, were doing fine, however, and they were gaining on us.

I was about to leap off the beetle to lighten the load for Choona and Booloo, cling to the vines that grew down the side of the ravine, and take my chances with the mantises, when I realized they were close, but not actually pursuing. They had given up on us and were now practicing the art of survival. Perhaps without their giant comrades, their masters, they felt little obligation to continue their pursuit of us. Whatever their intent, they veered off and rode their beetles down the side of the canyon, dipped away into darkness.

WHEN WE CAME to the bottom of the ravine, I was surprised to discover that there was not only a run of water, but crashing rapids. Booloo directed our beetle to the edge of the river, and forced it into the churning water. I thought this the height of insanity, not to mention stupidity, but a moment later the beetle was flowing up and down with the route of the water as if it were a raft. Now and again, the beetle's legs would rise from the water and slash, and our direction would turn slightly. As we proceeded, the flames from the fire on the rise above diminished, and finally there was nothing but blackness and wetness; the water sloshed against us and sometimes rolled over our beetle. I determined that the creature was able to see in the dark, and was also smarter than it looked. It could navigate between rocks and swells quite deftly. This is not to say that I felt we were safe, or that the beetle was fail proof, but I did decide after a few moments of bobbing up and down in the racing river that we were far better off than we had been moments before.

I don't know how long we rafted down the river on our beetle, but eventually the creature, perhaps tiring, made landfall. We were exhausted. No sooner had we dismounted and found a place to tie out our mount so that it might graze than we collapsed on the ground and fell fast asleep.

—

FOR THE NEXT few days we stayed close to the base limb that amounted to our terra firma. We tried to stay out of the trees that grew up from it. Our beetle, though it had the strength to carry the three of us into the trees, wasn't designed to accommodate comfortably, and securely, more than two for great distances in that manner. No doubt, had we tried to climb with all of us on its back, I would have tumbled off and been squashed into the foliage below.

We didn't come across any of the other escapees as we went, and I hoped that they, like us, had been fortunate. I can't tell you exactly how long we traveled. I know that I meant to count days, and did for some time, but eventually lost tally.

I found that much of my time was spent in observing Choona as we rode on the beetle. Her back was all that was visible to me, and sometimes she was in the front of the beetle with Booloo between us. I couldn't help but stare at her well-shaped shoulders over which her hair tumbled like a waterfall of blood.

When we paused for meals, I observed her as carefully as I could, without seeming to stare. She and Booloo spoke to each other often, but there never seemed to be any overly affectionate moments, which, though they certainly would have had the right to have them, would have pained me as deeply as if a knife were stuck in my ribs. On one hand, I wanted to get away from them because of my feelings, and on the other, I couldn't stand the thought of being away from her luminous presence.

The region we were traveling through, though well-wooded, was less thick than where Booloo and I had wandered, and at night there were areas where I could clearly see the sky. One night, after a long day of riding, we stopped to rest and eat. I chewed on a root given to me, and drank juice from a large gourd that I had harvested from one of many trees that held them; the liquid inside was almost pure water, but with a slight taste that I can only equate with lemon. As I ate and drank, I sat and looked up at the alien sky. It was littered with stars, but there was nothing about the constellations that was familiar, and there was a huge moon that floated high up and green as grass. I assumed this was due to the pollen that was a constant in the air here. There were a couple of other moons, smaller, that moved swiftly, zipping by and close together as if in a race. They were a tarnished gold, with a veneer of green about them. These sights were amazing and confusing. But there was also this: the great star that Booloo had shown me, the one he had tried to explain to me, was now very visible, and large to the point of distraction. It glowed red and blue, as if it were an alternating neon light. In clearings, its light, combined with that of the moons, was astonishing. If you looked at the ground (or again, what passed as the ground, the bough of a tremendous tree), you could not only see the fine glow of the moons, but the light from the blue-red star; it lit the place up like a floor show.

As we traveled, I made it a point each night—when the foliage allowed—of locating the star and observing it. I felt as if I acquired strength from it, as well as from the trees, the air, and even the pollen; this world was for me like a personal generator that made me not only strong, but made me agile, swift, and gave me the ability to learn and retain things more quickly than on Earth. And though the days were exhausting, I found that only a few hours' rest reinvigorated me. Some of this may have been an illusion, but the rest of it was irrefutable. There was another thing. My beard didn't grow. I was as smooth-faced now as I was the day I entered the machine that tossed me through space and time and nestled me here amongst the world of trees.

I came to anticipate the evenings with enthusiasm, not only because it gave me a chance to study those magnificent heavens, but because Booloo and Choona took it upon themselves to begin teaching me their language. I once had someone tell me that most languages have only about eight hundred words that matter as far as conversation goes, that the other words were adornments, and therefore, if you set your mind to it, a language could easily be acquired. Having tried learning Spanish and Italian, I can't say that I found this so. But, on this world, with my mental and physical faculties intensified, or perhaps by my actual need to learn the language, I discovered I was a very apt pupil indeed.

I first learned the basics, asking simple questions, and then I learned the names of certain plants, the gourds we drank from, the roots we ate, the plant that could start fires, and so on. Then I began to learn more conversational language. It was done mostly by show and tell.

What I soon discovered was that this world on which I now lived was called Juna, and that the star I was so infatuated with was called Badway de Moola. This, of course, Booloo had told me before, but I had been uncertain then if he actually meant this as a name, or a description of the star. Turned out it was both. The star was called the Warrior Star.

As they explained this to me, Choona reached out and touched my chest. The touch was like an electric shock, so much did I enjoy it. She spoke a few words. They were words I had learned, but it took me a moment to translate them in my mind, and then I got it. She was saying that I was a Son of the Warrior Star. That she was a Daughter of the Warrior Star, and Booloo was a Brother of the Warrior Star.

It took a moment for me to wrap my mind around that concept, but then I realized that this was a great compliment, and that this was in fact a part of their belief system; the star was their totem, or perhaps, to them, some kind of god.

A few days out and we received a pleasant surprise. Or at least I did. I can't say that Booloo was as sentimental about the event, and, of course, Choona knew nothing of Butch. But as we rounded a bend in a well-traveled trail, there, on the edge of it, punching a wad of grass, was Butch. His reins dangled and he still had his saddle. I can't say that I would have known for certain it was him, or it, or her, without those accouterments, but I fancied there was a distinct look on the beetle's mug that allowed me to distinguish my bug from others, even without that identifiable riding rig. It also seemed to me that Butch was glad to see me. Butch's presence was certainly a convenience, and gave me a mount of my own, though I was a little bewildered when Choona chose to ride with me.

Chapter Eight
The City in the Trees

EVENTUALLY THE GREAT limb on which we rode narrowed, and became smaller, more like a spit of earth stuck out over a great chasm. The trees that grew up from the limb thinned and became fewer. Finally there was only the limb, and it was perhaps the width of a dozen football fields. Clouds rolled around us, and above us was the great clear sky, tinted with that faint pollen-green haze. The sun looked like a huge pus-filled blister, but the air was no warmer than before.

Behind us were miles and miles of thick jungle, and rising way above the jungle were the base trees that were the foundation of this world.

Joe R. Lansdale

Moving toward the tip of the limb on which we rode, we saw a drop of miles. Down below there was green darkness. I was amazed I didn't feel any shortage of breath or any kind of mountain sickness. Instead, I felt better than I had ever felt in my life.

Looking from our limb into the great distance beyond the drop, were more forests, and between two of the great base trees on the far side, something glittered like a wet diamond necklace, dotted with blots of silver and gold. I couldn't make it out exactly, but Choona explained to me that it was a city, Goshon, and it was their home.

In the next moment, we were moving to our left toward the edge of the limb, and when we got there, I saw a great tangle of vines that hung off the edge of the limb and went down, down, down, until they wadded away into the distance.

That was our route. I made sure I was strapped in tight on Butch's saddle, and down I went, this time riding alone, with Choona seated behind Booloo on their beetle, taking the lead.

We spent the night in the nest of vines. When the wind blew—and that night it blew intensely—the great netting swayed like a massive hammock. It might have been a nice way to sleep, had the rain not come, blasting us like a fire hose. For the first time, I felt truly cold.

As morning came, the water was sucked up by the vines, and the air cleared, and turned pleasant. I found that I was drying out quickly. We descended again, and this time Choona chose to ride with me. She put her arms around me as we went, and I glanced at Booloo once or twice, but he seemed not to notice. Perhaps the idea of a mate was different here than on Earth. Which might not be a bad thing, considering on Earth I had injured a rival with a sword over a woman; it wasn't something I wanted to repeat.

After several days we stopped going down, leveled off, and proceeded across a net of closely interwoven vines that went for miles and was perhaps as wide as five acres. As we rode, the vines swayed precariously, but Butch and the other beetle handled the trail without effort.

Eventually, we came to where we could see the city quite clearly. It took my breath away. What had glistened in the distance had not been diamonds or silver and gold, but the constructs of a wall, and buildings that rose up above it. All of it was made of plants; the assemblies were of twists of cable-like gold- and silver-colored vines, and hardened wood, as bright and shiny as diamonds. We rode on a pathway of flattened gold gourds that served in the same manner as stones. From a distance, Goshon looked not too unlike the fabled city of El Dorado that so many lost souls had searched for back home.

When we were within sight of the city gate, guards from the top of the wall let out a cheer. I was amazed at this reception. The gate lowered and warriors dressed in bright red tunics overlapped with wood-plated armor and helmets poured forth. They went directly toward Choona and Booloo, who had dismounted from the beetles, and dropped to their knees and bowed. Soon the path was full with warriors, and then citizens, dressed in all manner of finery.

Booloo walked among the crowd. Men and women reached out to touch his hand. I was uncertain of what to do, so I slipped off Butch, and to stay within custom, got down on my knees as well, realizing that Choona and Booloo were royalty of some kind.

As I dropped to my knee, Booloo grabbed my arm and indicated that I should rise. He yelled out to the people.

"We return. And this man, Brax, saved me, and then Choona. He fought with us to help our people. We are, as far as we know, the only survivors, thanks to him. We owe him our lives. Honor him."

A great cheer was thrown to the sky and I was lifted on the hands and backs of the crowd and carried inside the city of Goshon in a manner of much pomp and circumstance.

—

I HAD PRESUMED Booloo and Choona were some kind of king and queen of Goshon, but I soon learned otherwise. They were in fact, prince and princess, brother and sister. Their parents were king and queen. I'm going to pause here to explain something about the people of Goshon, and I presumed it was true of everyone on the world of Juna. There were no old people. There were children, but no one who was elderly.

I was to discover from Choona that her people lived to be thousands of years old. They aged only slightly, and when their time came, unless of course they were felled by violence, or the rare disease, they just ceased to live; died and crumbled into dust.

To put it mildly, I found it strange.

But I had a suspicion that the very air and pollen here that had given me my new muscles, reflexes, sharper senses, may well have made me like my newfound friends, and perhaps more so. And considering that a day here was much longer than those on Earth, and therefore a year was much longer as well, a person's life span could be near immeasurable. It was merely a surmise, but from the way I felt, and having noticed that old scars from my sword training on Earth had disappeared, I suspected I just might be right.

But what was most exciting to me was this simple, and now obvious, fact: Choona was Booloo's sister.

I was given nice private quarters in a large building, that was, I presume, the equivalent of a palace. It was a several stories up. It wasn't the highest spot in the place, but it was tall. It was comfortable. There was a large window, minus glass, that overlooked the city. A cool breeze rolled through it and the air tasted like a sweet dessert.

For a bed there was a huge hammock fastened to the ceiling. The furniture, including the hammock, like most things on this world, was constructed of plants.

After I was shown my room, food was brought. I sat and ate, felt considerably better and refreshed. I was finishing up a large gourd of that liquid that reminded me of milk, but which I found far more refreshing, when three young women came in. They were beautiful, as they all were. They wore only loincloths, and they spoke to me in their musical language. Many of their words were foreign to me, but I was beginning to understand more and more.

It turned out they were there to bathe me. They pulled back a curtain from an area I hadn't bothered yet to investigate, and behind it was a deep tub. They pulled one of two long ropes and water began to gush from a spout and fill it. It was hot water, and as it flowed into the tub it steamed and hissed. A moment later they pulled the other rope, and from a spout on the opposite side cooler water gushed.

The women immediately set about trying to determine how to remove my clothes. I resisted. Slightly. And then showing them how buttons and zipper worked, I let them undress me, remove my shoes, and help me into the tub. Once I was seated there—the water feeling wonderful on my skin—they removed their loincloths and climbed in with me, took vegetable sponges from the sides of the tub, and went about scrubbing me. The sponges not only felt good, but they provided a light soap. They washed my hair, and much to my embarrassment, and simultaneous delight, they scrubbed every inch of my body. They seemed fascinated with the hair on my chest, and elsewhere. When they finished they wanted me to return the favor, and being within their hospitality, I felt I couldn't deny them, and didn't want to. I went about making sure they were very clean.

When we finished bathing, they climbed out of the tub laughing like babies at bath time, and produced from a nook in the wall a huge towel, handed it to me, then grabbed others for themselves.

I was being dried off by one of the women, while a second stood behind me and dried my hair. I was just about to pass into a heavenly realm, when Choona entered the room and smiled at me.

"Was your bath satisfactory?" she asked.

I felt an embarrassment that she didn't share. I think I flushed a little. "Yes…" I said. "It was quite refreshing."

"Good," she clapped her hands, and the women, like crows startled on a fence, moved away from me and folded the towels and departed, left me in all my naked glory.

Choona appraised whatever physical assets I might have with a bold examination that made me feel more than little uncomfortable. I did my best not to show it, realizing their customs were nowhere as prudish as those from where I came.

As for Choona, she was dressed quite differently. Her long hair was well-brushed and cascaded over her shoulders like a mountain fire running down-hill. She wore a white cloth over her breasts, tied behind her back, exposing her stomach. Her navel was circled by a painting of blue and yellow stars. She wore a gold sarong. On her feet were fine sandals that looked to be made of leather, but from my experience on this world, I determined were most likely made of some vegetable material.

"Come," she said.

Being nude, I eyed the folded towels, but finally gave in, and boldly followed her, resisting the desire to cover certain parts of my anatomy with my hands. She led me to a large closet, opened it, and took out a white cloth. She brought it to me, and proceeded without comment to wrap it between my legs and around my thighs. It was a loincloth. I just stood there stunned.

Finished with this project, she went back to the wardrobe and threw the doors wide so that I might see what was hanging on a rod—a series of colorful robes. She paused, picked out a long, hot pink one, turned with it and held it before me.

I might be nearly nude, but I wasn't going to wear that garish thing. I shook my head. She grinned and hung the robe back in place, and finally settled on a dark blue one. She came over with it, and standing behind me, held it so that I might slip my arms through the sleeves. Then she came around front and pulled it across me and fastened the belt. It fit very comfortably. She then returned to the wardrobe and picked up a pair of sandals from the floor. They looked too small, but she came over and dropped down on one knee and measured them against my foot. They were, in fact, too small. She grabbed them at tip and heel, tugged gently. They stretched like chewing gum. I slipped into them. They were soft and the bottoms of them were warm; they were like living tissue. They wrapped comfortably around my feet. It was easy to figure they were not only designed for comfort, they were constructed in such a way that climbing and leaping from limb to limb could be accomplished without slippage. My tennis shoes had served me, but these were even better designed to move about amongst the trees and vines of this world.

She took my hand and led me to a chair, and had me sit. In front of me was a mirror. It lacked the reflective quality of those on Earth, but it was a mirror nonetheless, crude as a sheet of shiny metal, though I doubted it was metal at all. She picked up a short, sharp stick—the only way I can describe it—and used it to part my hair. There was also a brush there, and though it was a little rough on my scalp, it served the purpose of putting my hair into a kind of 'do. Considering my hair had not been that long, but was now quite lengthy, I had some idea of how long I had been here. But, my beard had still not grown, though I could see there was a faint outline of it. I decided that it had not ceased growing at all, but for some odd reason facial hair didn't grow that well here. I couldn't make the sense of it.

I also had learned from my bath with the ladies that body hair was not that prevalent on women, and I decided it was most likely the same for the men, and this was why they had such an interest in my chest hair, and that which grew otherwise.

The way Choona had combed my hair made me look a little too much like a rooster, so I borrowed the brush and whipped it into something that resembled my simple, parted, and otherwise left alone, style at home.

I could see Choona in the mirror, studying me. She turned her head, pursed her lips, nodded.

"I like it," she said.

"Thank you," I said.

"You are to be formally introduced to the king and queen, my mother and father, and honored for saving us."

"I would love to meet them, but no honor is necessary."

"For us, it is a necessity."

—

My ability to absorb the language seemed to increase by the hour. I was glad of that when I went before the king and queen. I said that people don't age here, but they do age in the sense that people reach adulthood, and once there, they begin to age slowly until they might look as if they are forty or so, but a very healthy forty. In fact, I didn't see one overweight or infirm person amongst them. I attributed that to their diet, which was mostly, and perhaps exclusively, made up of plants and plant derivatives, many of which appeared to be high in protein.

So, when I came before the king and queen, they were among those who had grown to that appearance, fortyish. The King was dressed in great finery, gold and silver robes with strands of pink threaded throughout it, and the Queen, who looked very much like Choona, though her hair was longer, almost to her waist, was dressed in equal finery.

I was led to them with great procession, a blowing of horns and a thumbing of two stringed instruments that made a sound that I was uncertain I could ever comfortably accustom myself to.

Choona and Booloo escorted me, she on my right, he on my left. I went before them, and copying Choona and Booloo, I knelt and dipped my head, then rose up and stood before them.

I won't bother with all they said that day, but it was flattering and pleasing, and I was given full citizenship in Goshon, and then there was a ceremony of some sort, the particulars I was uncertain of, followed by music and dancing. I was given an excellent meal, and then it was over and I was led back to my room. I followed these events with a short nap.

When I was awakened by Choona, she was dressed in a short, loose tunic with a thick yellow sash, thrown across her shoulder that supported a sheathed sword at her hip. She tossed a dark tunic on the bed, along with a harness similar to hers, and told me it was time to go to work.

Though I had been honored before the king and queen in a hall filled with hundreds of people, most of them royalty, I was now being drafted into the service of their military. It too was an honor, according to Choona. It suited me fine. I was a fighting man, and on my world I had been like a tiger in a cage. Here, I could follow my true course, as instructor of the sword and hand-to-hand combat.

Chapter Nine

A Cultural Problem

WHEN I WAS before the warriors, they eyed me with what I can only call suspicion. I didn't blame them. It was the way of the fighting man and woman, for their warriors were of both sexes, to doubt the skills of an outsider that had been placed in a role of authority without having earned it in front of them.

Their former general, for lack of a better word, was a man named Tallo. He came forward and looked at me in a manner that I didn't mistake for friendly.

"I know you are something special to the princess. I respect that. But, you are nothing to us, and you are nothing to me. Yet."

I grinned at him. "Shall we work out a bit? Just you and I."

He smiled. "Why not."

A circle of warriors formed around us, and many of them moved back to where there were arena seats and seated themselves there. Tallo drew his sword and I drew mine.

"Shall we?" I said.

"First blood," he said.

Tallo moved. And let me tell you, he was quick. Very quick. He was the fastest swordsman I had seen, with the exception of my instructor, Jack Rimbauld. But speed isn't always the answer. It is an important part of the equation, but distance is also important. He was the first to attack, and his speed, as I said, was impressive, but he had to cover six feet to touch me with the sword. I had but to move a few inches to parry, and as soon as I did, I glided over the ground like a bullet, lifted the pommel of my sword under his chin and knocked him down. And out.

There was a murmur from the crowd of warriors. I sheathed my sword and lifted him to a sitting position, and placed my knee in the small of his back, and reached over and pushed my hands up and down on his chest to revive him. It was actually a technique to revive an unconscious person from being choked out, but I had found that it was also good for bringing a knocked out person around; it let their bodies know they should be awake.

When Tallo revived, shook his head, he tried to stand, and I helped him. On his feet, he reached out with one hand and clasped my shoulder and dipped his head. He said, "I am your servant."

Moments later, I began their training.

—

DAY IN AND day out, I showed them the art of the sword. Don't misunderstand me. They were warriors. They were willing and they were serviceable with their weapons, and they had a number of methods, techniques I had not seen before. But they were lacking in discipline. Here in Goshon, training was regular, but somewhat lax.

Tallo became my right-hand man. I used him to show my approach. The Goshon warriors fought not as a unit, but as individuals. In battle, they chose whoever they wanted to fight, and fought on a personal basis. They had a good initial attack, but from that moment on, they were defensive. It's a good way to be, but there are times when the other is appropriate, and in war, more so. I taught them there was more than just a quick initial lunge, like Tallo had tried on me.

The Goshon sword is not a short sword, nor is it a long sword. It is, frankly, any length the user chooses. I changed that. Soon I had them all bearing three-foot swords. I taught them patterns akin to that of the Romans; it was methodology Jack Rimbauld had made me study. I taught them to hold their ground by pressing together behind a shield. Before I started training them, some had shields, some did not. Now, I insisted everyone bear a shield. I also taught them that when they were no longer on flat "ground," or Father Tree, as they called what was beneath them, they should resort to a more free style of fighting, but with an awareness of teamwork and the concept of staying as close together as possible.

I went at this work with great and joyful deliberation, discovering as I went better and better methods for them to be warriors, better methods for fighting the Juloon, which was their name for the giants, and the Norwat, the mantis-like creatures. One of these methods was the use of the long spear, or pike. I taught them that in the case of the giants, it was better strategy to cut them down from below instead of trying to reach their vital organs with spears and swords. Instead, the cutting of muscles behind the ankle and calf, and thrusts to the arteries inside the legs, were essential methods of bringing the giants down to size, causing them to fall and end up on their faces, or at the least, on their knees where new opportunities were available. The lungs, liver, heart, throat, eyes. All the vital points. For that matter, a good thrust to the artery inside the leg, especially close to the groin, could end a fight immediately, as your victim would bleed out in seconds.

At the end of each day of training I ate with the men and women in the mess, for there was no segregation of sex, but when they returned to their barracks, I returned to the quarters Choona had arranged for me. I felt somewhat guilty about this, but no doubt the softness of my bed, and the fact that each night Choona joined me there, made it a lure I could not resist. We had fallen into this pattern quite naturally, as if we had known each other all our lives.

Each night, before bed, I would strip down nude, and Choona would watch as I meditated, the way Rimbauld had shown me. After a time, she too would strip down and join me. We always chose the middle of the room, in line with the window through which a sweet breeze came and cooled, and invigorated us. I did my best to explain to her what it was I was doing, and how I was doing it. She was a quick study. Unfortunately for her, I didn't feel I had that much to teach her.

It was a nice life, but I knew it would not stay nice forever. The reason for this was simple. War was coming. The Juloon and the Norwat were constantly waging war against the city of Goshon, taking slaves for food, and far worse reasons. It would soon happen again. The reason for this was Dargat, which loosely translates as the Masters. These were the plant-squid-like things I had seen on the backs of their necks and skulls. They were the ones who directed things. The giants were dangerous enough, but on their own they were not particularly organized. Some years back, the Masters and the Juloon had made a sort of unspoken pact. The Masters supplied the brains and the will, and the Juloon the muscle. The Norwat were the scavengers, the low among the low.

"The Juloon and the Norwat, they are the yuloo for the Dargat," Choona explained to me.

"The what for the what?" I said.

It took a bit of explaining, but apparently, yuloo is a word for a kind of worm that eats its own excrement, makes houses of it, and births its young in piles of the same. It's a large creature, and smells, and isn't edible, which was something I ascertained well before Choona finished explaining them to me.

After this insult, she explained the Masters to me in greater detail, and finally, the One. To put it in as small a nutshell as I possibly can, way out where the woods grew the thickest, where the woods were chopped and burned and used without worry, because they grew back so incredibly fast, there was a group of plant beings.

I know no other way to describe them. Large, plump, white plants with vines, thick as octopus tentacles, with suckers on their tips; I've described them before, clinging to the backs of the giants' necks. The creatures on the backs of the giants' necks were a kind of hive mind, and they were in turn ruled by a creature that Choona called the One. The One was of their sort, but like a Queen Bee, a creature that lived off Goshon slaves by fastening to them with its tentacles and sucker mouths. It sucked their blood, and brains, bone marrow, and energy; it took from their very core of being until they were withered shells, dead and useless. Some of the humans were kept to breed with each other, to keep a supply of food when the Master's lackeys were not raiding Goshon. Simply put, they farmed the humans for the Masters and the One, and the giants got a portion of the stock, and the mantises got the scraps.

This had gone on for years, the giants and mantises attacking and raiding Goshon, and the warriors of Goshon protecting them-selves enough to keep their population and way of life alive. Still the giants and mantises came, and the population of Goshon shrunk while the population of their enemies grew.

I quizzed Choona some more, and it was, to say the least, a baf-fling discussion. "So how do you fight them?" I asked.

"When they come, we fight," Choona said.

"You say there are many more of them than there are of you?"

"Yes," she said.

"So they come, and breach the walls, and you fight them, and they take slaves and retreat?"

"That is correct."

"And then you go after them, to rescue the captives?"

I had an idea what the answer to this would be, as I had learned some of their culture's thinking in the time I had been training the warriors, but I wanted to know for sure.

Choona considered this. "It is thought to be pointless to go after them."

"You were rescued."

225

She nodded. "Booloo escaped. You helped him. He came back for me, and you were with him."

"So, why don't your people do that, come for the captured ones I mean?"

"Because it is pointless."

"You are home, and so is Booloo."

"Once the giants have us, that does not happen."

"But it did."

"Thanks to you."

"Thanks to Booloo, he went back for you, and I was with him. He chose to do things different."

This confused Choona's way of thinking. I realized it wasn't lack of intelligence, it was culture. Their culture was accustomed to fending for itself in the city, but outside the city, if something happened to one of their people, they were on their own, unless one or two warriors chose, by their own choice, to do something out of the ordinary. It was a thing that happened, but according to Choona, not often.

I found this way of thinking frustrating. "But why don't you just go after the captives?"

"It is not done," she said.

"Except when it is."

"Yes. But that is the choice of the individual. Not the king or queen. Not the city."

Our discussion was becoming circuitous, but I tried to stay with it.

"Why?" I asked. "Why is it only done now and again? Why is it not always done?"

"Because it is not done."

I knew I was repeating myself, but I couldn't help but think if I phrased the question simply, and correctly, I would receive what I thought of as a more common-sense answer.

"No one goes after the captives?" I asked.

"Sometimes. But not far. This is our home. We live on the forest around us, and we live in Goshon. We do not go into the lands of the giants, and we certainly do not go into the lands of the Dargats."

"You should."

"But why? Once captives are taken, they rarely come back."

"But sometimes they do."

"Sometimes they escape," she said.

"Or they are rescued."

"Yes."

"But no one goes after them as a force, as an army?"

She walked to the window and pointed. Where she was pointing was the forest on the other side of the bridge. "We go there, and a ways beyond that. No more."

"That doesn't make sense," I said.

"It is how we do it."

"Change it."

She gave me a perplexed look. "Why?"

I took her hands and led her to what served as a couch. When we were seated, I continued to hold her hands. I said, "If we go after them, we turn the tables. Instead of waiting for them to attack, we can attack them. If a few warriors now and then are rescued, then why not many by a larger force?"

She thought about it.

"No one has ever done that," she said.

I tried not to sigh too audibly.

"Did you make me the leader of your warriors?"

"Yes."

"Why?"

"You have great skill."

"Do you trust my judgment?"

"Of course."

"Then, what you have to do is discard cultural barriers that have kept you in the position you are in now with your enemies. This way of thinking may even have been beneficial in the past, may have become a way of doing things because at one point it worked well, or well enough. It's not working now. Gradually, you, and all of your people, will be enslaved or destroyed. Bravery, and even skill with weapons, is not enough against enemies like this."

She nodded slowly. "We have considered this."

"But you haven't changed. If you do something and it isn't working, and you keep doing it, you get the same results. You know that, right?"

"We still exist."

"Yes, but you are being slowly whittled down, like cutting chunks from a large tree. No matter how big the tree, if you keep cutting, it will fall down."

"And then grow back."

I realized that on this world my analogy was not a good one. The growth rate was so tremendous you couldn't get ahead of it.

"Let me put it like this. The cultural reason you do not leave the city is buried in memory. You do not even know why it is that way anymore, do you?"

She wrinkled her pretty brow.

"Because it has always been that way. The gods made us that way, and left us that way, and we follow the law of the gods."

"But you are warriors. You worship the Warrior Star."

She let go of my hands. "We are warriors."

"No doubt. But you have to be proactive warriors."

I had spoken in her language, but not knowing any other word for proactive, that was the word I had used. I tried to explain it to her in her language, but found it difficult.

"We shall take the fight to them first," I said.

"But it has never been done that way."

I was becoming frustrated.

"Then, Choona, my dear one, we will change things, you and I, and Booloo, and the warriors of Goshon."

Chapter Ten
Meditation and the Arts of War

BEFORE THE KING and queen, I presented my ideas.

The queen said, "But we have never done it that way before."

"It would go against custom," said the king.

Choona was with me, and so was Booloo.

Booloo, an immediate convert to the idea, said, "Brax saved us from our enemies. His training of our warriors has improved them dramatically. He has discarded many old methods, and his new methods are making our warriors superior. Perhaps it is time we change some of our views."

"But those views are what make us...us," the king said.

"Yes," Booloo said, "but Father, there are a whole lot less of us now. Once we fought a certain way against a certain enemy. But the Dargats, the Juloons, and the Norwats are a different kind of enemy. They have killed many other clans all across our great forests. To the best of my knowledge, we are the last of our kind."

The queen said, "We protect our walls. We stay in our place."

"Commendable," I said. "No one should want war or start war or war against those who are not threatening them. But these creatures have come to you and taken your people for food, for slaves. It is time to take the fight to them."

I was amazed at how complicated this was for them. It seemed obvious to me. But to those of the city of Goshon it was not. What would have been a silly discussion at home was dead serious here.

"Father," Booloo said. "All things change. It is the way of the jungle. It grows. It dies. It rebirths. But there must be something left of it, a seed, a root, a stalk, the breath of the plant (he was referring to the pollen) to bring it back. When we are gone our bones will not rebirth our flesh. Our stalks will be dried and rotted."

"They will become one with all others," said the king.

"Yes," Booloo said, nodding. "But it will not be our people. Our people's remains will be no different from the remains of all things."

"That is the way of all death," the king said.

"Yes, Father," Choona said. "But it is not the way of all life. It is change. It is different. But I see Brax's way. His way is our way now. He is the trainer of our warriors. His is the greatest sword we have ever seen. He is Goshon now."

The king and queen sat silent for a long time. The king looked at the queen. Something passed between them that only passes between those who have lived with one another so long words are not always necessary.

"Very well," said the king. "It is strange, but if this is what Brax believes, we will take the fight to them."

—

Each night after training the warriors, I went about my ritual, and before bed, I meditated as Jack Rimbauld had taught me. Choona still meditated with me. She wanted to learn the ways of meditation because I told her it was part of what Jack Rimbauld had taught me, and that it made me a better warrior.

I was mostly speaking in a rote way, because, except for a certain calm that meditation gave me, I had yet to glean the real merits of the art. And then, one night while I was meditating, and was in a deep state, Choona said, "Brax." I opened my eyes. I was looking down on her.

"You..." she said. "You...you are floating."

And so I was. I was a good six feet off the ground, hovering in the air, legs crossed, nothing to support me. The moment I realized it, I crashed painfully to the floor.

"I was not sure I believed you," she said. "When you told me your master trainer could float in the air, and make many of himself. But, you, Brax. You were floating."

I gathered myself together and sat on the couch, stunned. "I was," I said. "I was indeed. And I was not sure I believed it when I told you either."

She laughed.

"I am more than a little glad that I did not turn out to be a liar," I said.

We soon went to bed, chattering excitedly about what had happened. It took awhile, but finally we ceased talking, and Choona drifted off to sleep. I could not sleep. I arose, went to a spot beneath the window, and sat cross-legged, and concentrated, and this time, immediately I rose up from the floor. I went up and down at will for some time, practicing. I begin to think about all that Jack had taught me. If I could do this, why not astral projection, all manner of skills he had possessed.

I was so excited I couldn't sleep that night.

Despite this lack of visitation from Morpheus, I was energized the next day. I fenced with warrior after warrior, finding that I was moving with greater ease and skill than ever before. I couldn't decide if years of practice had finally paid off, or if it was that along with a combination of the environment that accelerated my skills. The only thing that mattered now was that I was different, and better.

The next night, while Choona slept, I sat before the open window in my cross-legged position, tried to send my thoughts out across the city, over the walls and the web bridge, back the way we had come, back to where I had first seen the giants. Nothing happened.

I thought about it longer and harder, and then, in my mind, my naked body was moving through the forest, or rather the forest was moving through me. I was still sitting cross-legged, but it was as if I were a ghost. I opened my eyes. It was not all in my head. I was in the air and I was traveling swiftly, right through tree trunks and boughs and vines and all manner of growth; traveling through them without so much as rustling a leaf.

I was a spirit, an astral body flowing across this world of great vegetation with the swiftness of thought. My mind sought out my target. I came to a monumental tree. It was the size of a continent, and on it lived the giants, the mantises, and most importantly, the Dargots, and among the Dargots, more importantly, the One. I could sense him the way animals sense oncoming rain.

I can't explain how I went there, as it was a place I didn't know. But my thoughts were pulled across that vast expanse toward the One, as if it were calling me to it as diligently as I was trying to find it.

It touched me, probed with its mind. It was as if the One was a boulder and I was a river, and I flowed around it. Images flashed in my mind; they came from all directions, so fast I couldn't organize them: I saw the Dargots, the Masters, on the necks and backs of the giants. I saw the mantises, lurking about on the fringes, clothed in shadow, and then...once again, I felt before I saw...the One.

I saw a great pile of human skulls and broken bones and desiccated corpses, living humans who thrashed and withered and appeared little more than mummies, the naked bodies of hundreds, the bones of thousands, and on top of them, writhing and twisting, was something I could recognize as a Dargot, but different, larger. It was the One. A thing that was like them, and not. Monstrous, dark as the night, oily as the slick on-water remains of a sunken tanker. Forty feet high. Its long, dark tentacles waved at the air and the suckers that lay beneath them drew at the air as if they could pull it completely out of being, suck the atmosphere, and the world, and the very moon and stars, and the blackness of space into it. Roots near its base coiled and uncoiled, dripped the gooey remains of the humans below them.

Closer and closer I came, traveling across the gap between space and time, hurtling toward the One. Those tentacles reached out and touched me, the roots caressed me, a dry tongue flicked out of what served as its face, and tasted me. I felt as if my brain were being shocked with an electric current. Foul sensations, like the rotting innards of the dead licked about in my brain. I could momentarily feel what it felt, a kind of dark superiority, a brilliance of mind that was directed toward the simplicity of one single purpose—survival.

There was a sensation of falling down a long, cold, dark tunnel, followed by exhaustion; it was as if my brain cells struck an invisible wall and exploded in all directions.

And then—

—nothing.

When I awoke, Choona was wiping my brow with a wet towel.

"Brax, are you sick?"

"No," I said. "I am far worse than sick. The Dargots and their lackeys. And the One. They are coming. We must go forward. As soon as possible."

In the morning I set about pushing the Goshon warriors hard. We worked the pikes, we worked the swords. We drilled as a wall of men and weapons, learned to break apart and attack, and come together and attack. As the night came and the Warrior Star rode high in the sky, I led the warriors off the training field and out into the city plaza. There were perhaps no more than three thousand, but we filled the plaza.

In the camp of the Dargots I had sensed many more. Counting the giants, the mantises, and the Masters, and the One, they were perhaps ten thousand. They were formidable, but there wasn't any true organization about them, just a hive mind that directed them in a general manner; there was no individuality of thought.

I climbed up on a prominent stone wall that surrounded a fountain spewing water. I pointed up at the Warrior Star. Criers throughout the group carried my words across the mass of humanity as I spoke.

"Tomorrow, we will go after our enemies. We will go after them before they come to us. You are the warriors of that star. You are trained, and you have the hearts of true warriors. I pledge by that star that I will lead you into battle. I will say, come after me, warriors, follow me, not go after them and I will wait here for you. I will be there with you. All of us, together, as one."

Tallo came forward. He stepped up on the rim around the fountain and touched my shoulder.

"I have known this man, Brax, for only a short time. But he is a great warrior. He is a great teacher of the arts of war. You know that. You have seen. I will follow him anywhere. That is my word, and that is all of my word."

Then the commanders in the army, the men and women who directed groups of our soldiers, came forward, and each in his turn promised me their support, and vowed to die in my service. They bowed before me, and I went to each of them, took hold of them and helped them to a standing position. I walked back to my place on the fountain, and I called those leaders up, men and women. I had them stand on the fountain wall with me.

"No warrior here bows before another warrior," I said. "It is a new time. It is a new war. And we are the new warriors. We are one."

Choona came forward. She was dressed only in a white sarong. The light of the moon and the Warrior Star made it luminous. Her dark body and red hair were like a beautiful sculpture.

She said, "As of this moment, I, Choona, and my brother, Booloo, we are warriors, like you. We are not the prince and princess. We are warriors, and we too will follow Brax into battle, and we will fight to the bloody end."

A wild cheer went up.

As we used to say in grade school: It was on.

Chapter Eleven

Preparations

THE NEXT MORNING the warriors of Goshon—with the exception of a well-trained skeleton force left to protect the city—were riding their beetles or marching outside of the walls, heading toward the enemy. Individual warriors had done this sort of thing, guerrilla tactics, but never as a group, never as a war party. For them, this was an amazing event, and it was going against all they had been taught as part of their survival.

By now, however, they were convinced. Or convinced enough to follow me. We were ready, and we were at war.

I had been reunited with Butch, and though it may well have been my imagination, I felt certain that the beast recognized me, and was glad to see me. I know I was glad to see him...or her...or it. I made a mental note to ask Choona at some point what Butch's sex actually was.

There were a number of our warriors who bore cloaks made from the web of the spider. Since these spiders were not the approachable sort, and lived deep within the forests, only those who had ventured out in search of food, or singular adventure—which was far more prized here than accomplishments in packs—ever came across them and their webs. So there was very little of this material available. But there were at least a hundred of these cloaks, and Choona, Booloo, and myself each possessed one. It would have been better, of course, if everyone in my army had one, for it goes without saying that being invisible is a great boon in battle. But this was not an option.

Although I had taught the warriors how to work as a unit, I began to realize there was a reason these kinds of tactics had not been used before. On this world, to travel, one must move up and down and all around. A path for one was not always a path fit for two, let alone thousands. It occurred to me then why the idea of individuality, except as part of the city, was so important. On this world it was difficult to work as a unit; the world worked against you.

The environment dictated our route. We were a unit, but a unit not always in sight or position of one another. The plan, of course, was to fight on a solid limb, some broad space surrounded by jungle. A cavalry charge followed by foot soldiers. Before that, I planned to use the invisible one hundred to wreak havoc on the enemy, to have them in a state of flux before the main attack occurred.

Joe R. Lansdale

If we failed, our city and its small clutch of defenders would be at the mercy of their enemies. It was an all-out assault, and it was up to us to hit our foes hard and finish it.

In my head it was simple, but I realized, though I had studied strategy from Jack Rimbauld, read and reread *The Art of War*, and *The Book of Five Rings*, Caesar's memoirs, reading strategy and experiencing war first hand were two different things.

There's no point in telling you about all the problems we ran up against, but suffice it to say there were numerous encounters with wild creatures, great gaps to traverse by natural vine webbings, as well as a number of warriors lost to accident. But we persisted. At night we would camp, and I would meditate. I could see the place where our enemy was gathered by astral travel, and in the morning, as if by instinct, I could lead us in that direction.

Each time I drifted out of my body in my astral state, I could sense and feel the power of the Dargats, and most specifically the power of the One.

"Are we close?" Choona asked from time to time.

"Closer," I would say.

"We will defeat them," she would say.

"Yes," I would say.

And each night we would repeat this, like a mantra. It was akin to boxers working themselves up before a fight.

When we were within a day's march, and could arrive there by midday, I halted our party, had them camp. My plan was to come at them on the fringe of the morrow. Sleep during the day, then move the last bit of distance to where they waited, and just before morning, come at them like the flames of hell.

I slept uncomfortably. I did not try to meditate. I knew where we were. I knew how close we were, and the path to arrive at our destination. But the One reached out for me. It was probing my mind. I could sense it, and I didn't want to give anything away. I built brick walls in my brain, and I would see its tentacles grab at them and move them aside. I would rebuild. It would probe again, cracking through.

I sat up and shook Choona awake.

"What is it, Brax?"

"Talk to me," I said.

"What?"

"About anything."

She saw the look on my face, nodded. She began to talk. She talked for an hour, telling me all manner of information about her world, her city, her parents and brother, and herself. She talked until I felt the One's mental tentacles retreat in defeat from my thoughts. When it was over, I explained to Choona what had happened.

"Does that mean they know we are coming?"

"It means he knows that I have been prying at its thoughts. It has known that from the first time I touched its mind. As for the other, I cannot say. I hope not."

"Should we pull back?"

I shook my head. "No. We have come this far, and even if they know we are coming, they still have to defeat us. If we go home, then all we are doing is waiting for them to come to us, same as before."

"To the death," she said.

"Let us hope things are not that severe, though I fear that tomorrow many warriors will fall."

"They know their duty," she said.

"Yes," I said. "Soldiers always do. But the leaders, they are a little less certain."

I said this knowing I had put fuel to their pride, and that I was pushing them toward battle. On Earth I had seen it many times. Wars fought for political gain. Wars fought for pride. I hoped my war, the one I had created, my self-defense war, was worth it, and that in the end, Goshon would have peace.

—

WE, THE INVISIBLE One Hundred, left our mounts among the main body of the army. Wearing our cloaks of invisibility, I led our undercover band of warriors into position for an advance attack. Among the one hundred were, of course, Booloo and Choona, and Tallo.

Choona was a warrior, but the idea of having the woman you love exposed to danger is a hard concept to swallow. Choona, however, did not give me a choice.

We crept through the woods where water gathered around the roots. Though we blended in quite well in our cloaks, showing our heads so that we could stay in contact with one another, we had to be careful not to make too much noise; our feet sloshing in the water would give us away in an instant. Therefore, our progress was slow and tedious.

Along the way, I left some of the warriors behind to form a kind of relay. When it was time for the beetle-backed cavalry to ride forward, they would be informed by one of our cloaked runners. The cavalry would ride down the middle, where it was clear. This would happen after our advance attack, where we would hit our targets clandestinely, hidden behind our cloaks of invisibility. We would dent them, the cavalry would tear them, and our foot soldiers would come from all sides and break them completely apart.

As the open field became visible through the trees, I halted our group, handed my cloak to Choona, and climbed up a thin tree, nimble as a monkey, if I say so myself, and I do. I positioned myself on a high limb, peeled back the leaves and took a look.

There were great fires all over the field, and the field was many acres wide and many acres deep. I could see the giants squatting by the fires, and as before, many were partaking of horrible meals made of humans. I could see the strange, treelike growths clutched to the backs of their heads, tentacles, thrashing at the air as if in enjoyment of the meals the giants ate. As before, the mantises lurked outside the circle, just within firelight, hoping for scraps. Nearby, in a kind of makeshift corral of vines and sticks, were the beetles that made up the mantis cavalry. There were thousands of the beasts.

I closed my eyes briefly, tried to remember what I had seen when I had traveled in my astral body. I knew that at the far end of the field, in the shadows, the One waited. I could sense it, and I could visualize it, but not in a complete way. It was akin to reaching down in dark water and clutching at something loathsome, something you could not quite describe in shape or size, but something that squirmed and touched a place in the soul that made you weak and afraid.

I made it a point to make the One my mission. Maybe I could even attack and destroy it before our enemy knew we were among them. I had a feeling that with the One gone, it might not end the battle, but it would certainly cause problems for the enemy. For without the One, I knew from my astral sensations that the tree creatures and their hosts, as well as the scavenger mantises, would be less willful. The One was the master of the hive, and they were the drones.

When I was on the ground, Choona returned my cloak.

I gathered my band around me. I said, "We will go silently among them. We will leave a trail of warriors here, so we can carry our messages to the others. But the bulk of us, we will split up in threes, and we will go in and do our damage under the cover of the cloaks. Once they know to look for us, though they will have some trouble seeing us, it won't be the same as when we're not expected. We cannot use the swords without revealing ourselves to some degree. So mind your attacks. Make them quick. Make them simple."

"It will be done," Tallo said.

"Good," I said. "Tallo, you are with me."

"And so am I," Booloo said.

"No," said Choona, "he is my man, and it is right that I should go with him."

I didn't say it, but I was glad of this. The idea of Choona being out of my sight was a terrible thought, especially during battle. Yet, it was not a suggestion I would have made. Now that it was made by her, I accepted it gladly.

"Booloo," I said. "You will break the others into groups. Do it now. We must be ready to move forward in moments."

"It is done," he said, and moved away, the cloak wrapped around his shoulders, only his head visible, floating among the trees and undergrowth.

Chapter Twelve

The Great Battle

WE WRAPPED OUR cloaks around our bodies and our heads, tied them close around our faces with straps so that only our eyes were visible. Our swords were inside our cloaks, our hands near their hilts. Under the light of the Warrior Star, we moved to the outskirts of the fires, toward the mantises, and moving like apparitions, we attacked the creatures with their backs to us. We came upon them slowly and with great precision. A half-dozen were dead before any of the others realized something was wrong.

All along the outer circle, the mantises fell dead. One after another, swords seemingly reaching out from another dimension brought them down. By the time they realized something was amiss—and I must state that these creatures are not the sharpest knives in the drawer—a good fifty or so were dead.

I revealed my face to Choona and Tallo, beckoned with my head for them to follow me. I pulled the cloak tight around my face again, charged toward where the beetles were kept in a corral.

As we approached, one of the guards, a blue giant, retched his meal, his stomach most likely soured by some sort of crude alcoholic drink. He paused, shook his head, and looked in our direction. I knew what he saw. The light of the moons and the Warrior Star were revealing our footprints in the soft bed of needles and rotting leaves.

By the time he realized what was going on, it was too late.

The giant bellowed and drew his sword. I raced toward him, but not as fast as Tallo, who flung back his cloak and revealed himself, causing the giant to lurch after him. The giant's huge sword came crashing down with a tremendous chop. Tallo deftly sidestepped and stuck the giant's hand with his own sword, causing the colossus to bellow loud enough to cause the other giants by the fires to stir.

Tallo dodged a swing of the giant's sword, darted between his legs, jabbed up with the sword, finding a most delicate target. The giant slashed down between his own legs, trying to nail Tallo, but in his haste, he managed to cut off a portion of his own foot.

By this time, Choona and I had arrived to Tallo's aid. He didn't need us. The giant had dropped to one knee, and grasped his ruined foot. With a deft leap, Tallo thrust his blade deep within the giant's liver.

The giant wobbled and fell.

I grabbed up Tallo's cloak and shoved it at him. "Your bravery is appreciated. But your survival is even more needed."

Grinning, he slung the cloak over his shoulders. When I looked up, the corral gate was opening, and I could hear the invisible Choona yelling inside. She was stampeding the beetles. The startled creatures thundered out of the enclosure, filling the open gap until they were pushing against the railings, knocking the whole thing down.

Mantises and giants were surging toward the corral. Our invisible guerrilla team was engaging them, and for the moment, the battle was one-sided in our favor.

I pulled from my belt pack a bit of the igniting plant, got it to flame to life. I waved it above my head. I knew that from the protection of the woods our relay team could only see a bit of fire moving back and forth in the dark, and I hoped they were alert enough to notice. If they saw my warning, the relay was already being carried, and soon our cavalry would appear, riding down the middle of the plain, hitting our adversaries while they were engaged with invisible fighters and escaping beetles.

Since we could not see one another without revealing ourselves, I made no effort to let Choona or Tallo know what I was doing next. We, the invisible, were all on our own. Our job was to harass and confuse the enemy until the real action started. I ran as fast as I could across the field, engaging panicked mantises along the way, cutting them down with what seemed to them a disembodied sword.

I glanced back to see the giants slashing at the night, trying to score on my invisible warriors. I saw at least two of my soldiers cut from their cloaks by great broadswords, sent to the ground and pinned there by blades.

It was all I could do not to turn back and engage the giants, but I knew I had a bigger goal, and I could not be deterred from it. As I moved away from the lights of the fire, the darkness enveloped me. I went more by instinct than design.

And then I felt it.

The One. It was like being hit by a lightning bolt. I dropped to my knees, losing my sword, grabbing my head. The One had caught me off guard. It had sensed me.

It was nearby, and being this near, its power was strong.

—

INSIDE MY SKULL the thing moved and twisted and sought the core of my being. I fought back. I built walls, but the walls were torn down. I put up a forest, swamp water around the trunks. But that was not enough. The water was sucked away, as if by a vacuum, and the trees were felled by an invisible axe.

Before, I had been able to hold it at bay. My powers were stronger at a distance. But mind against mind I could feel that the One was superior. I was growing weaker. Roots broke up from a dark surface and wound themselves around me. Vines drooped down and enveloped my head. I felt as if I were being crushed. My lungs were shutting down.

It's all in your mind, I told myself.

But that was cold comfort. In my head or not, the One was slowly killing me.

I imagined the light at daybreak, pushing away the darkness like an anxious child tossing off covers.

I imagined Choona, in our bedroom, back in the city of Goshon. I could see her smile. I could hear her voice and her musical laugh. Her naked body was a delight. Vines wrapped around me, dark and seeking, pushing into my imaginings, turning the day slowly black. The air filled with a stench. I could smell it as surely as if I had been dropped into a sewage pit. My head was a dark cloud. It was becoming harder and harder to breathe. I tried to concentrate on where I really was. Lying on the ground, battling the One with my mind.

But it was useless.

All I could see was that cloud, and all I could feel were those tentacles, the life slowly being crushed out of me, the deepest recesses of my thoughts being touched by something awful and polluted.

And I hadn't so much as seen my enemy.

In the background, I heard a great clash of warriors, tremendous shouts. I concentrated on those noises, and they brought me back a little. The cloud receded slightly. I put my thoughts back on the beautiful Choona, our most intimate moments. The cloud pulled back, the tentacles recoiled. The positive thoughts in my brain had repulsed it.

Now I was breathing again, rising, taking up my sword, moving in the direction from which I felt the power.

It tried to stop me with another mental push.

I threw up a wall of light, not bricks, and I felt the tentacles recoil and retreat at a savage pace. I began to run.

Still, it wasn't easy. There were moments when I felt I was trying to swim through an ocean of peanut butter. Each step made me grunt with exertion. Each breath made my lungs burn as if they were stuffed with hot coals. The One's foul smell stuffed up my head and made me pause to throw up. It projected heat, like something that had been set on fire and smoldered down to coals and ash and wafts of fetid smoke. But that was alright. I followed the stink, the heat.

Into the shadows I went, and then the shadows began to move, and they were not shadows at all. They were the One. Sight of it almost made me drop my sword. It was shrouded in darkness, but, wearing my cloak, so was I. But neither mattered. The One's darkness or my invisibility. We could, in our way, see each other clearly.

It writhed and coiled on top of the great mound of flesh and bones that I had seen in my astral journey. There were bare skulls mounded up around living beings who could barely move, fluttering arms, kicking legs. Wriggling down from that thing at the top of the pile were thousands of vibrating roots; the tips of the roots were in the eyes and noses and mouths and ears of the living. When the little moons passed quickly across the sky, I could see their desperate thrashings clearly. Some of them were little more than mummified flesh.

I dropped the cloak from my shoulders for greater mobility. I climbed onto the mound, onto the skulls and bones and dying flesh, and went upwards.

Behind me the war was in full swing. I could hear the cries of warriors, both Goshon warriors and giants. The screeching and clicking of the mantises. The clashing of swords and shields and the thumping of flesh and bone. But that was not my mission. My mission was the One.

Tentacles slashed at me and knocked me back, sent me rattling down the pile of meat and bones. I got my feet under me and put my new abilities to work, leaping and bounding, until I was even with the creature, perching at the top of the mound. I stuck my sword in its body. It was like sticking a toothpick through gelatin. It did about as much damage as vile remarks.

A stinging sensation made my face go numb. A root from the One had popped up from below and struck my face; it was like being hit by an angry jellyfish.

Leaping upwards, my feet landed on the middle of the thing. I grabbed at one of its tentacles to steady myself, and then I thrust forward with my sword. The tentacle burned my arm where it held me, and my sword thrust was useless. I hacked at the tentacles that popped at me like whips, managing to cut a few of them apart. Tentacles and roots snatched at me and picked me up and tore my feet free of the One's base. The great beast tossed me like I was nothing more than a worrisome flea.

I smashed into the bones and flesh of the dead and the dying, and then I was up again, scrambling to the peak of that pile, toward the One.

And when those fast moons sailed across the sky again, I saw its one hard, yellow eye peeking out from under a hood of flesh that protected it, and below that I saw spittle sparkle on its beak, which was huge, like that of the largest parrot you could imagine.

But more importantly, I saw coming up behind it, leaping like a grasshopper, her cloak falling away from her like a snake shedding skin, Choona, my lovely warrior.

During its preoccupation with me, she had come from the rear, and now she was bringing her sword down violently on its head. There was a noise like a gunshot, followed by the cracking of Choona's sword, and then the thing's tentacles and roots grabbed her.

I gave it all I had, leaping, and gliding, using the abilities Jack had taught me, abilities I didn't know I possessed until that moment. I went up, and along with me went multiple projections of myself, three to be exact. Three and me. I was as much the core of a hive mind as the One now. My multiple selves charged up with me. Straight up we went. When we were even with that hard, yellow, boiled egg eye, we threw our swords, all of them solid, made with the power of my mind; we threw them with all our strength. We were greeted with a happy sight. Our swords buried to the hilt in that eye, down deep in that powerful and repulsive brain. The tentacles and roots went loose, letting go of Choona, causing her to tumble down the mound.

I had lost my footing as well. I was weak from the mental exertion. The multiple Braxs faded. My legs were like rubber, and then they folded under me.

I bounced and bumped until I hit the ground. When I looked up, the One's tentacles were tearing my sword out of its skull; the other swords, though they had been real enough on contact, had gone the route of my astral selves.

I grabbed up a human skull from the mound, cocked back and threw it like a football. It was a good throw. It hit the injured, wobbling beast and knocked it off its pedestal. It went tumbling backwards from the mound.

I rushed around the mound after it. Choona was on her feet and heading in the same direction. When we came to the One, it was no longer moving.

I took a deep breath, let my thoughts loose. They reached out and touched—

—nothing.

The One was finished.

THE WAR HAD gone well. It was a riot. And with the death of the One, the Dargat lost their grips on the blue giants; their hive minds died, and they dropped off of their hosts like bloated dog ticks. The giants were now about their own devices. They and the mantises retreated, or were captured, and I must admit, killed without mercy. It would not have been my will, but before I could stop it, all of them were slain. This was not a world of great consideration for the enemy.

There was much celebration that daybreak, and all through the day, and night. The following morning, before we moved out, we set fire to the One's corpse. The flames turned it to black cinders in instants. Those humans who were alive in the mound were so far gone they were put to death as a form of mercy. They were no longer human. They weren't really living. They were existing. They were shells that writhed, their brain matter turned to mush.

—

WE WERE A day out from our victory when it happened.

Booloo, Choona, and myself drifted off from the others to a spot where the great limb we were on ended, at least on that far side. We dismounted and stood on the edge and looked out over the great world of trees. Below we could see mountains and clouds and little thin lines of water that had to be raging rivers.

We were enjoying the sights, though I was feeling kind of woozy. I thought perhaps it was due to my battle with the One. I wasn't exactly sick, but I felt a little disoriented.

Then there was an eruption of arms and legs from a growth of foliage nearby, and one of the mantises, wounded, crazed, charged out of it with a sword.

I wheeled.

I was in direct line with it.

I drew my sword and sidestepped and planted it so that it went straight though the mantis's chitin chest. But, as fate would have it, my disorientation slowed me down, didn't allow me to dodge fully out of the way. The thing collided with me in a whiplash motion, knocking the both of us off the edge of the limb, out into the void of what might as well have been a bottomless world.

Chapter Thirteen

Back to the Beginning

I GLANCED UP as I fell. I saw Choona and Booloo, on their knees, looking over the edge, their eyes wide, and just to the side and above me, the lighter body of the mantis drifted like chaff. And then something even more unexpected happened. I had become so much a part of their world, I had forgotten mine.

I had temporarily forgotten the ball and that at some point it would call me back. That had been the source of the disorientation I had felt. It was happening. I was being pulled back.

I saw my hands and arms turn to light, and then there was brief sensation of being back in the ball, and the next moment I was striking the wall of the laboratory so hard the ball burst apart, shattering all over the floor and dropping me like a ton of bricks.

When I gathered myself enough to sit up, I saw that I was in the room from where I had departed. The place had been ravaged. And across the way, the glass that had been between this room and the room that held the universe was knocked out, leaving only pieces of jagged glass. The universe was gone.

—

I SEARCHED THE place from one end to the other. It was wrecked. Computers were smashed; all of the equipment was destroyed. Rooms were emptied out and there was no one present. I walked around confused and dazed. What had happened here?

The kitchen was still pretty much intact, though everything in the refrigerator was spoiled. I found candles for light. As the night fell, I sat in the kitchen at the counter where the cooks had worked, and ate potted meat from a can by the light of those candles.

That night, I slept in my old room.

I had no idea what I was going to do. Everything that meant anything to me was in that universe, on that world, in the eyes of that woman, Choona. Now it was all lost to me, including, it appeared, the entire universe. Had that been why I had been sucked back? The universe had been destroyed?

I couldn't wrap my mind around it.

And then I heard movement down the hall. I had a flashlight I had found, and I carried it with me, but didn't turn it on. I had it for a weapon. I didn't need its light. Even in the dead dark I knew my way along that hall. I had traversed it often when I was healing up from the plane crash.

I saw light shining through a crack in the kitchen door, peaked through and saw a bearded man sitting there. His hair was stringy, his clothes looked ragged. He had a large battery-powered lantern light sitting on the counter. He was eating from a can with a spoon.

It was Dr. Wright.

I pushed the door open.

I said, "Hello, Dr. Wright."

———

"MY GOD," HE said, "you're alive."

"Yes."

"It brought you back?"

"Not what I wanted. How long have I been gone?"

"I don't know. I've lost count. Six months maybe. I've been hiding here. I've no place to go. I have perhaps three or four months worth of food left. They destroyed most things, but there are a lot of canned goods all over the place."

"What happened here?"

"They shut us down."

"The government?"

He nodded. "The special ops. We were...eliminated. The workers were killed, the place was trashed... All gone."

"But you?"

"I had a hiding place for just that sort of situation," he said. "They probably have no idea I wasn't killed. You see... It was such a mess. Terrible weapons. People blown apart."

"You're the only survivor?" I moved to the counter and stood near him.

"Yes," he said. "You really went? You went into the universe we created?"

Joe R. Lansdale

Using English again felt strange. "I didn't want to come back. I liked it there. But the ball brought me back, and now it's destroyed. Of course, it doesn't matter, so is the universe and the world, the Warrior Star, Choona."

"What? Who?"

I told him briefly of my adventures. When I finished, he said, "Not all is lost."

"What do you mean?" I asked.

"The universe. I stored it the week before they came."

"Stored it?"

"You'll like this. In a bottle."

"A bottle?"

"You sound like a parrot," he said.

I grabbed his arm. "Explain yourself, now."

"You're hurting me."

"And I'll hurt you worse if you don't tell me about the universe… In a bottle."

"Superman comics. The old ones. He put the city of Kandor in a big bottle. I realized that with a bit of mathematical formulae, a lot of instrumentation, I could do the same. I had a feeling that we were soon to be put out of operation. I thought I had more time. I was going to make it portable, take it with me. Now, I have no place to go."

"Show it to me," I said.

—

THE DOCTOR'S OFFICE was trashed, but he touched something close to the baseboards, a hidden button, and the wall slid back. It smelled like sweat and old food in there. It was large enough to house a desk and a chair. There were empty shelves and a few books.

He sat the battery lantern on his desk. It lit up the room a little. In the corner was a large jar, and inside were the cosmic swirls of a universe. I bent down and looked inside. The contents seemed to go on forever, and in the center of one of millions of solar systems was a little dot. That was the sun of Juna, and there was a large star that I decided must be the Warrior Star. It was all speculation on my part. From my point of view they were nothing more than dots in the foreground. The bottle had a wooden cork jammed into its mouth. That made me smile.

"How does it exist here?"

"It takes care of itself, just like our universe, our solar system. Once it was put into play, as long as it's contained, it exists."

"Then I can go back?"

"No. The machinery, the device and the equipment that allowed that... All destroyed."

"Then you can rebuild it?"

"No. No, I can't. It would take billions of dollars and a lot of help. It can't be done."

—

THAT NIGHT I slept in my old room and thought about things, and in the middle of the night I got up and went to Dr. Wright's hideaway. He had left it open; the wall still slid back.

I awoke him. I said, "I can go back."

He stirred, half awake. "I'm sorry, Brax. You can't."

"I can," I said, and I explained to him about the meditation, my ability to travel by astral projection. He looked at me like I was crazy. I sat on the floor, legs crossed, and within seconds, effortlessly floated.

"My God," he said.

He reached out to touch me. But there was nothing there. I tapped him on the shoulder from behind.

"Heavens," he said. "You can really do it. I thought it was impossible."

"So did I," I said. "But now I think I can go back to Juna, just by using my mind."

"It's an amazing idea, but..."

"Listen," I said. "If I do, what will become of the bottle? What will become of you?"

"I don't know. I've thought about that a lot."

"You believe they think you're dead?" I said.

"I do."

"Then walk out and take the bottle with you. Protect it. It's your greatest work. There is a world inside of that bottle, inside that universe, and I know now that it's my home. No telling how many other worlds are there, inside that silly corked bottle."

—

So NOW I sit here writing all that has happened to me. I don't know if anyone will ever read it. When I finish writing it, the doctor will take it with him. He knows a writer named Joe Lansdale that he believes might be able to do something with it, though he assumes, and perhaps correctly, that no one will believe it's a true story, just something from his imagination. Of course, he has to get out of here and make his way down to the southern United States where Lansdale lives. That's a tall order right now.

As for this being believed, it doesn't matter. I have recorded this for my own satisfaction.

But tonight, before I sat down to finish this, I finished something else. Dr. Wright and I have been planning for several days now. We have put together enough supplies, found enough clothes and necessary items for him to in fact walk out. The weather is at its best. It's summer here. I gave him a map. I know this area enough to at least set him off in the right direction. We even found a rifle and ammunition so that he can protect himself if the need should arise.

I know of a cabin where he can stay. A place my old boss owns. He seldom uses it. It will most likely be empty. It's a chance worth taking. It's a place to pause before he moves on. And if he's lucky, he will make his way to some place more permanent, someplace safe. There he will protect the universe he has created; I depend on his ego for that.

When I finish this, I am going to say goodbye to Dr. Wright. And then, if I am fortunate, if what Jack Rimbauld taught me is well learned, I will try to imagine the world of Juna, the city of Goshon, and my sweet Choona.

If my abilities allow, I will concentrate, meditate, and I will send my astral self across time and space to my new home. I will separate that self from my body here. If I do it right, my former true self will die, and my new self will become solid and permanent on Juna.

If not, then I will go blindly into the jar and lose my way and cease to exist.

For me, the chance of being with Choona again is worth it.

So I go now to sit cross-legged on the floor in front of the jar. I will close my eyes and imagine the world of Juna and myself being there.

If Lady Luck is with me, I will leave this worthless husk behind, and I will return to Choona, my one true love, and live the life that is truly meant for me.

If you read this, I hope you have wished me luck.

THE WIZARD OF THE TREES

I AM HERE because of a terrible headache. I know you will want more of an explanation than that, but I can't give it to you. I can only say I was almost killed when the great ship Titanic went down. There was an explosion, a boiler blowing, perhaps. I can't say. When the ship dove down and broke in half, I felt as if I broke in half with it.

An object hit me in the head underwater. I remember there was something down there with me. Not anyone on the ship, not a corpse, but something. I remember its face, if you can call it that: full of teeth and eyes, big and luminous, lit up by a light from below, and then I was gasping water into my lungs, and then this thing was pulling me toward a glowing pool of whirling illumination. It dragged me into warmth and into light, and my last sight of the thing was a flipping of its fish-like tail, and then my head exploded.

Or so it seemed.

When I awoke, I was lying in a warm muddy mire, almost floating, almost sinking. I grabbed at some roots jutting out from the shoreline and pulled myself out of it. I lay there with my headache for awhile, warming myself in the sunlight, and then the headache began to pass. I rolled over on my belly and looked at the pool of mud. It was a big pool. In fact, pool is incorrect. It was like a great lake of mud. I have no idea how I managed to be there, and that is the simple truth of it. I still don't know. It felt like a dream.

With some difficulty I had managed a bunk in steerage on the Titanic, heading back home to my country, the United States of America. I had played out my string in England, thought I might go back and journey out west where I had punched cows and shot buffalo for the railroad. I had even killed a couple of men in self-defense, and dime novels had been written about me, The Black Rider Of The Plains. But that was mostly lies. The only thing they got right was the color of my skin. I'm half-Black, half-Cherokee. In the dime novels I was described as mostly white, which is a serious lie. One look at me will tell you different.

I was a rough rider with Buffalo Bill's Wild West Show, and when it arrived in England to perform, they went back and I had stayed on. I liked it for awhile, but as they say, there's no place like home. Not that I had really had one, but we're speaking generally here.

I managed to my feet and looked around. Besides the lake of mud, there were trees. And I do mean trees. They rose up tall and mighty all around the lake, and there didn't seem anything to do but to go amongst them. The mud I wouldn't go back into. I couldn't figure what had happened to me, what had grabbed me and pulled me into that glowing whirlpool, but the idea of it laying its grip on me again was far less than inviting. It had hauled me here, wherever here was, and had retreated, left me to my own devices.

The mud I had ended up in was shallow, but I knew the rest of the lake wasn't. I knew this because as I looked out over the vast mire, I saw a great beast moving in it; a lizard, I guess you'd call it. At least that was my first thought, then I remembered the bones they had found out in Montana some years back, and how they were called dinosaurs. I had read a little about it, and that's what I thought when I saw this thing in the mud, rising up gray and green of skin, lurching up and dipping down, dripping mud that plopped bright in the sunlight. Down it went, out of sight, and up again, and when it came up a third time it had a beast in its mouth; a kind of giant slick, purple-skinned seal, its blood oozing like strawberry jam from between the monster's teeth.

It may seem as if I'm nonchalant about all this, but the truth is I'm telling this well after the fact and have had time to accept it. But let me jump ahead a bit.

The world I am on is Venus, and now it is my world.

—

MY ARRIVAL WAS not the only mystery. I am a man of forty-five, and in good shape, and I like to think of sound mind. But good as I felt at that age, I felt even better here on this warm, damp, tree-covered world. I would soon discover there was an even greater mystery I could not uncover. But I will come to that, even if I will not arrive at a true explanation.

I pulled off my clothes, which were caked with mud, and shook them out. I had lost both my shoes when the ship went down; they had been sucked off of me by the ocean's waters with the same enthusiasm as a kid sucking a peppermint stick. I stood naked with my clothes under my arm, my body covered in mud, my hair matted with it. I must have looked pretty foolish, but there I was with my muddy clothes and nowhere to go, but I was bound to go there.

I glanced back at the muddy lake, saw the great lizard and his lunch were gone. The muddy lake, out in the center, appeared to boil. My guess was it was hot in the middle, warm at the edges. My host, the thing that had brought me here, had fortunately chosen one of the warm areas for me to surface.

I picked a wide path between the trees, and took to the trail. It was shadowy on the path. I supposed it had been made by animals, and from the prints, some of them very large. Had I gone too far off the path I could easily have waded into darkness. There was little to no brush beneath the trees because there wasn't enough sunlight to feed them. Unusual birds and indefinable critters flittered and leaped about in the trees and raced across my trail. I walked on for some time with no plans, no shoes, my clothes tucked neatly under my arm like a pet dog.

Now, if you think I was baffled, you are quite correct. For a while I tried to figure out what had nabbed me under the waters and taken me through the whirling light and left me almost out of the mud, and then disappeared. No answers presented themselves, and I let it go and set my thoughts to survival. I can do that. I have a practical streak. One of the most practical things was I was still alive, wherever I was. I had survived in the wilderness before. Had gone up in the Rocky Mountains in the dead of winter with nothing but a rifle, a knife, and a small bag of possibles. I had survived, come down in the spring with beaver and fox furs to sell.

I figured I could do that, I could make it here as well, though later on I will confess to an occasional doubt. I had had some close calls before, including a run-in with Wyatt Earp that almost turned ugly, a run-in with Johnny Ringo that left him dead under a tree, and a few things not worth mentioning, but this world made all of those adventures look mild.

Wandering in amongst those trees, my belly began to gnaw, and I figured I'd best find something I could eat, so I began looking about. Up in the trees near where I stood there were great balls of purple fruit, and birds about my size, multi-colored and feathered, with beaks like daggers. They were pecking at those fruits. I figured if they could eat them, so could I.

My next order of plan was to skinny up one of those trees and lay hold of my next meal. I put my clothes under it, the trunk of which was as big around as a locomotive, grabbed a low-hanging limb, and scuttled up to where I could see a hanging fruit about the size of a buffalo's head. It proved an easy climb because the limbs were so broad and so plentiful.

The birds above me noticed my arrival, but ignored me. I crawled out on the limb bearing my chosen meal, got hold of it and yanked it loose, nearly sending myself off the limb in the process. It would have been a good and hard fall, but I liked to think all that soft earth down there, padded with loam, leaves and rot, would have given me a soft landing.

I got my back against the tree trunk, took hold of the fruit, and tried to bite into it. It was as hard as leather. I looked about. There was a small broken limb jutting out above me. I stood on my perch, lifted the fruit, and slammed it into where the limb was broke off. It stuck there, like a fat tick with a knife through it. Juice started gushing out of the fruit. I lifted my face below it and let the nectar flood into my mouth and splash over me. It was somewhat sour and tangy in taste, but I was convinced that if it didn't poison me, I wouldn't die of hunger. I tugged on the fruit until it ripped apart. Inside it was pithy and good to eat. I scooped it out with my hands and filled up on it.

I had just finished my repast, when above me I heard a noise, and when I looked up, what I saw was to me the most amazing sight yet in this wild new world.

—

SILVER.

A bird.

But no, it was a kind of flying sled. I heard it before I saw it, a hum like a giant bee, and when I looked up the sunlight glinted off of it, blinding me for a moment. When I looked back, the sled tore through the trees, spun about and came to light with a smack in the fork of a massive limb. It was at an angle. I could see there were seats on the sled, and there were people in the seats, and there was a kind of shield of glass at the front of the craft. The occupants were all black of hair and yellow of skin, but my amazement of this was nothing compared to what amazed me next.

Another craft, similar in nature came shining into view. It glided to a stop, gentle and swift, like a gas-filled balloon. It floated in the air next to the limb where the other had come to a stop. It was directed by a man sitting in an open seat who was like those in the other machine, a man with yellow skin and black hair. Another man, similar in appearance sat behind him, his biggest distinction a large blue-green half moon jewel on a chain hung around his neck. This fellow leaped to his feet, revealing himself nude other than for the sword harness and the medallion, drew a thin sword strapped across his back, dropped down on the other craft and started hacking at the driver who barely staggered to his feet in time to defend himself. The warriors' swords clanged together. The other two occupants of the wrecked craft had climbed out of the wells of their seats with drawn swords and were about to come to their comrade's aid when something even more fantastic occurred.

Flapping down from the sky were a half-dozen winged men, carrying swords and battle axes. Except for the harness that would serve to hold their weapons, and a small hard, leather-looking pouch, they, like the others, were without clothes. Their eyes were somewhat to the side of their heads, there were beak-like growths jutting from their faces, and their skin was milk-white, and instead of hair were feathers. The colors of the feathers were varied. Their targets were the yellow men in the shiny machine on the tremendous tree limb.

It became clear then that the man with the necklace, though obviously not of the winged breed, was no doubt on their side. He skillfully dueled with the driver of the limb-beached craft, parried deftly, then with a shout ran his sword through his opponent's chest. The mortally wounded warrior dropped his weapon and fell backwards off his foe's sword, collapsed across the fore of his vessel.

The two warriors in league with the dead man were fighting valiantly, but the numbers against them were overwhelming. The man with the medallion, or amulet, stood on the fore of the craft, straddling the carcass of his kill, and it was then that I got a clear view of his face. It has been said, and normally I believe it, that you can't judge someone by their appearance. But I tell you that I have never seen anyone with such an evil countenance as this man. It wasn't that his features were all that unusual, but there was an air about him that projected pure villainy. It was as if there was another person inside of him, one black of heart and devious of mind, and it seemed that spectral person was trying to pressure itself to the surface. I have never before or since had that feeling about anyone, not even Comanche and Apache warriors that had tried to kill me during my service with the Buffalo Soldiers.

It was then that one of the two defenders, having driven back a winged warrior he had been dueling with, pulled with his free hand a pistol. It was a crude looking thing, reminiscent of an old flintlock. He raised the pistol in the direction of his adversary and fired. The pistol's bark was like the cough of a tubercular man. The winged man spouted blood, dropped his sword, brought both hands to his face, then relaxed and fell, diving head-first like a dart. As the winged man dove between the limbs near me, crashed through some leaves, and plummeted to the earth, the sword he dropped stuck conveniently in the limb before me. I took hold of it thinking that now I had a weapon for self-defense, and that it was a good time to depart. I told myself that this fight, whatever it was about, was not my fight. They were so busy with one another, I had not even been seen. So, of course, casting aside common sense, I decided I had to get into the thick of it.

It may well have been the fact that the men in the craft were outnumbered, but I must admit that one glance at the man with the jeweled medallion and I knew where my sentiments lay. I know how that sounds, but I assure you, had you seen his face you would have felt exactly the same way.

Why I thought one more sword might make a difference, considering the horde of winged men assisting the evil-faced man was enormous, I can't explain to you. But with the thin, light sword in my teeth, I began to climb upwards to aid them.

This is when I realized certain things, certain abilities that I had sensed upon arrival, but were now proving to be true. I felt strong, agile, not only as I might have felt twenty years earlier, but in a manner I had never experienced. I moved easily, squirrel-like is what I thought, and in no time I reached the craft caught in the fork of the limb.

The winged men were fluttering about the two survivors like flies on spilled molasses. The man with the necklace had paused to watch, no longer feeling the need to engage. He observed as his birds flapped and cawed and swung their weapons at his own kind. It was then that he saw me, rising up over the lip of the limb, finding my feet.

I removed the sword from my teeth and sprang forward with a stabbing motion, piercing the heart of one of the winged attackers. It fluttered, twisted, and fell.

The yellow-skinned couple glanced at me, but accepted my help without question or protest for obvious reasons. I must have been a sight. Naked, having left my clothes at the base of the great tree. My skin and hair matted with mud. I looked like a wild man. And it was in that moment I noticed something I should have noticed right off, but the positioning and the leaves and smaller limbs of the tree had blocked my complete view. One of the yellow skins was a woman. She was lean and long and her hair was in a rough cut, as if someone had just gathered it up in a wad and chopped it off with a knife at her shoulders. She was not nude as her opponents were. She wore, as did her companion, a sort of black skirt, and a light covering of black leather breast armor. She had a delicate, but unquestionably feminine shape. When I saw her face I almost forgot what I was doing. Her bright green, almond-shaped eyes sucked me into them. I was so nearly lost in them that a winged man with an axe almost took my head off. I ducked the axe swing, lunged forward, stretching my leg way out, thrusting with my sword, sticking him in the gut. When I pulled my sword back, his guts spilled out along with a gush of blood. As he fell out of view, more of the things came down from the sky and buzzed around us, beating their wings. They were plenty, but it was soon obvious our skills with weapons were superior to theirs. They used the swords and axes crudely. They handled them with less skill than a child with a mop and a broom.

My partners—such as they were—were well versed in the use of the blade, as was I, having learned swordsmanship from an older man while I was amongst the Buffalo Soldiers. My teacher was a Black man, like me, and had once lived in France. There he had been trained well in the use of the steel, and I in turn had learned this skill from him. So it was not surprising, that in short order, we had killed most of our attackers, and sent the others soaring away in fear. The necklace wearing man, who had been observing, now joined in, attempting to take me out of the fray, and I engaged him. He was good with the sword, quick. But I was quicker and more skilled, blessed with whatever strange abilities this world gave me. He caused me a moment's trouble, but it only took me a few parries to grasp his method, which was not too unlike my own. A high and low attack, a way of using the eyes to mislead the opponent. I was gradually getting the better of him when his driver coasted his machine next to the limb. My opponent gave out with a wild cry, came at me with a surge of renewed energy, driving me back slightly, then he wheeled, leaped onto his machine, and slid quickly into his seat, smooth as a woman slipping sleek fingers into a calf-skin glove. The winged men, or bird-men as I had come to think of them, had had their fill as well, and now they flew up and away, darting after the sled with the two yellow men in it.

I turned, lowered my blood-stained blade, and looked at those whose side I had joined. The woman spoke, and her words, though simple, hit me like a train.

She said, "Thank you."

—

It was another side effect of my arrival here. I was not only stronger and more agile, I could understand a language I had never heard before. As soon as the words left her mouth they translated in my head. It was so immediate it was as if their language was my native tongue.

"You're welcome," I said. This seemed a trite thing to say, me standing there on a limb holding a sword, mud-covered and naked, with my business hanging out, but I was even more astonished to have my words understood by her without any true awareness that I was speaking my own language.

"Who are you?" the woman asked.

"Jack Davis," I said. "Formerly of the United States Buffalo Soldiers."

"The United States?" she asked.

"It's a bit hard to explain."

"You are covered in mud," the man said, sheathing his sword.

"You are correct," I said. I decided to keep it simple. "I fell into a mud lake."

The man grinned. "That must have took some doing."

"I consider myself a man of special talents," I said.

The young woman turned her head in a curious fashion, glanced down at me. "Is your skin black, or is it painted?"

I realized what part of me she was studying. Under all that mud had I been Irish and not part Negro, my blush would have been as bright as the sinking sun. Before long it would become obvious to me that on this world nudity was not something shameful or indecent in their minds. Clothes for them were ornaments, or were designed to protect them from the weather, but they were not bothered by the sight of the flesh.

"Correct," I said. "I am black. Very much so."

"We have heard of black men," she said. "But we have never seen them."

"There are others like me?" I said.

"We have heard that this is so," said the woman. "In the far south, though I suspect they are less muddy."

"Again," said the man, "we thank you. We were very much outnumbered and your sword was appreciated."

"You seem to have been doing well without me, but I was glad to help," I said.

"You flatter us," he said. "I am Devel, and this is my sister, Jerrel."

I nodded at them. By this time Devel had turned to the sled and to the dead man lying on its front, bleeding. He bent down and touched his face. "Bandel is dead by Tordo's hand, the traitor."

"I'm sorry," I said.

"He was a warrior, and there is nothing else to say," said Jerrel, but she and Devel, despite their matter-of-fact tone were obviously hurt and moved. That's why what happened next was so surprising.

Devel dragged the corpse to the edge of the sled, and then the limb, and without ceremony, flipped it over the side. "To the earth again," he said.

This seemed more than unusual and disrespectful, but I was later to learn this is their custom. When one of their number dies, and since they live in high cities and populate the trees, this is a common method. If they die on the ground, they are left where they fell. This treatment was considered an honor.

I processed this slowly, but kept my composure. My survival might depend on it. I said, "May I ask who these men were, and why they were trying to kill you?"

Jerrel glanced at Devel, "He chose to help us without question. He is bonded to us in blood."

"True," Devel said, but I could tell he wasn't convinced.

Jerrel, however, decided to speak. "They are the Varnin. And we are warriors of Sheldan. Prince and princess, actually. We are going to their country, in pursuit of the talisman."

"You're warring over a trinket?" I said.

"It is far more than a trinket," she said. "And since there are only us two, it is hardly a war."

"I would call in reinforcements."

She nodded. "If there was time, but there is not."

She did not elaborate. We left it at that for the time being, and set about releasing the silver craft from the limbs where it had lodged. This seemed like a precarious job to me, but I helped them do it. The craft proved light as air. When it came loose of the limbs it didn't fall, but began to hum and float. Devel climbed into the front seat position, where the dead man had been, touched a silver rod, and the machine hummed louder than before.

Jerrel climbed into one of the seats behind him, said, "Come with us."

Devel glanced at her.

"We can't leave him," she said. "He looks to be lost."

"You have no idea," I said.

"And he helped us when we needed it," she said. "He risked his life."

"We have our mission," he said.

"We will find a safe place for him," she said. "We still have a long distance to go. We can not just abandon him."

This discussion had gone on as if I were not standing there. I said, "I would appreciate you taking me somewhere other than this tree."

Devel nodded, but I could tell he wasn't entirely convinced.

I stepped into the machine, took a seat. Devel looked back at me. I could tell this was a development he was not fond of, in spite of the fact I had taken their side in the fight.

But he said nothing. He turned forward, touched the rod. The machine growled softly, glided away through a cluster of leaves and limbs. I ducked so as not to be struck by them. When I looked up the machine had risen high in the sky, above the tree line, up into the sunny blue. I was astonished. It was such a delicate and agile craft, so far ahead of what we had achieved back home. This made me consider that, interestingly enough, their understanding of fire-arms was far behind ours. There was a part of me that felt that it would be nice if it stayed that way. It seemed humans and bird-men were quite capable of doing enough damage with swords and axes. As for the pistol Devel had fired, he had discarded it as if it had been nothing more than a worn out handkerchief.

I glanced over the side, saw below all manner of creatures. There were huge leather-winged monsters flying beneath us, and in the clear areas between the trees. On the ground in the rare open spaces I could see monstrous lizards of assorted colors. The beasts looked up at the sound of our humming machine, their mouths falling open as if in surprise, revealing great rows of massive teeth. We passed over muddy lakes boiling and churning with heat. Huge snakes slithered through the mud and onto the land and into the trees. It was beautiful and frightening. In short time I had survived the sinking of a great ocean liner, an uncommon arrival in a hot mud lake, climbed a tree to eat, found a fight against a yellow man with a strange talisman who was assisted by winged creatures, and I had taken sides in the fight. Now, here I was, lost and confused, flying above massive trees in a feather-light craft at tremendous speed, my body feeling more amazing than ever, as if someone had split open my skin and stuck a twenty-year-old inside of me. It made my head spin.

"Exactly where are you going?" I had to raise my voice to be heard above the wind.

"Perhaps it is best we do not speak of it," Devel said. "You aided us, but our mission is personal. You know what you know about the talisman and need know no more."

"Understood, but where are you taking me?"

"I am uncertain," Devel said.

"Very well," I said, not wishing to be put out of the craft and left to my own devices. I needed to try and stay with them as long as I could to learn more about this world. Here was better than wandering the forest below; how much better off remained to be seen. As an old Sergeant told me around a wad of chewing tobacco once, "If you ain't dead, you're living, and that's a good thing." It was one of the few bits of advice he had given me I had taken to heart, as he was always jealous of my education, which he called white man's talk. I had been blessed with a Cherokee mother who had learned reading and writing in white man's schools and had become a teacher. She always said education didn't belong to anyone other than the one who was willing to take it. She also said education was more than words and marks on paper. She taught me the customs of the Cherokee, taught me tracking, about living in the wild. All the things I might need to survive.

That said, I preferred the comfort of the flying sled to the rawness of the wild world below. This way I had time to consider and plan, though I must admit my considerations and planning were not accomplishing a lot. It was more as if wheels were spinning inside my head, but wouldn't gain traction.

Besides, let me be entirely honest. The woman was why I wanted to remain. I was smitten. Those green eyes were like cool pools and I wanted to dive right into them. I wanted to believe there had been some kind of connection on her part, but considering my current appearance the only person or thing that might love me was a hog that had mistaken me for a puddle to wallow in.

I can't say how long we flew, but I feel certain it was hours. I know that exhaustion claimed me after a while; the cool wind blowing against me, me snug in my seat. I may have felt better and stronger, but I had swam in the cold ocean, pulled myself from a hot mud pit, climbed a great tree and fought a great fight, so I was tired. I drifted asleep for awhile.

When I awoke the sun had dipped low in the sky, and so had we. We were coasting down between large gaps in the great trees. We came to trees so huge they would have dwarfed the redwoods of home. There was even one with shadowy gaps in it the size of small caves.

That's when I saw nearly all the trees had large gaps in them, from head to foot. It was part of their natural construct. As the sun finally set, we flew into one of those tight wooden caverns, Devel parked his air ship, and we stepped out.

The night was dark as in the inside of a hole. No moon was visible. What stars there were made a thin light. But then, as I stood there looking out of the gap, soaking in the night, an amazing thing happened. It was as if there was suddenly dust in the air, and the dust glowed. I was confused for a moment, then some of the dust landed on me. It wasn't dust at all, but little bugs that were as silver as the flying sled, shinier. The entire night was filled with them. They gave a glow to everything, bright as the missing moonlight.

I should pause here and jump ahead with something I later learned. There was no moonlight because there was no moon. This world was without one. Of all the things I had trouble getting used to, that was the one that most pained me. No bright coin of light coasting along in the night sky. In place of it were glowing insects, lovely in their own way, but they could not replace in my mind the moon that circled Earth.

Jerrel pulled a length of dark cloth from inside a container in the craft, fastened it to the top and bottom of our cavern. It stuck to where she put it without button or brace or tack or spike. The cloth was the same color as the tree we were in. I realized immediately, that at night, and perhaps in day at a decent distance, it would appear to be a solid part of the tree. We were concealed.

There were cloaks inside the craft's container, red and thick. Jerrel gave Devel one, me one, took one for herself. She turned on a small lamp inside the craft. The source of its power I assumed was some kind of storage battery. It lit up the interior of our cavern quite comfortably.

Jerrel broke out some food stuffs, and though I couldn't identify what she gave me, except for a container of water, I lit into that chow like it was my last meal. For all I knew it was. It wasn't good, but it wasn't bad either.

Before long, Devel lay down and pulled his cloak over him and fell asleep. I was near that point myself, but I could tell Jerrel wanted to talk, that she was interested in me. She began with a few simple questions, most of which I couldn't answer. I told her about the great ocean liner and what had happened to me, how I thought I might be in a dream. She assured me she was real, and not a dream. When she laughed a little, the way she laughed, sweet and musical, it assured me my ears were hearing a real voice, and that my eyes were seeing a strange and rare beauty.

Jerrel tried her best to explain to me where I was. She called the world she knew Zunsun. She took a slate from the craft with a marker, drew a crude drawing of the sun, then placed her planet two places from it. I knew enough basic astronomy to know she was talking about the planet we called Venus.

I learned there was only one language on Zunsun, and everyone spoke it, with varying degrees of accent according to region. I told her about the moon I missed, and she laughed, saying such a thing seemed odd to her, and it was impossible for her to grasp what it was I so sorely missed.

After a time, she opened the back of the sled and took out a large container of water. She also found a cloth and gave that to me to clean up with. I was nervous wiping myself down in front of her, but as she seemed disinterested, I went about it. Running water through my hair and fingers, wiping myself as clean as possible with what was provided. When I was nearly finished, I caught her eye appraising me. She was more interested than I had first thought.

I don't know why, but Jerrel took me into her confidence. Had Devel been awake, I don't know she would have. But I could tell she trusted me. It was an immediate bond. I have heard of and read of such things, but never believed them until then. Love at first sight was always a romantic writer's foolishness to me, but now I saw the idea in an entirely new light, even if it was the light from a battery.

"Tordo has taken our half of the talisman," she said. "The other half is in the city of the bird-men. Once it was whole, and its powers gave the bird-men a great advantage against us. Our people warred constantly against them. We had no real land to call our own. We moved among the trees, for we couldn't defend ourselves well in a direct fight against the bird-men, not with them having both halves of the talisman, and aided by wings."

"Where does it come from?" I said. "What does it do?"

"I can only speak of legend. The halves have been separated a long time. One half was with our people, the other with theirs. It is said that in the far past the two tribes, weary of war, divided the talisman. This was not something the bird-men had to do, as they were winning the conflict, and we would not have lasted. But their warrior-king, Darat, felt we could live together. Against the advice of his counsel, he gave our people one half of the talisman and kept the other half. Divided, it is powerless. United it was a dangerous tool of war. No one remembers how it was made or of what it was made, or even what powers it possesses. When Darat died the tradition of peace carried on for many years with new rulers, but then the recent king of the bird-men, Canrad, was of a different mind. After many generations he wanted the lost power back."

"And one of your people, Tordo, betrayed you?" I said.

Jerrel nodded. "He was a priest. It was his job to protect our half of the talisman. It was kept in a house of worship."

"You worship half of a talisman?"

"Not the talisman. The peace it gives us. Peace from the bird-men, anyway. There are others who war against us, but they are less powerful. The bird men could be a true threat. It surprises me that Canrad has taken this approach. The peace between us had worked for so long.

"What we are trying to do is stop Tordo before he delivers our half of the talisman. My father, King Ran, sent us. We did not want to alarm our people. We thought to overtake the thief swiftly, as we got news of his treachery immediately, Tordo's and that of the lesser priest, the one who was with him in the flier. But it turned out Tordo was prepared for our pursuit. His actions hadn't been of the moment, but were long prepared. He had the winged men waiting. An assistance given him by King Canrad. Tordo knows how my father thinks, knew he would try and catch him with as little alarm as possible by using a small force. He knew this because Tordo is my father's brother, our uncle."

"Betrayed by family," I said. "There isn't much worse."

"We could go back and raise an army, but it would be too late. Two days and he will be in the city of the Varnin, and they will have both pieces of the talisman, and all of its power."

"Seems to me, that being the case, you should have flown all night."

Jerrel grimaced. "You may be telling the truth about being from another world."

"You doubt me?" I asked.

She smiled, and it was brighter than the light from the battery. I melted like butter on a hot skillet.

"Let me show you why we do not fly at night. Why no one in their right mind does."

She took hold of the cloth she had placed over the entrance to the tree cave, tugged it loose at one edge, said, "Come look."

I looked, and what I saw astonished me. The sky was bright with the glowing insects, thicker than before. Their light showed me the sky was also full of great bat-like creatures, swooping this way and that. They were the size of Conestoga wagons, but moved more lightly than the flying sled. They were snapping and devouring the shiny bugs in large bites, gulping thousands at a time.

"Fly at night, they will make sure you do not fly for long. We call them Night Wings. They rule the sky from solid dark until near first light, and then they go away, far beyond the trees and into the mountains where they dwell."

"This means your uncle has to stop for the night as well," I said.

"Exactly," she said. "When the Night Wings depart in the early morning, we will start out again, hope to catch up with them. They don't have a tremendous lead, but it's lead enough if they are able to arrive at the city of the Varnin and my uncle delivers the talisman."

"Were you and your uncle ever close?"

"Close?" she said. "No. He was not close to my father. He felt he should have his place of rule. My guess is he hopes to do just that, under the agreement of Canrad of Varnin. He would rather rule with a cloud over his head than not rule at all."

"I would like to assist you. I have a good sword arm. I can help you stop your uncle. I pledge my allegiance to you."

Jerrel grinned when I said that.

"I accept," she said. "But Devel must accept as well."

"That sounds good to me," I said.

"For now, let us rest."

We took our cloaks, stretched out on the floor of our wooden cave. I tried to sleep, and thought I would have no trouble, exhausted as I was. But I merely dozed, then I would awake thinking I was fighting the waters of the Great Atlantic, only to find I was indeed on Venus, sleeping in a tree, and sleeping not far away was the most beautiful and enticing woman I had ever known.

—

I WAS UP when Jerrel and Devel rose.

It was partially dark, but some light was creeping through the cloth over the gap in the tree. Jerrel pulled it loose, let the beginnings of early morning seep in.

Jerrel and Devel moved to an area of our cave away from me and whispered. As they did, Devel would glance at me from time to time. His face was a mixture of emotions, none of them appeared to be amused.

After a moment Devel came to me, said, "Jerrel trusts you. I feel I must. Her judgment is generally sound."

"I assure you," I said, "I am trustworthy."

"Words are easy, but you will have your chance to prove your loyalty," he said. "Don't let us down."

"Did I let you down in the fight?"

"No. But what we face from here on out will be much worse. It will try all of us."

"Then put me to the test," I said.

—

WE FLEW AWAY from the tree and into the morning sky. As we went, the sun grew large and the sky grew bright. The glowing bugs were long gone to wherever they go—some in the gullets of the Night Flyers—and the hungry bat things were gone as well. We sailed on into the bright light and before long it was less bright and the clouds above were dark and plump with rain. Finally, the rain came, and it came hard and fast and began to flood the seats on the craft.

Devel guided our flying sled down and under the lower limbs of the trees. We dodged in between them swiftly, and close to limbs that for a moment looked like inevitable crash sites. But he avoided them, flicked us through clusters of leaves, and then down under a series of trees that were smaller in height than the others, yet wide and numerous of branch with leaves so thick the rain could hardly get through. It was as if a great umbrella had been thrown over us. As we went, the sky darkened more and the rain hammered the trees and shook the leaves; random drops seeped through. Then came the lightning, sizzling across the sky with great gongs of thunder. There was a great crack and a flash, a hum of electricity, and a monstrous limb fell from one of the trees.

The lightning, as if seeking us out for dodging the rain, flicked down through a gap in the larger trees and hit one of the smaller ones just before we glided under it. A spot on the limb burst into a great ball of flame and there was an explosion of wood. It struck the front of the craft, hit so hard it was as if a great hand had taken hold of the front of the flying machine and flung it to the ground.

Fortunately we were not flying high at the time, but it was still a vicious drop. Had it not been for the centuries build up of loam from leaves and needles and rotting fruit to cushion our fall, we would have burst apart like a tossed china cup.

We smacked the ground hard enough to rattle our teeth. The machine skidded through the loam like a plow breaking a field. It went along like that for a great distance beneath the trees, then hit something solid that caused us to veer hard left and wreck against the trunk of one of the smaller trees.

It was such an impact, that for a long moment I was dazed. When I gathered my thoughts and put them into some reasonable shape of understanding, I examined my surroundings. I was in the middle seat of the flying sled, Devel ahead of me, Jerrel behind. But she wasn't. She was missing. I struggled out of my seat, got up close to Devel. He wasn't moving. He couldn't. He was dead. A short limb jutting out from the tree had been driven securely through his chest, bursting his heart. His body was painted in blood.

I fell off the crumpled craft, landed on the ground and started to crawl. When I got enough strength back to manage my feet under me. I searched around for Jerrel, screamed her name.

"Here," she said. I turned, saw her rising up from behind a pile of leaves and branches. She was scratched up, but from where I stood she looked well enough, all things considered.

When I got to her she surprised me by taking me into her arms, clutching me to her.

"Devel?" she asked.

I gently freed myself from her embrace, shook my head. She made a squeaking noise and fell to her knees. I squatted beside her, held her as she shook and cried. As if to mock us, the sky grew light and the rain stopped. The world took on a pleasant, emerald glow.

—

I WAS STILL astonished to find that at death all that was done in way of ceremony was that the dead were placed on the ground. I assumed in the humid air of Venus, aided by insects and internal decay, bodies would soon lose their flesh and find their way into the soil. But it was still disconcerting to see Devel pulled from the machine by Jerrel, stretched out on the soil to be left. Jerrel weeped over him, violently, and then she was through. She left him, as she said, to Become One With the All. I convinced her to stretch his cloak over him, though she thought it was a waste of material. I know how this makes her sound, but I assure you, this was custom. I guess it was a little bit similar to some American Indian tribes leaving the corpses of the dead on platforms to be consumed by time and elements.

We traveled forward. The sky had completely cleared and the storm had moved on. We could hear it in the distance, roaring at the trees and the sky. I don't know how long we walked, but finally we came to a clearing in the wilderness, and in the clearing were mounds of giant bones. Some were fresh enough that stinking flesh clung to them, others had almost disappeared into the ground itself. Teeth gleamed in the sunlight. In the distance the dark rain clouds moved as if stalking something, lightning flashed and thunder rolled and the wind sighed.

"It's a kind of graveyard for the great beasts," Jerrel said, looking around.

It was indeed. It went on for what I estimated to be a ten or fifteen miles long, a half mile wide.

We had brought some supplies from the crippled flying sled with us, and we found the shade of some very large and well-aged bones, sat down in the shade the bones made, ignored the smell from still rotting flesh, and ate our lunch. It was an odd place for a meal, but our stamina had played out. We sat and Jerrel talked about Devel. It was minor stuff, really. Childhood memories, some of it funny, some of it poignant, some of it just odd, but all of it loving. She talked for quite a while.

When our strength was renewed, we continued. I guess we had walked about a mile among the bones when we found her uncle's airship. It was blackened and twisted and smacked down among a rib cage that looked like the frame of a large ship. The man I had seen before, the one who had been driving the craft, was still in it, though some creature had been at him; had actually sucked the flesh from his head and face. But it was him. I could tell that, and if I had any doubts Jerrel dismantled them. She drew her sword and cut off his fleshless head and kicked it into a pile of the bones.

"Traitor," she said. I saw then not only the beautiful woman I had fallen in love with, but the warrior, and it frightened me a little.

"The question," I said, "is where is your uncle? Wait. Look there."

A little farther up, among the bones, were the wrecked bodies of several bird-men, blackened and twisted and scorched by fire.

"The lightning hit them same as us," I said. "Maybe your uncle was killed."

But we didn't locate his body. Perhaps a beast had found him, but it was also possible that he was journeying on foot to the kingdom of the Varnin.

"This means we may catch up with him," I said.

Before long I spied his tracks in the soft soil, pointed them out. Jerrel could find Varnin without tracking her uncle, but it was him and the talisman we wanted, so the tracks were encouraging.

—

IT WAS NEAR night when we finally passed the lengthy stacks of bones. We edged toward the forest. The trees, low down and high up, were full of ravaging beasts, but the open land worried me most. Anyone or anything could easily spot us there.

Edging along the trees, moving swiftly and carefully as possible, we were suddenly taken aback by the sudden appearance of half a dozen beasts with men mounted on them. My fear had been realized. They spotted us. The beasts they were riding looked remarkably like horses, if horses could have horns and were shorter and wider with red and white stripes. They were guided in a way similar to horses as well, bits and bridles, long, thin reins. The riders were seated in high-set saddles, and as they came closer it became apparent they were not human at all.

Humans have flesh, but these things had something else. Their skin was yellow like Jerrel's skin, but it was coarse and gave one the impression of alligator hide. They had flaring scales around their necks. Their features were generally human-like, but their noses were flat as a coin, little more than two small holes. Their foreheads slanted and the tops of their heads peaked. Their mouths were wide and packed with stained teeth and their round eyes were red and full of fiery licks of light. They were carrying long lances tipped with bright tips of metal. Short swords with bone handles bounced in scabbards at their hips. Closer yet, I saw there were little glowing parasites flowing over their skin like minnows in a creek.

Jerrel said, "Galminions. They are eaters of human flesh. Robbers. They run in packs. And they smell."

They came ever closer. Jerrel was right. They did smell, like something dead left under a house.

"Ah," said the foremost rider, reining his mount directly in front of us. The others sat in a row behind him, smiling their filthy teeth. "Travelers. And such a good day for it."

"It is," Jerrel said. "We thought a stroll would be nice."

The one who had spoken laughed. The laugh sounded like ice cracking. He had a peculiar way of turning his head from side to side, as if one eye were bad. When the sunlight shifted I saw that was exactly the problem. He was blind in that eye; no red flecks there. It was white as the first drifts of snow in the Rockies.

"How is your stroll?" said Dead Eye.

"It's been warm, and it's quite the hike," Jerrel said, "but it has been amusing. It has been so good to speak to you. We must be on our way. We wish you good day."

"Do you now?" said Dead Eye. He turned in his saddle and looked back at his companions. "They wish us good day."

The companions laughed that similar laugh, the one that sounded like ice cracking, then made leathery-shifts in their saddles.

"It's good to see we're all in a cheery mood," Jerrel said.

When Dead Eye turned back to us, he said, "I am cheery because we are going to kill you and eat you and take your swords. But mainly we're going to kill you and eat you. Maybe we'll start eating you while you're alive. Of course we will. That's how we like it. The screams are loud and the blood is hot."

"You will dance on the tip of my sword," I said. "That is what you will do."

"And what are you exactly?" said Dead Eye.

"A Black man."

"I can see that. Were you burned?"

"By the fires of hell. Perhaps you would like a taste of hell itself."

"What is hell?"

I had wasted my wit. "Never mind," I said. "Let us pass, or—"

"I will dance on the tip of your sword," Dead Eye said.

"Exactly," I said.

"What about the rest of us?" he said. "Shall they dance as well?"

"I suppose that between our two swords there will be dancing partners for all of you."

This really got a laugh.

"He is not joking," said Jerrel.

"We will be the judge of that," Dead Eye said. "For we are not jokesters either."

"Oh, I don't know," I said. "You look pretty funny to me."

My comment was like the starter shot.

They came as one in a wild charge. Jerrel and I worked as one. We seemed to understand the other's next move. We dodged into the trees, and the Galminions followed. The trees made it difficult for them to maneuver their beasts, but we moved easily. I sprang high in the air and came down on the rider nearest me with a slash of my sword, severing his head, spurting warm blood from his body like the gush from a fountain.

Jerrel lunged from behind a tree, and avoiding the ducking horned head of one of the mounts, stuck it in the chest. With a bleating sound it stumbled and fell, rolled about kicking its legs, tumbling over the fallen rider, crushing him with a snap of bone and a crackle of bumpy skin.

That was when Dead Eye swung off his steed and came for me, driving his lance directly at my chest. I moved to the side, parried his lance with my sword. The tip of his weapon stuck deep in a tree, and the impact caused him to lose his footing. When he fell, it was never to rise again. I bounded to him and drove my sword deep in his throat. He squirmed like a bug stuck through by a pin. His white eye widened. He half spun on my sword, spat a geyser of blood, shook and lay still.

The others fled like deer.

"Are you all right?" she asked.

"I am, and believe it or not," I said, "fortune has smiled on us."

—

For Jerrel riding one of the beasts was uncomfortable and she rode awkwardly. For me it was like being back in the cavalry. I felt in control. The creatures handled very similar to horses, though they seemed smarter. There isn't much that isn't smarter than a horse, by the way. That said, they had a gait similar to mules, making for a less smooth ride.

"You call this fortune?" Jerrel said.

"If your uncle is on foot, yes," I said.

As we rode on, in front of us the clearing went away and a mountain range rose before us. It was at first a bump, then a hump, and finally we could see it for what it was. The mountain was covered in dark clouds and flashes of lightning, all of it seen to the sound of rumbling thunder. The patches of forest that climbed up the mountain were blacker than the trees that gave the Black Hills of the Dakotas their name.

The day moved along, the sun shifted, and so did the shadows. They fell out of the forests and grew longer, thicker, cooler and darker. A few of the shiny bugs came out. We shifted into the woods, found a spot where old wood had fallen and made a kind of hut of trees and limbs. We dismounted and led our animals inside through a gap. I found some deadwood and pulled it in front of the opening. I chopped a lean but strong limb off a tree with my sword and used it to stretch from one side of our haven to the other. On one side of it I placed our mounts, the limb serving as a kind of corral. After removing their saddles and bridles, I used bits of rope from the bag of supplies we had brought from the wreck of the sled to hobble them, a trick Jerrel had never seen before.

Finally we stretched out on our side of the barrier with our cloaks as our beds. We lay there and talked, and you would have thought we had known each other forever. In time the Night Wings were out. They flew down low and we could hear their wings sweeping past where we were holed up. Many of the bugs outside slipped in between the gaps of fallen wood and made our little room, such as it was, glow with shimmering light.

Jerrel and I came together at some point, and anything beyond that is not for a gentleman to tell. I will say this, and excuse the dime novel feel to it. My soul soared like a hawk.

—

NEXT MORNING WE were up early, just after the Night Wings and the glowing bugs abandoned the sky. We saddled up and rode on out. From time to time I got down off my critter and checked the ground, found signs of our quarry's tracks, remounted and we continued. By the middle of the day we had reached the mountain and were climbing up, riding a narrow trail between the great dark trees.

The weather had shifted. The dark clouds, the lightning and thunder had flown. As we rode from time to time I saw strange beasts watching us from the shadows of the forest, but we were not bothered and continued on. Late in the day I got down and looked at our man's tracks, and they were fresh. Our mounts were giving us the final edge on his head start.

"He is not far ahead," I said, swinging back into the saddle.

"Good. Then I will kill him."

"Maybe you could just arrest him."

"Arrest him?"

"Take him prisoner."

"No. I will kill him and take back the talisman."

I figured she would, too.

The trail widened and so did our view. Up there in the mountains, nowhere near its peak, but right in front of us at the far end of the wide trail, we could see the city of the bird-men. The great trees there had grown, or been groomed, to twist together in a monstrous wad of leaves and limbs, and mixed into them was a rock fortress that must have taken thousands of bird-men and a good many years to build. It was like a castle and a nest blended together with the natural formations of the mountain; in places it was rambling, in others tight as drum.

I said, "Before we come any closer, we had best get off this trail and sneak up on our man. If we can jump him before he enters the city, then that's the best way, and if he is inside already, well it's going to be difficult, to put it mildly."

Jerrel nodded, and just as we rode off the trail and into the dark forest, a horde of bird men came down from the sky and into the thicket with a screech and a flash of swords.

Surprised, we whirled on our mounts and struck out at them. It was like swatting at yellow jackets. I managed to stick one of the creatures and cause him to fall dead, but as he fell his body struck me and knocked me off my mount. I hustled to my feet just as Jerrel ducked a sword swing, but was hit in the head by the passing hilt of the sword. She fell off her beast and onto her back and didn't move.

I went savage.

I remember very little about what happened after that, but I was swinging my sword with both skill and insane fury. Bird men lost wings and limbs and faces and skulls. My sword stabbed and slashed and shattered. I was wet and hot with the blood of my enemies.

To protect themselves they flapped their wings, lifted up higher, and dove, but they were never quick enough and were hindered by the thickness of the trees and my speed was beyond measure. I leaped and dodged, parried and thrust. I raged among the flapping demons like a lion among sheep.

Finally it was as if all the bird-men in the world appeared. The sky darkened above me and the darkness fell over me, and down they came in a fluttering wave of screeches and sword slashes and axe swings.

I was a crazed dervish. I spun and slung my blade like the Reaper's scythe, and once again they began to pile up, but then I was struck in the head from the side, and as I tumbled to the ground, I thought it was the end of me.

I couldn't have been down but for a moment when I felt a blade at my throat and heard a voice say, "No. Bring him."

Jerrel and I were lifted up and carried. My sword was gone. I was bleeding. I saw walking before the pack of bird-men, Tordo, Jerrel's traitorous uncle.

We were hoisted out of the forest and onto the trail, carried up toward the amazing twists of forest and stone. As we neared I saw small clouds of smoke rising from stone chimneys, and in loops of groomed limbs I saw large nests made of vines and sticks and all manner of refuse. The nests were wide open, but they were built under the great limbs and leaves of trees that served as a roof. Beyond them there was an enormous tree, the biggest I had seen on my world or this one, and there was a gap in it that served as an opening into the city proper. A great drawbridge had been dropped, and it stretched out over a gap between trees and mountain, and the gap was wide and deep beyond comprehension. Over the drawbridge we were carried, and into the great fortress of wood and stone.

—

MY THOUGHT WAS that Jerrel was already dead and I was next, and let me tell you true as the direction north, I didn't care if I died. With Jerrel lost, I wished to die.

As it turned out, I didn't die. And neither did Jerrel. I didn't realize she was alive until we found ourselves in the bowels of the fortress in a prison that was deep inside the cave of a tree, a series of metal bars served as our doorway. Looking through the bars I could see a long corridor that was also the inside of a tree, and there were two guards nearby, one with a lance, one with an axe, both with expressions that would make a child cry.

In our cell they dropped us down on some limbs and leaves that served as beds. There was a peculiar odor. The only thing I can equate it with is the smell of a hen house on a hot damp afternoon.

I knelt over Jerrel, lifted her head gently. "My love," I said.

"My head hurts," she said. The sound of her voice elated me.

"I guess so. You took quite a lick."

She sat up slowly. "Are you okay?"

"I got a bump myself, behind my ear."

She gingerly touched it with the tip of her fingers. "Ow," she said.

"My sentiments exactly. What I don't understand is why they didn't kill us."

"I think, in my case, my uncle wants me to see the ceremony."

"What ceremony?"

"The linking of the two halves of the talisman. The acquisition of the greatest power on our planet. He wants me to see what he has achieved before he puts me to death. Wants me to know the deed is done, and I have failed to prevent it, and then we die."

"If you ain't dead, you're living, and that's a good thing," I said.

It took her a moment to take that in. It was as if whatever power allowed my words to be translated to her language had lost a beat. After a moment she laughed her musical laugh. "I think I understand."

"We won't give up until we're beyond considering on the matter one way or the other," I said.

"I love you, Jack," she said.

"And I love you." We allowed ourselves a kiss. Yet, in spite of my bravado, in spite of the repeating of my old sergeant's words, I feared it might be our last.

"Love is a wonderful steed," said a voice, "ride it as long as you can."

We looked up, and there above us, sitting on a ridge of stone was a bird-man, his feet dangling. He looked youngish, if I can claim any ability of judging the age of a man who looks a lot like a giant chicken crossed with the body of a man. A very weak looking chicken. He appeared near starved to death. His head hung weak. His ribs showed. His legs were skinny as sticks, but there was still something youthful about him.

"Who are you?" I asked. It wasn't a brilliant question, but it was all I had.

"Gar-don," he said, and dropped off the ledge, his wings taking hold with a fanning of air. He settled down near us, his legs weak and shaky. He sat down on the floor, his head sagged, he sighed. "I am a prisoner, same as you."

"Gar-don," Jerrel said. "The former king's son. His heir."

"That was how it was supposed to be, but no longer. I was usurped."

"Canrad," said Jerrel.

"Yes," Gar-don said, "Now he is king. And I am here, awaiting the moment when he is able to acquire the rest of the talisman, and from what I overheard, that moment has arrived."

"Yes," Jerrel said. "For all of us. I am Jerrel, Princess of Sheldan."

Gar-don lifted his head, took a deep breath, said, "I know of you. I am sorry for your fate, and his."

"Jack," I said. "I am called Jack."

"I shall go out as a prince," Gar-don said. "I will not beg. My horror is not my death, but what the two halves of the talisman can do. Canrad will possess immense power."

"What does this power do?" I asked.

"We only have legend to explain it to us. It gives him the power over spirits and demons from the old trees."

"The old trees?" I said.

"Giant trees that contain spirits of power," Jerrel said. "Those kind of trees no longer exist. They ceased to exist before I was born, before my father was born, his grandfather and so on. The spirits are contained in the two halves of the talisman."

"Canrad will be able to control the people then," Gar-don said. "They, like my father, and myself, were perfectly happy with our peace treaty. Only an insane being wants war. The people only follow Conrad because they fear him. All uprisings have been destroyed, or the participants have gone into hiding. After today, they might as well never have existed, for he will control anyone and everyone with his new powers. He will not be able to be defeated."

"But you don't know actually know how he will do that?" I said.

"I have only heard of the legend," Gar-don said. "The power of the spirits, the demons of the trees. Exactly what they are capable of, I do not know. Our people have always feared the talisman, and knowing now that it will be united, no one will resist him. It would be useless."

There was a clatter of sound in the hallway. Gar-don stood weakly, said, "It seems we are about to find out the exactness of the talisman's power."

They came for us, unlocking our cell, entering quickly. To be sure of our compliance there was a horde of them with long spikes and strong nets and an angry attitude. I managed to hit one with my fist, knocking him to the floor in a swirl of dust and feathers. Jerrel kicked another. Gar-don tried to fight, but he was as weak as a dove. They netted the three of us, bagged us, kicked us awhile, then hauled us away like trapped vermin being taken to a lake to be drowned.

—

WE WERE BROUGHT to a large throne room, that like the overall stronghold was made of stone and was combined with the natural strength of trees and limbs and leaves. Enormous branches jutted out of the walls high above our heads, and perched on them like a murder of ravens, were bird-men and bird-women—the first females I had seen of that race. An occasional feather drifted down from above, coasted in the light.

Above that perch on which the bird-people were seated was a tight canopy of leaves, so thick and layered it would have taken an army of strong warriors many days to hack their way through it; actually, I'm not even sure they could do it in years.

They brought us in and held us close to the floor in our nets. We could see through the gaps in the netting. Besides the bird-people on the limbs above, the throne room was packed with others, some of them warriors, many of them nobles, and some citizens. We were the spectacle, and all of the bird-people had been summoned to witness whatever ceremony was at hand. I assumed it would not be a parade in our honor.

On a dais was a throne and on the throne was a large winged man who looked as if an ancient human being, fat of body, thin of legs, with a head like a warped melon, had been mated to a condor and a buzzard, all of him swathed over with warts and scars and age. A golden cloak draped his shoulders, and except for half the talisman on a chain around his neck, he wore nothing else. His eyes were dark and the color of old, dried pine sap. This, of course, was King Canrad.

Tordo stood near the throne, one hand on its back support. There were guards on either side of King Canrad and Tordo. The room was full of warriors as well.

Canrad nodded at Tordo. Tordo stepped to the center of the dais, removed his half of the talisman from his neck, and lifted it up with both hands. Sunlight coming through an open gap behind the king glittered across the talisman like sunlight on a trout's back.

"What say you?" said the king.

The crowed cheered. It sounded like the sort of cheers we Buffalo Soldiers used to give the lieutenant when he rode by on horseback. A white man who led us like we couldn't lead ourselves, as if our color tainted our intelligence. It was a cheer, but it came from the mouth, not the soul.

The king said, "The old order is here. Gar-don, son of the former king, who was not worthy and shall not be named is also here. He will see how a true king shows his power."

"It is you who is not worthy," Gar-don called out from his netted position on the floor.

"Strike him," said the king. One of the warriors stepped forward and brought the staff of his spear sharply across Gar-don's back. Gar-don grunted.

"We also have among us the daughter of King Ran of the Sheldan," said the king. "A rather inferior race in my opinion. Add a black man-thing that I cannot define, nor can anyone else, and we have three enemies of the throne. The gods will welcome their deaths. They will be the first to die by the power of the talisman. I will call up all the demons of the trees and they will render these worthless creatures into wet rags."

"I know your law," Jerrel said, pushing herself to her knees under the net. "I ask my right to challenge you, or your second. If I win, our lives will be spared."

"I am too old to be challenged," said the king. "I have no intention of sullying myself with a duel. Nor will I sully one of my men. Why should I? You have the right by our law to make a challenge, and I, as King, have the right to refuse. I refuse. Be silent."

King Canrad leaned forward on his throne. I could almost hear his bones creak. His wings trembled slightly. He looked like a gargoyle rocking on its ledge. He said to Tordo, "Bring me the power."

Tordo hesitated, then moved toward him. King Canrad held out his hand. "Give it to me."

Tordo held his half of the talisman forward with his left hand, and as the king reached to take it, Tordo sprang forward, snatched at the talisman around the king's neck, yanked it loose of its chain.

Links of chain clattered on the floor as Tordo slammed the two pieces of the talisman together with a loud click. He lifted it above his head with a smile. He yelled out a series of words, an incantation. I understood the words, but not their jumbled purpose.

And then the spell was finished, and...

...Well, nothing. It was as quiet in the throne room as a mouse in house slippers. From somewhere in the crowd there was a cough, as if someone had a mouthful of feathers, which considering who was in the room, could have actually been the case.

Tordo's gleeful expression died slowly. He said a word that didn't translate, but I had an idea what it meant. He turned slowly and looked over his shoulder. He had gone from a potential wizard of the trees to a fool with two connected pieces of jewelry.

The guards hustled up from the bottom of the dais, their spears raised, ready to stick Tordo.

"No," said the King. "Give me the talisman first."

One of the warriors tugged it from Tordo's hands, removed his sword as well, gave the talisman to the king. The king held it in his hands. He looked at it the way a fisherman might look at his catch, realizing it had appeared much larger under water. "It is useless. It is a lie." He lifted his eyes to Tordo. "I will make your death a long one."

While they were so engaged, and all eyes were on them, I lifted an edge of the net, crawled out from under it and seized one of the bird-men. I drew his sword from its sheath and shoved him back. I sprang toward the dais. A warrior stepped in front of me, but I jabbed quickly and the sharp blade went through his eye and down he went.

With my newfound abilities renewed, I leaped easily to the dais and put my sword to the king's throat.

The guards on either side of the throne started toward me.

I said to the king, "Give the order to free the lady and Gar-don, or I will run this through your throat."

The king's body shook. "Free them," he said.

The net was lifted. The warriors around them parted. I noticed there was a rearranging of soldiers, some shifted out of one group and into another. It was a good sign. They were showing their division.

I said, "Those who wish the king well, fear the point of my sword. Those who wish him ill, perhaps you would enjoy my sword thrust. We shall see which is more popular."

There was a slight murmur.

By this time Jerrel and Gar-don had joined me on the dais. They stood near me and the king. Jerrel picked up the pike of the guard I had killed. Tordo hadn't moved; he feared to move.

Gar-don said, "I am your king. I am the son of the true king, who was the son of a king, and the king before that. Today the talisman failed Canrad and Tordo. The spirits within it do not wish their will to succeed. They do not wish their powers used for something so pointless as killing and destruction and war. It is peace they want. It is peace they have allowed. And I suggest we obey their will and continue on that path, least they turn on us and destroy us all."

Someone said, "Gar-don, our king."

A moment latter this was repeated, and then someone else said the same, and then voices rose up from the crowd and they filled the room, and the voices came not from the mouths of the frightened, but from the souls of true believers.

—

THERE WERE A few who for a moment seemed unwilling to make the change to Gar-don, but they were vastly outnumbered, and those who tried to defend Canrad were quickly dispatched in a wave of bloody anger. If there was a lesson to be learned from Gar-don's remarks about the talisman, they hadn't actually learned it, which meant the bird-people were as human as the wingless. They were not ready to accept the talisman was nothing more than an ancient myth.

Gar-don took the talisman, held it up as Tordo had done. He was still weak and struggled to hold it aloft. But his spirit was strong. He spoke so loudly his words could be heard at the back of the room and up into the leafy canopy.

"The power of the talisman will remain unused. Half of it will go back with Princess Jerrel, back to her city and her king, where it will continue to remain powerless, and our peace will continue."

"What of him?" said a bird woman, stepping forward to point a long finger at Tordo.

Gar-don turned his head to Tordo, studied him. He was about to speak when Jerrel beat him to it. "Gar-don, King of the Varnin," she said. "I ask you to sanction my right to combat with Tordo. He has stolen from my family. He has insulted my family. And I desire to insult him with the edge of my blade."

"And if you lose?" said Gar-don.

"I won't," Jerrel said. "But if I do, let him go. Banish him."

"Don't do this," I said. "Let me take your place."

"I am as good a warrior as any other, my love."

"Very well," said Gar-don. "But before that…"

He turned to the former King Canrad.

"I banish you. As of now, you will rise and you will go away, and you will never come back."

The old man rose, and in that moment, seeing how weak he was, I almost felt sorry for him. Then a blade came out from under his cloak and he stabbed at Gar-don. I caught Canrad's arm just in time, twisted. It snapped easily. He screeched and dropped the dagger. I let him go.

Gar-don leaned forward and looked into Canrad's eyes. "I see emptiness."

Gar-don weakly picked up the dagger Canrad had dropped. He seemed strong all of a sudden. "It will not matter what I do, Canrad, you are dead already." With that, he jammed the blade into the former king's chest. The old man collapsed in a cloaked wad, and immediately a pool of blood flowed around him.

"Give Tordo a sword," Gar-don said, turning back to the situation at hand. "Death is your loss, Tordo. Banishment is your victory."

Jerrel dropped the pike and was given a sword.

—

TORDO WAS GIVEN a sword. All of the disappointment of the moment, every foul thing he was, bubbled up and spewed out of him. He attacked with a yell. He bounced forward on the balls of his feet, attempting to stick Jerrel. Jerrel glided back as if walking on air.

Everyone on the dais moved wide of their blades as they battled back and forth, the throne sometimes coming between them.

291

Once Jerrel slipped in Canrad's blood, and in spite of this being a private duel, I almost leapt to her aid, but Gar-don touched me on the arm.

"It is not done," he said.

Tordo put one boot on Canrad's lifeless neck and used it as a kind of support to lift him up and give him more of a downward thrust. But Jerrel slipped the lunge.

Tordo sprang off Canrad's lifeless neck and made a beautiful thrust for her face. I let out a gasp of air. It was right on target.

At the last moment Jerrel dropped under his thrust, which lifted the hair on her head slightly, and drove her weapon up and into his belly. He held his position, as if waiting for his form to be admired, then made a noise like an old dog with a chicken bone in its throat, and fell flat on his face. Blood poured out of him and flowed into the puddle of gore that had fanned out from beneath Canrad.

Jerrel studied the corpse of Tordo for a moment. She took a deep breath, said, "I have drawn my kin's own blood, but I have avenged Tordo's treachery and honored my father."

Gar-don stepped forward and surveyed the crowd. He lifted his chin slightly. The response to this was another cheer from the multitude, and this one was more than from the throat. It was from deep within the soul.

—

THERE WERE GREAT celebrations, and we were part of it. It was pleasant and necessary to the new agreement between kingdoms, but I was glad when it ended and we were given back the mounts we had taken from the Galminions, sent on our way with supplies, fanfare, and of course Jerrel's half of the talisman.

As we rode along the wide trail in the morning light, winding down from the great lair of the bird-people, I said, "Do you think Gar-don's people believed what he said about the talisman?"

"Perhaps they did," Jerrel said. "Perhaps some did. Perhaps none did. The only thing that matters is there was no great power when the two pieces were united. It's just a legend."

"Designed to prevent war between your people and theirs," I said. "That seems like a legend worth believing. The halves of a great power divided so neither has a unique and overwhelming power over the other."

"Devel would be amused," she said.

We experienced a few adventures on our way to Jerrel's kingdom, but they were minor, mostly involving brigands that we dispatched with little effort, a few encounters with wild beasts. When we arrived in the land of Sheldan and Jerrel explained all that had happened to her father, I was afforded much curiosity, mostly due to the color of my skin.

I was thanked. I was rewarded with a fine sword and scabbard. I was given a prominent place at King Ran's table, and it was there that Jerrel told him that we were to marry.

It was the first I had heard of it, but I was delighted with the idea.

That was some time ago. I am sitting now at a writing desk in a great room in this Sheldan castle made of clay and stone. It is dark except for a small candle. I am writing with a feather pen on yellow parchment. My wife, the beautiful warrior Jerrel, sleeps not far away in our great round bed.

Tonight, before I rose to write, I dreamed, as I have the last three nights. In the dream I was being pulled down a long bright tunnel, and finally into the cold, dark waters of the Atlantic, washing about in the icy waves like a cork. The great light of a ship moved my way, and in the shadows of that light were the bobbing heads of dying swimmers and the bouncing of the Titanic's human-stuffed rafts. The screams of the desperate, the cries of the dying filled the air.

I have no idea what the dream means, or if it means anything, but each night that I experience it, it seems a little clearer. Tonight there was another part to it. I glimpsed the thing that brought me here, pulled me down and through that lighted tunnel to Venus. I fear it wishes to take me back.

I finish this with no plans of it being read, and without complete understanding as to why I feel compelled to have written it. But written it is.

Now I will put my pen and parchment away, blow out the candle, lie gently down beside my love, hoping I will never be forced to leave her side, and that she and this world will be mine forever.

ABOUT THE AUTHOR

WELL KNOWN AND loved for his Texas Mojo storytelling style, JOE R. LANSDALE (1951-) is the author of more than forty novels and two hundred short works, including *Act of Love*, *The Nightrunners*, *Cold in July*, *Savage Season*, *The Bottoms*, and the "Hap and Leonard" and "Drive-In" series of novels, as well as scripts for both comics and film. Two of his stories, the cult classic "Bubba Ho-Tep" and "Incident On and Off a Mountain Road," have been adapted for film, as well as his novel *Cold in July*. His "Hap and Leonard" series of novels was turned into a television series. He has had the honor of being chosen to complete an unfinished Tarzan novel by Edgar Rice Burroughs, one of the founding authors of the sword and planet genre, published in 1995 as *Tarzan: The Lost Adventure*. Lansdale has also been a student of the martial arts for more than fifty-four years—learning how to take a punch being a self-admitted ingredient of good Mojo storytelling—and he is an inductee into the International Martial Arts Hall of Fame as well as the United States Hall of Fame. He has won the Edgar Award, the British Fantasy Award, the Spur Award, the American Mystery Award, the Grinzani Prize for Literature, the International Horror Guild Award, and nine Bram Stoker Awards, and in 2007 he was named a Grand Master of Horror, and has achieved the Lifetime Achievement Award.